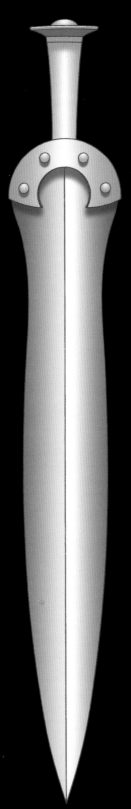

THE SWORD

EARTH

JOSHUA LUNA
Story, Script, Layouts, Letters

JONATHAN LUNA
Story, Illustrations, Book Design

SPECIAL THANKS TO:

Rommel Calderon
Randy Castillo
Dan Dos Santos
Timothy Ingle
Fenn Kao
Marc Lombardi
Jordan Millner
Victoria Stein
Giancarlo Yerkes

IMAGE COMICS, INC.

Robert Kirkman Chief Operating Officer
Erik Larsen Chief Financial Officer
Todd McFarlane President
Marc Silvestri Chief Executive Officer
Jim Valentino Vice-President
ericstephenson Publisher
Joe Keatinge PR & Marketing Coordinator
Branwyn Bigglestone Accounts Manager
Sarah deLaine Administrative Assistant
Tyler Shainline Traffic Manager
Allen Hui Production Manager
Drew Gill Production Artist
Jonathan Chan Production Artist
Monica Howard Production Artist

www.imagecomics.com
www.lunabrothers.com

THE SWORD, VOL. 3: EARTH
ISBN: 978-1-60706-073-4
First Printing

International Rights Representative: Christine Jensen (christine@gfloystudio.com)

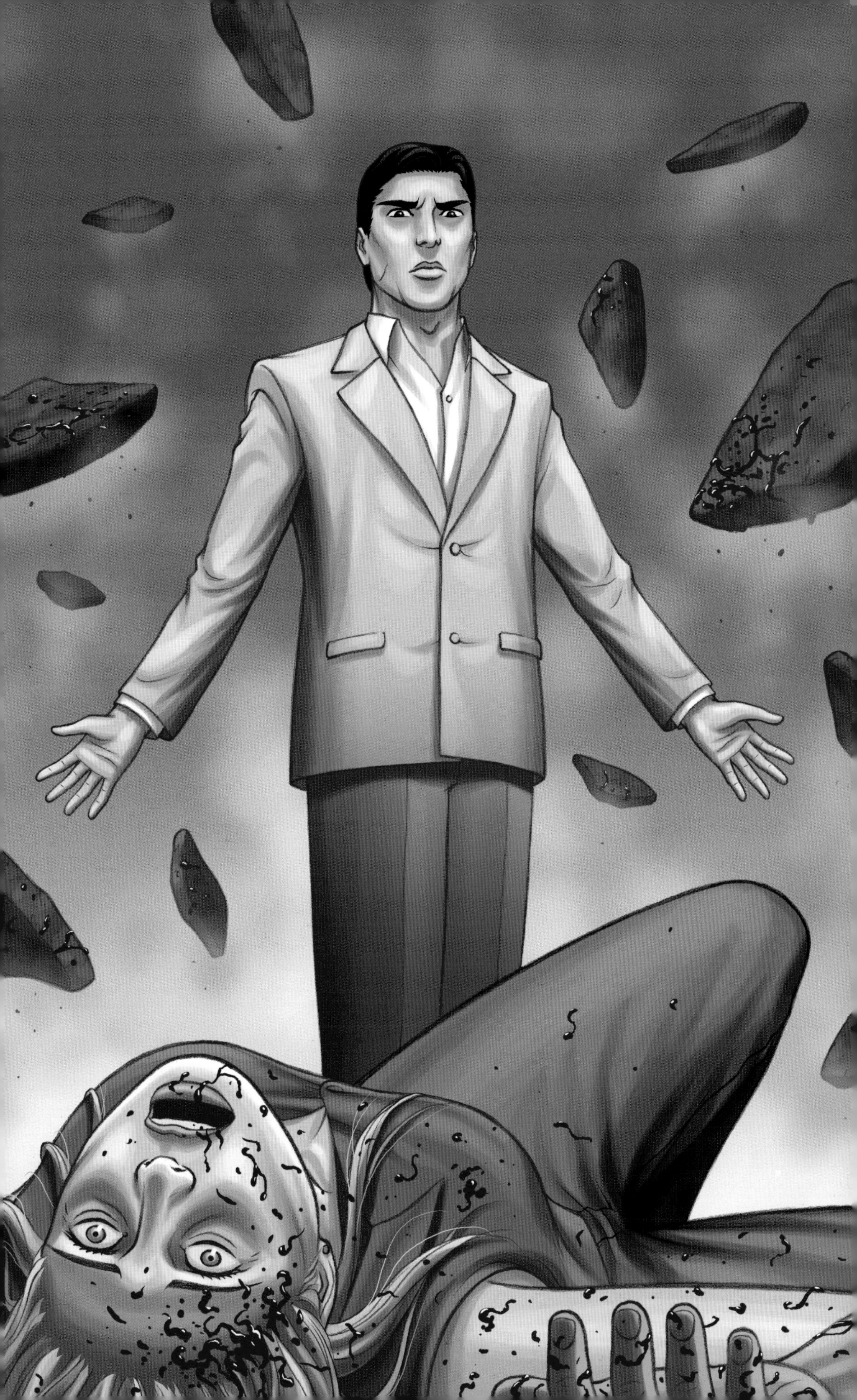

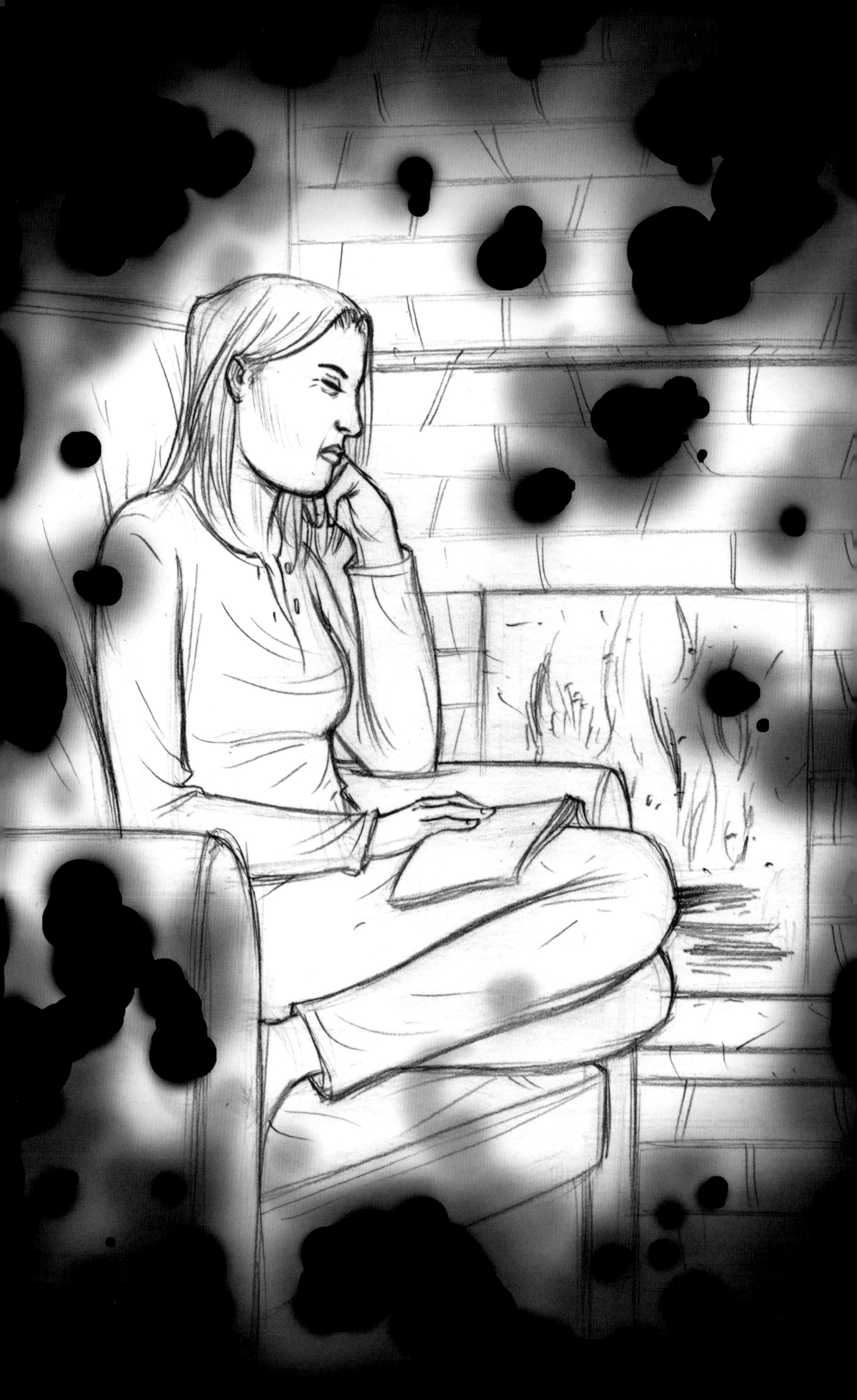

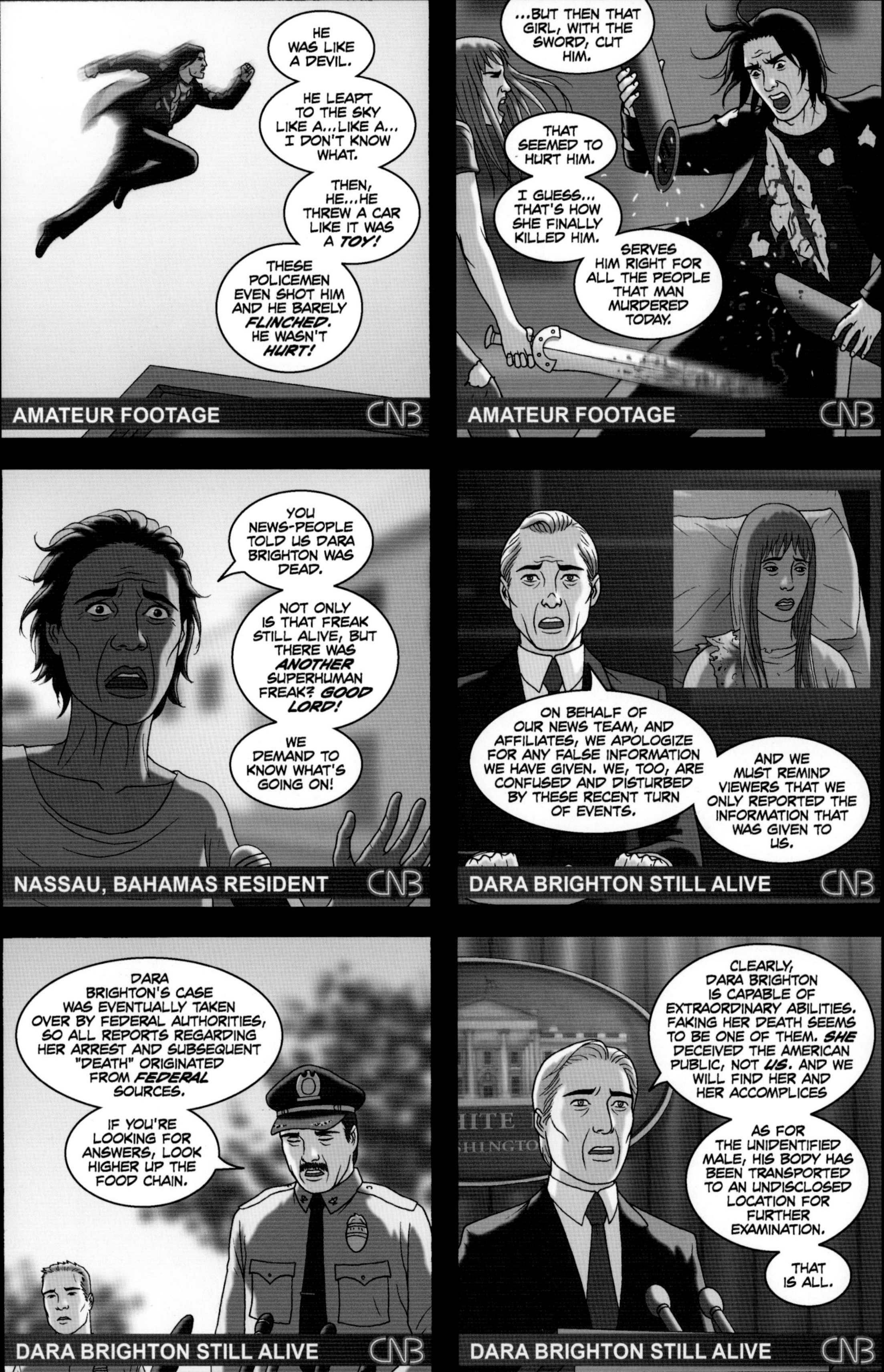
HE WAS LIKE A DEVIL.
HE LEAPT TO THE SKY LIKE A...LIKE A... I DON'T KNOW WHAT.
THEN, HE...HE THREW A CAR LIKE IT WAS A *TOY!*
THESE POLICEMEN EVEN SHOT HIM AND HE BARELY *FLINCHED.* HE WASN'T *HURT!*
AMATEUR FOOTAGE
CNB
...BUT THEN THAT GIRL, WITH THE SWORD, CUT HIM.
THAT SEEMED TO HURT HIM.
I GUESS... THAT'S HOW SHE FINALLY KILLED HIM.
SERVES HIM RIGHT FOR ALL THE PEOPLE THAT MAN MURDERED TODAY.
AMATEUR FOOTAGE
CNB
YOU NEWS-PEOPLE TOLD US DARA BRIGHTON WAS DEAD.
NOT ONLY IS THAT FREAK STILL ALIVE, BUT THERE WAS *ANOTHER* SUPERHUMAN FREAK? *GOOD LORD!*
WE DEMAND TO KNOW WHAT'S GOING ON!
NASSAU, BAHAMAS RESIDENT
CNB
ON BEHALF OF OUR NEWS TEAM, AND AFFILIATES, WE APOLOGIZE FOR ANY FALSE INFORMATION WE HAVE GIVEN. WE, TOO, ARE CONFUSED AND DISTURBED BY THESE RECENT TURN OF EVENTS.
AND WE MUST REMIND VIEWERS THAT WE ONLY REPORTED THE INFORMATION THAT WAS GIVEN TO US.
DARA BRIGHTON STILL ALIVE
CNB
DARA BRIGHTON'S CASE WAS EVENTUALLY TAKEN OVER BY FEDERAL AUTHORITIES, SO ALL REPORTS REGARDING HER ARREST AND SUBSEQUENT "DEATH" ORIGINATED FROM *FEDERAL* SOURCES.
IF YOU'RE LOOKING FOR ANSWERS, LOOK HIGHER UP THE FOOD CHAIN.
DARA BRIGHTON STILL ALIVE
CNB
CLEARLY, DARA BRIGHTON IS CAPABLE OF EXTRAORDINARY ABILITIES. FAKING HER DEATH SEEMS TO BE ONE OF THEM. *SHE* DECEIVED THE AMERICAN PUBLIC, NOT *US.* AND WE WILL FIND HER AND HER ACCOMPLICES
AS FOR THE UNIDENTIFIED MALE, HIS BODY HAS BEEN TRANSPORTED TO AN UNDISCLOSED LOCATION FOR FURTHER EXAMINATION.
THAT IS ALL.
DARA BRIGHTON STILL ALIVE
CNB

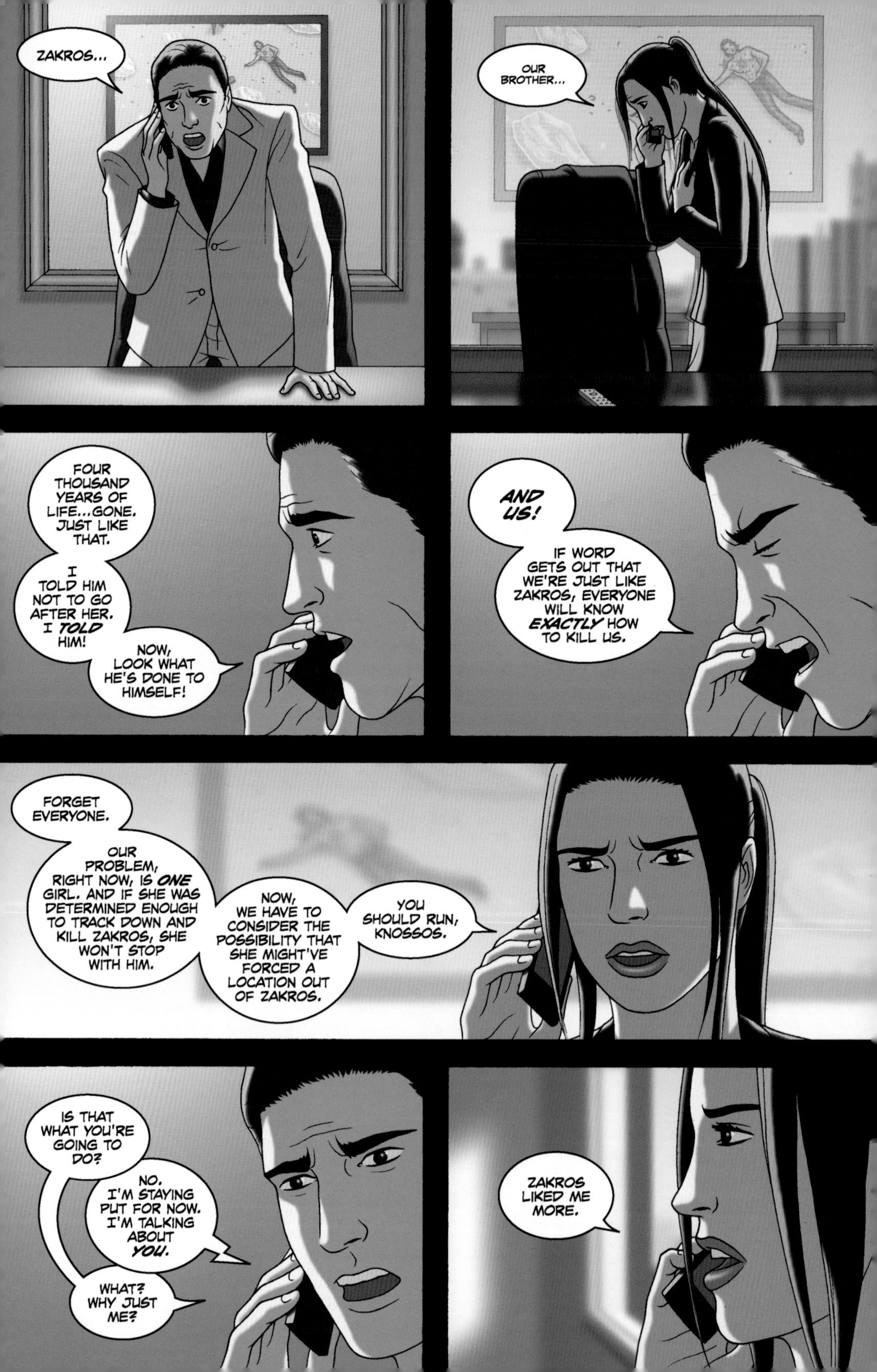
ZAKROS...
OUR BROTHER...
FOUR THOUSAND YEARS OF LIFE...GONE. JUST LIKE THAT.
I TOLD HIM NOT TO GO AFTER HER. I TOLD HIM!
NOW, LOOK WHAT HE'S DONE TO HIMSELF!
AND US!
IF WORD GETS OUT THAT WE'RE JUST LIKE ZAKROS, EVERYONE WILL KNOW EXACTLY HOW TO KILL US.
FORGET EVERYONE.
OUR PROBLEM, RIGHT NOW, IS ONE GIRL. AND IF SHE WAS DETERMINED ENOUGH TO TRACK DOWN AND KILL ZAKROS, SHE WON'T STOP WITH HIM.
NOW, WE HAVE TO CONSIDER THE POSSIBILITY THAT SHE MIGHT'VE FORCED A LOCATION OUT OF ZAKROS.
YOU SHOULD RUN, KNOSSOS.
IS THAT WHAT YOU'RE GOING TO DO?
NO. I'M STAYING PUT FOR NOW. I'M TALKING ABOUT YOU.
WHAT? WHY JUST ME?
ZAKROS LIKED ME MORE.

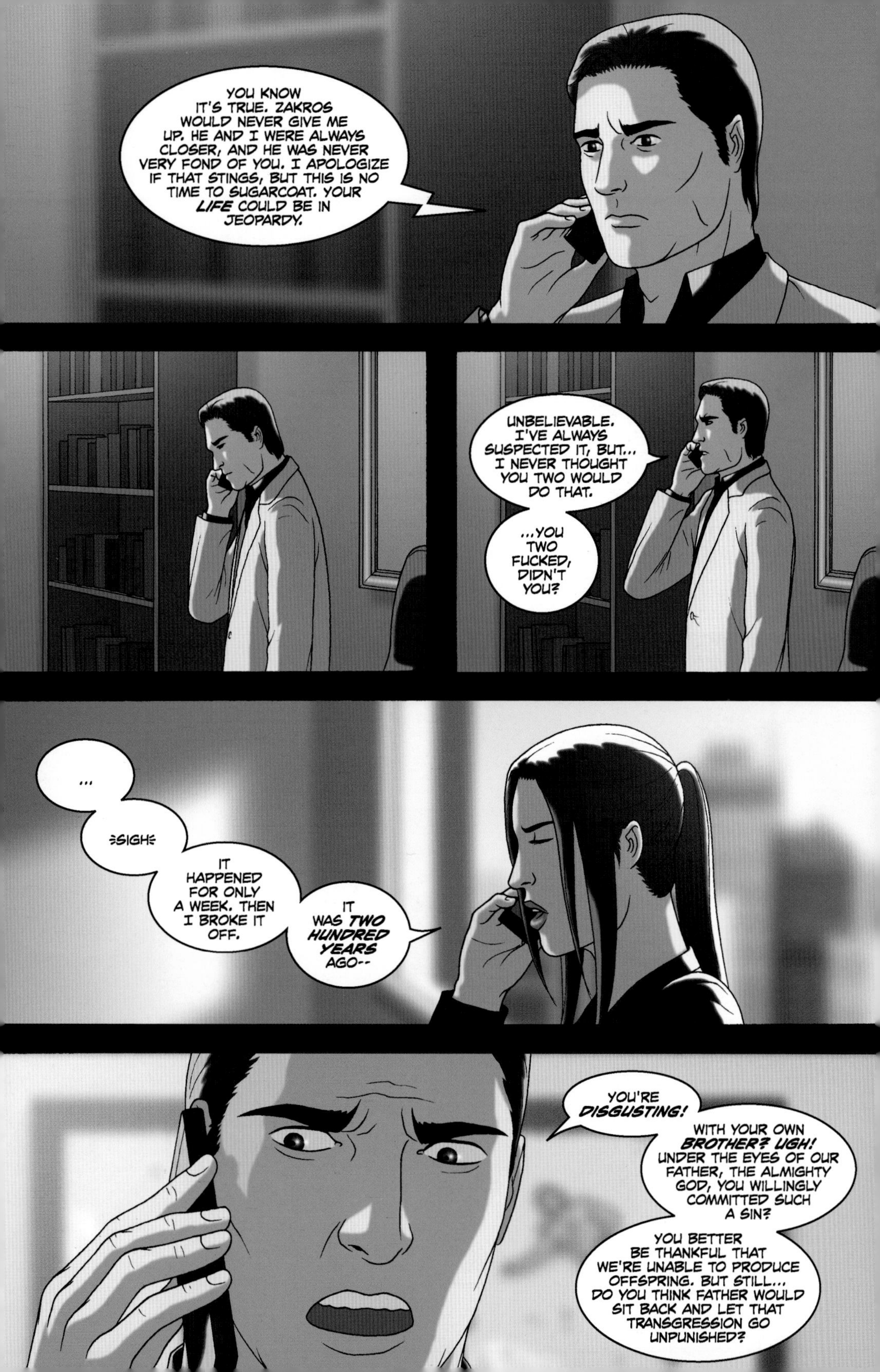
YOU KNOW IT'S TRUE. ZAKROS WOULD NEVER GIVE ME UP. HE AND I WERE ALWAYS CLOSER, AND HE WAS NEVER VERY FOND OF YOU. I APOLOGIZE IF THAT STINGS, BUT THIS IS NO TIME TO SUGARCOAT. YOUR *LIFE* COULD BE IN JEOPARDY.
UNBELIEVABLE. I'VE ALWAYS SUSPECTED IT, BUT... I NEVER THOUGHT YOU TWO WOULD DO THAT.
...YOU TWO FUCKED, DIDN'T YOU?
...
SIGH
IT HAPPENED FOR ONLY A WEEK. THEN I BROKE IT OFF.
IT WAS ***TWO HUNDRED YEARS*** AGO--
YOU'RE ***DISGUSTING!***
WITH YOUR OWN ***BROTHER? UGH!*** UNDER THE EYES OF OUR FATHER, THE ALMIGHTY GOD, YOU WILLINGLY COMMITTED SUCH A SIN?
YOU BETTER BE THANKFUL THAT WE'RE UNABLE TO PRODUCE OFFSPRING. BUT STILL... DO YOU THINK FATHER WOULD SIT BACK AND LET THAT TRANSGRESSION GO UNPUNISHED?

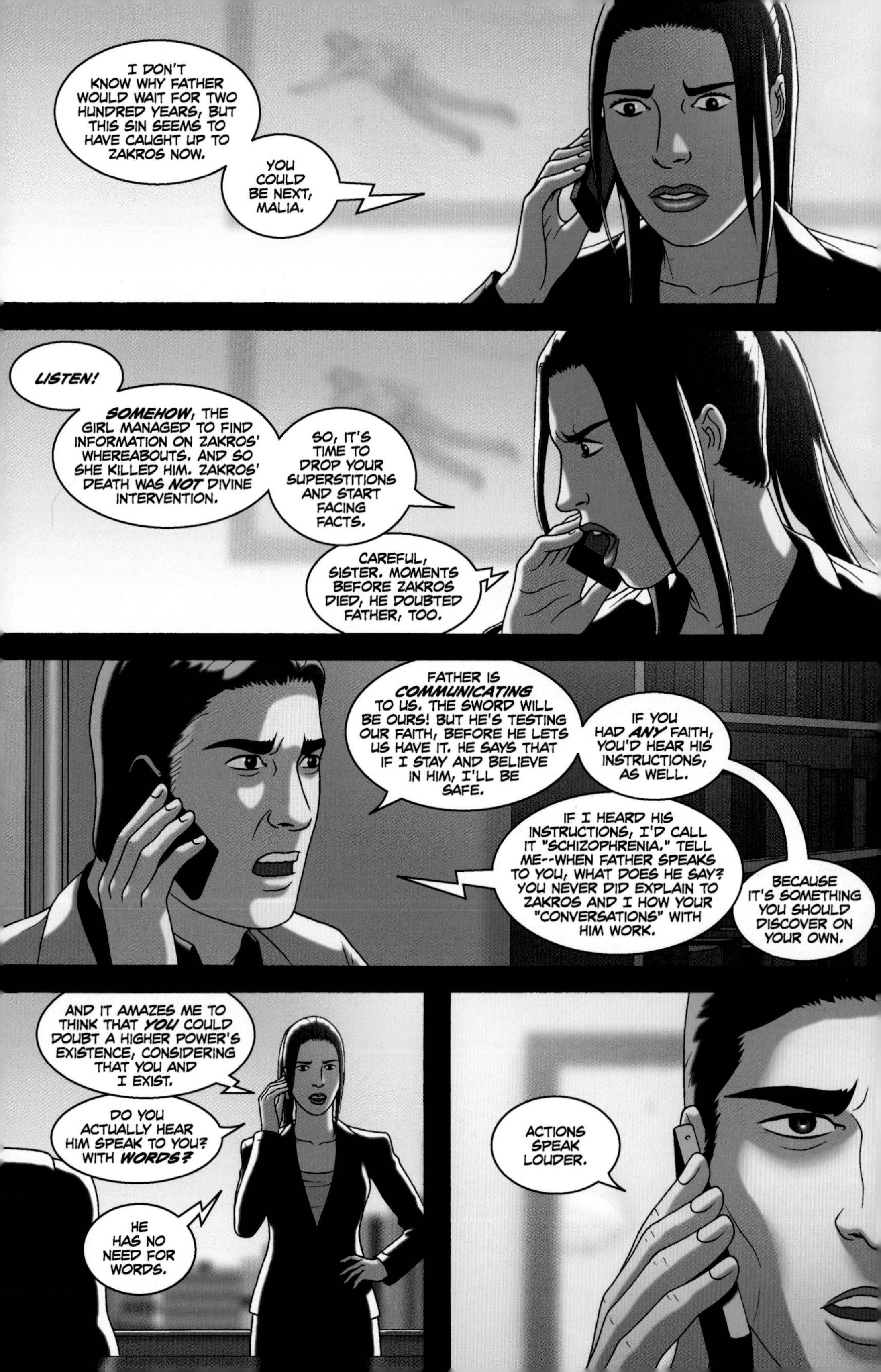
I DON'T KNOW WHY FATHER WOULD WAIT FOR TWO HUNDRED YEARS, BUT THIS SIN SEEMS TO HAVE CAUGHT UP TO ZAKROS NOW.
YOU COULD BE NEXT, MALIA.
LISTEN!
SOMEHOW, THE GIRL MANAGED TO FIND INFORMATION ON ZAKROS' WHEREABOUTS. AND SO SHE KILLED HIM. ZAKROS' DEATH WAS NOT DIVINE INTERVENTION.
SO, IT'S TIME TO DROP YOUR SUPERSTITIONS AND START FACING FACTS.
CAREFUL, SISTER. MOMENTS BEFORE ZAKROS DIED, HE DOUBTED FATHER, TOO.
FATHER IS COMMUNICATING TO US. THE SWORD WILL BE OURS! BUT HE'S TESTING OUR FAITH, BEFORE HE LETS US HAVE IT. HE SAYS THAT IF I STAY AND BELIEVE IN HIM, I'LL BE SAFE.
IF YOU HAD ANY FAITH, YOU'D HEAR HIS INSTRUCTIONS, AS WELL.
IF I HEARD HIS INSTRUCTIONS, I'D CALL IT "SCHIZOPHRENIA." TELL ME--WHEN FATHER SPEAKS TO YOU, WHAT DOES HE SAY? YOU NEVER DID EXPLAIN TO ZAKROS AND I HOW YOUR "CONVERSATIONS" WITH HIM WORK.
BECAUSE IT'S SOMETHING YOU SHOULD DISCOVER ON YOUR OWN.
AND IT AMAZES ME TO THINK THAT YOU COULD DOUBT A HIGHER POWER'S EXISTENCE, CONSIDERING THAT YOU AND I EXIST.
DO YOU ACTUALLY HEAR HIM SPEAK TO YOU? WITH WORDS?
HE HAS NO NEED FOR WORDS.
ACTIONS SPEAK LOUDER.

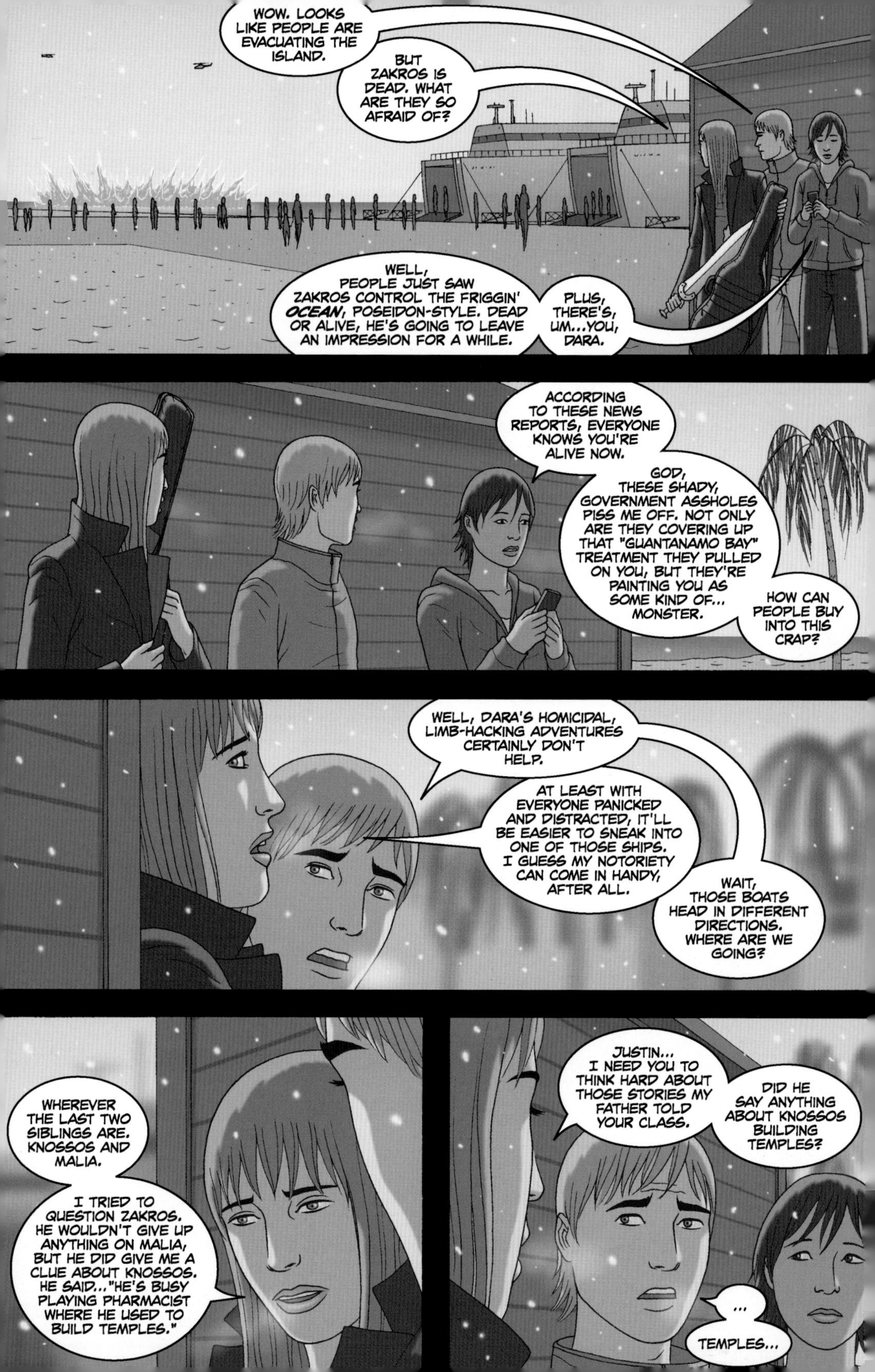
WOW. LOOKS LIKE PEOPLE ARE EVACUATING THE ISLAND.
BUT ZAKROS IS DEAD. WHAT ARE THEY SO AFRAID OF?
WELL, PEOPLE JUST SAW ZAKROS CONTROL THE FRIGGIN' OCEAN, POSEIDON-STYLE. DEAD OR ALIVE, HE'S GOING TO LEAVE AN IMPRESSION FOR A WHILE.
PLUS, THERE'S, UM...YOU, DARA.
ACCORDING TO THESE NEWS REPORTS, EVERYONE KNOWS YOU'RE ALIVE NOW.
GOD, THESE SHADY, GOVERNMENT ASSHOLES PISS ME OFF. NOT ONLY ARE THEY COVERING UP THAT "GUANTANAMO BAY" TREATMENT THEY PULLED ON YOU, BUT THEY'RE PAINTING YOU AS SOME KIND OF... MONSTER.
HOW CAN PEOPLE BUY INTO THIS CRAP?
WELL, DARA'S HOMICIDAL, LIMB-HACKING ADVENTURES CERTAINLY DON'T HELP.
AT LEAST WITH EVERYONE PANICKED AND DISTRACTED, IT'LL BE EASIER TO SNEAK INTO ONE OF THOSE SHIPS. I GUESS MY NOTORIETY CAN COME IN HANDY, AFTER ALL.
WAIT, THOSE BOATS HEAD IN DIFFERENT DIRECTIONS. WHERE ARE WE GOING?
WHEREVER THE LAST TWO SIBLINGS ARE. KNOSSOS AND MALIA.
I TRIED TO QUESTION ZAKROS. HE WOULDN'T GIVE UP ANYTHING ON MALIA, BUT HE DID GIVE ME A CLUE ABOUT KNOSSOS. HE SAID..."HE'S BUSY PLAYING PHARMACIST WHERE HE USED TO BUILD TEMPLES."
JUSTIN... I NEED YOU TO THINK HARD ABOUT THOSE STORIES MY FATHER TOLD YOUR CLASS.
DID HE SAY ANYTHING ABOUT KNOSSOS BUILDING TEMPLES?
...
TEMPLES...

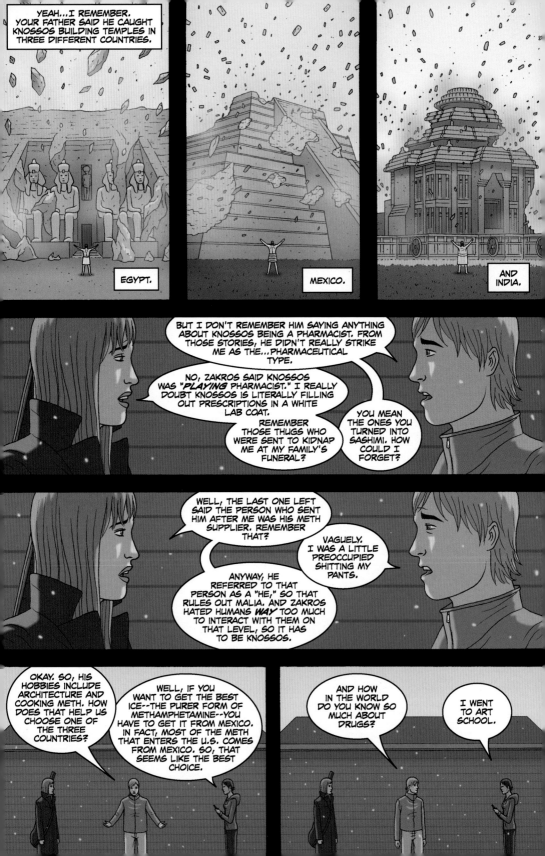

YEAH...I REMEMBER. YOUR FATHER SAID HE CAUGHT KNOSSOS BUILDING TEMPLES IN THREE DIFFERENT COUNTRIES.

EGYPT.

MEXICO.

AND INDIA.

BUT I DON'T REMEMBER HIM SAYING ANYTHING ABOUT KNOSSOS BEING A PHARMACIST. FROM THOSE STORIES, HE DIDN'T REALLY STRIKE ME AS THE...PHARMACEUTICAL TYPE.

NO, ZAKROS SAID KNOSSOS WAS *"PLAYING* PHARMACIST." I REALLY DOUBT KNOSSOS IS LITERALLY FILLING OUT PRESCRIPTIONS IN A WHITE LAB COAT.

REMEMBER THOSE THUGS WHO WERE SENT TO KIDNAP ME AT MY FAMILY'S FUNERAL?

YOU MEAN THE ONES YOU TURNED INTO SASHIMI. HOW COULD I FORGET?

WELL, THE LAST ONE LEFT SAID THE PERSON WHO SENT HIM AFTER ME WAS HIS METH SUPPLIER. REMEMBER THAT?

VAGUELY. I WAS A LITTLE PREOCCUPIED SHITTING MY PANTS.

ANYWAY, HE REFERRED TO THAT PERSON AS A "HE," SO THAT RULES OUT MALIA, AND ZAKROS HATED HUMANS *WAY* TOO MUCH TO INTERACT WITH THEM ON THAT LEVEL, SO IT HAS TO BE KNOSSOS.

OKAY. SO, HIS HOBBIES INCLUDE ARCHITECTURE AND COOKING METH. HOW DOES THAT HELP US CHOOSE ONE OF THE THREE COUNTRIES?

WELL, IF YOU WANT TO GET THE BEST ICE--THE PURER FORM OF METHAMPHETAMINE--YOU HAVE TO GET IT FROM MEXICO. IN FACT, MOST OF THE METH THAT ENTERS THE U.S. COMES FROM MEXICO. SO, THAT SEEMS LIKE THE BEST CHOICE.

AND HOW IN THE WORLD DO YOU KNOW SO MUCH ABOUT DRUGS?

I WENT TO ART SCHOOL.

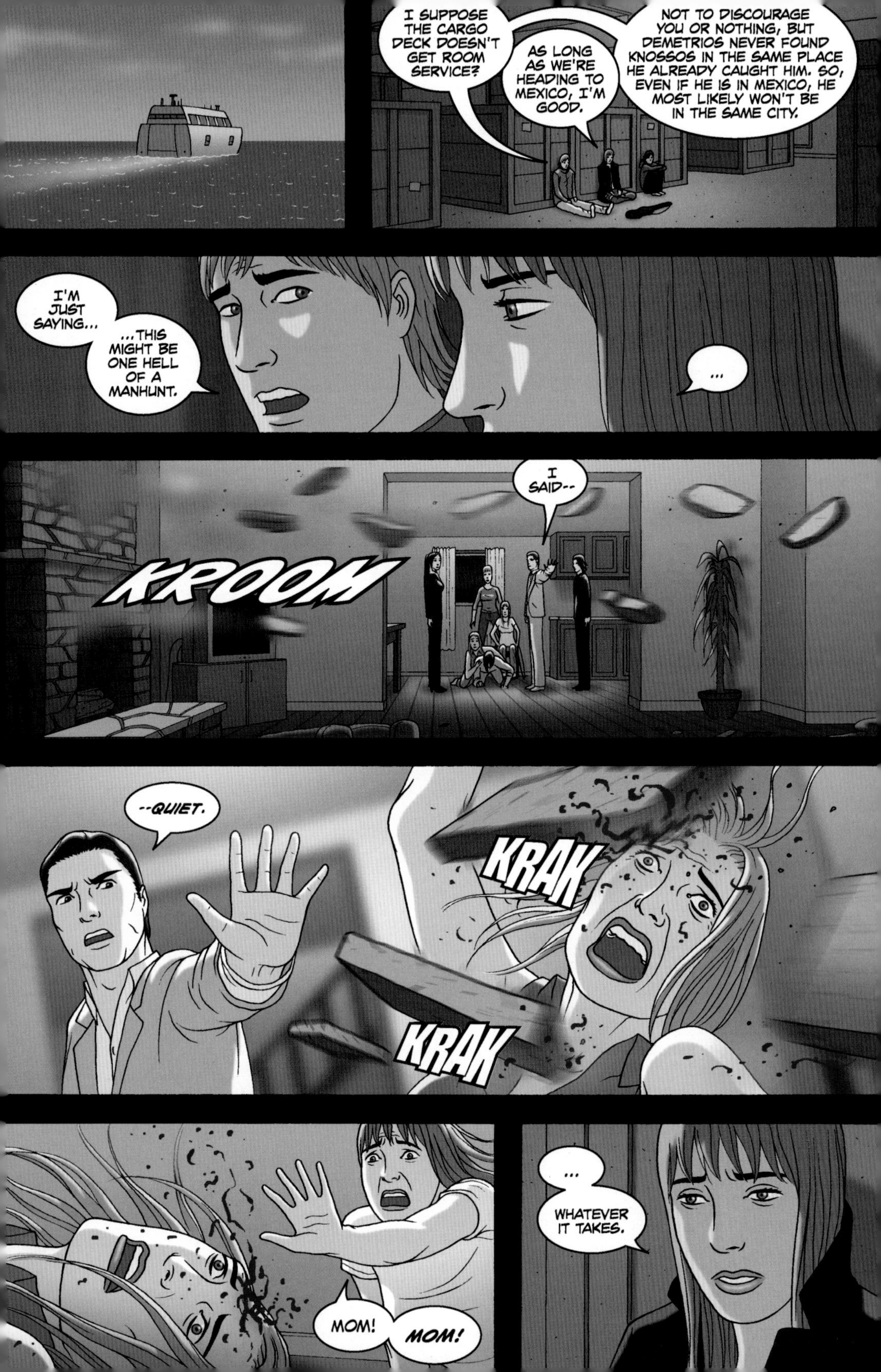
I SUPPOSE THE CARGO DECK DOESN'T GET ROOM SERVICE?
AS LONG AS WE'RE HEADING TO MEXICO, I'M GOOD.
NOT TO DISCOURAGE YOU OR NOTHING, BUT DEMETRIOS NEVER FOUND KNOSSOS IN THE SAME PLACE HE ALREADY CAUGHT HIM. SO, EVEN IF HE IS IN MEXICO, HE MOST LIKELY WON'T BE IN THE SAME CITY.
I'M JUST SAYING...
...THIS MIGHT BE ONE HELL OF A MANHUNT.
...
KROOM
I SAID--
--QUIET.
KRAK
KRAK
MOM!
MOM!
...
WHATEVER IT TAKES.

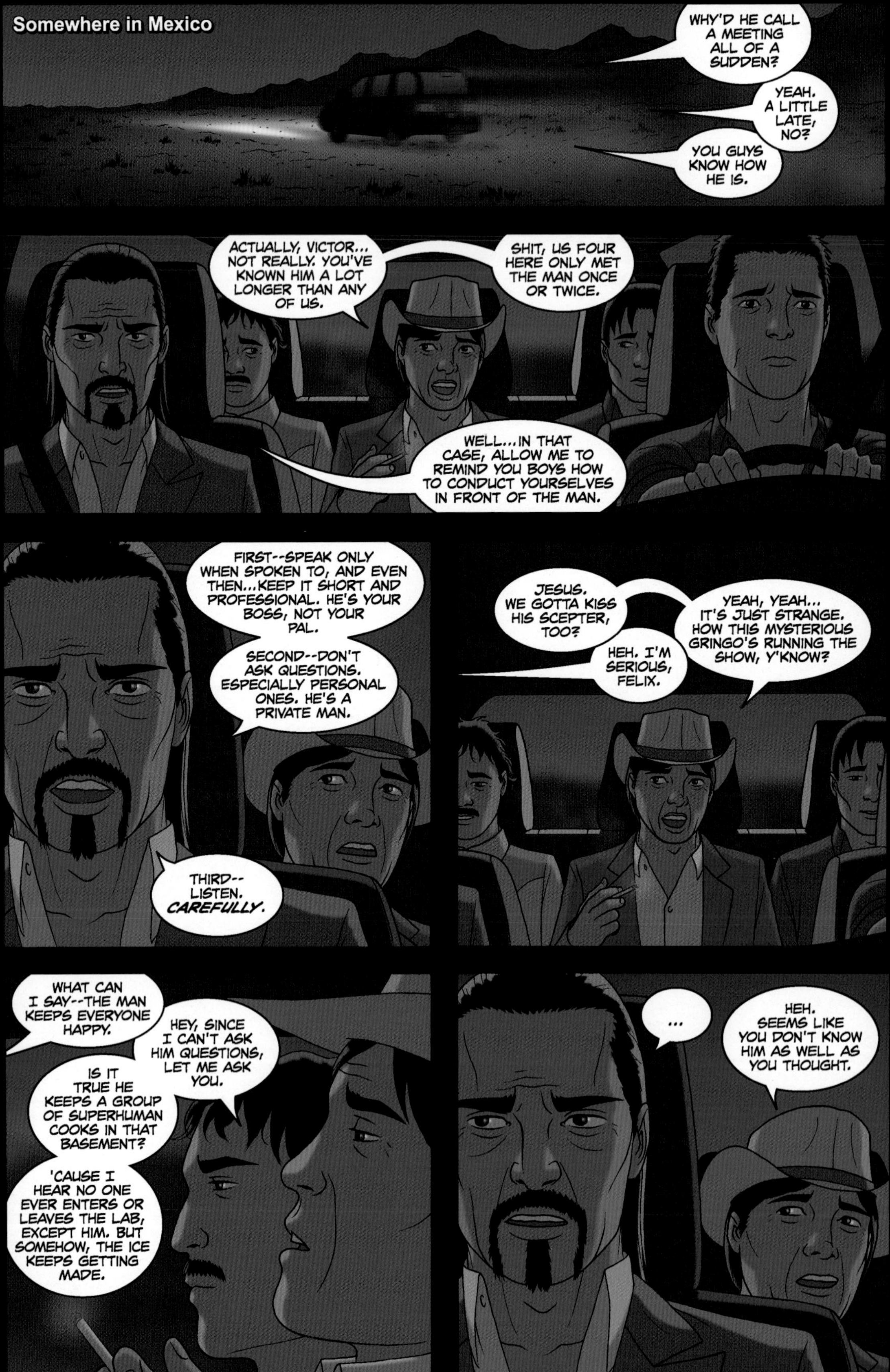
Somewhere in Mexico
WHY'D HE CALL A MEETING ALL OF A SUDDEN?
YEAH. A LITTLE LATE, NO?
YOU GUYS KNOW HOW HE IS.
ACTUALLY, VICTOR... NOT REALLY. YOU'VE KNOWN HIM A LOT LONGER THAN ANY OF US.
SHIT, US FOUR HERE ONLY MET THE MAN ONCE OR TWICE.
WELL...IN THAT CASE, ALLOW ME TO REMIND YOU BOYS HOW TO CONDUCT YOURSELVES IN FRONT OF THE MAN.
FIRST--SPEAK ONLY WHEN SPOKEN TO, AND EVEN THEN...KEEP IT SHORT AND PROFESSIONAL. HE'S YOUR BOSS, NOT YOUR PAL.
SECOND--DON'T ASK QUESTIONS. ESPECIALLY PERSONAL ONES. HE'S A PRIVATE MAN.
THIRD-- LISTEN. *CAREFULLY*.
JESUS. WE GOTTA KISS HIS SCEPTER, TOO?
HEH. I'M SERIOUS, FELIX.
YEAH, YEAH... IT'S JUST STRANGE. HOW THIS MYSTERIOUS GRINGO'S RUNNING THE SHOW, Y'KNOW?
WHAT CAN I SAY--THE MAN KEEPS EVERYONE HAPPY.
HEY, SINCE I CAN'T ASK HIM QUESTIONS, LET ME ASK YOU.
IS IT TRUE HE KEEPS A GROUP OF SUPERHUMAN COOKS IN THAT BASEMENT?
'CAUSE I HEAR NO ONE EVER ENTERS OR LEAVES THE LAB, EXCEPT HIM. BUT SOMEHOW, THE ICE KEEPS GETTING MADE.
...
HEH. SEEMS LIKE YOU DON'T KNOW HIM AS WELL AS YOU THOUGHT.

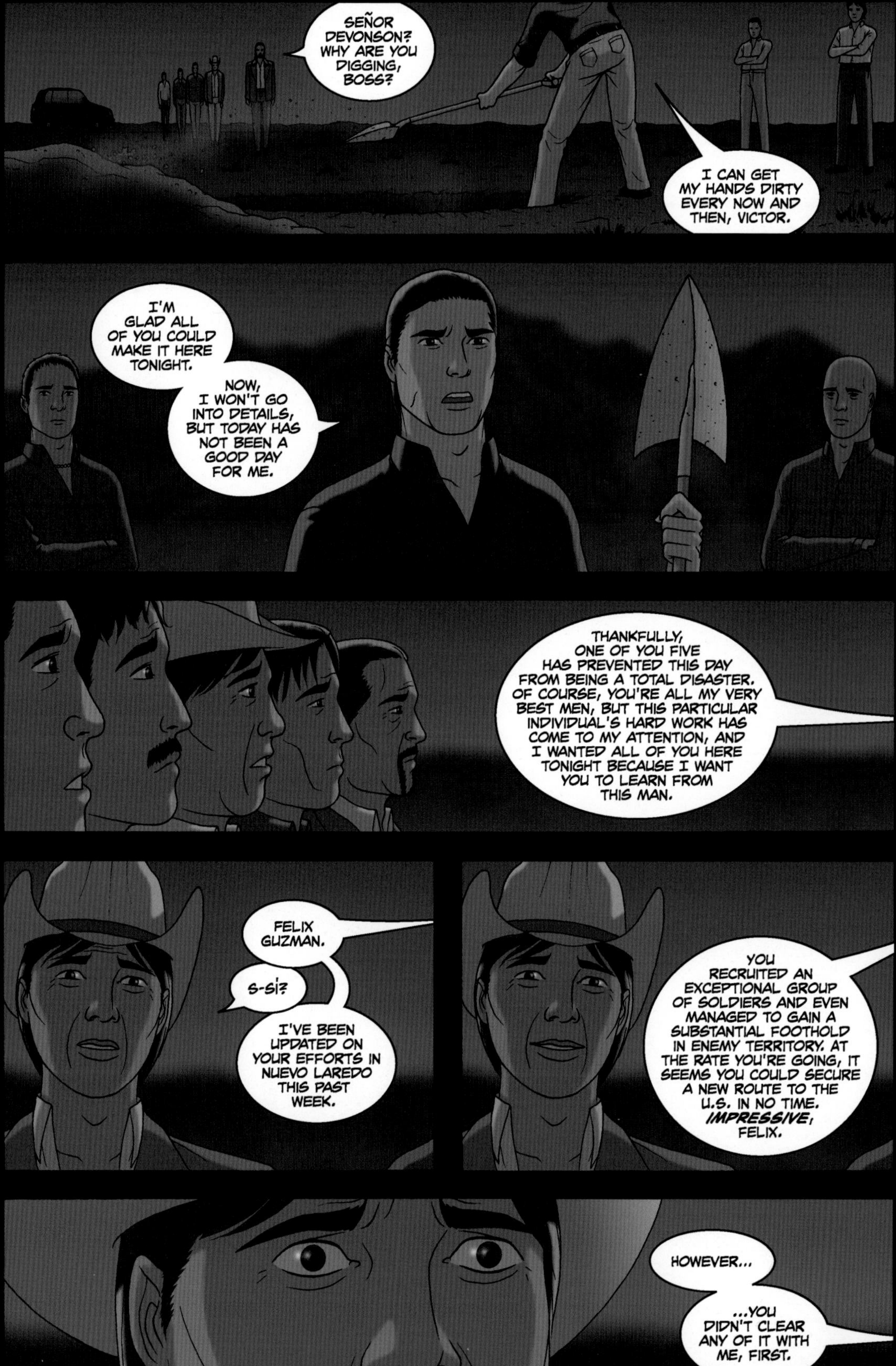
SEÑOR DEVONSON? WHY ARE YOU DIGGING, BOSS?
I CAN GET MY HANDS DIRTY EVERY NOW AND THEN, VICTOR.
I'M GLAD ALL OF YOU COULD MAKE IT HERE TONIGHT.
NOW, I WON'T GO INTO DETAILS, BUT TODAY HAS NOT BEEN A GOOD DAY FOR ME.
THANKFULLY, ONE OF YOU FIVE HAS PREVENTED THIS DAY FROM BEING A TOTAL DISASTER. OF COURSE, YOU'RE ALL MY VERY BEST MEN, BUT THIS PARTICULAR INDIVIDUAL'S HARD WORK HAS COME TO MY ATTENTION, AND I WANTED ALL OF YOU HERE TONIGHT BECAUSE I WANT YOU TO LEARN FROM THIS MAN.
FELIX GUZMAN.
S-SÍ?
I'VE BEEN UPDATED ON YOUR EFFORTS IN NUEVO LAREDO THIS PAST WEEK.
YOU RECRUITED AN EXCEPTIONAL GROUP OF SOLDIERS AND EVEN MANAGED TO GAIN A SUBSTANTIAL FOOTHOLD IN ENEMY TERRITORY. AT THE RATE YOU'RE GOING, IT SEEMS YOU COULD SECURE A NEW ROUTE TO THE U.S. IN NO TIME. *IMPRESSIVE*, FELIX.
HOWEVER...
...YOU DIDN'T CLEAR ANY OF IT WITH ME, FIRST.

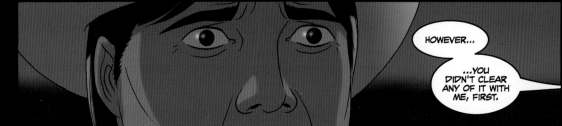

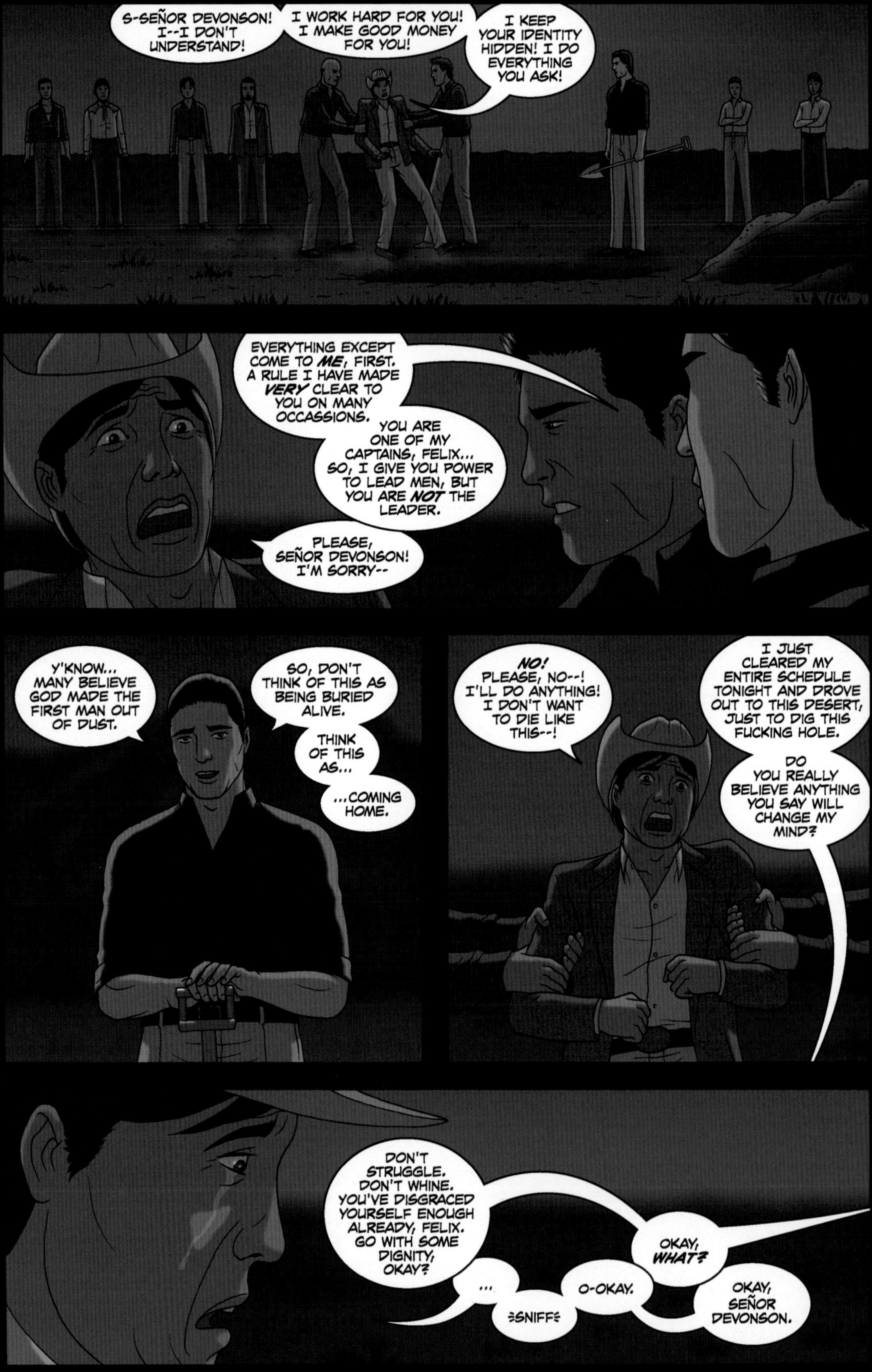
S-SEÑOR DEVONSON! I--I DON'T UNDERSTAND!
I WORK HARD FOR YOU! I MAKE GOOD MONEY FOR YOU!
I KEEP YOUR IDENTITY HIDDEN! I DO EVERYTHING YOU ASK!
EVERYTHING EXCEPT COME TO *ME*, FIRST. A RULE I HAVE MADE *VERY* CLEAR TO YOU ON MANY OCCASSIONS.
YOU ARE ONE OF MY CAPTAINS, FELIX... SO, I GIVE YOU POWER TO LEAD MEN, BUT YOU ARE *NOT* THE LEADER.
PLEASE, SEÑOR DEVONSON! I'M SORRY--
Y'KNOW... MANY BELIEVE GOD MADE THE FIRST MAN OUT OF DUST.
SO, DON'T THINK OF THIS AS BEING BURIED ALIVE.
THINK OF THIS AS...
...COMING HOME.
NO! PLEASE, NO--! I'LL DO ANYTHING! I DON'T WANT TO DIE LIKE THIS--!
I JUST CLEARED MY ENTIRE SCHEDULE TONIGHT AND DROVE OUT TO THIS DESERT, JUST TO DIG THIS FUCKING HOLE.
DO YOU REALLY BELIEVE ANYTHING YOU SAY WILL CHANGE MY MIND?
DON'T STRUGGLE. DON'T WHINE. YOU'VE DISGRACED YOURSELF ENOUGH ALREADY, FELIX. GO WITH SOME DIGNITY, OKAY?
...
≡SNIFF≡
O-OKAY.
OKAY, *WHAT?*
OKAY, SEÑOR DEVONSON.

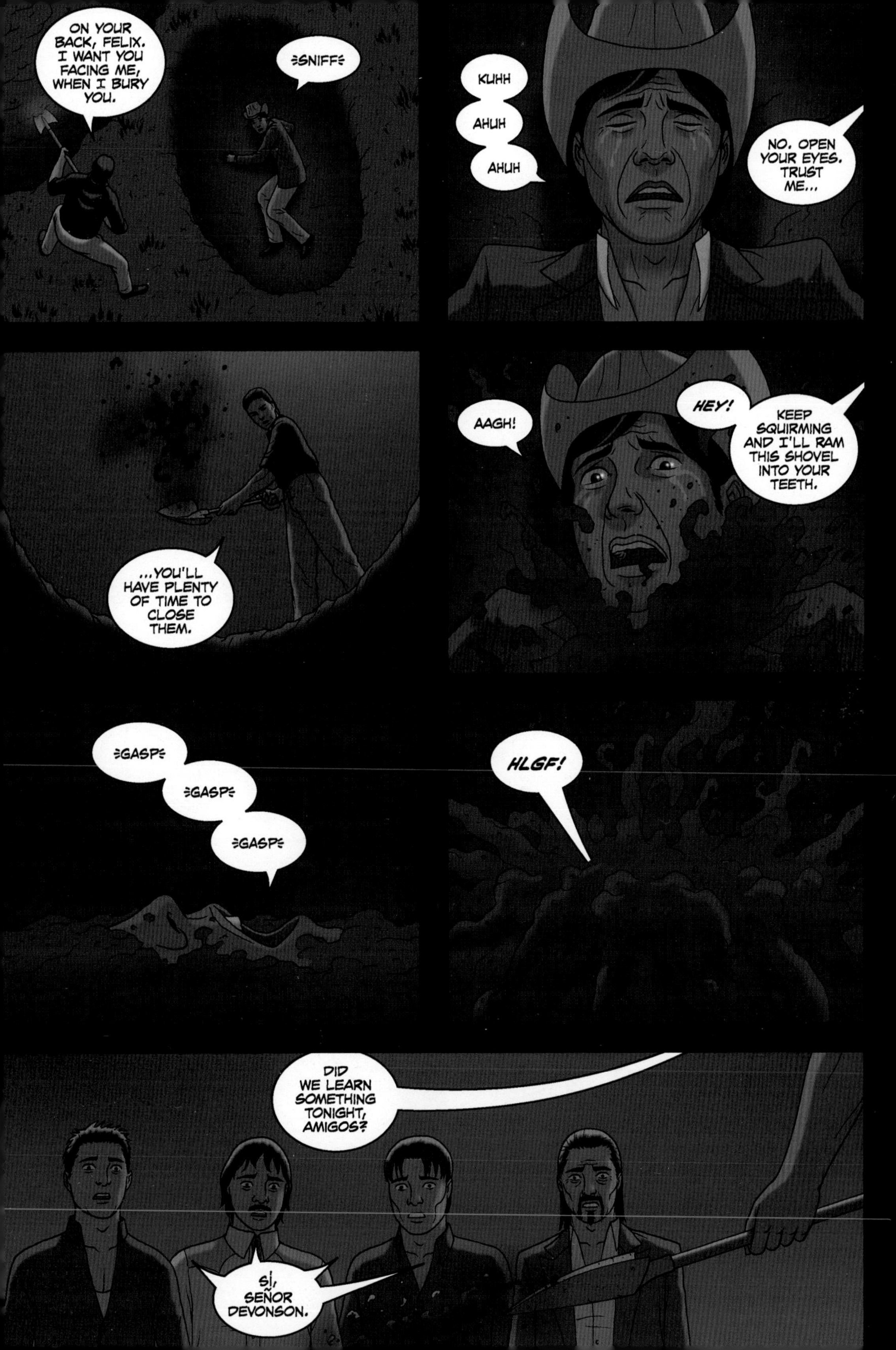
ON YOUR BACK, FELIX. I WANT YOU FACING ME, WHEN I BURY YOU.
SNIFF
KUHH
AHUH
AHUH
NO. OPEN YOUR EYES. TRUST ME...
...YOU'LL HAVE PLENTY OF TIME TO CLOSE THEM.
AAGH!
HEY!
KEEP SQUIRMING AND I'LL RAM THIS SHOVEL INTO YOUR TEETH.
GASP
GASP
GASP
HLGF!
DID WE LEARN SOMETHING TONIGHT, AMIGOS?
SÍ, SEÑOR DEVONSON.

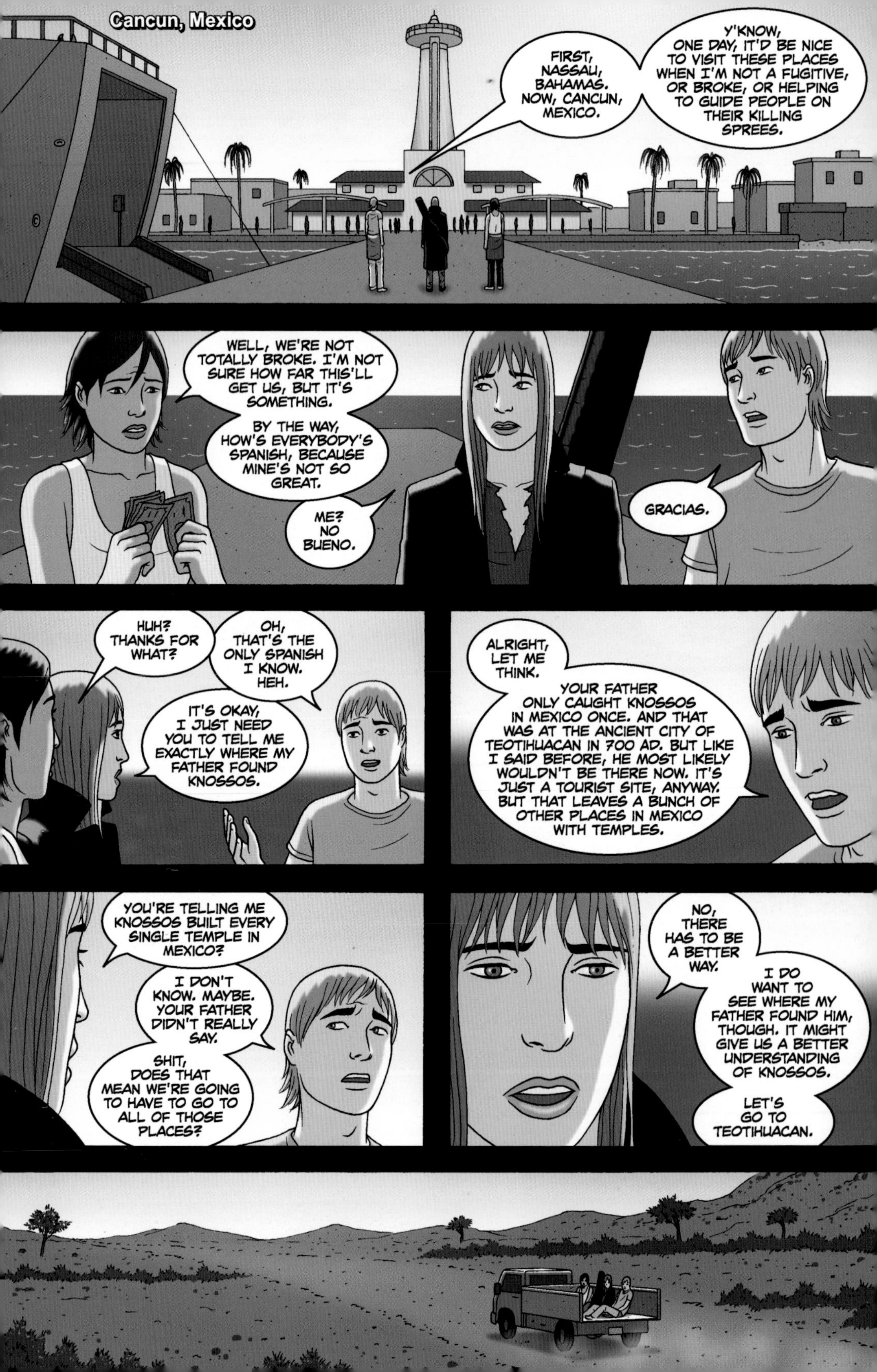
Cancun, Mexico
FIRST, NASSAU, BAHAMAS. NOW, CANCUN, MEXICO.
Y'KNOW, ONE DAY, IT'D BE NICE TO VISIT THESE PLACES WHEN I'M NOT A FUGITIVE, OR BROKE, OR HELPING TO GUIDE PEOPLE ON THEIR KILLING SPREES.
WELL, WE'RE NOT TOTALLY BROKE. I'M NOT SURE HOW FAR THIS'LL GET US, BUT IT'S SOMETHING.
BY THE WAY, HOW'S EVERYBODY'S SPANISH, BECAUSE MINE'S NOT SO GREAT.
ME? NO BUENO.
GRACIAS.
HUH? THANKS FOR WHAT?
OH, THAT'S THE ONLY SPANISH I KNOW. HEH.
IT'S OKAY, I JUST NEED YOU TO TELL ME EXACTLY WHERE MY FATHER FOUND KNOSSOS.
ALRIGHT, LET ME THINK.
YOUR FATHER ONLY CAUGHT KNOSSOS IN MEXICO ONCE. AND THAT WAS AT THE ANCIENT CITY OF TEOTIHUACAN IN 700 AD. BUT LIKE I SAID BEFORE, HE MOST LIKELY WOULDN'T BE THERE NOW. IT'S JUST A TOURIST SITE, ANYWAY. BUT THAT LEAVES A BUNCH OF OTHER PLACES IN MEXICO WITH TEMPLES.
YOU'RE TELLING ME KNOSSOS BUILT EVERY SINGLE TEMPLE IN MEXICO?
I DON'T KNOW. MAYBE. YOUR FATHER DIDN'T REALLY SAY.
SHIT, DOES THAT MEAN WE'RE GOING TO HAVE TO GO TO ALL OF THOSE PLACES?
NO, THERE HAS TO BE A BETTER WAY.
I DO WANT TO SEE WHERE MY FATHER FOUND HIM, THOUGH. IT MIGHT GIVE US A BETTER UNDERSTANDING OF KNOSSOS.
LET'S GO TO TEOTIHUACAN.

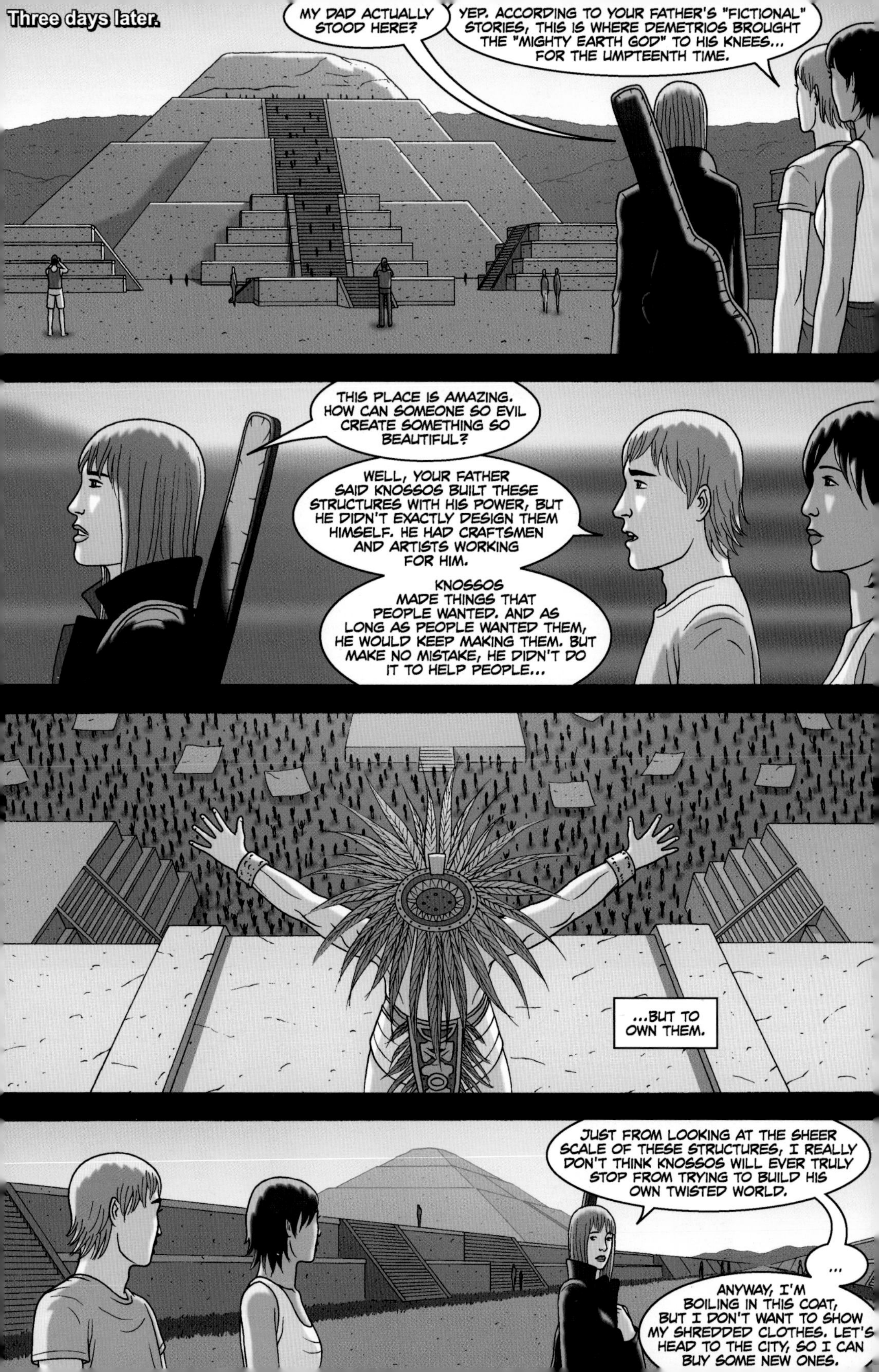
Three days later.
MY DAD ACTUALLY STOOD HERE?
YEP. ACCORDING TO YOUR FATHER'S "FICTIONAL" STORIES, THIS IS WHERE DEMETRIOS BROUGHT THE "MIGHTY EARTH GOD" TO HIS KNEES... FOR THE UMPTEENTH TIME.
THIS PLACE IS AMAZING. HOW CAN SOMEONE SO EVIL CREATE SOMETHING SO BEAUTIFUL?
WELL, YOUR FATHER SAID KNOSSOS BUILT THESE STRUCTURES WITH HIS POWER, BUT HE DIDN'T EXACTLY DESIGN THEM HIMSELF. HE HAD CRAFTSMEN AND ARTISTS WORKING FOR HIM.
KNOSSOS MADE THINGS THAT PEOPLE WANTED. AND AS LONG AS PEOPLE WANTED THEM, HE WOULD KEEP MAKING THEM. BUT MAKE NO MISTAKE, HE DIDN'T DO IT TO HELP PEOPLE...
...BUT TO OWN THEM.
JUST FROM LOOKING AT THE SHEER SCALE OF THESE STRUCTURES, I REALLY DON'T THINK KNOSSOS WILL EVER TRULY STOP FROM TRYING TO BUILD HIS OWN TWISTED WORLD.
...
ANYWAY, I'M BOILING IN THIS COAT, BUT I DON'T WANT TO SHOW MY SHREDDED CLOTHES. LET'S HEAD TO THE CITY, SO I CAN BUY SOME NEW ONES.

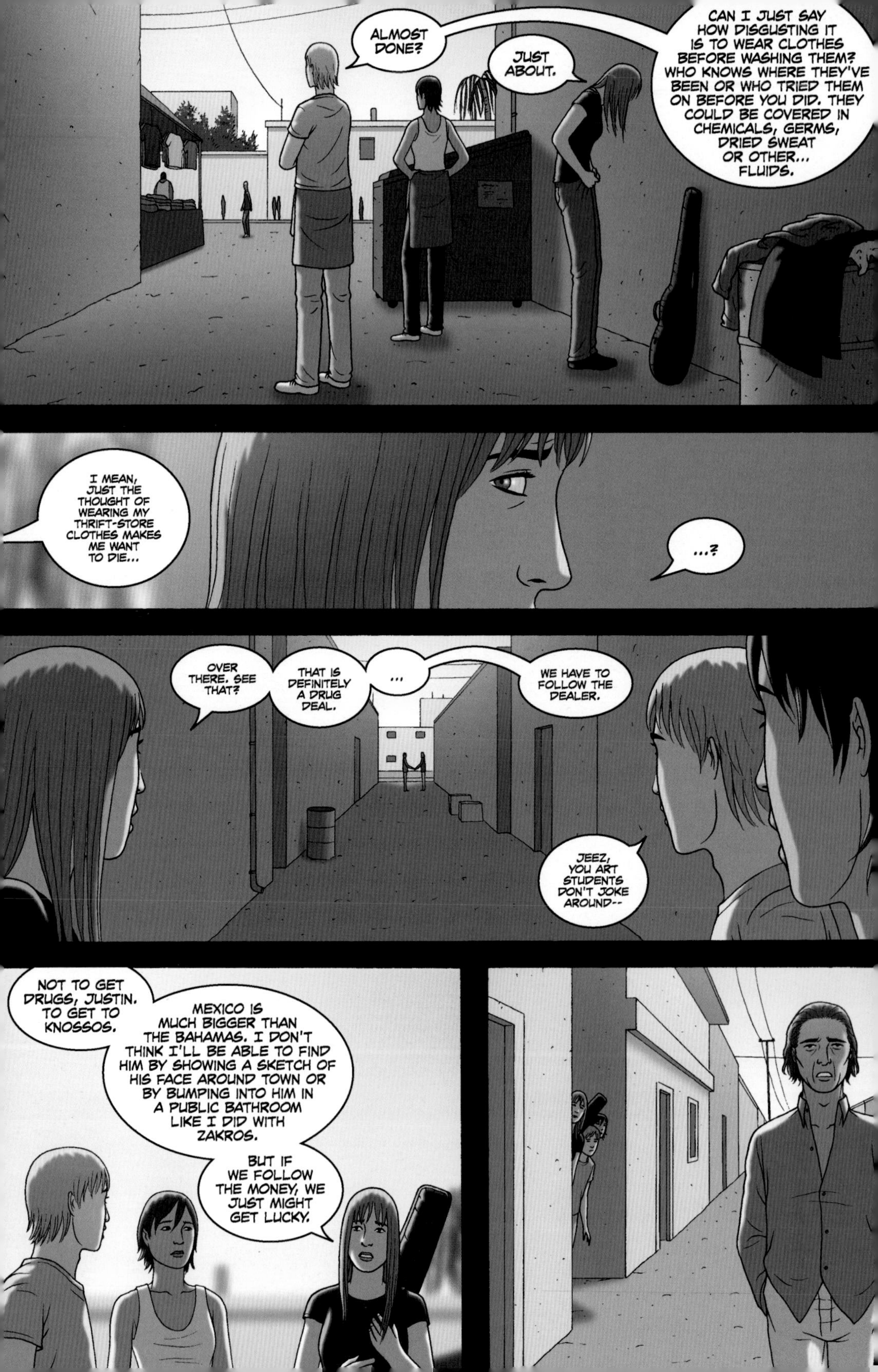
ALMOST DONE?
JUST ABOUT.
CAN I JUST SAY HOW DISGUSTING IT IS TO WEAR CLOTHES BEFORE WASHING THEM? WHO KNOWS WHERE THEY'VE BEEN OR WHO TRIED THEM ON BEFORE YOU DID. THEY COULD BE COVERED IN CHEMICALS, GERMS, DRIED SWEAT OR OTHER... FLUIDS.
I MEAN, JUST THE THOUGHT OF WEARING MY THRIFT-STORE CLOTHES MAKES ME WANT TO DIE...
...?
OVER THERE. SEE THAT?
THAT IS DEFINITELY A DRUG DEAL.
...
WE HAVE TO FOLLOW THE DEALER.
JEEZ, YOU ART STUDENTS DON'T JOKE AROUND--
NOT TO GET DRUGS, JUSTIN. TO GET TO KNOSSOS.
MEXICO IS MUCH BIGGER THAN THE BAHAMAS. I DON'T THINK I'LL BE ABLE TO FIND HIM BY SHOWING A SKETCH OF HIS FACE AROUND TOWN OR BY BUMPING INTO HIM IN A PUBLIC BATHROOM LIKE I DID WITH ZAKROS.
BUT IF WE FOLLOW THE MONEY, WE JUST MIGHT GET LUCKY.

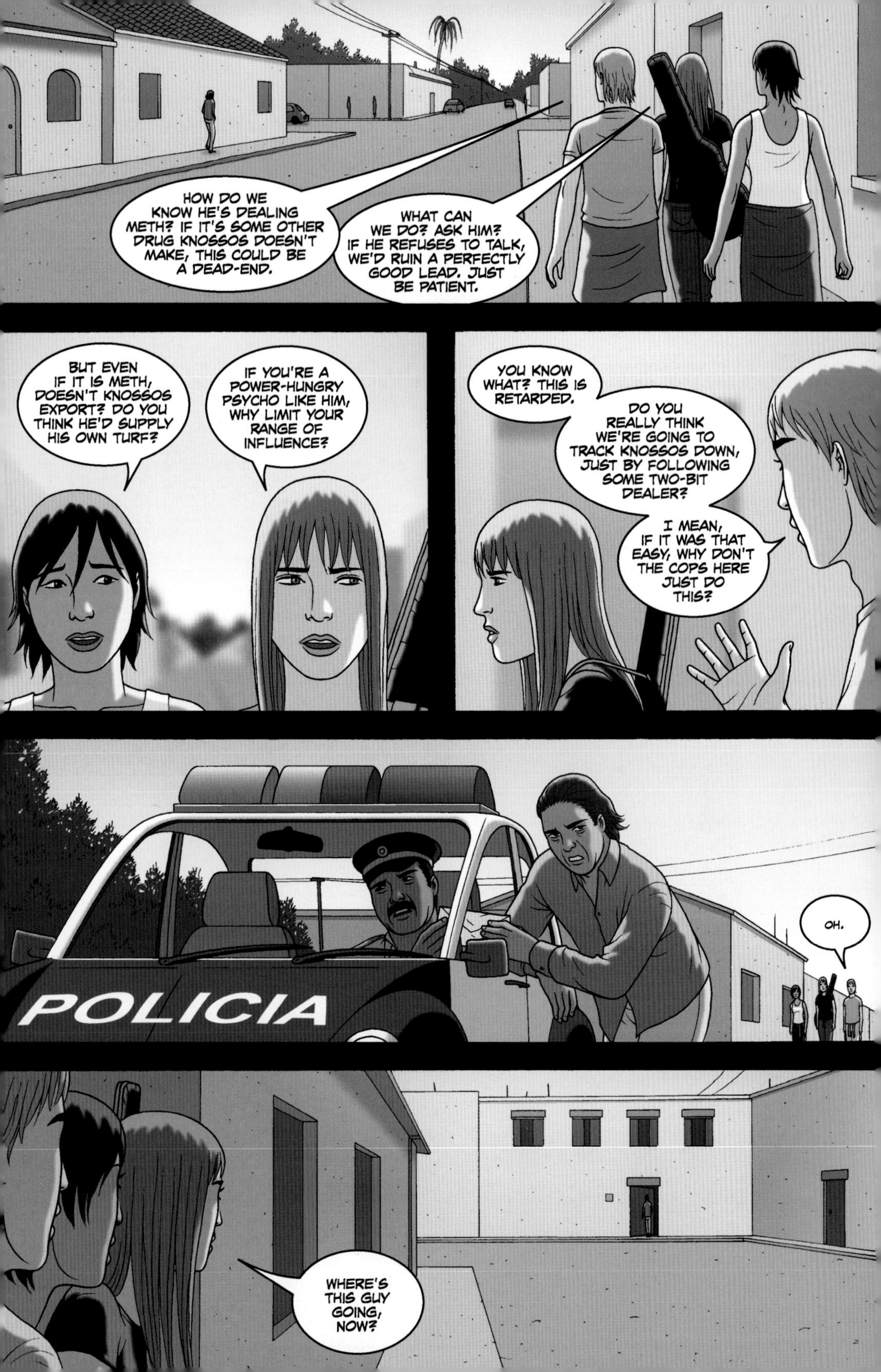
HOW DO WE KNOW HE'S DEALING METH? IF IT'S SOME OTHER DRUG KNOSSOS DOESN'T MAKE, THIS COULD BE A DEAD-END.
WHAT CAN WE DO? ASK HIM? IF HE REFUSES TO TALK, WE'D RUIN A PERFECTLY GOOD LEAD. JUST BE PATIENT.
BUT EVEN IF IT IS METH, DOESN'T KNOSSOS EXPORT? DO YOU THINK HE'D SUPPLY HIS OWN TURF?
IF YOU'RE A POWER-HUNGRY PSYCHO LIKE HIM, WHY LIMIT YOUR RANGE OF INFLUENCE?
YOU KNOW WHAT? THIS IS RETARDED.
DO YOU REALLY THINK WE'RE GOING TO TRACK KNOSSOS DOWN, JUST BY FOLLOWING SOME TWO-BIT DEALER?
I MEAN, IF IT WAS THAT EASY, WHY DON'T THE COPS HERE JUST DO THIS?
POLICIA
OH.
WHERE'S THIS GUY GOING, NOW?

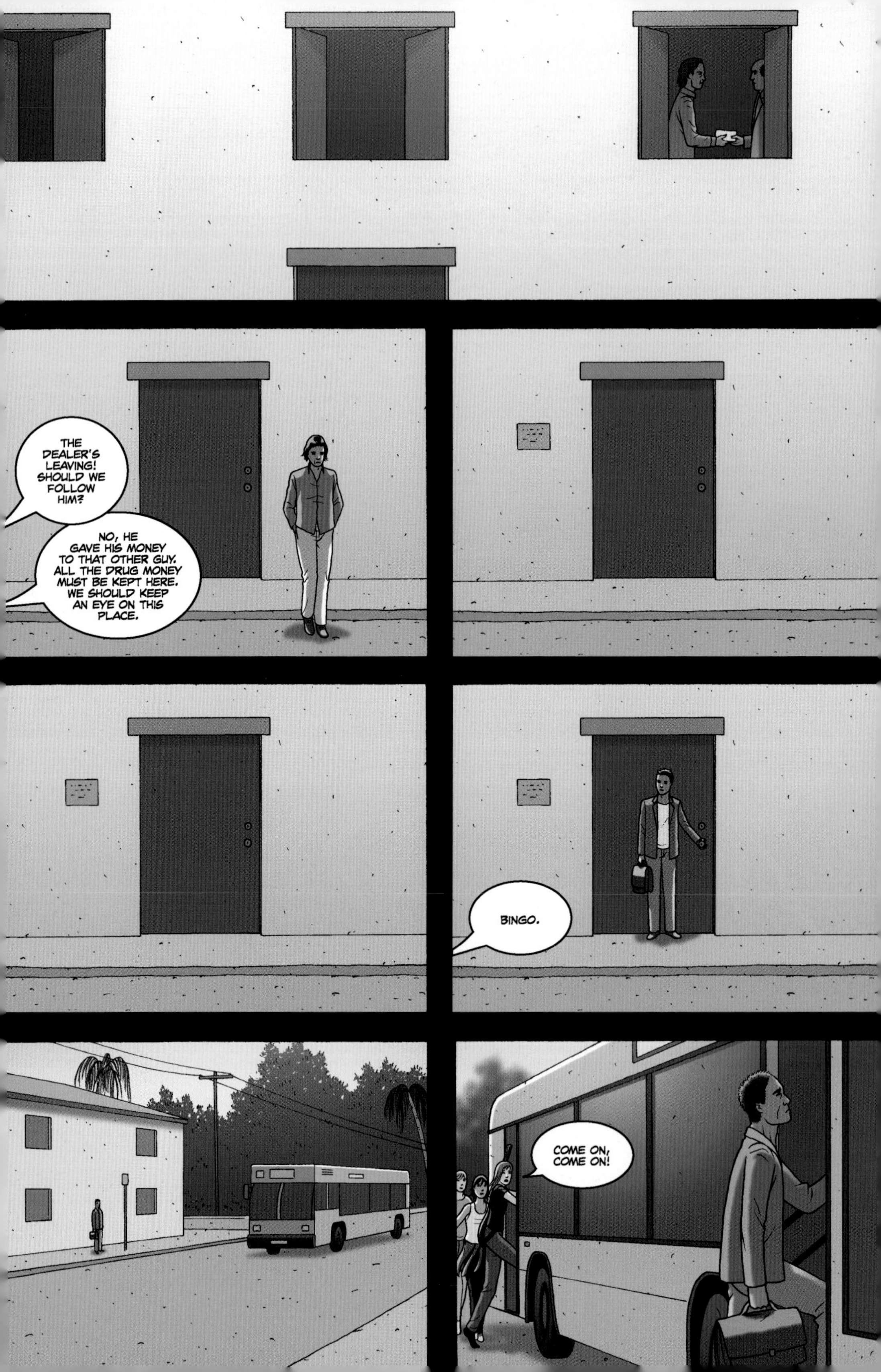

THE DEALER'S LEAVING! SHOULD WE FOLLOW HIM?
NO, HE GAVE HIS MONEY TO THAT OTHER GUY. ALL THE DRUG MONEY MUST BE KEPT HERE. WE SHOULD KEEP AN EYE ON THIS PLACE.
BINGO.
COME ON, COME ON!

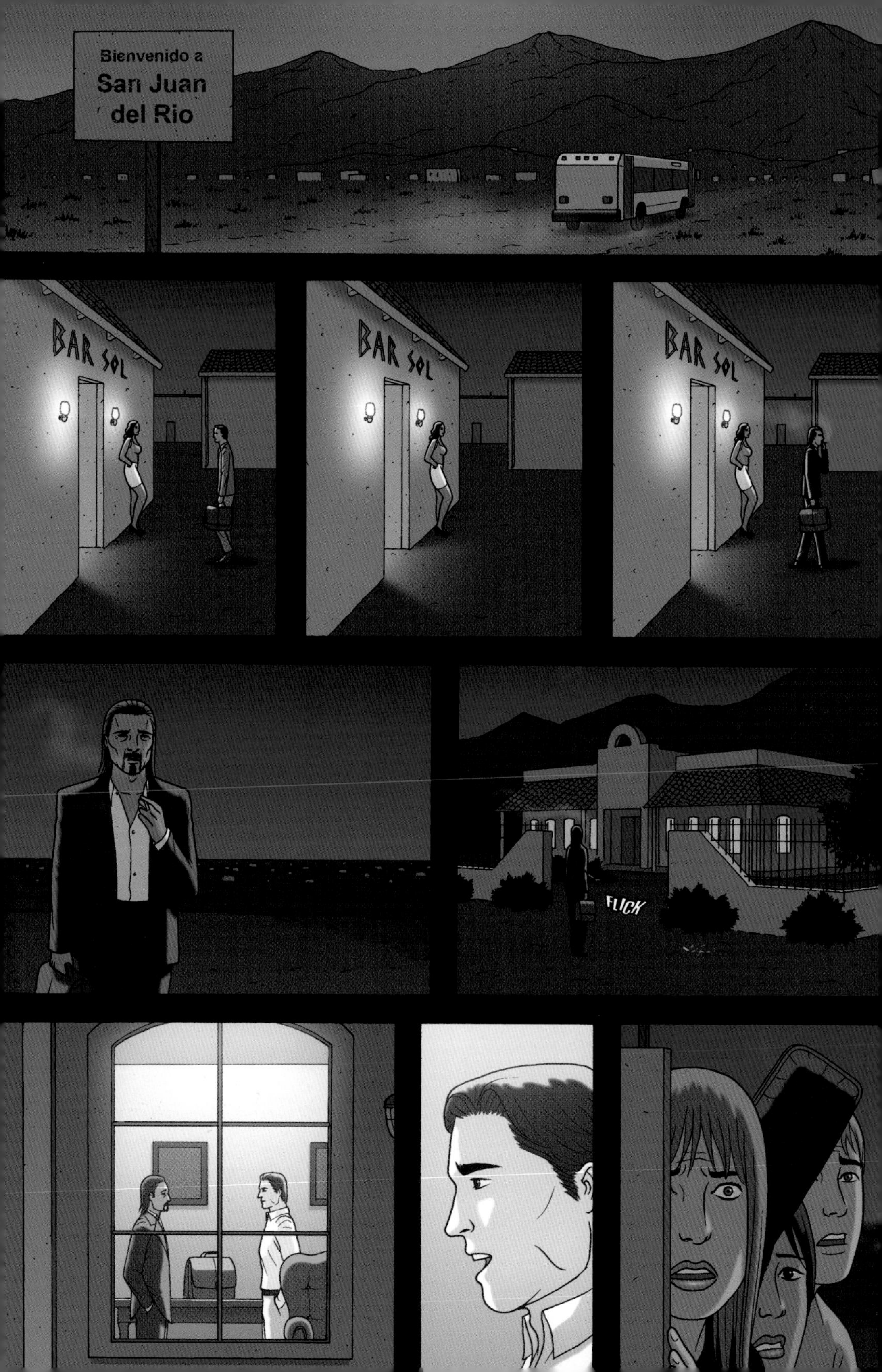

Bienvenido a
San Juan
del Rio
BAR SOL
BAR SOL
BAR SOL
FLICK

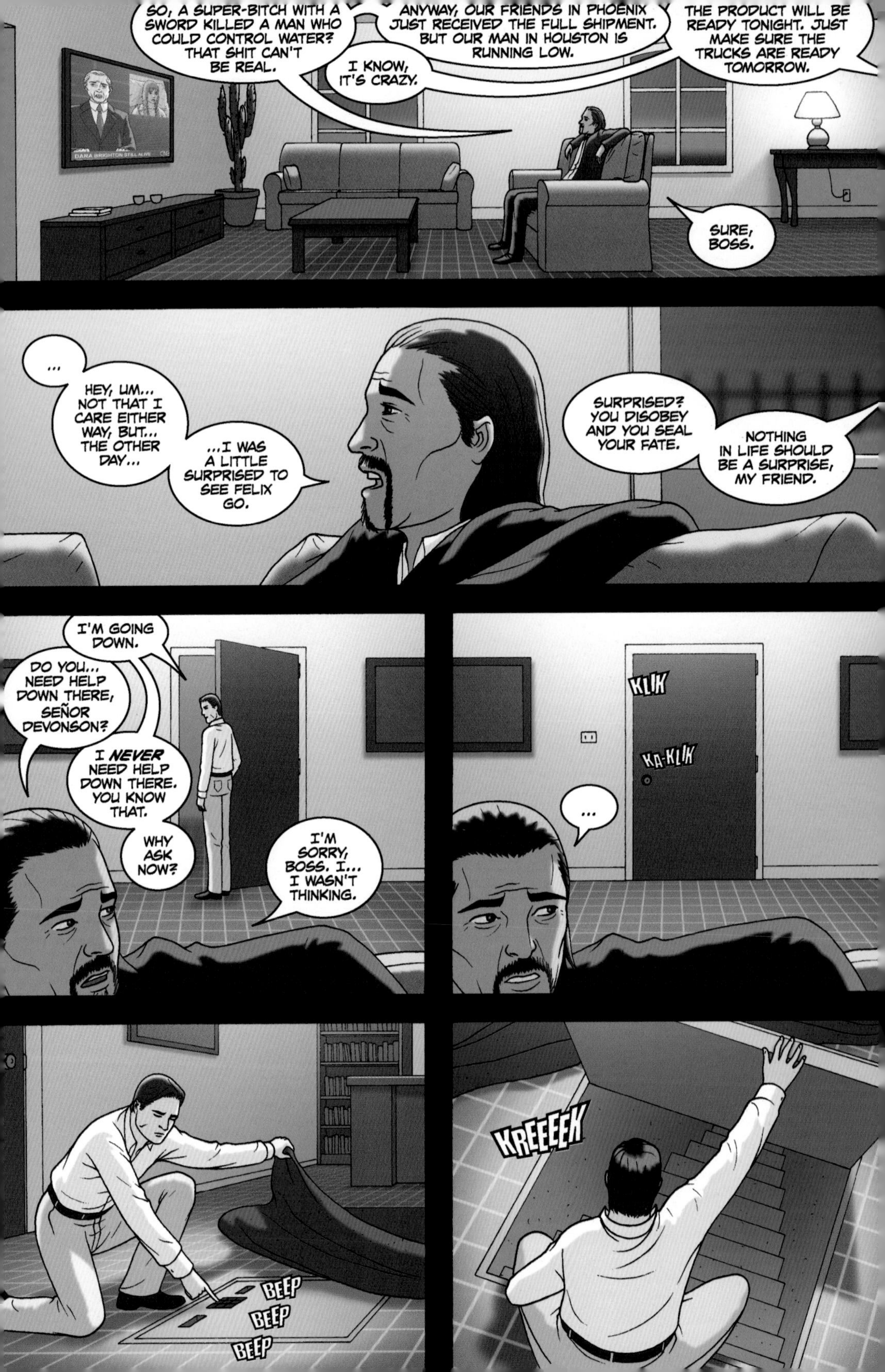
SO, A SUPER-BITCH WITH A SWORD KILLED A MAN WHO COULD CONTROL WATER? THAT SHIT CAN'T BE REAL.
I KNOW, IT'S CRAZY.
ANYWAY, OUR FRIENDS IN PHOENIX JUST RECEIVED THE FULL SHIPMENT. BUT OUR MAN IN HOUSTON IS RUNNING LOW.
THE PRODUCT WILL BE READY TONIGHT. JUST MAKE SURE THE TRUCKS ARE READY TOMORROW.
DARA BRIGHTON STILL ALIVE
SURE, BOSS.
...
HEY, UM... NOT THAT I CARE EITHER WAY, BUT... THE OTHER DAY...
...I WAS A LITTLE SURPRISED TO SEE FELIX GO.
SURPRISED? YOU DISOBEY AND YOU SEAL YOUR FATE.
NOTHING IN LIFE SHOULD BE A SURPRISE, MY FRIEND.
I'M GOING DOWN.
DO YOU... NEED HELP DOWN THERE, SEÑOR DEVONSON?
I *NEVER* NEED HELP DOWN THERE. YOU KNOW THAT.
WHY ASK NOW?
I'M SORRY, BOSS. I... I WASN'T THINKING.
KLIK
KA-KLIK
...
BEEP
BEEP
BEEP
KREEEEEK

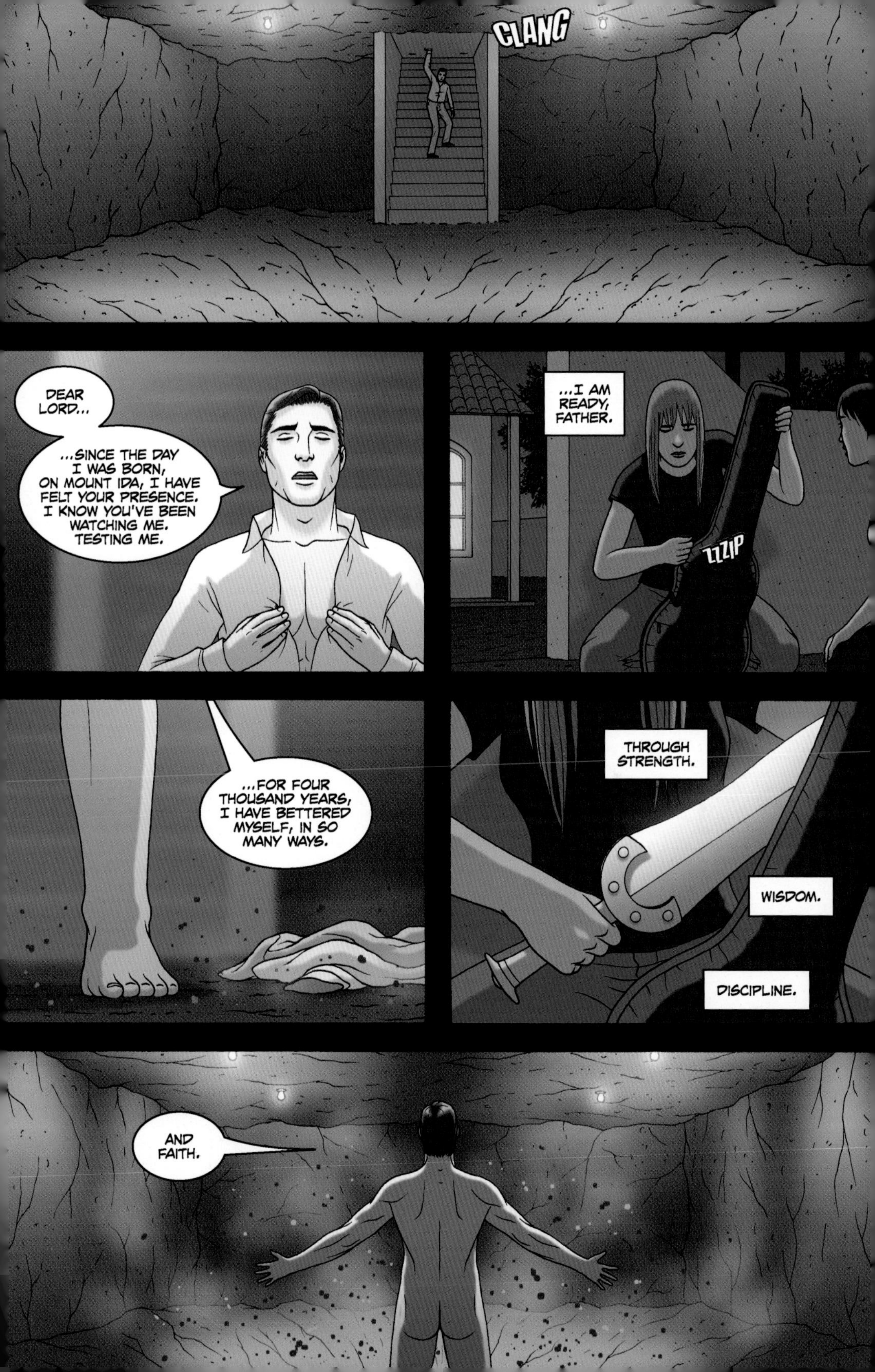
CLANG
DEAR LORD...
...SINCE THE DAY I WAS BORN, ON MOUNT IDA, I HAVE FELT YOUR PRESENCE. I KNOW YOU'VE BEEN WATCHING ME. TESTING ME.
...I AM READY, FATHER.
ZZZIP
...FOR FOUR THOUSAND YEARS, I HAVE BETTERED MYSELF, IN SO MANY WAYS.
THROUGH STRENGTH.
WISDOM.
DISCIPLINE.
AND FAITH.

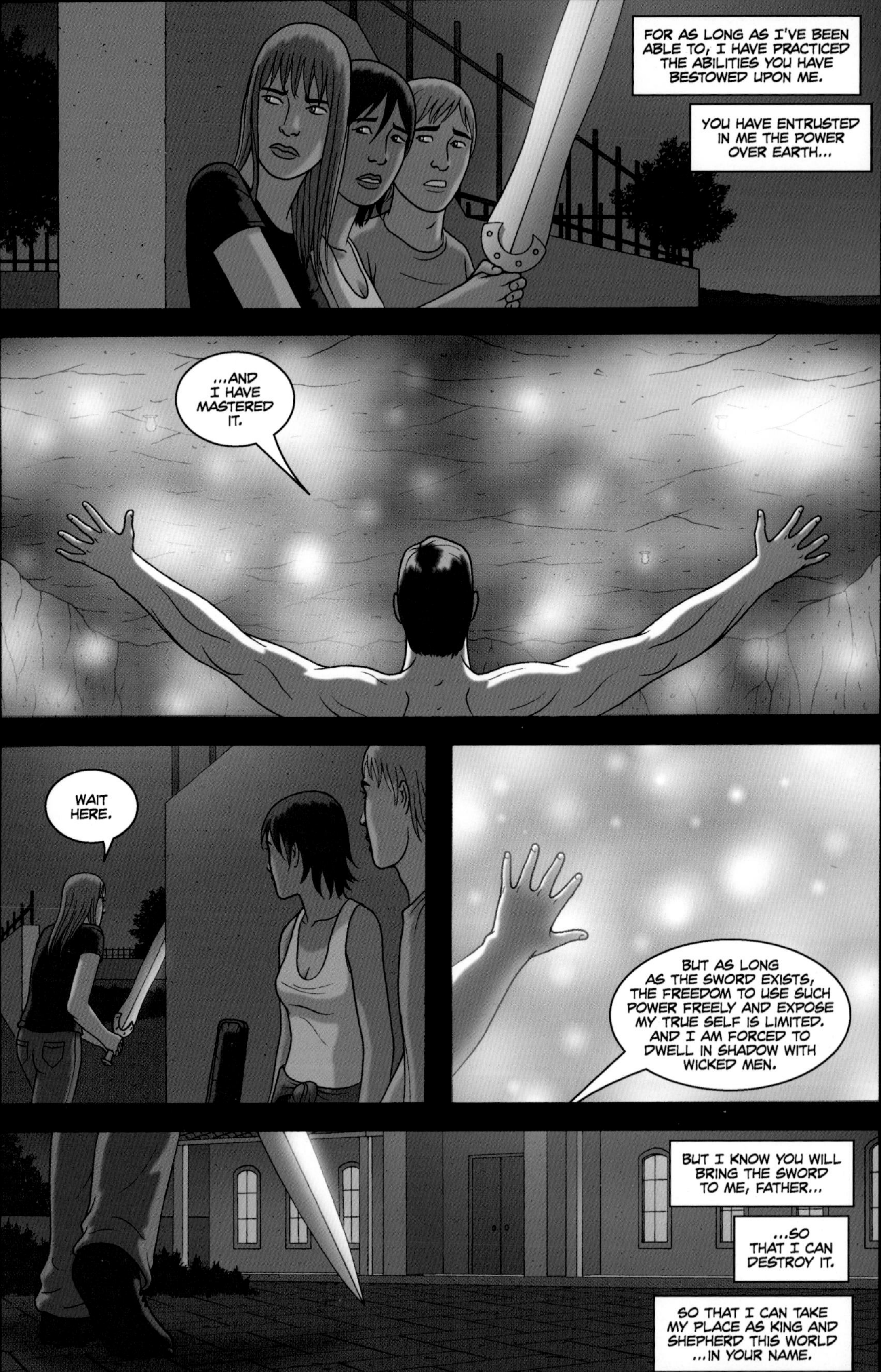
FOR AS LONG AS I'VE BEEN ABLE TO, I HAVE PRACTICED THE ABILITIES YOU HAVE BESTOWED UPON ME.
YOU HAVE ENTRUSTED IN ME THE POWER OVER EARTH...
...AND I HAVE MASTERED IT.
WAIT HERE.
BUT AS LONG AS THE SWORD EXISTS, THE FREEDOM TO USE SUCH POWER FREELY AND EXPOSE MY TRUE SELF IS LIMITED. AND I AM FORCED TO DWELL IN SHADOW WITH WICKED MEN.
BUT I KNOW YOU WILL BRING THE SWORD TO ME, FATHER...
...SO THAT I CAN DESTROY IT.
SO THAT I CAN TAKE MY PLACE AS KING AND SHEPHERD THIS WORLD ...IN YOUR NAME.

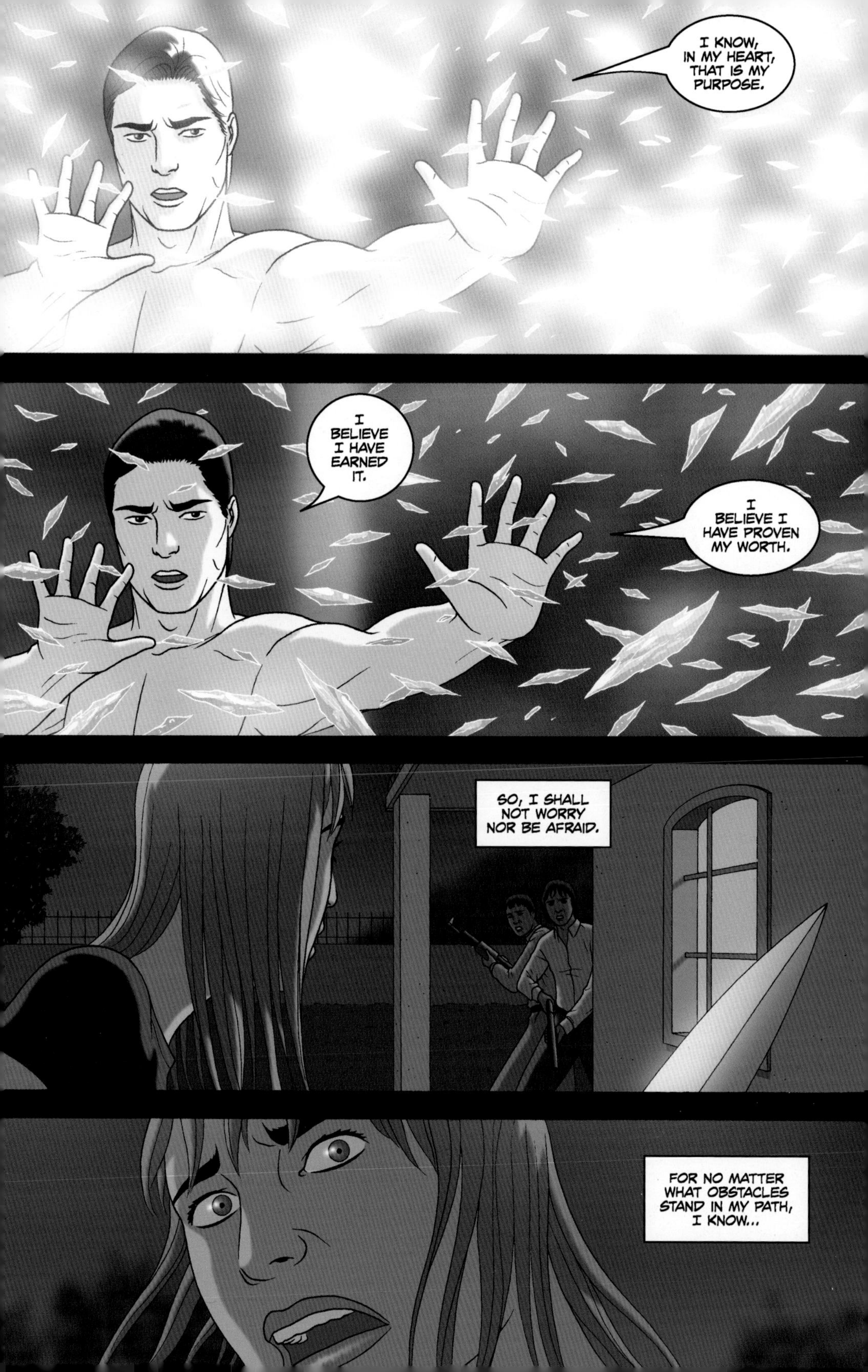
I KNOW, IN MY HEART, THAT IS MY PURPOSE.
I BELIEVE I HAVE EARNED IT.
I BELIEVE I HAVE PROVEN MY WORTH.
SO, I SHALL NOT WORRY NOR BE AFRAID.
FOR NO MATTER WHAT OBSTACLES STAND IN MY PATH, I KNOW...

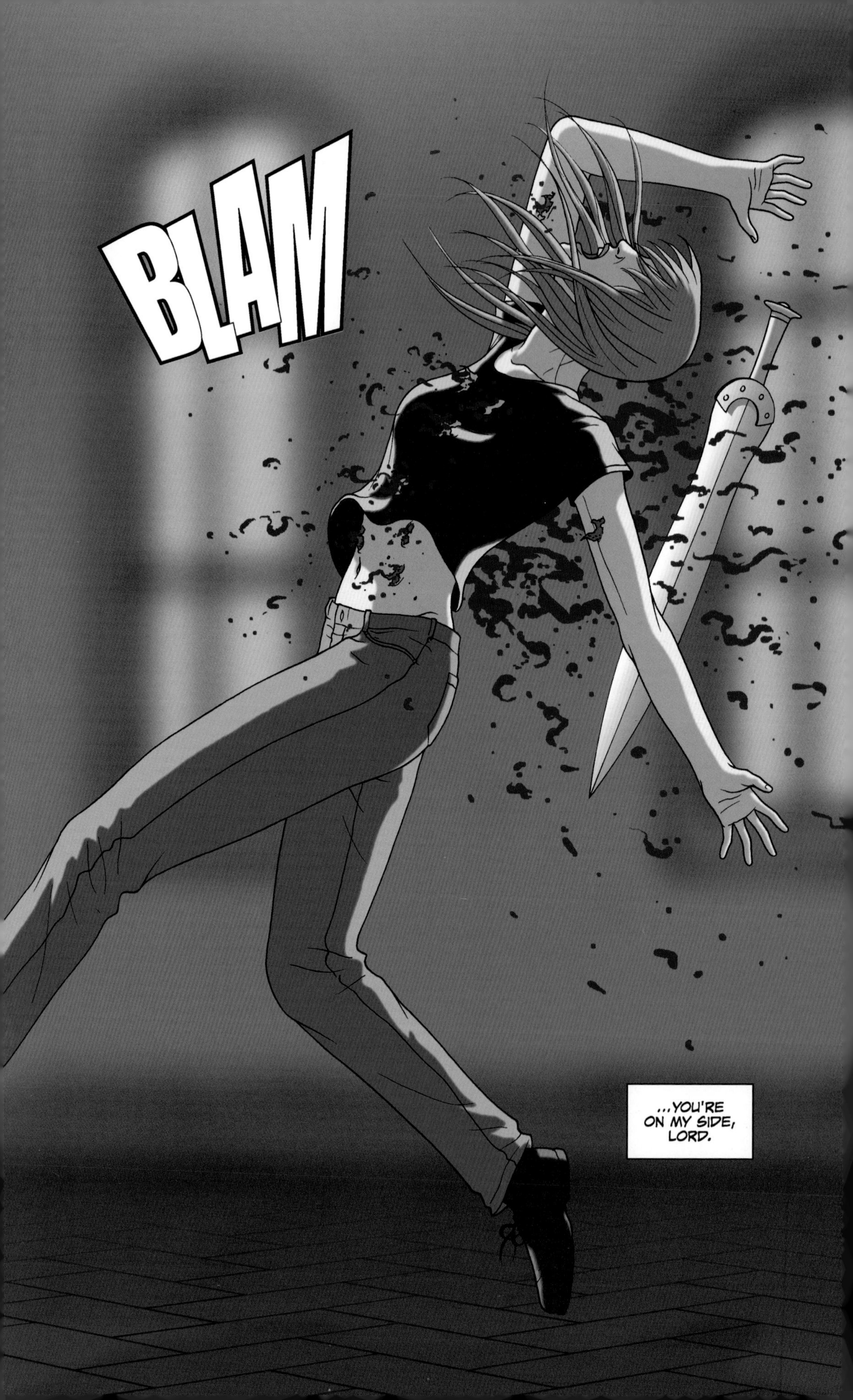
BLAM
...YOU'RE ON MY SIDE, LORD.

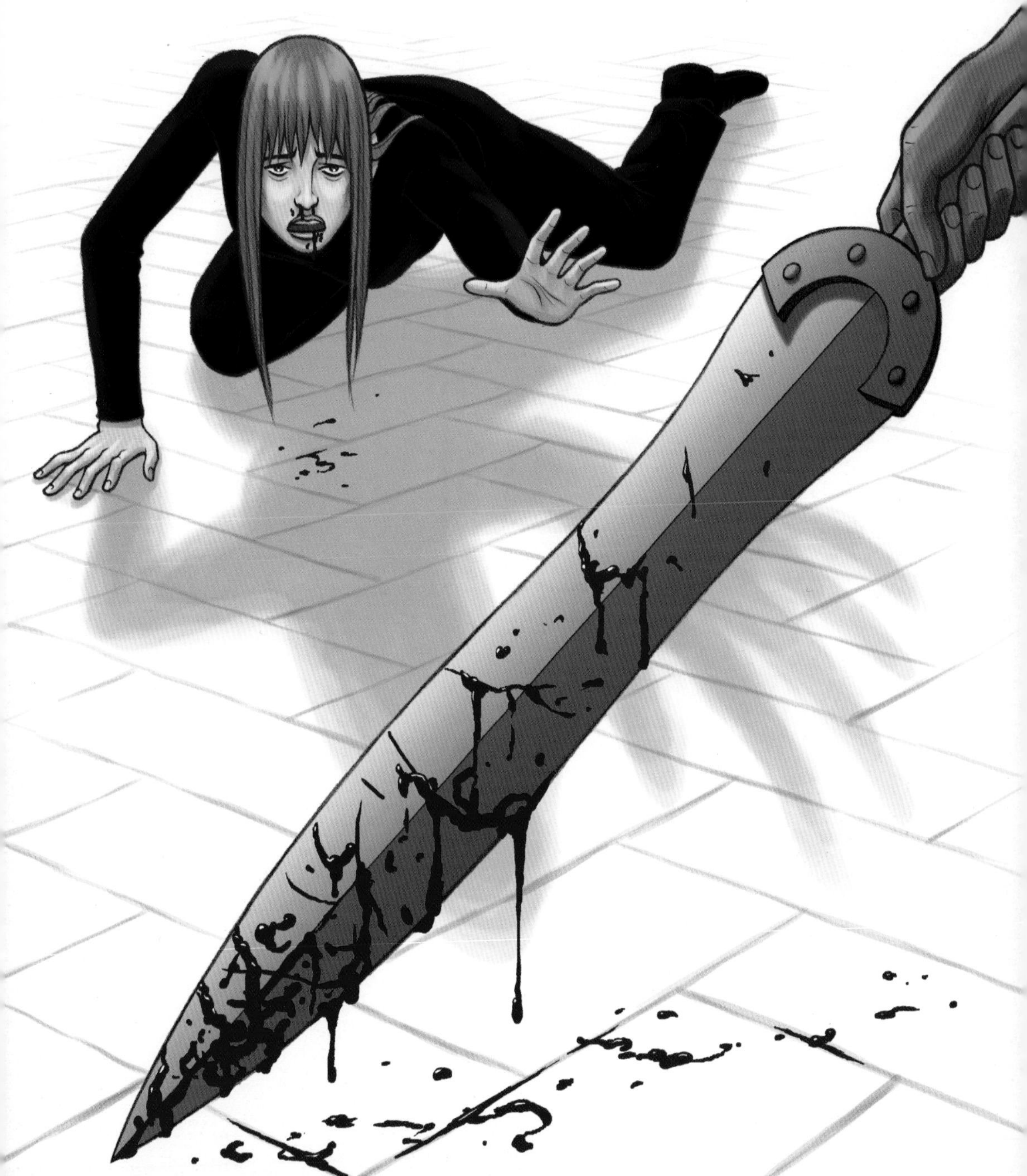

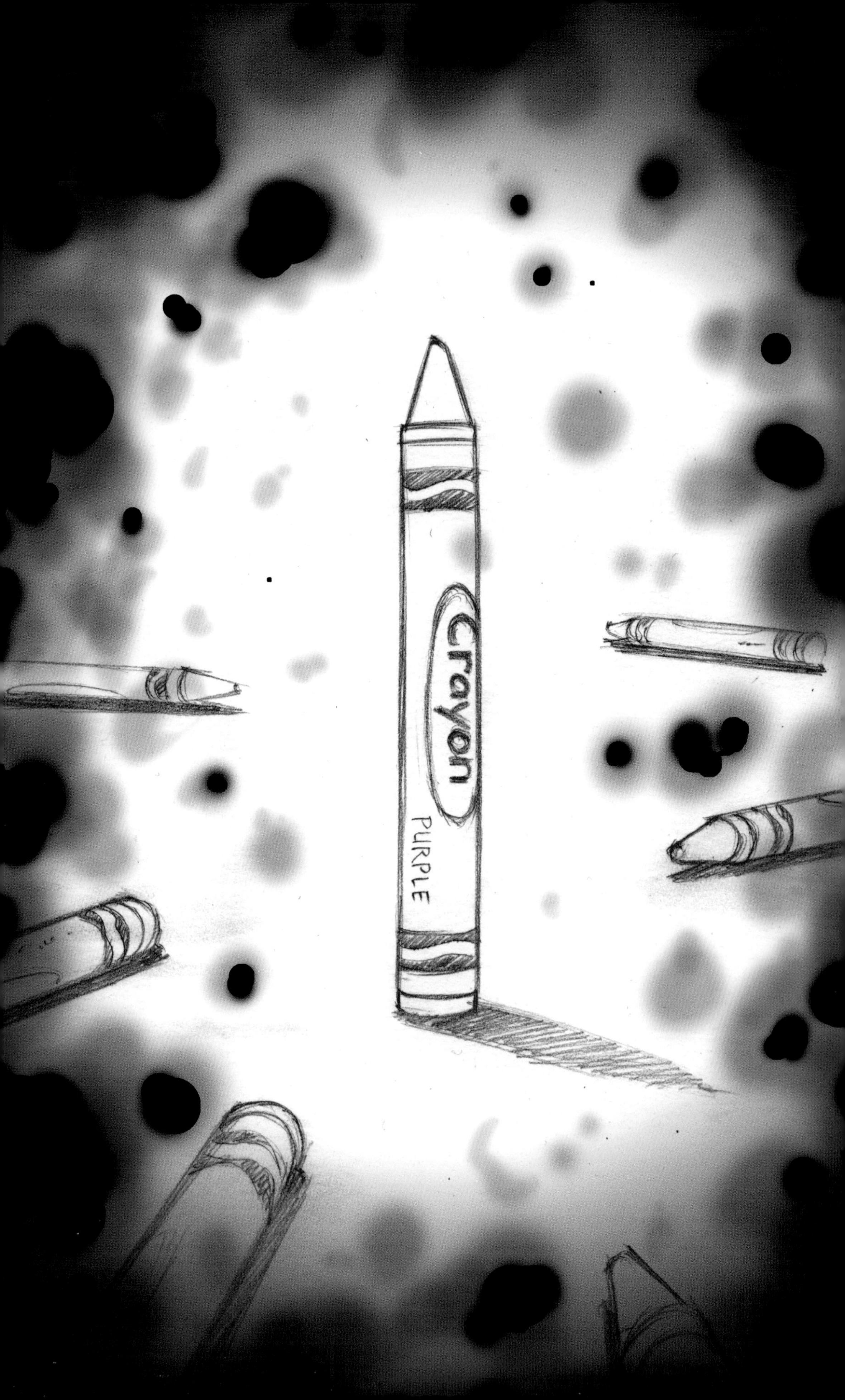
Crayon
PURPLE

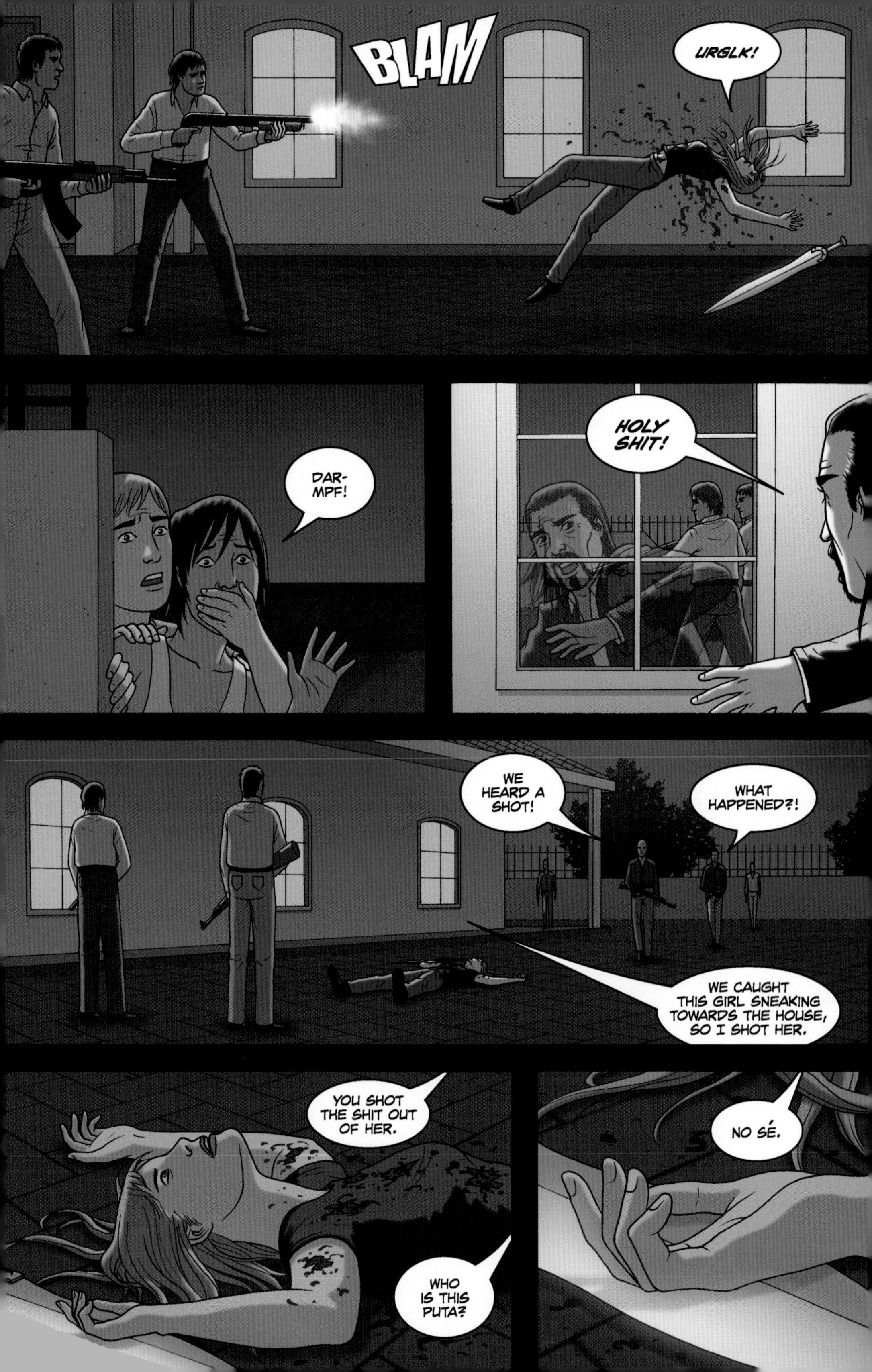
BLAM
URGLK!
DAR-MPF!
HOLY SHIT!
WE HEARD A SHOT!
WHAT HAPPENED?!
WE CAUGHT THIS GIRL SNEAKING TOWARDS THE HOUSE, SO I SHOT HER.
YOU SHOT THE SHIT OUT OF HER.
WHO IS THIS PUTA?
NO SÉ.

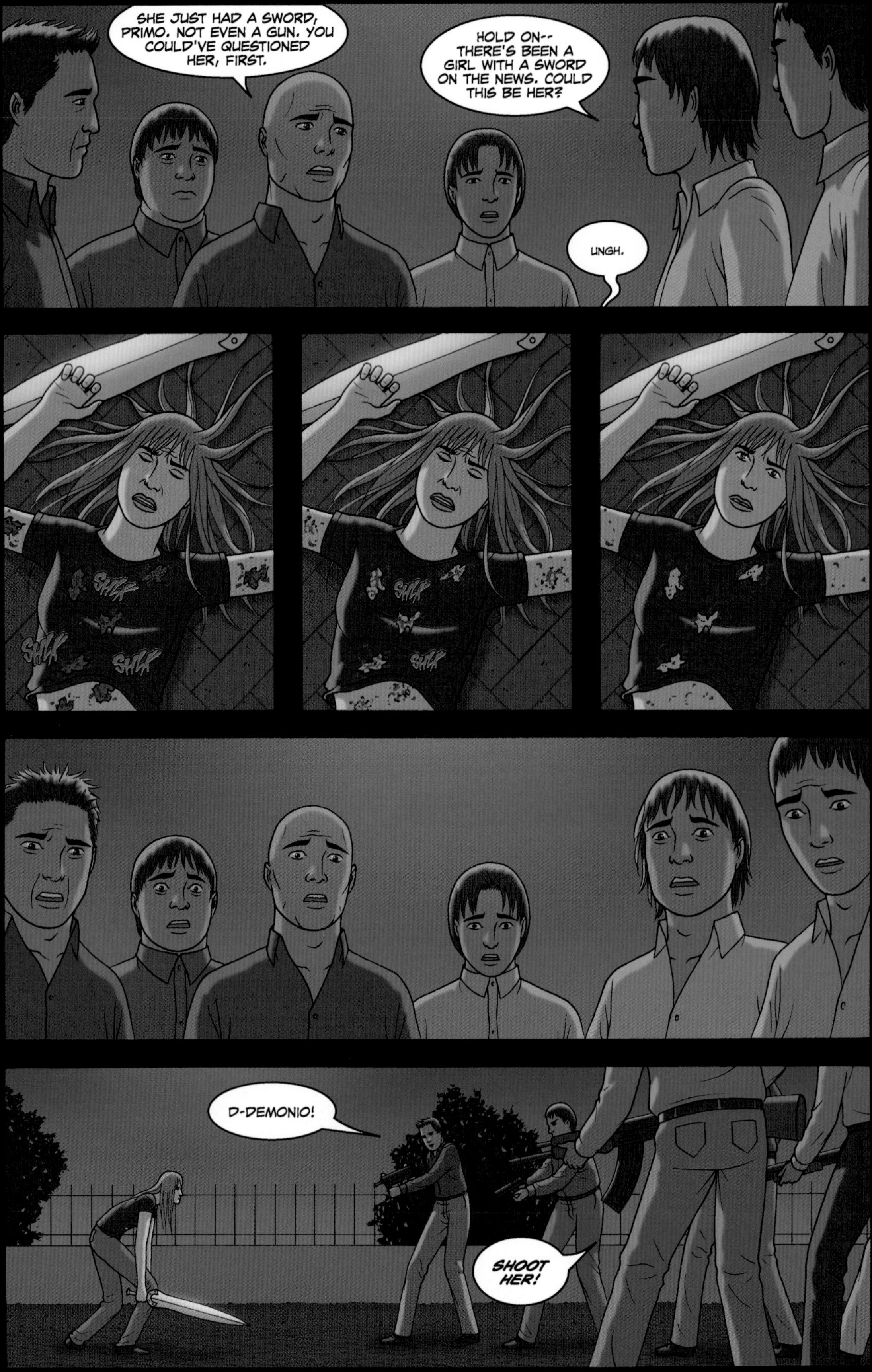
SHE JUST HAD A SWORD, PRIMO. NOT EVEN A GUN. YOU COULD'VE QUESTIONED HER, FIRST.
HOLD ON-- THERE'S BEEN A GIRL WITH A SWORD ON THE NEWS. COULD THIS BE HER?
UNGH.
SHLK
SHLK
SHLK
SHLK
SHLK
D-DEMONIO!
SHOOT HER!

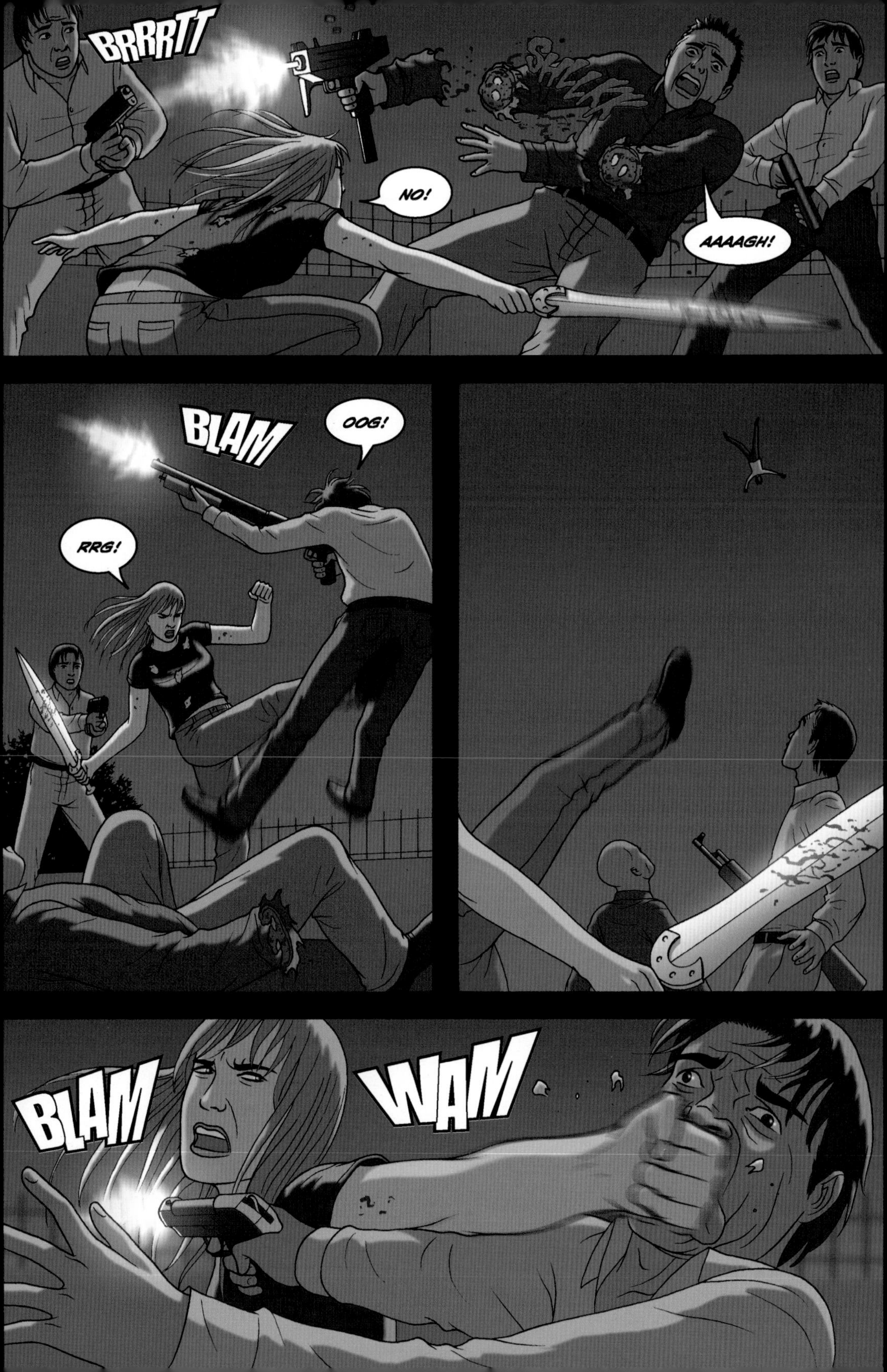
BRRRTT
NO!
AAAAGH!
BLAM
OOG!
RRG!
BLAM
WAM

AAAH!
SEÑOR DEVONSON! I'M SORRY TO BOTHER YOU, BUT THERE'S TROUBLE OUTSIDE!
CAN YOU HEAR ME IN THERE?!
BAM
BAM
SHIT!
TAKATAKA
BLAM BLAM
BACK UP! BACK UP! STAY AWAY FROM HER, AND DON'T STOP SHOOTING!
TAKATAKATAKA
PTING
PTING
PTING
PTING
PTING
PTING
PTING
PTING
AGH!
SPLK

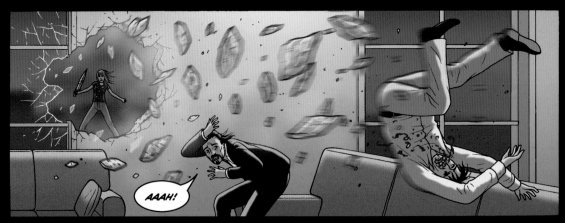

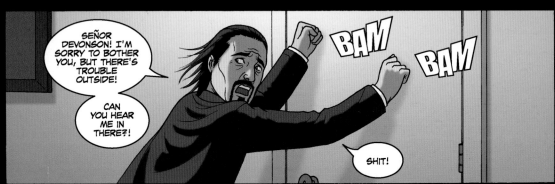

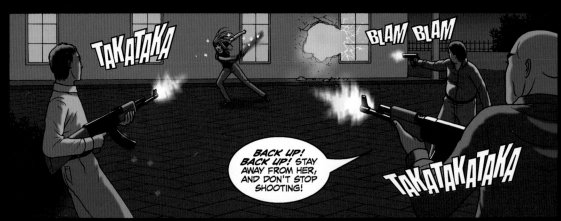

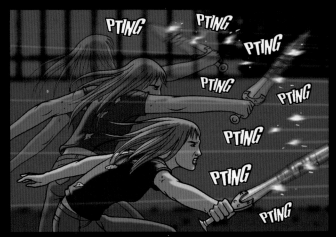

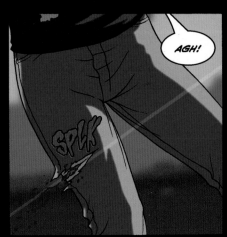

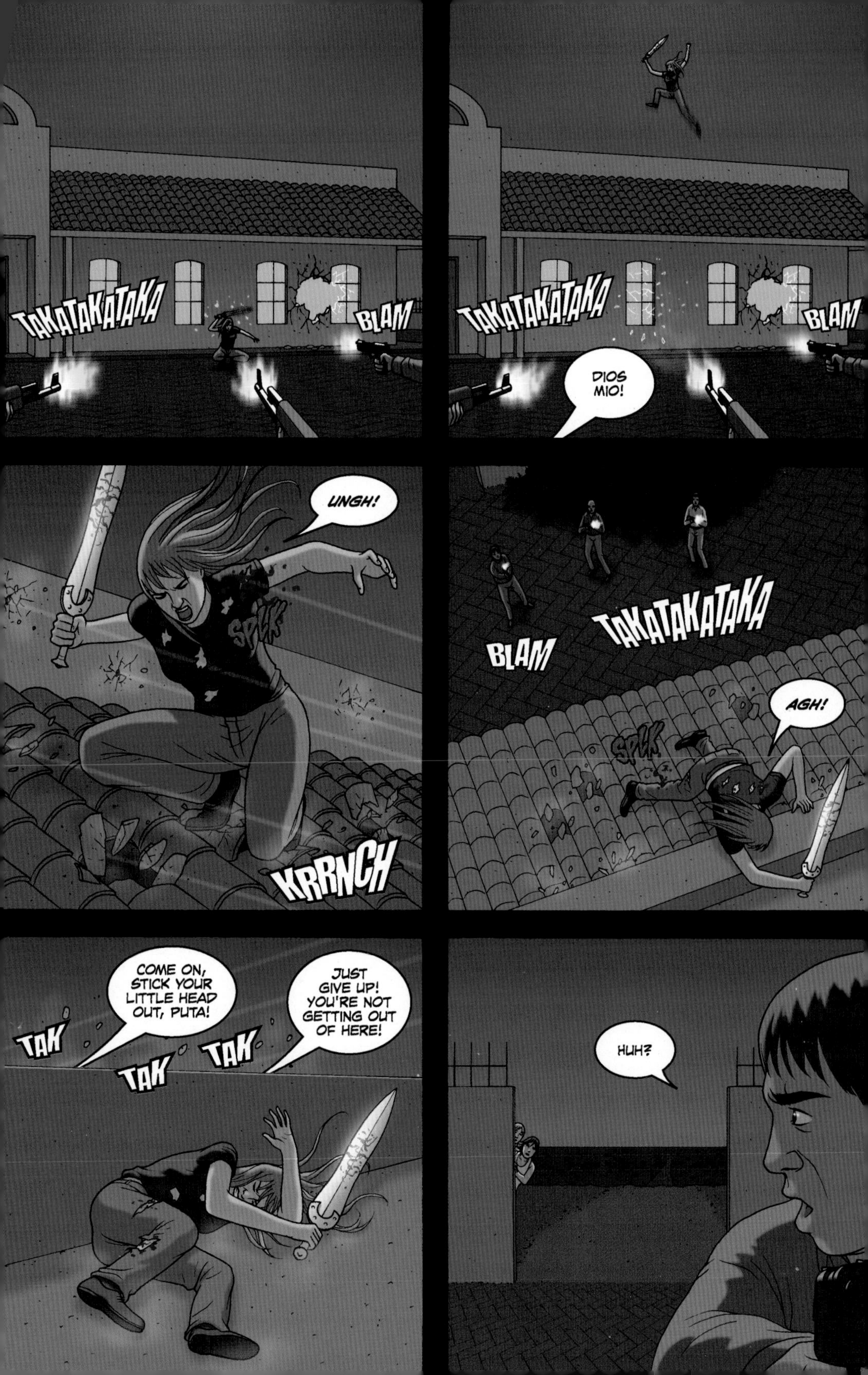
TAKATAKATAKA
BLAM
TAKATAKATAKA
BLAM
DIOS MIO!
UNGH!
SPLK
KRRNCH
BLAM
TAKATAKATAKA
AGH!
SPLK
TAK
COME ON, STICK YOUR LITTLE HEAD OUT, PUTA!
TAK
TAK
JUST GIVE UP! YOU'RE NOT GETTING OUT OF HERE!
HUH?

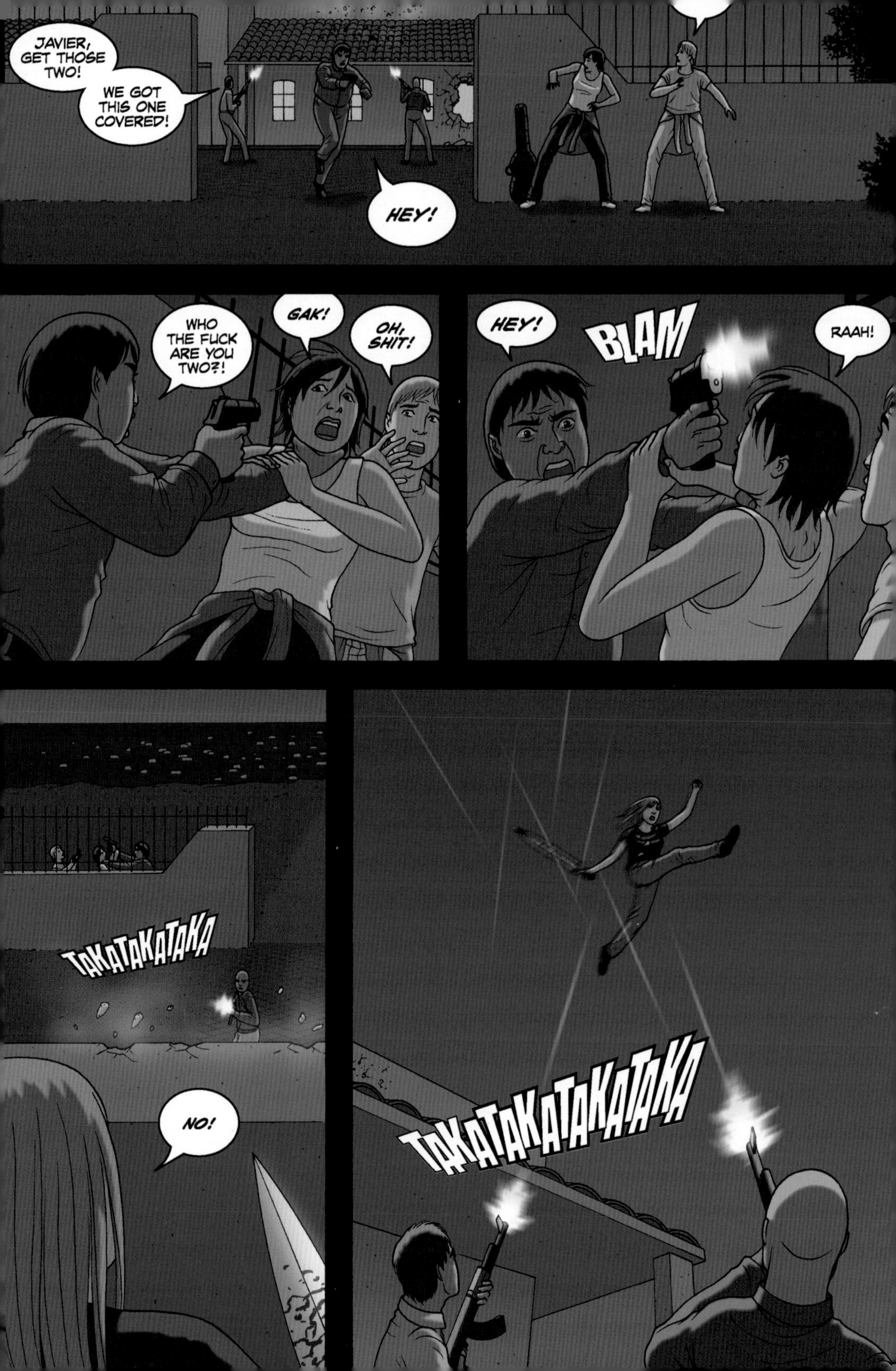
JAVIER, GET THOSE TWO!
WE GOT THIS ONE COVERED!
HEY!
WHO THE FUCK ARE YOU TWO?!
GAK!
OH, SHIT!
HEY!
BLAM
RAAH!
TAKATAKATAKA
NO!
TAKATAKATAKATAKA

AAAGH!
SPLAK
NO!
KLANG
AGH!
GRAH!
KLAK
DON'T SHOOT! YOU'LL HIT JAVIER!
THEN SHOULD WE GO THERE AND HELP HIM?
FUCK THAT! I'M NOT GOING NEAR THAT GIRL.
OOOMPF!
MIERDA! HOW DID SHE DO THAT CRAZY SHIT?!
WHO THE FUCK KNOWS?

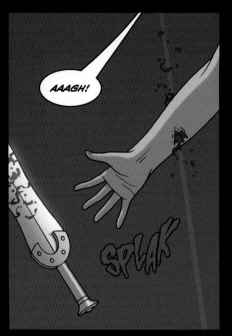

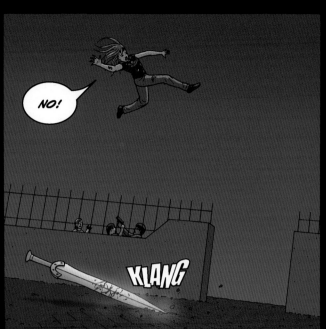

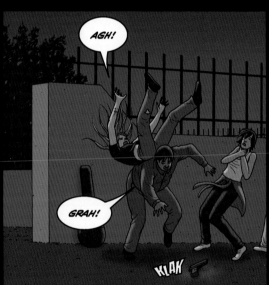

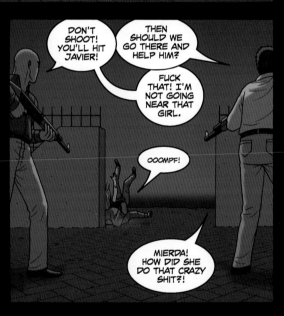

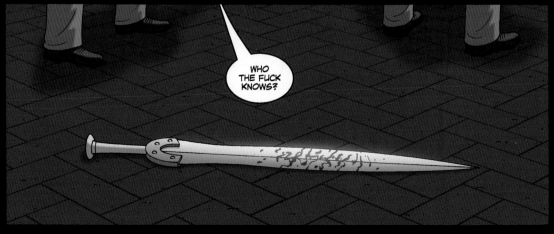

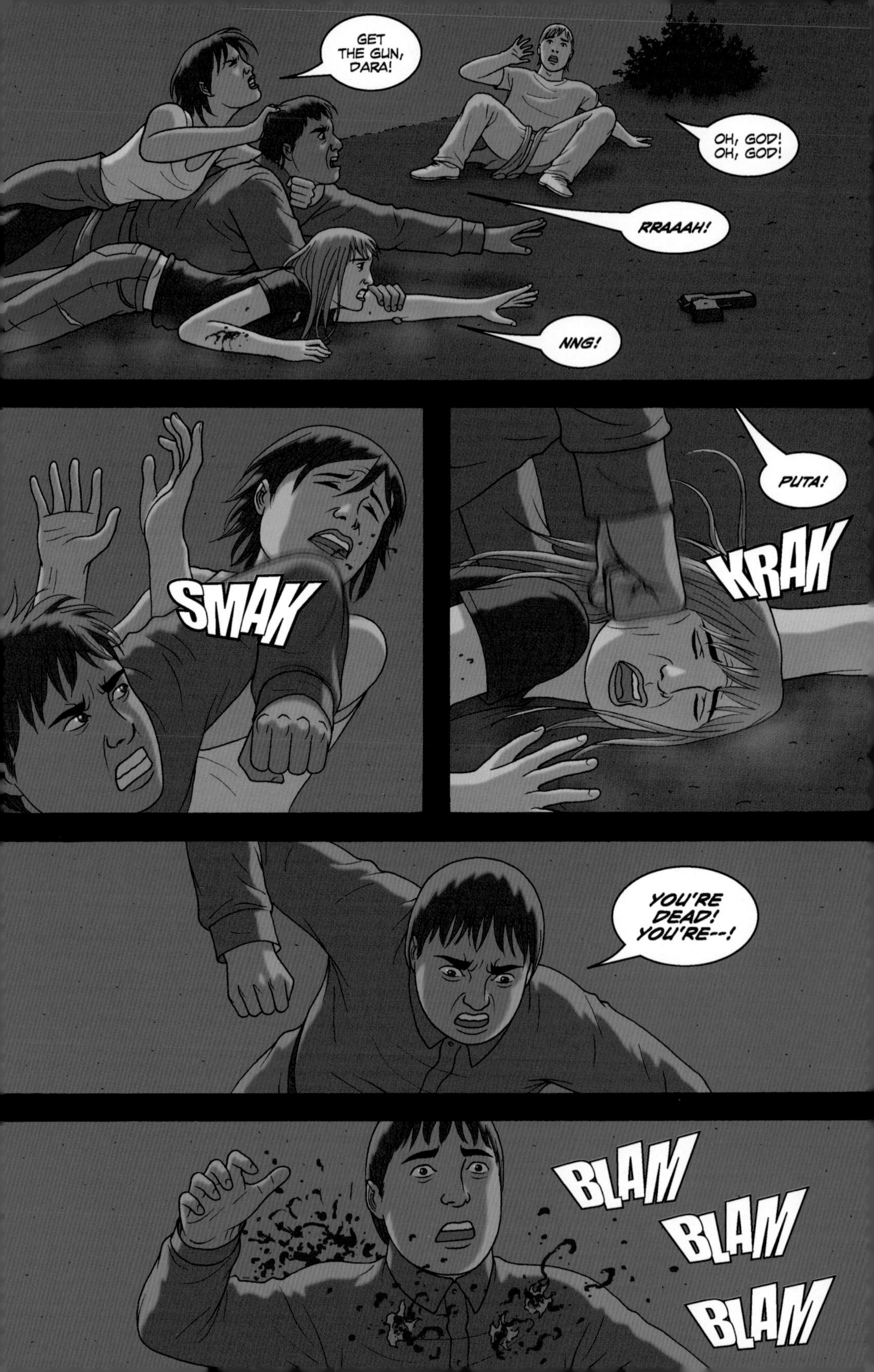
GET THE GUN, DARA!
OH, GOD! OH, GOD!
RRAAAH!
NNG!
SMAK
PUTA!
KRAK
YOU'RE DEAD! YOU'RE--!
BLAM
BLAM
BLAM

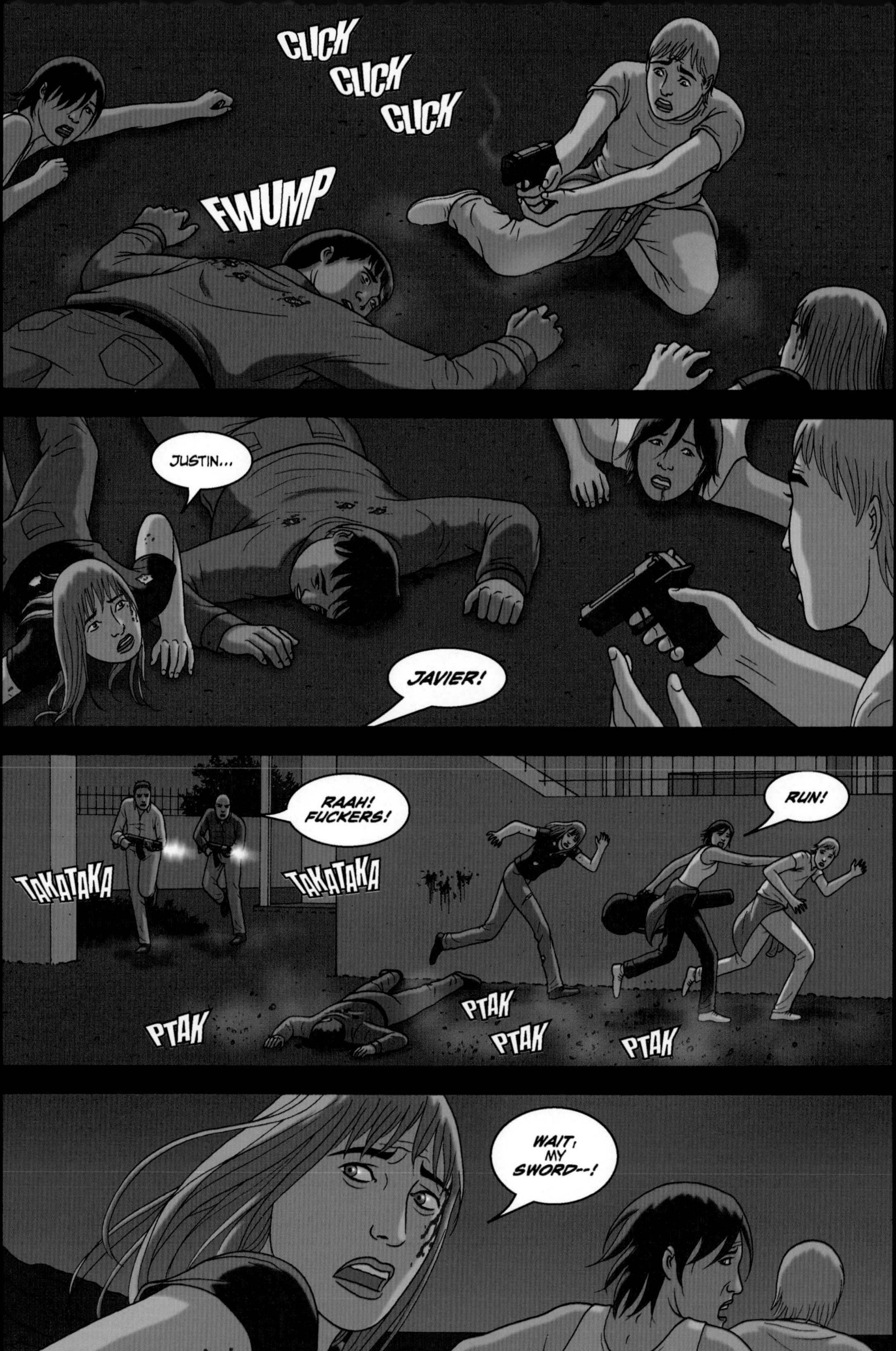
CLICK
CLICK
CLICK
FWUMP
JUSTIN...
JAVIER!
RAAH! FUCKERS!
TAKATAKA
TAKATAKA
RUN!
PTAK
PTAK
PTAK
PTAK
WAIT, MY SWORD--!

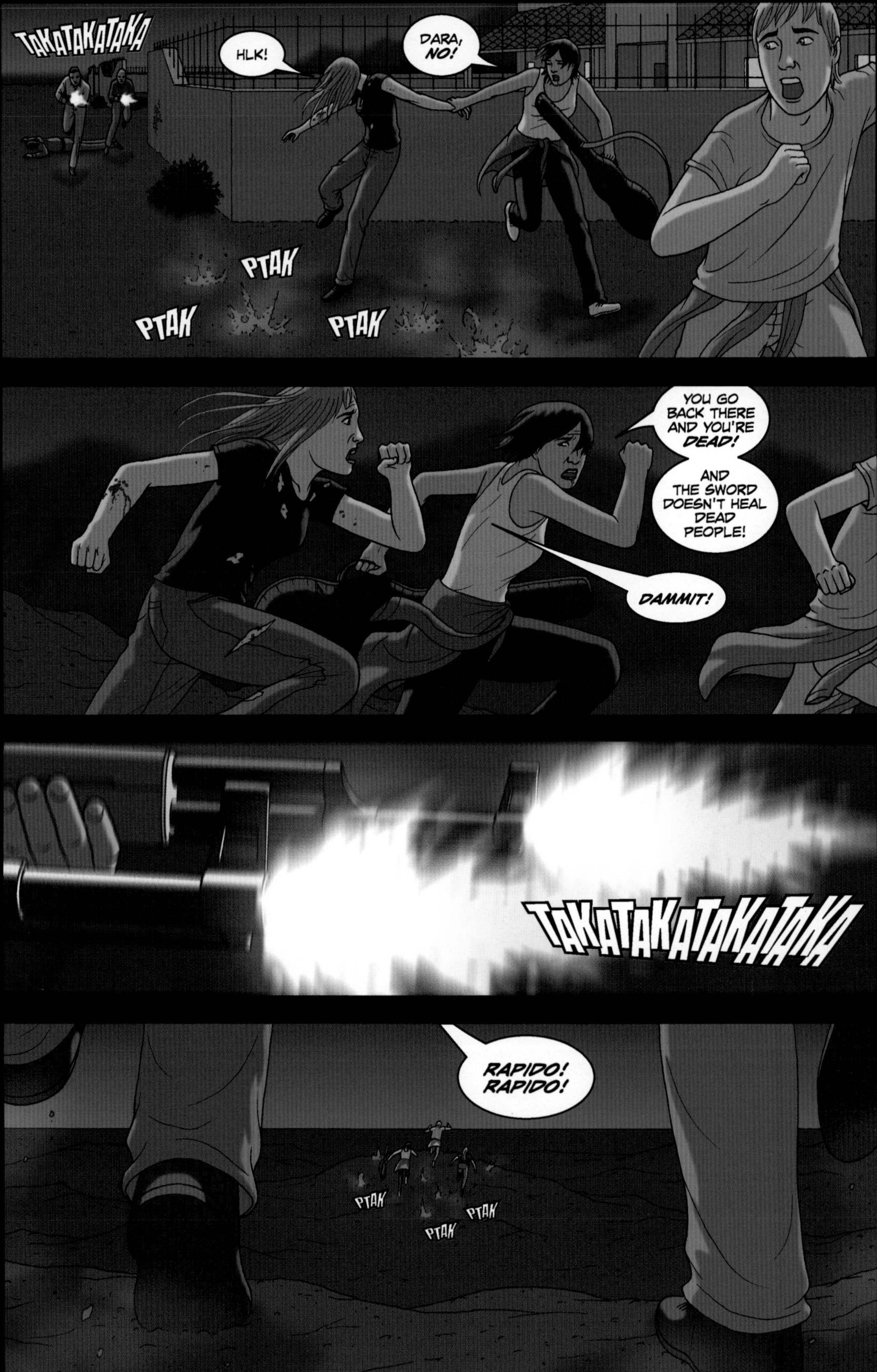
TAKATAKATAKA
HLK!
DARA, NO!
PTAK
PTAK
PTAK
YOU GO BACK THERE AND YOU'RE DEAD!
AND THE SWORD DOESN'T HEAL DEAD PEOPLE!
DAMMIT!
TAKATAKATAKATAKA
RAPIDO! RAPIDO!
PTAK
PTAK
PTAK

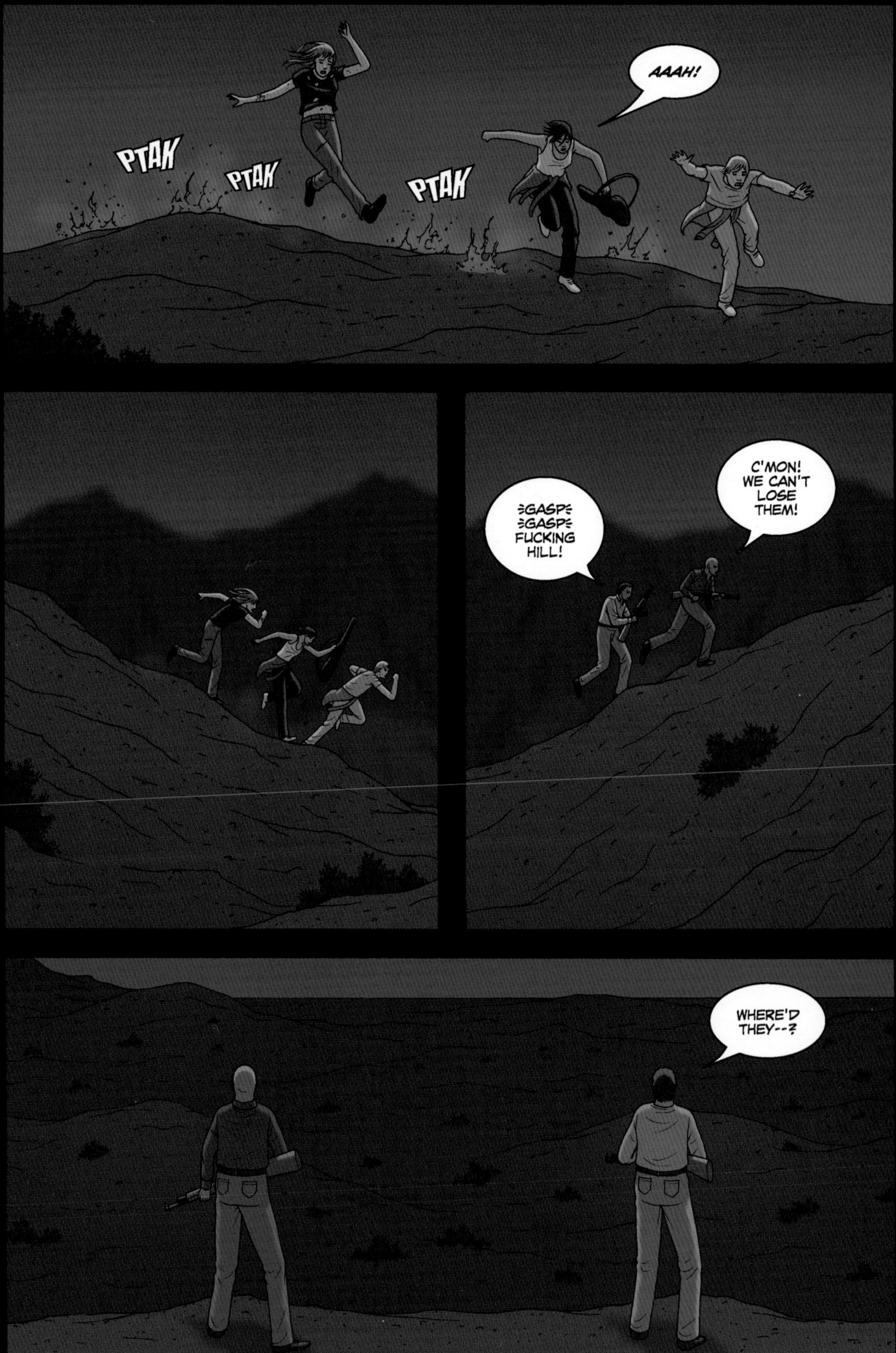
PTAK
PTAK
PTAK
AAAH!
=GASP=
=GASP=
FUCKING
HILL!
C'MON!
WE CAN'T
LOSE
THEM!
WHERE'D
THEY--?

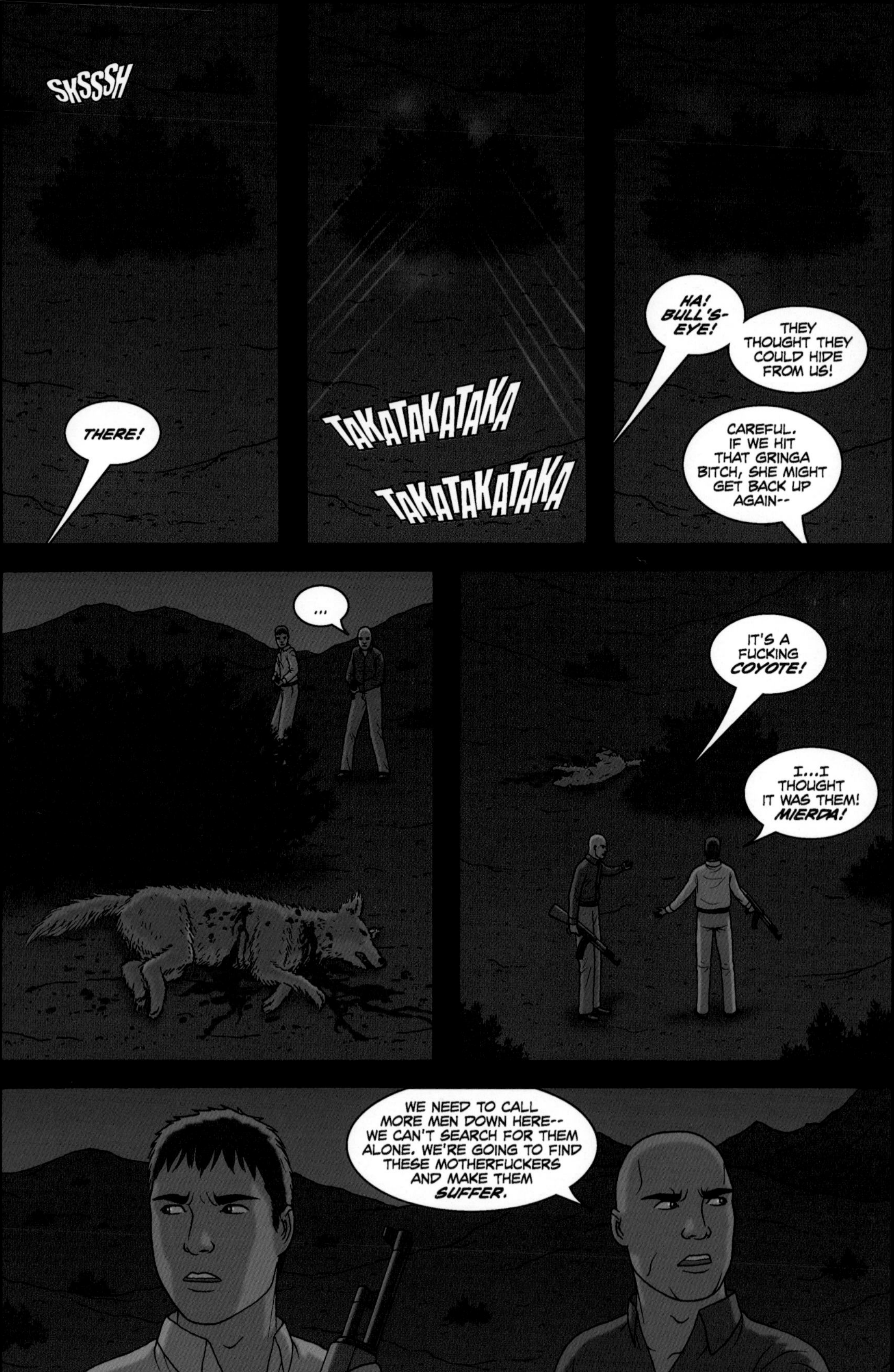
SKSSSH
THERE!
TAKATAKATAKA
TAKATAKATAKA
HA! BULL'S-EYE!
THEY THOUGHT THEY COULD HIDE FROM US!
CAREFUL. IF WE HIT THAT GRINGA BITCH, SHE MIGHT GET BACK UP AGAIN--
...
IT'S A FUCKING COYOTE!
I...I THOUGHT IT WAS THEM! MIERDA!
WE NEED TO CALL MORE MEN DOWN HERE-- WE CAN'T SEARCH FOR THEM ALONE. WE'RE GOING TO FIND THESE MOTHERFUCKERS AND MAKE THEM SUFFER.

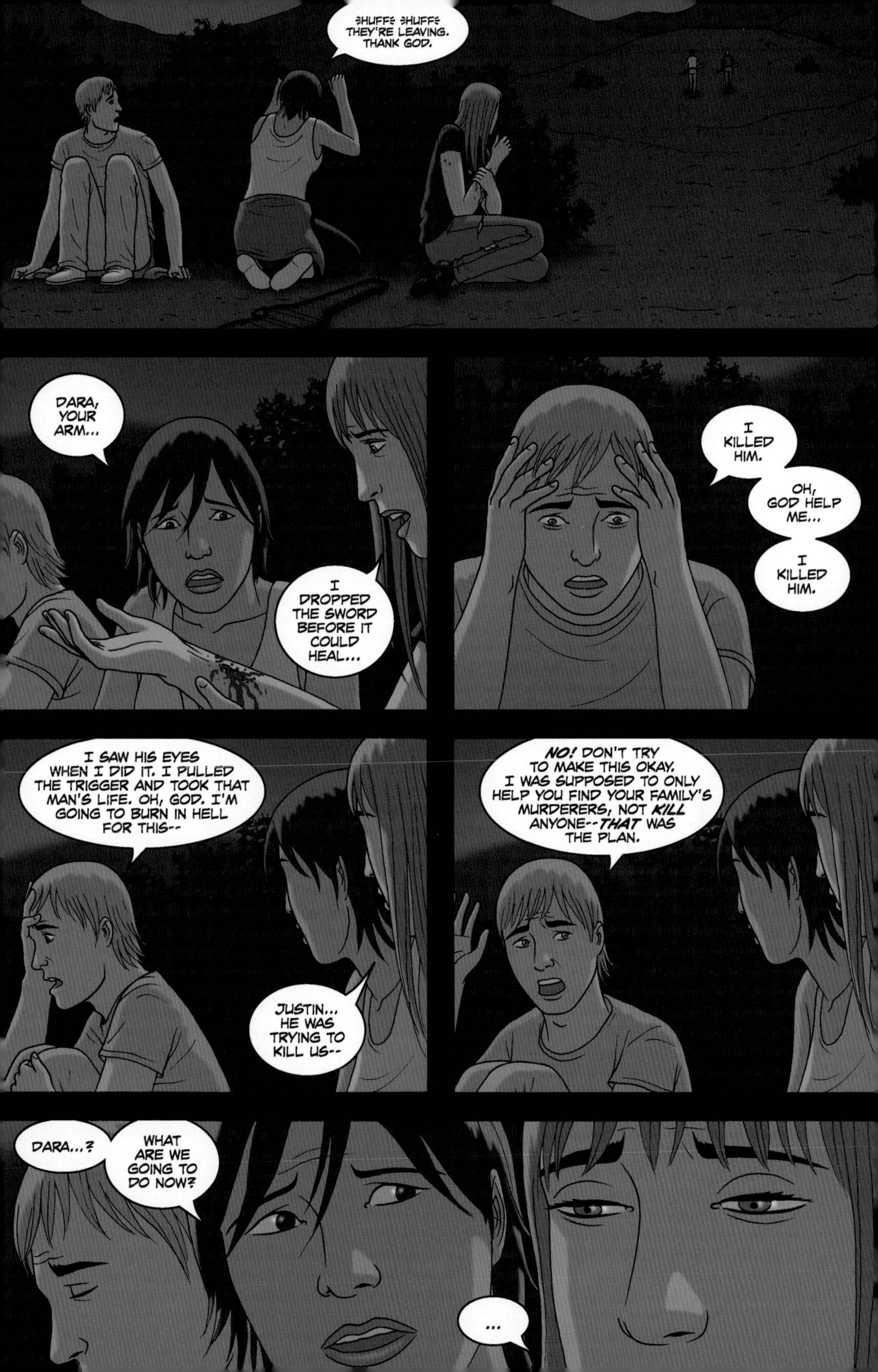

≠HUFF≠ ≠HUFF≠ THEY'RE LEAVING. THANK GOD.
DARA, YOUR ARM...
I DROPPED THE SWORD BEFORE IT COULD HEAL...
I KILLED HIM.
OH, GOD HELP ME...
I KILLED HIM.
I SAW HIS EYES WHEN I DID IT. I PULLED THE TRIGGER AND TOOK THAT MAN'S LIFE. OH, GOD. I'M GOING TO BURN IN HELL FOR THIS--
JUSTIN... HE WAS TRYING TO KILL US--
NO! DON'T TRY TO MAKE THIS OKAY. I WAS SUPPOSED TO ONLY HELP YOU FIND YOUR FAMILY'S MURDERERS, NOT KILL ANYONE--THAT WAS THE PLAN.
DARA...?
WHAT ARE WE GOING TO DO NOW?
...

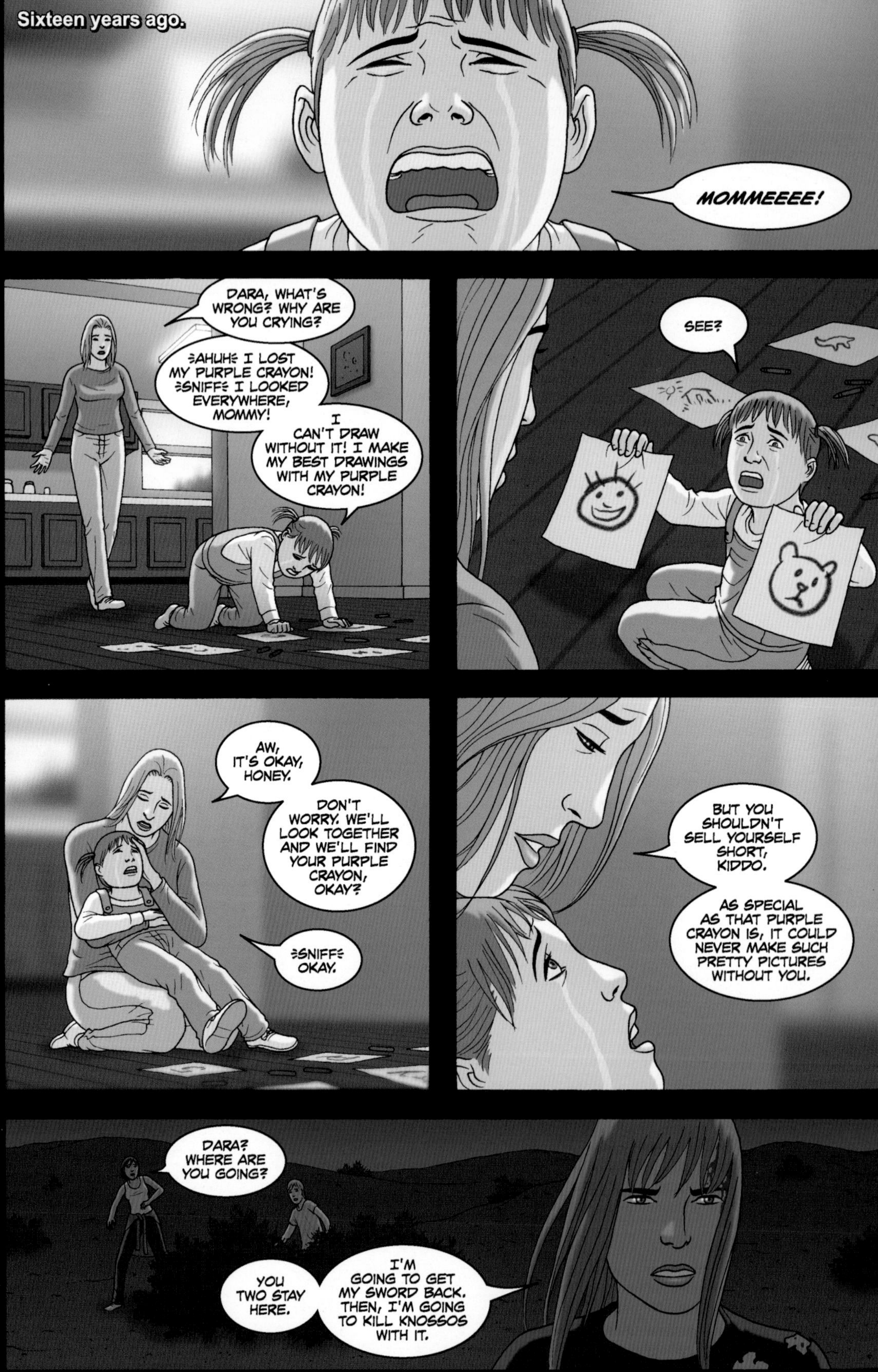
Sixteen years ago.
MOMMEEEE!
DARA, WHAT'S WRONG? WHY ARE YOU CRYING?
≠AHUH≠ I LOST MY PURPLE CRAYON! ≠SNIFF≠ I LOOKED EVERYWHERE, MOMMY!
I CAN'T DRAW WITHOUT IT! I MAKE MY BEST DRAWINGS WITH MY PURPLE CRAYON!
SEE?
AW, IT'S OKAY, HONEY.
DON'T WORRY. WE'LL LOOK TOGETHER AND WE'LL FIND YOUR PURPLE CRAYON, OKAY?
≠SNIFF≠ OKAY.
BUT YOU SHOULDN'T SELL YOURSELF SHORT, KIDDO.
AS SPECIAL AS THAT PURPLE CRAYON IS, IT COULD NEVER MAKE SUCH PRETTY PICTURES WITHOUT YOU.
DARA? WHERE ARE YOU GOING?
YOU TWO STAY HERE.
I'M GOING TO GET MY SWORD BACK. THEN, I'M GOING TO KILL KNOSSOS WITH IT.

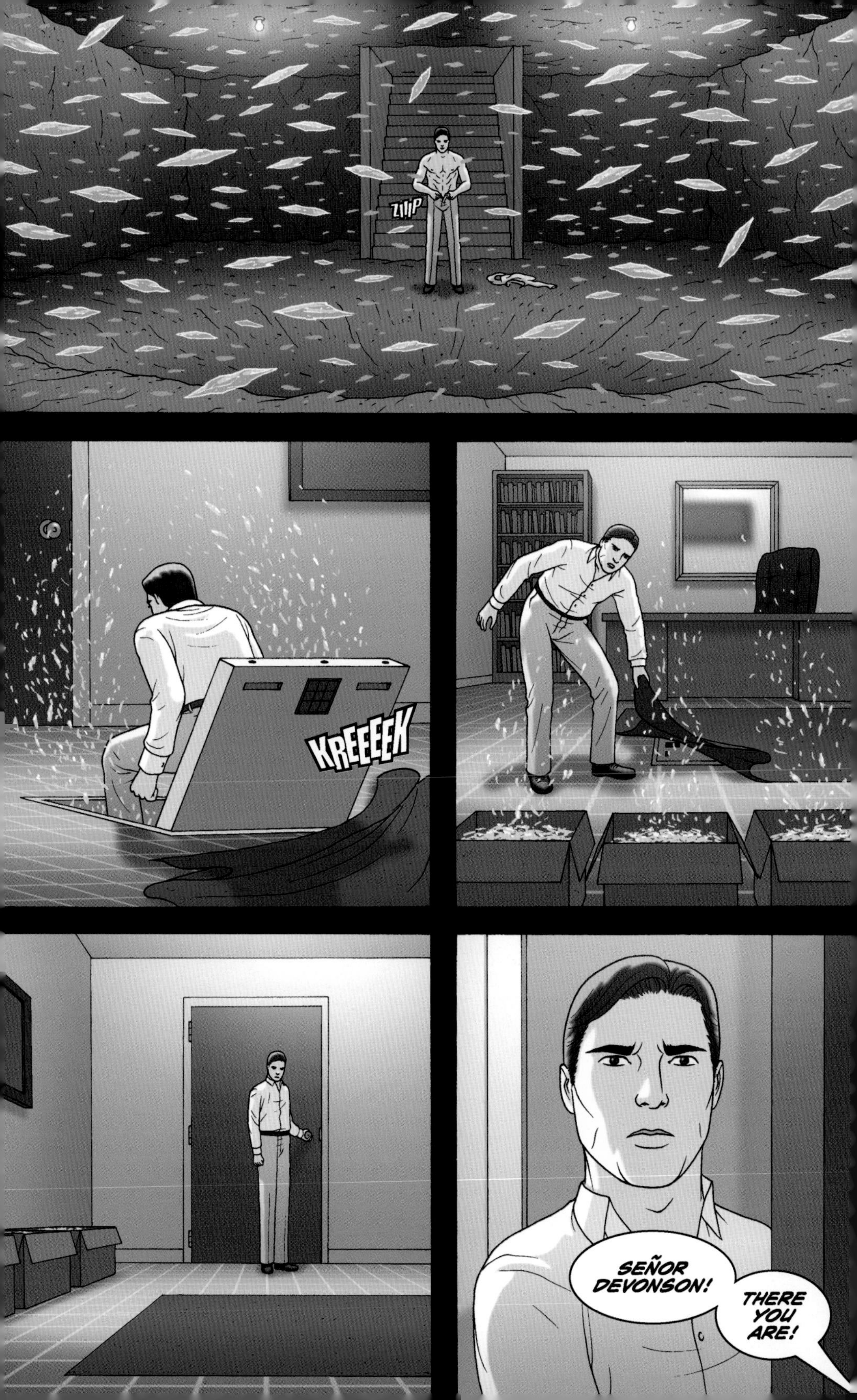
ZIIIP
KREEEEK
SEÑOR DEVONSON!
THERE YOU ARE!

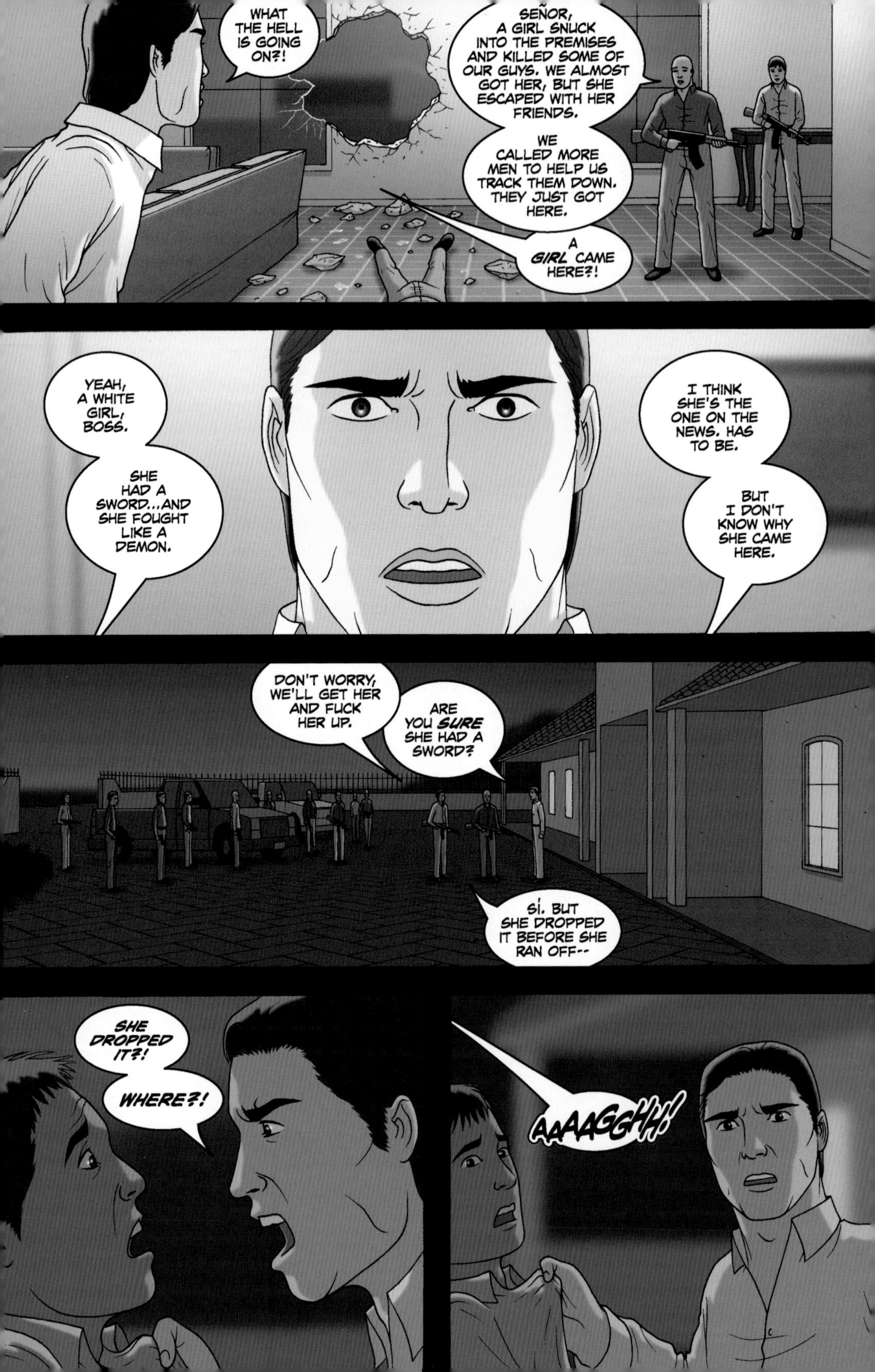
WHAT THE HELL IS GOING ON?!
SEÑOR, A GIRL SNUCK INTO THE PREMISES AND KILLED SOME OF OUR GUYS. WE ALMOST GOT HER, BUT SHE ESCAPED WITH HER FRIENDS.
WE CALLED MORE MEN TO HELP US TRACK THEM DOWN. THEY JUST GOT HERE.
A GIRL CAME HERE?!
YEAH, A WHITE GIRL, BOSS.
SHE HAD A SWORD...AND SHE FOUGHT LIKE A DEMON.
I THINK SHE'S THE ONE ON THE NEWS. HAS TO BE.
BUT I DON'T KNOW WHY SHE CAME HERE.
DON'T WORRY, WE'LL GET HER AND FUCK HER UP.
ARE YOU SURE SHE HAD A SWORD?
SÍ. BUT SHE DROPPED IT BEFORE SHE RAN OFF--
SHE DROPPED IT?!
WHERE?!
AAAAGGHH!

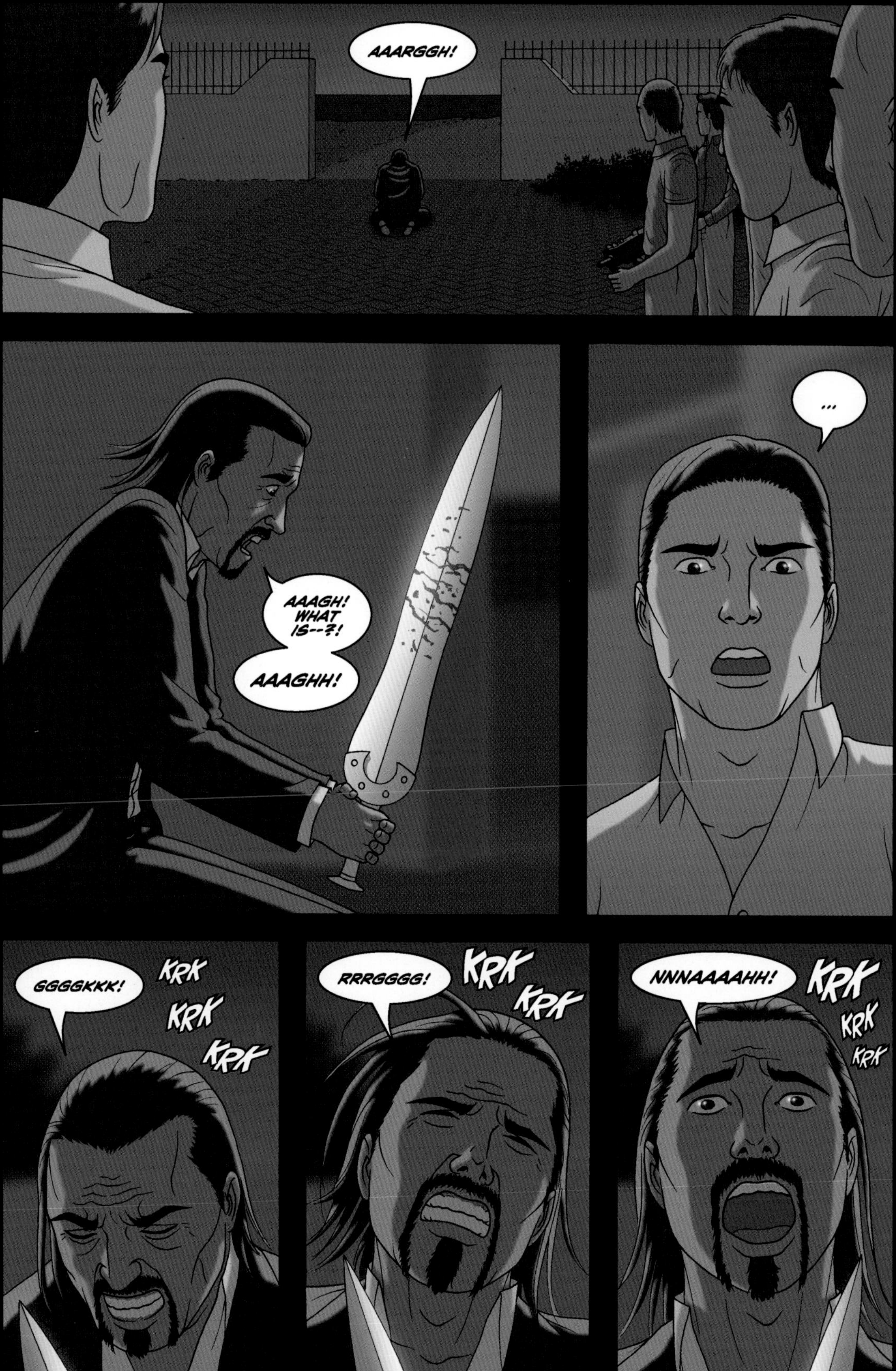
AAARGGH!
AAAGH! WHAT IS--?!
AAAGHH!
...
GGGGKKK!
KRK
KRK
KRK
RRRGGGG!
KRK
KRK
NNNAAAAHH!
KRK
KRK
KRK

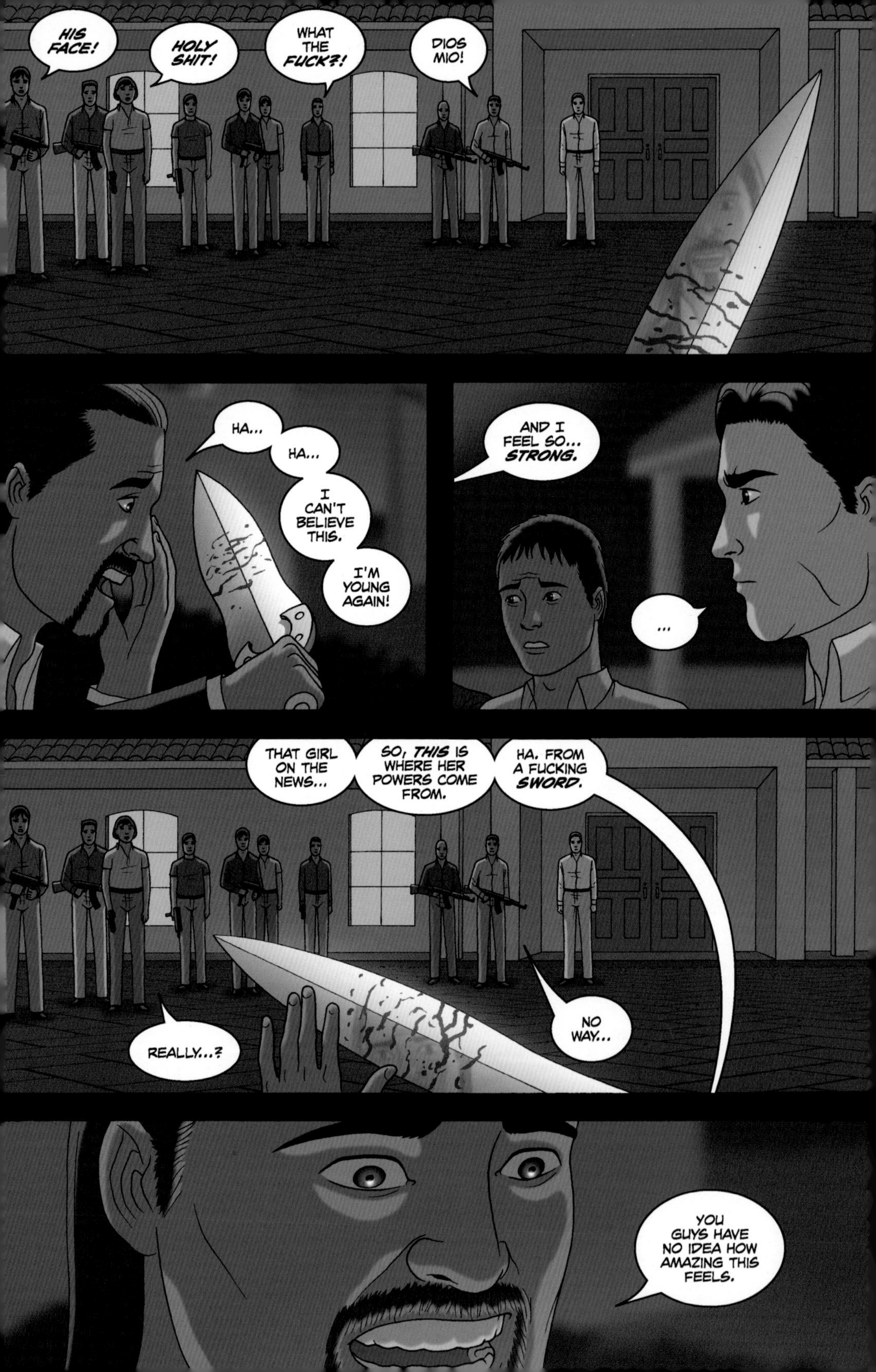
HIS FACE!
HOLY SHIT!
WHAT THE FUCK?!
DIOS MIO!
HA...
HA...
I CAN'T BELIEVE THIS.
I'M YOUNG AGAIN!
AND I FEEL SO... STRONG.
...
THAT GIRL ON THE NEWS...
SO, THIS IS WHERE HER POWERS COME FROM.
HA. FROM A FUCKING SWORD.
REALLY...?
NO WAY...
YOU GUYS HAVE NO IDEA HOW AMAZING THIS FEELS.

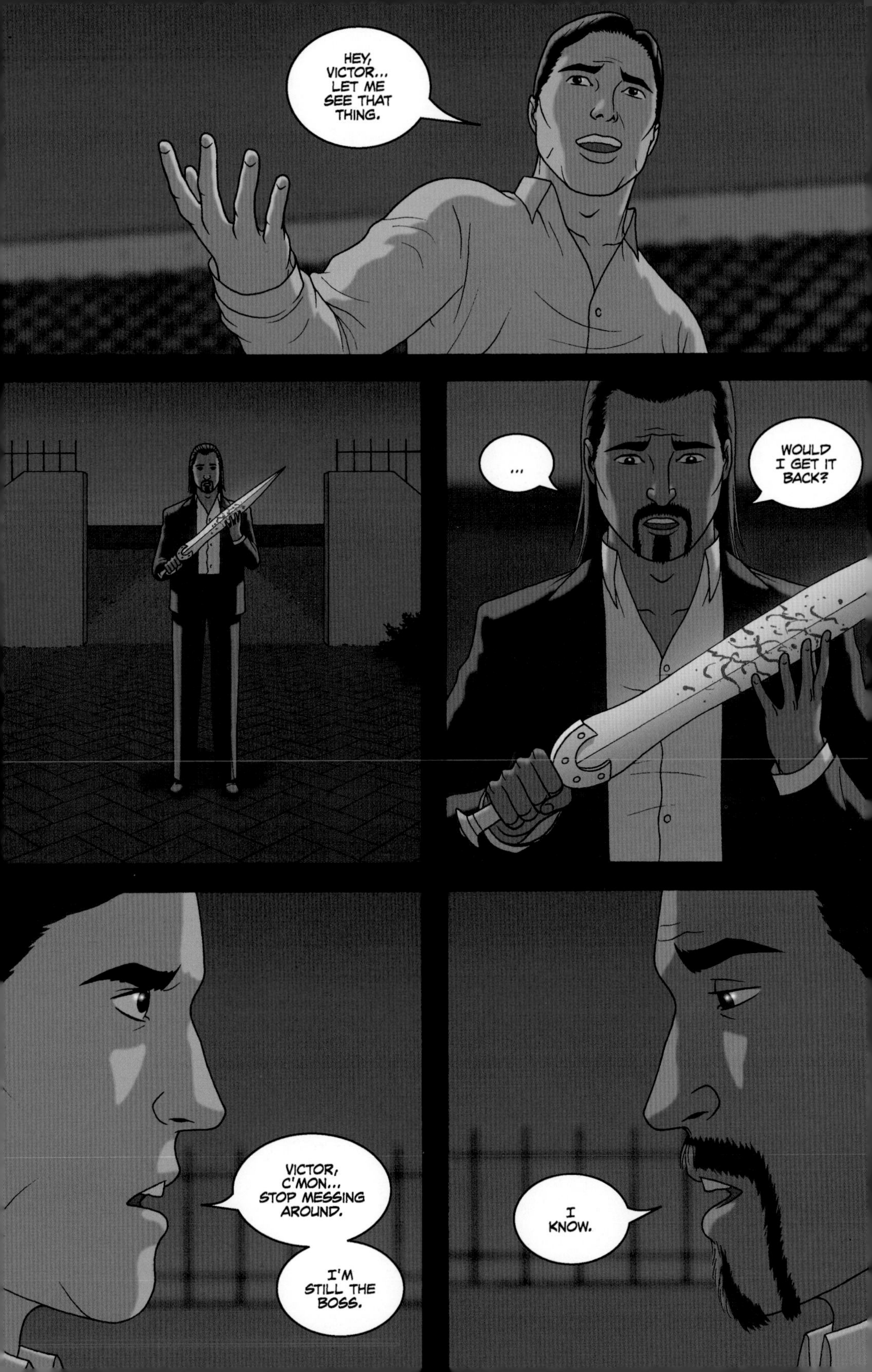
HEY, VICTOR... LET ME SEE THAT THING.
...
WOULD I GET IT BACK?
VICTOR, C'MON... STOP MESSING AROUND.
I'M STILL THE BOSS.
I KNOW.

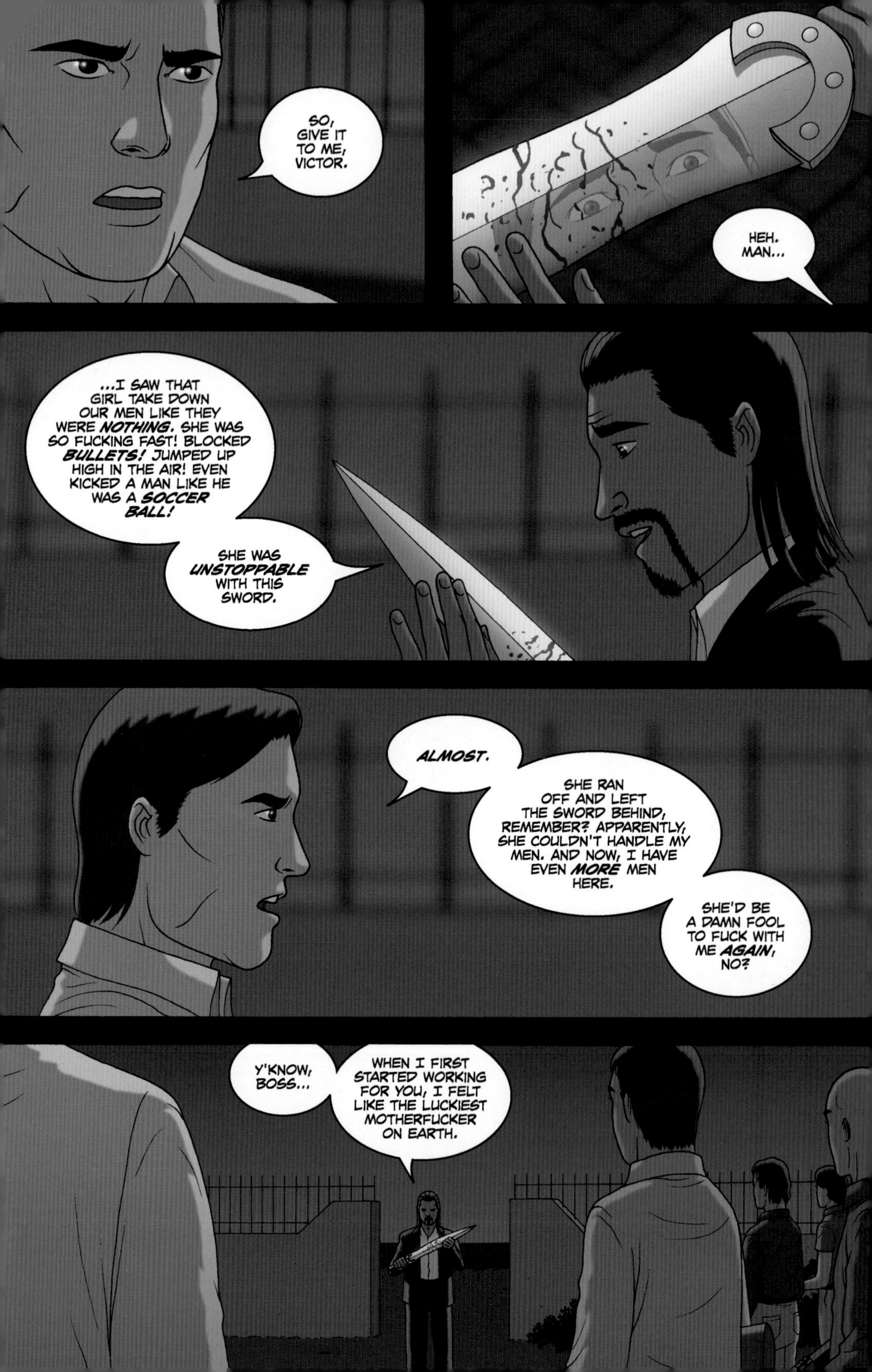
SO, GIVE IT TO ME, VICTOR.
HEH. MAN...
...I SAW THAT GIRL TAKE DOWN OUR MEN LIKE THEY WERE NOTHING. SHE WAS SO FUCKING FAST! BLOCKED BULLETS! JUMPED UP HIGH IN THE AIR! EVEN KICKED A MAN LIKE HE WAS A SOCCER BALL!
SHE WAS UNSTOPPABLE WITH THIS SWORD.
ALMOST.
SHE RAN OFF AND LEFT THE SWORD BEHIND, REMEMBER? APPARENTLY, SHE COULDN'T HANDLE MY MEN. AND NOW, I HAVE EVEN MORE MEN HERE.
SHE'D BE A DAMN FOOL TO FUCK WITH ME AGAIN, NO?
Y'KNOW, BOSS...
WHEN I FIRST STARTED WORKING FOR YOU, I FELT LIKE THE LUCKIEST MOTHERFUCKER ON EARTH.

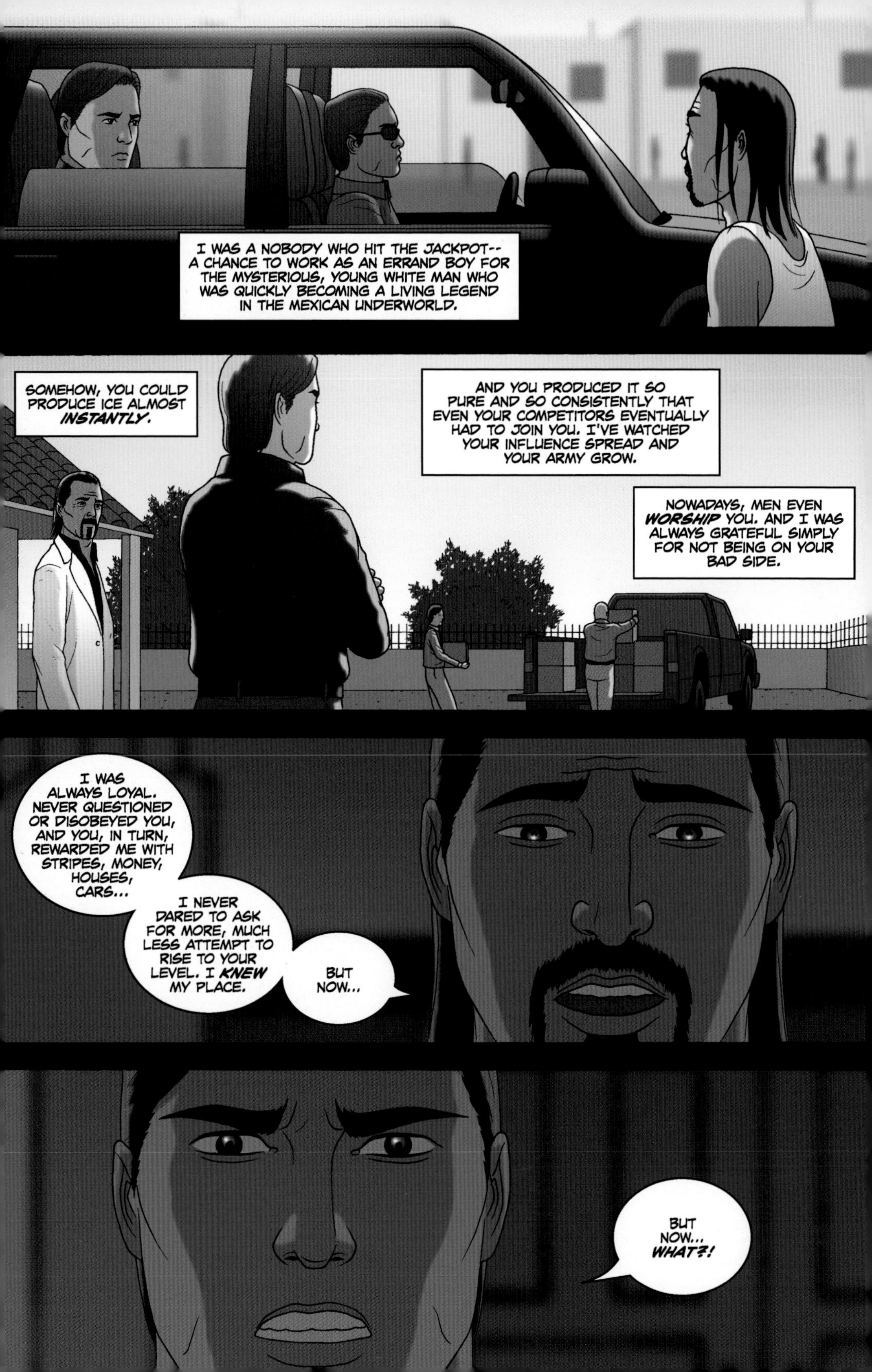
I WAS A NOBODY WHO HIT THE JACKPOT-- A CHANCE TO WORK AS AN ERRAND BOY FOR THE MYSTERIOUS, YOUNG WHITE MAN WHO WAS QUICKLY BECOMING A LIVING LEGEND IN THE MEXICAN UNDERWORLD.
SOMEHOW, YOU COULD PRODUCE ICE ALMOST *INSTANTLY*.
AND YOU PRODUCED IT SO PURE AND SO CONSISTENTLY THAT EVEN YOUR COMPETITORS EVENTUALLY HAD TO JOIN YOU. I'VE WATCHED YOUR INFLUENCE SPREAD AND YOUR ARMY GROW.
NOWADAYS, MEN EVEN *WORSHIP* YOU. AND I WAS ALWAYS GRATEFUL SIMPLY FOR NOT BEING ON YOUR BAD SIDE.
I WAS ALWAYS LOYAL. NEVER QUESTIONED OR DISOBEYED YOU, AND YOU, IN TURN, REWARDED ME WITH STRIPES, MONEY, HOUSES, CARS...
I NEVER DARED TO ASK FOR MORE, MUCH LESS ATTEMPT TO RISE TO YOUR LEVEL. I *KNEW* MY PLACE.
BUT NOW...
BUT NOW... *WHAT?!*

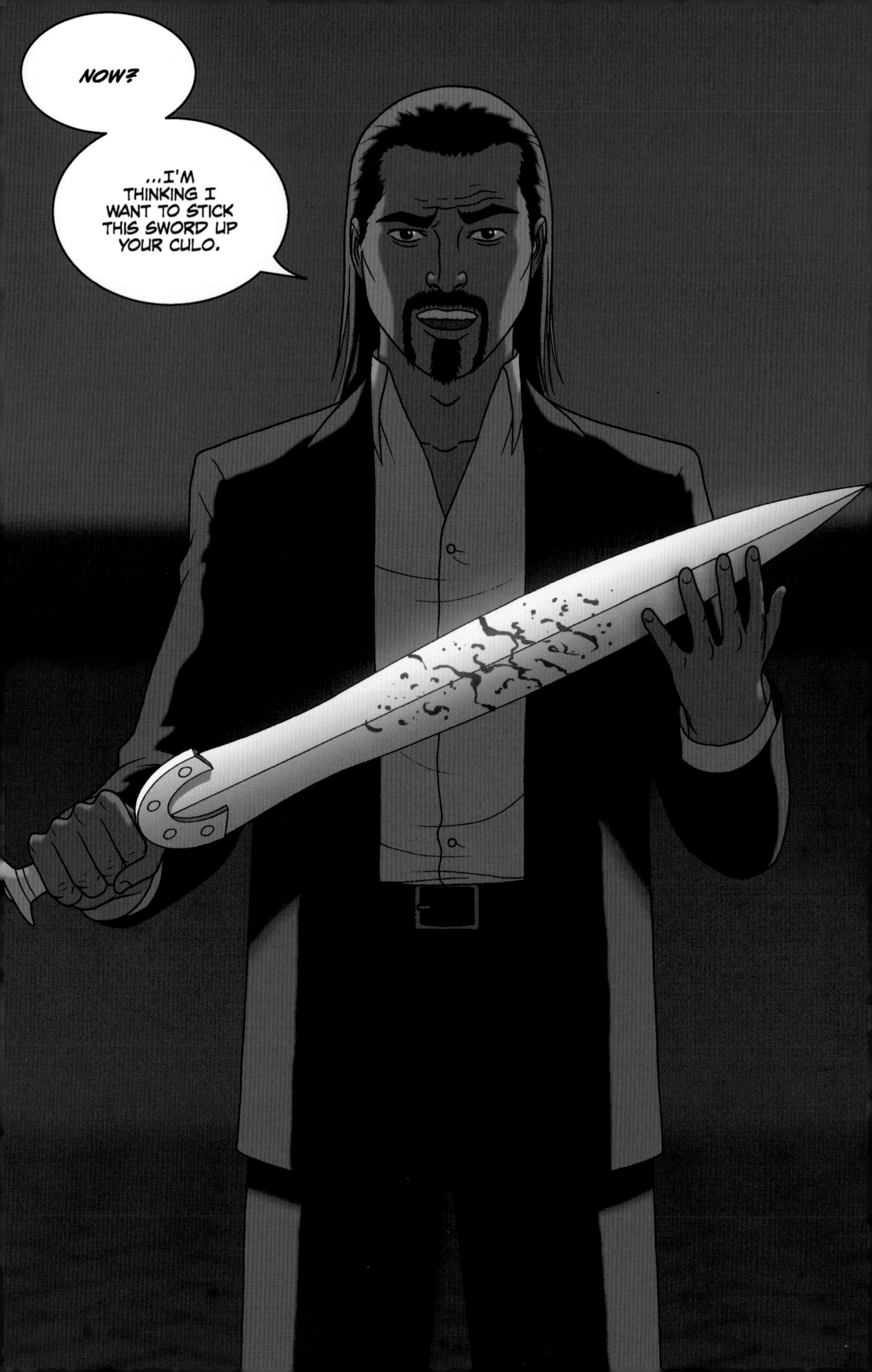
NOW?
...I'M THINKING I WANT TO STICK THIS SWORD UP YOUR CULO.

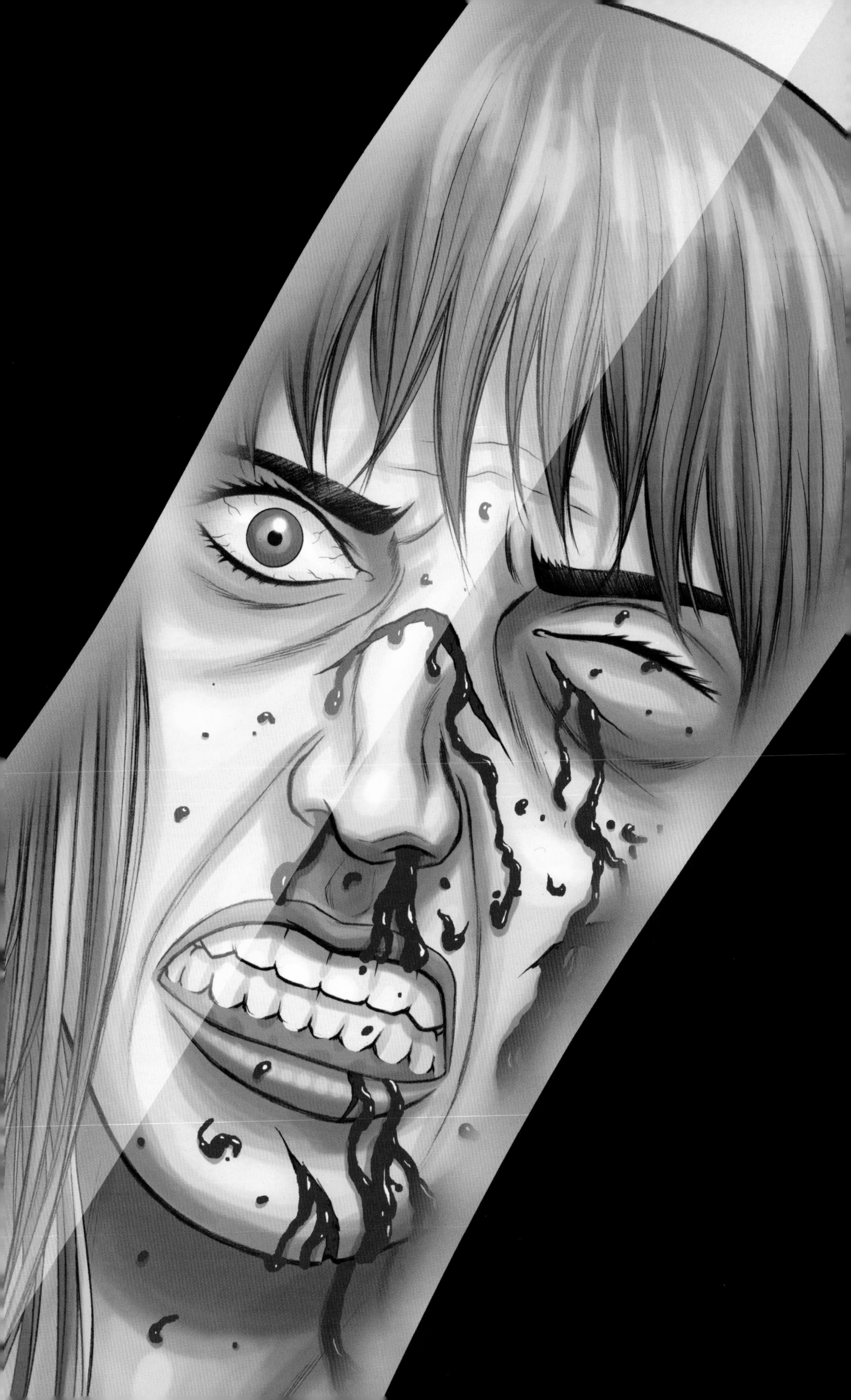

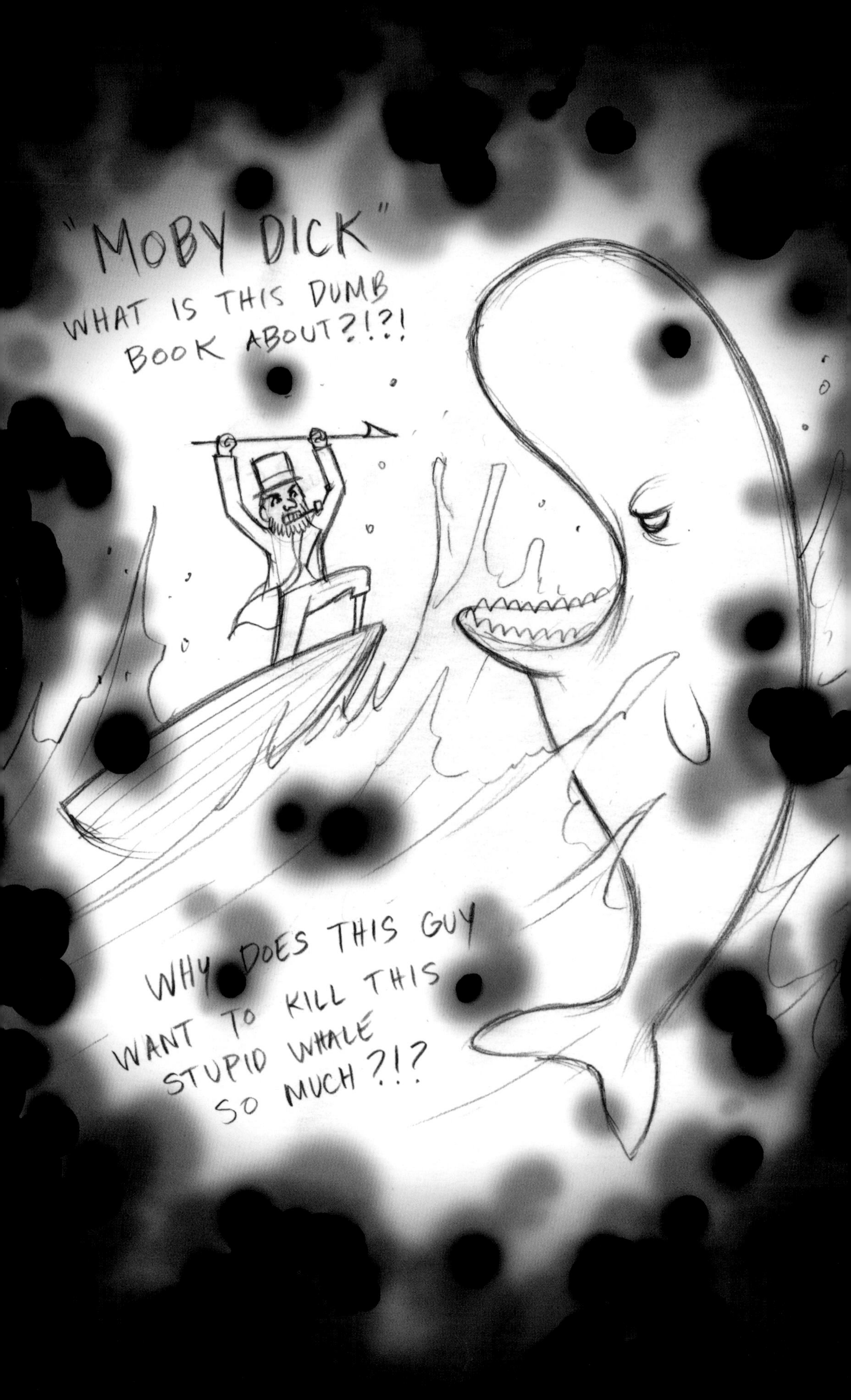
"MOBY DICK"
WHAT IS THIS DUMB BOOK ABOUT?!?!
WHY DOES THIS GUY WANT TO KILL THIS STUPID WHALE SO MUCH?!?

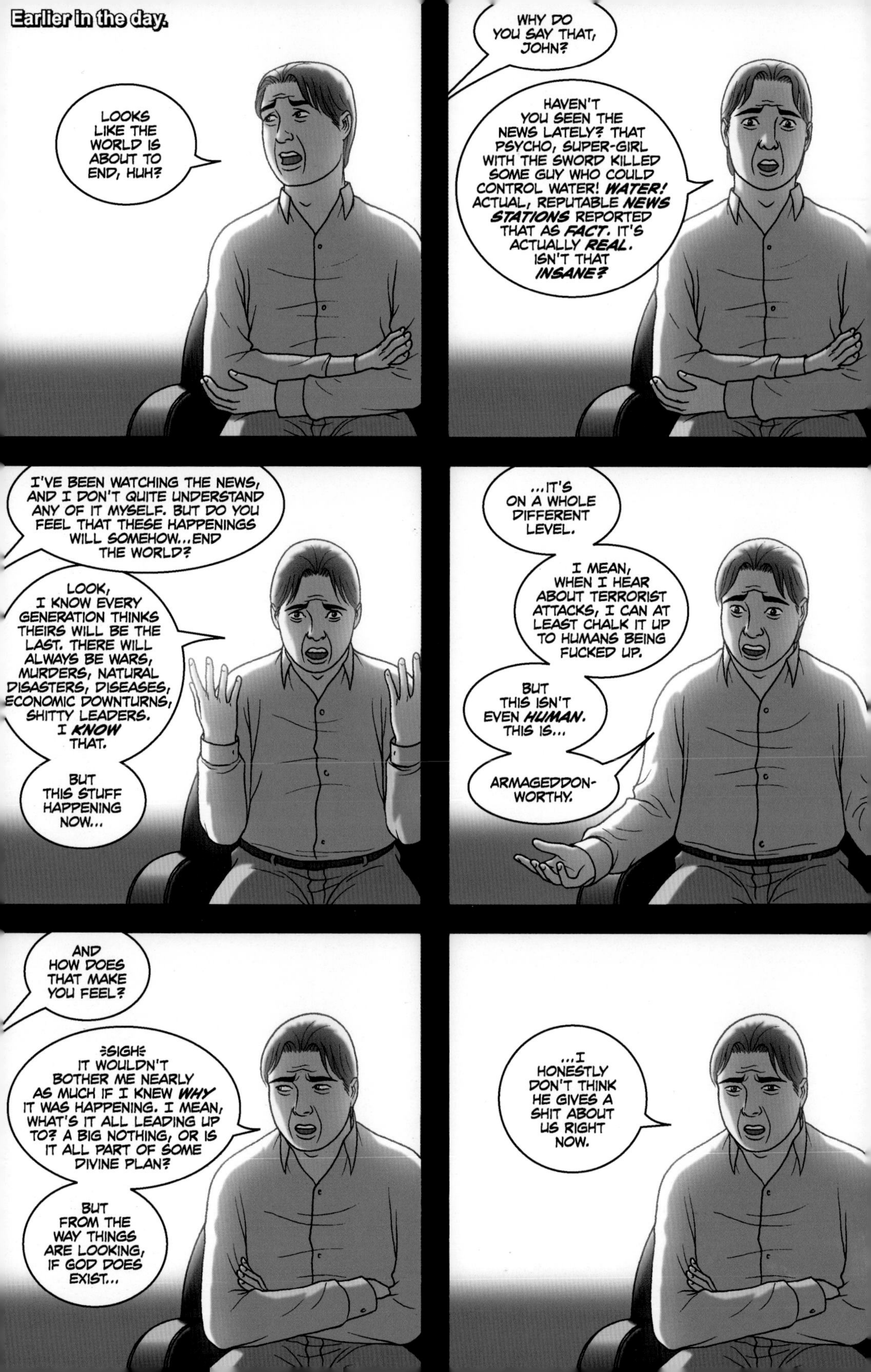
Earlier in the day.
LOOKS LIKE THE WORLD IS ABOUT TO END, HUH?
WHY DO YOU SAY THAT, JOHN?
HAVEN'T YOU SEEN THE NEWS LATELY? THAT PSYCHO, SUPER-GIRL WITH THE SWORD KILLED SOME GUY WHO COULD CONTROL WATER! WATER! ACTUAL, REPUTABLE NEWS STATIONS REPORTED THAT AS FACT. IT'S ACTUALLY REAL. ISN'T THAT INSANE?
I'VE BEEN WATCHING THE NEWS, AND I DON'T QUITE UNDERSTAND ANY OF IT MYSELF. BUT DO YOU FEEL THAT THESE HAPPENINGS WILL SOMEHOW...END THE WORLD?
LOOK, I KNOW EVERY GENERATION THINKS THEIRS WILL BE THE LAST. THERE WILL ALWAYS BE WARS, MURDERS, NATURAL DISASTERS, DISEASES, ECONOMIC DOWNTURNS, SHITTY LEADERS. I KNOW THAT.
BUT THIS STUFF HAPPENING NOW...
...IT'S ON A WHOLE DIFFERENT LEVEL.
I MEAN, WHEN I HEAR ABOUT TERRORIST ATTACKS, I CAN AT LEAST CHALK IT UP TO HUMANS BEING FUCKED UP.
BUT THIS ISN'T EVEN HUMAN. THIS IS...
ARMAGEDDON-WORTHY.
AND HOW DOES THAT MAKE YOU FEEL?
=SIGH= IT WOULDN'T BOTHER ME NEARLY AS MUCH IF I KNEW WHY IT WAS HAPPENING. I MEAN, WHAT'S IT ALL LEADING UP TO? A BIG NOTHING, OR IS IT ALL PART OF SOME DIVINE PLAN?
BUT FROM THE WAY THINGS ARE LOOKING, IF GOD DOES EXIST...
...I HONESTLY DON'T THINK HE GIVES A SHIT ABOUT US RIGHT NOW.

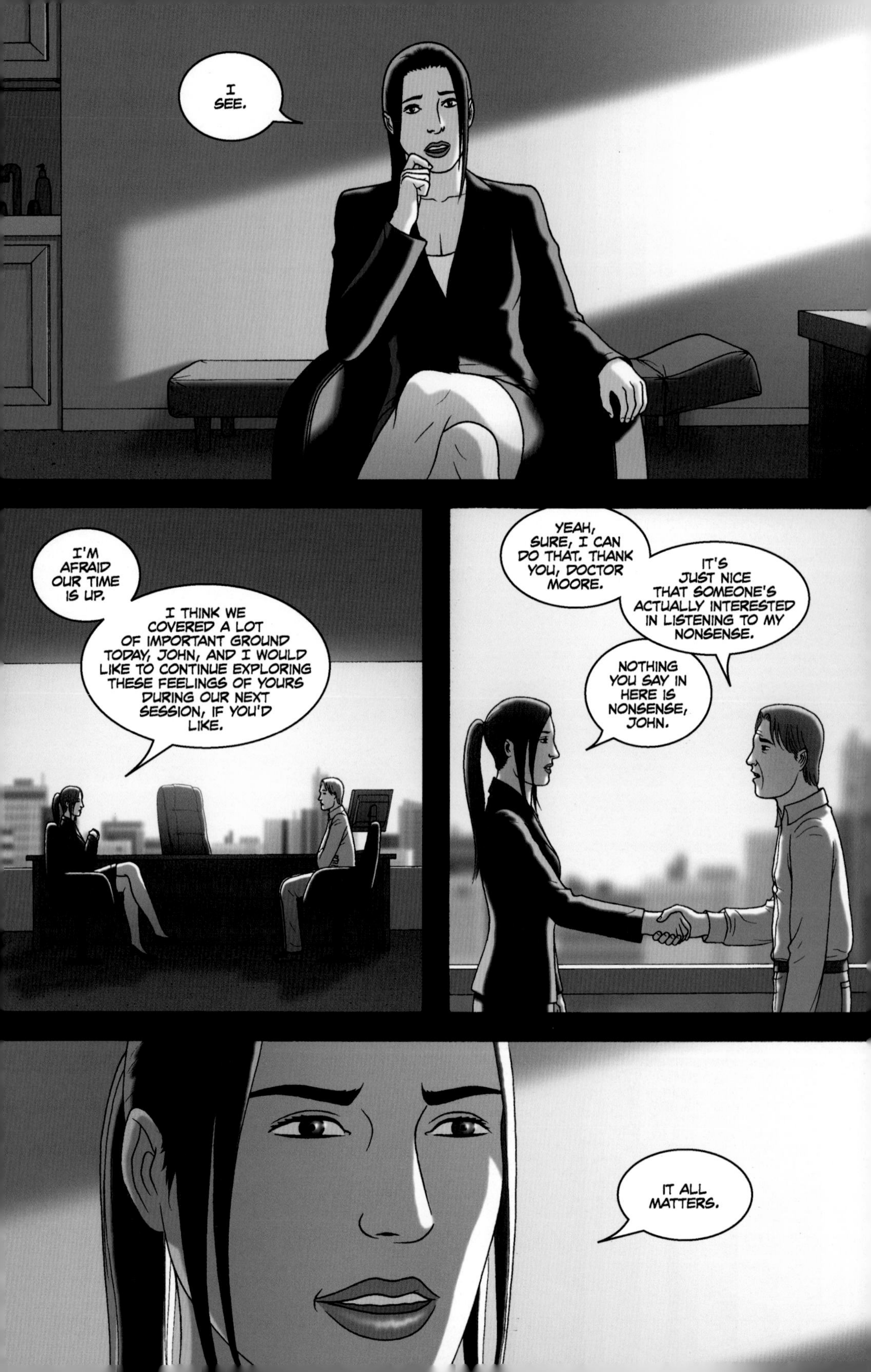
I SEE.
I'M AFRAID OUR TIME IS UP.
I THINK WE COVERED A LOT OF IMPORTANT GROUND TODAY, JOHN, AND I WOULD LIKE TO CONTINUE EXPLORING THESE FEELINGS OF YOURS DURING OUR NEXT SESSION, IF YOU'D LIKE.
YEAH, SURE, I CAN DO THAT. THANK YOU, DOCTOR MOORE.
IT'S JUST NICE THAT SOMEONE'S ACTUALLY INTERESTED IN LISTENING TO MY NONSENSE.
NOTHING YOU SAY IN HERE IS NONSENSE, JOHN.
IT ALL MATTERS.

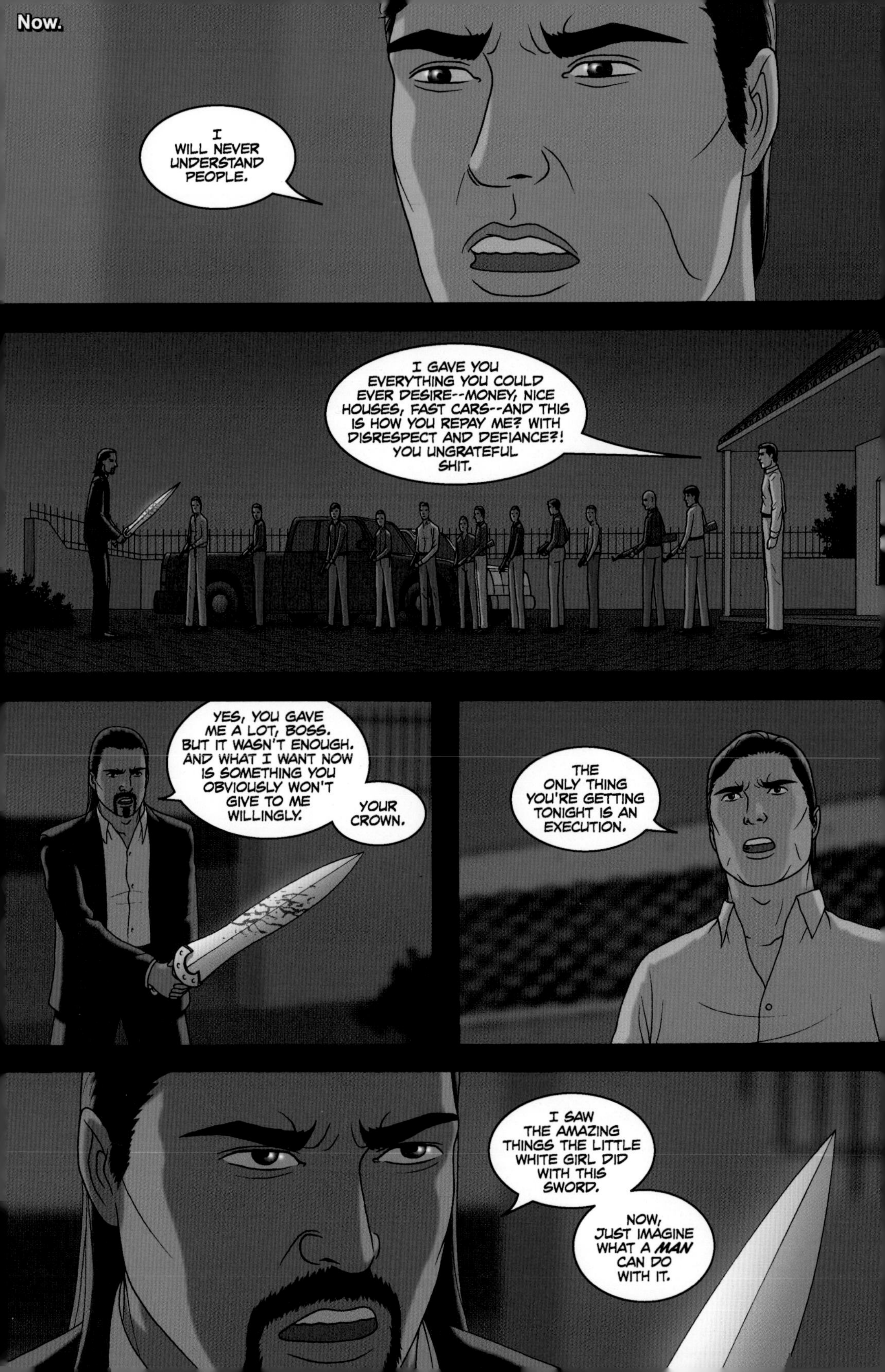
Now.
I WILL NEVER UNDERSTAND PEOPLE.
I GAVE YOU EVERYTHING YOU COULD EVER DESIRE--MONEY, NICE HOUSES, FAST CARS--AND THIS IS HOW YOU REPAY ME? WITH DISRESPECT AND DEFIANCE?! YOU UNGRATEFUL SHIT.
YES, YOU GAVE ME A LOT, BOSS. BUT IT WASN'T ENOUGH. AND WHAT I WANT NOW IS SOMETHING YOU OBVIOUSLY WON'T GIVE TO ME WILLINGLY.
YOUR CROWN.
THE ONLY THING YOU'RE GETTING TONIGHT IS AN EXECUTION.
I SAW THE AMAZING THINGS THE LITTLE WHITE GIRL DID WITH THIS SWORD.
NOW, JUST IMAGINE WHAT A *MAN* CAN DO WITH IT.

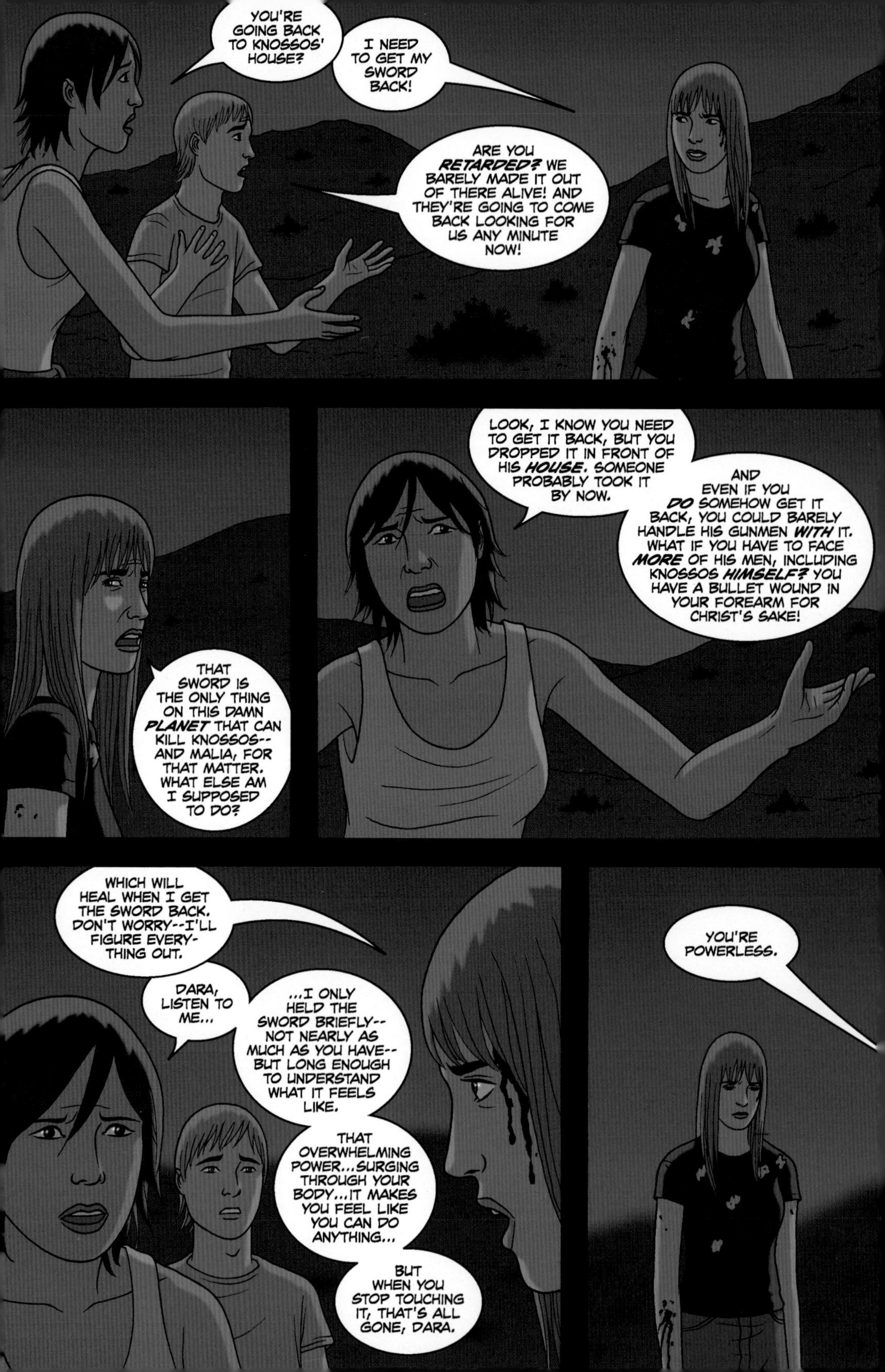
YOU'RE GOING BACK TO KNOSSOS' HOUSE?
I NEED TO GET MY SWORD BACK!
ARE YOU RETARDED? WE BARELY MADE IT OUT OF THERE ALIVE! AND THEY'RE GOING TO COME BACK LOOKING FOR US ANY MINUTE NOW!
LOOK, I KNOW YOU NEED TO GET IT BACK, BUT YOU DROPPED IT IN FRONT OF HIS HOUSE. SOMEONE PROBABLY TOOK IT BY NOW.
AND EVEN IF YOU DO SOMEHOW GET IT BACK, YOU COULD BARELY HANDLE HIS GUNMEN WITH IT. WHAT IF YOU HAVE TO FACE MORE OF HIS MEN, INCLUDING KNOSSOS HIMSELF? YOU HAVE A BULLET WOUND IN YOUR FOREARM FOR CHRIST'S SAKE!
THAT SWORD IS THE ONLY THING ON THIS DAMN PLANET THAT CAN KILL KNOSSOS--AND MALIA, FOR THAT MATTER. WHAT ELSE AM I SUPPOSED TO DO?
WHICH WILL HEAL WHEN I GET THE SWORD BACK. DON'T WORRY--I'LL FIGURE EVERY-THING OUT.
DARA, LISTEN TO ME...
...I ONLY HELD THE SWORD BRIEFLY--NOT NEARLY AS MUCH AS YOU HAVE--BUT LONG ENOUGH TO UNDERSTAND WHAT IT FEELS LIKE.
THAT OVERWHELMING POWER...SURGING THROUGH YOUR BODY...IT MAKES YOU FEEL LIKE YOU CAN DO ANYTHING...
BUT WHEN YOU STOP TOUCHING IT, THAT'S ALL GONE, DARA.
YOU'RE POWERLESS.

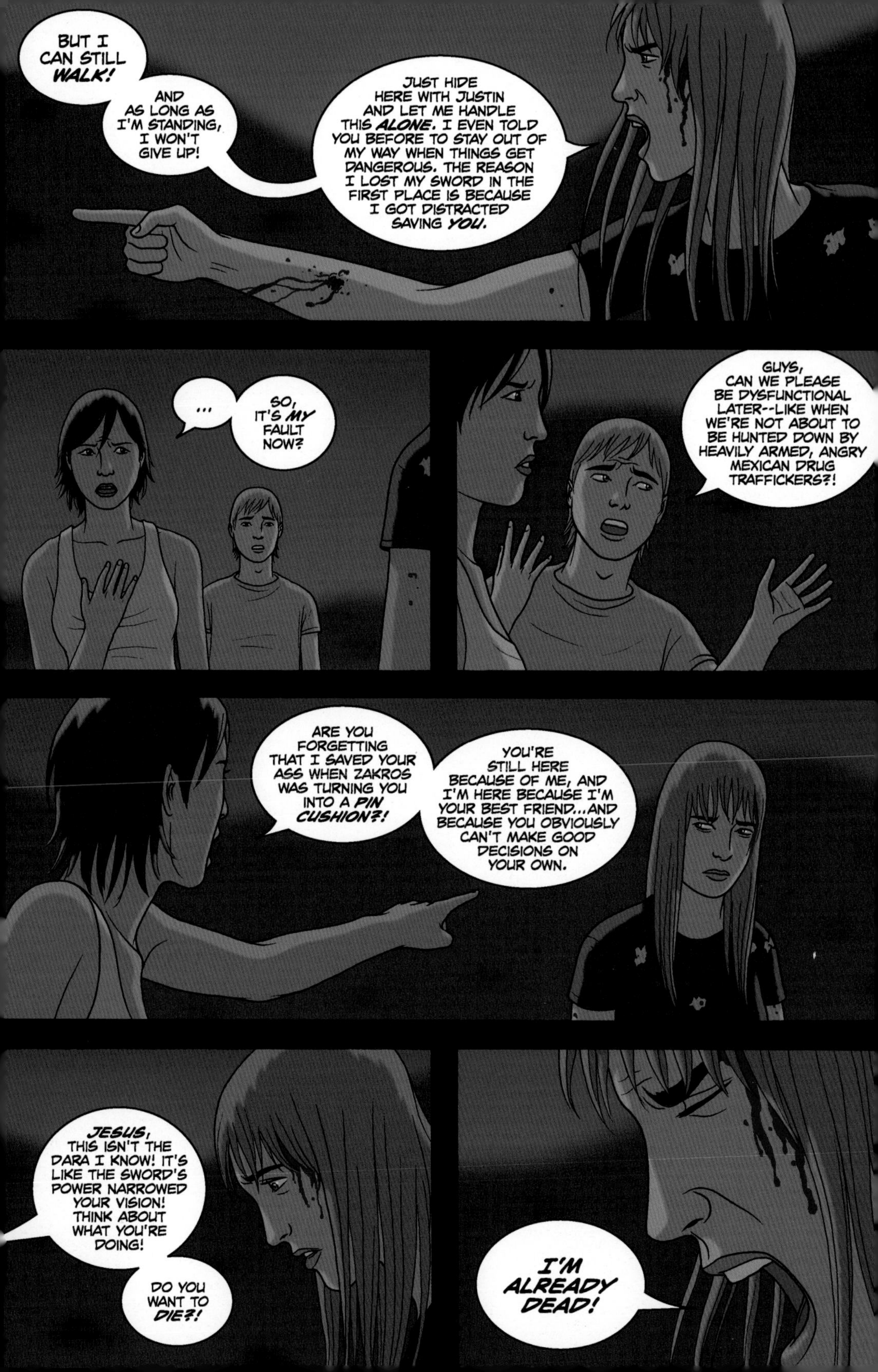

BUT I CAN STILL WALK!
AND AS LONG AS I'M STANDING, I WON'T GIVE UP!
JUST HIDE HERE WITH JUSTIN AND LET ME HANDLE THIS ALONE. I EVEN TOLD YOU BEFORE TO STAY OUT OF MY WAY WHEN THINGS GET DANGEROUS. THE REASON I LOST MY SWORD IN THE FIRST PLACE IS BECAUSE I GOT DISTRACTED SAVING YOU.
...
SO, IT'S MY FAULT NOW?
GUYS, CAN WE PLEASE BE DYSFUNCTIONAL LATER--LIKE WHEN WE'RE NOT ABOUT TO BE HUNTED DOWN BY HEAVILY ARMED, ANGRY MEXICAN DRUG TRAFFICKERS?!
ARE YOU FORGETTING THAT I SAVED YOUR ASS WHEN ZAKROS WAS TURNING YOU INTO A PIN CUSHION?!
YOU'RE STILL HERE BECAUSE OF ME, AND I'M HERE BECAUSE I'M YOUR BEST FRIEND...AND BECAUSE YOU OBVIOUSLY CAN'T MAKE GOOD DECISIONS ON YOUR OWN.
JESUS, THIS ISN'T THE DARA I KNOW! IT'S LIKE THE SWORD'S POWER NARROWED YOUR VISION! THINK ABOUT WHAT YOU'RE DOING!
DO YOU WANT TO DIE?!
I'M ALREADY DEAD!

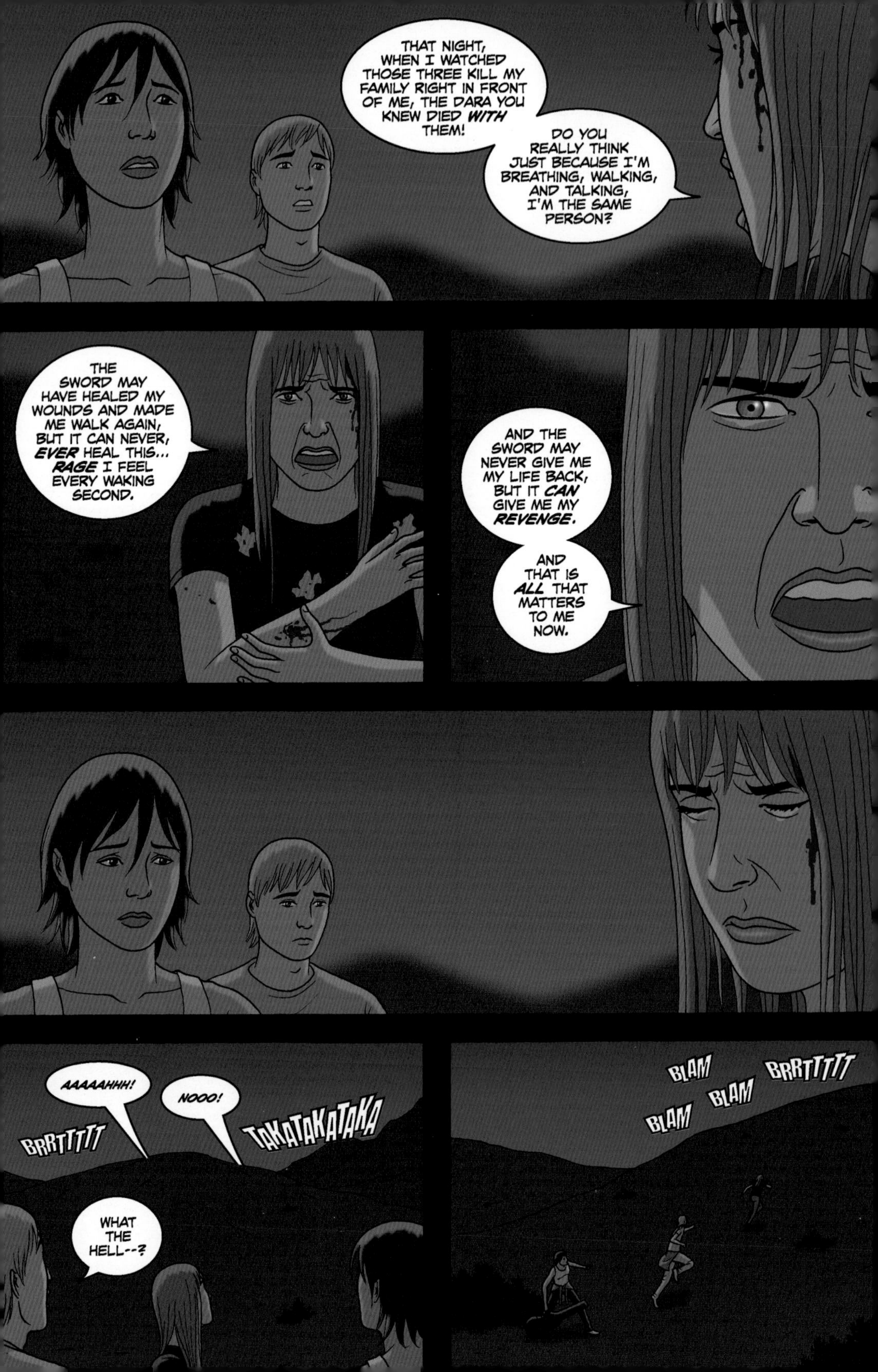
THAT NIGHT, WHEN I WATCHED THOSE THREE KILL MY FAMILY RIGHT IN FRONT OF ME, THE DARA YOU KNEW DIED *WITH* THEM!
DO YOU REALLY THINK JUST BECAUSE I'M BREATHING, WALKING, AND TALKING, I'M THE SAME PERSON?
THE SWORD MAY HAVE HEALED MY WOUNDS AND MADE ME WALK AGAIN, BUT IT CAN NEVER, *EVER* HEAL THIS... *RAGE* I FEEL EVERY WAKING SECOND.
AND THE SWORD MAY NEVER GIVE ME MY LIFE BACK, BUT IT *CAN* GIVE ME MY *REVENGE*.
AND THAT IS *ALL* THAT MATTERS TO ME NOW.
AAAAAHHH!
NOOO!
BRRTTTTT
TAKATAKATAKA
WHAT THE HELL--?
BLAM
BLAM
BLAM
BRRTTTTT

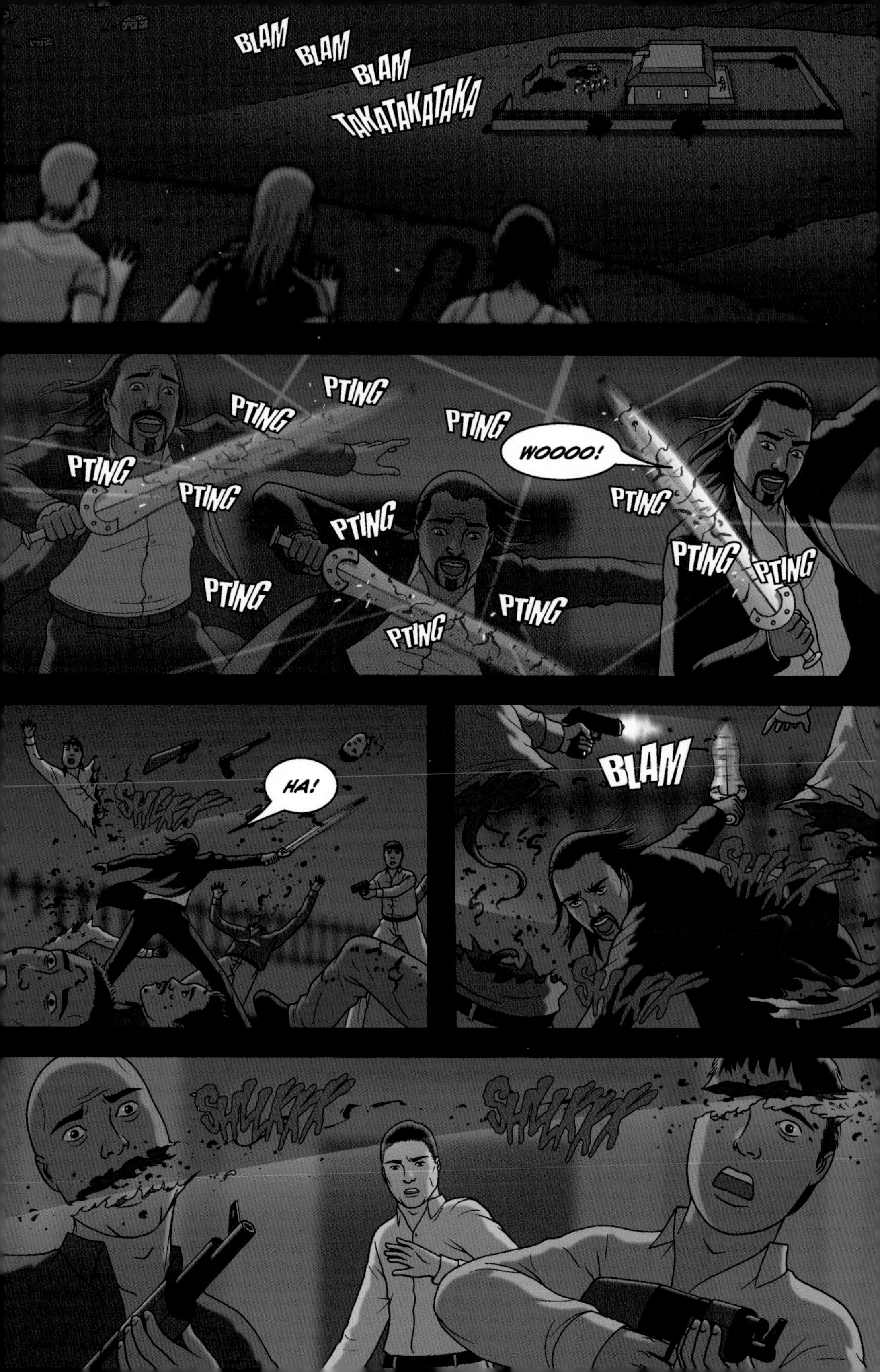

BLAM
BLAM
BLAM
TAKATAKATAKA
PTING
PTING
PTING
PTING
PTING
WOOOO!
PTING
PTING
PTING
PTING
PTING
PTING
PTING
HA!
BLAM

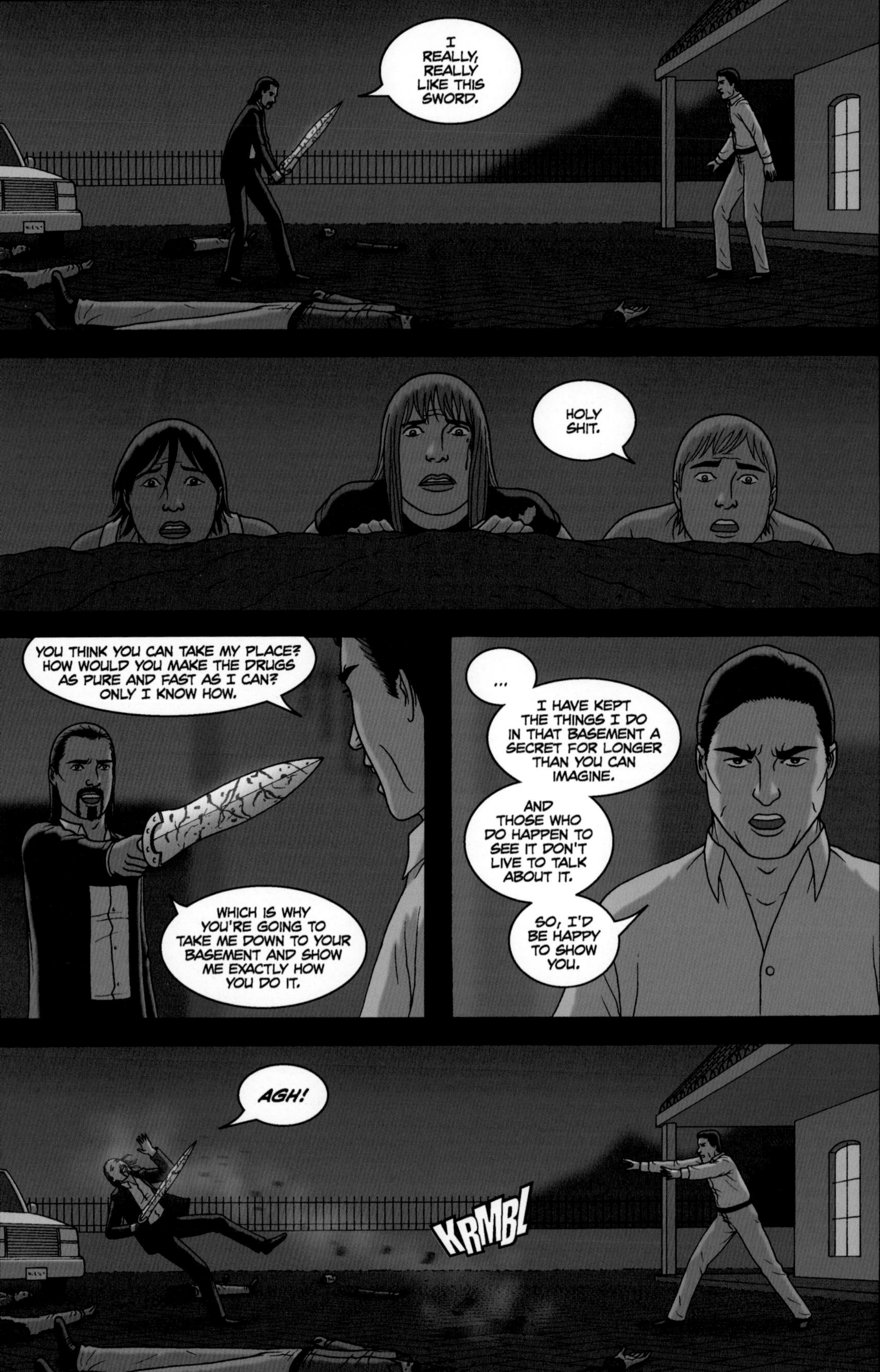
I REALLY, REALLY LIKE THIS SWORD.
HOLY SHIT.
YOU THINK YOU CAN TAKE MY PLACE? HOW WOULD YOU MAKE THE DRUGS AS PURE AND FAST AS I CAN? ONLY I KNOW HOW.
WHICH IS WHY YOU'RE GOING TO TAKE ME DOWN TO YOUR BASEMENT AND SHOW ME EXACTLY HOW YOU DO IT.
...
I HAVE KEPT THE THINGS I DO IN THAT BASEMENT A SECRET FOR LONGER THAN YOU CAN IMAGINE.
AND THOSE WHO DO HAPPEN TO SEE IT DON'T LIVE TO TALK ABOUT IT.
SO, I'D BE HAPPY TO SHOW YOU.
AGH!
KRMBL

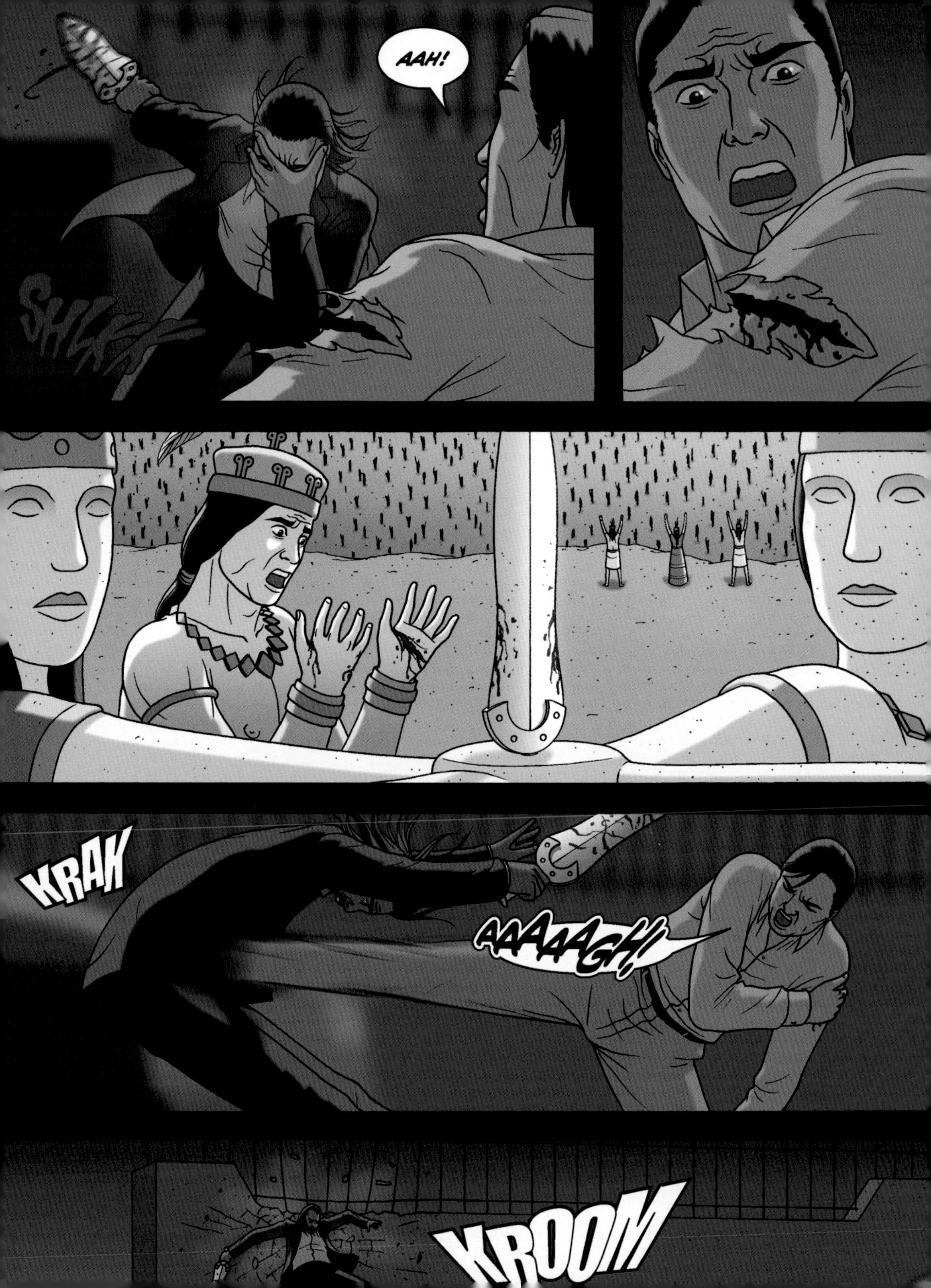

AAH!
KRAK
AAAAAGH!
KROOM

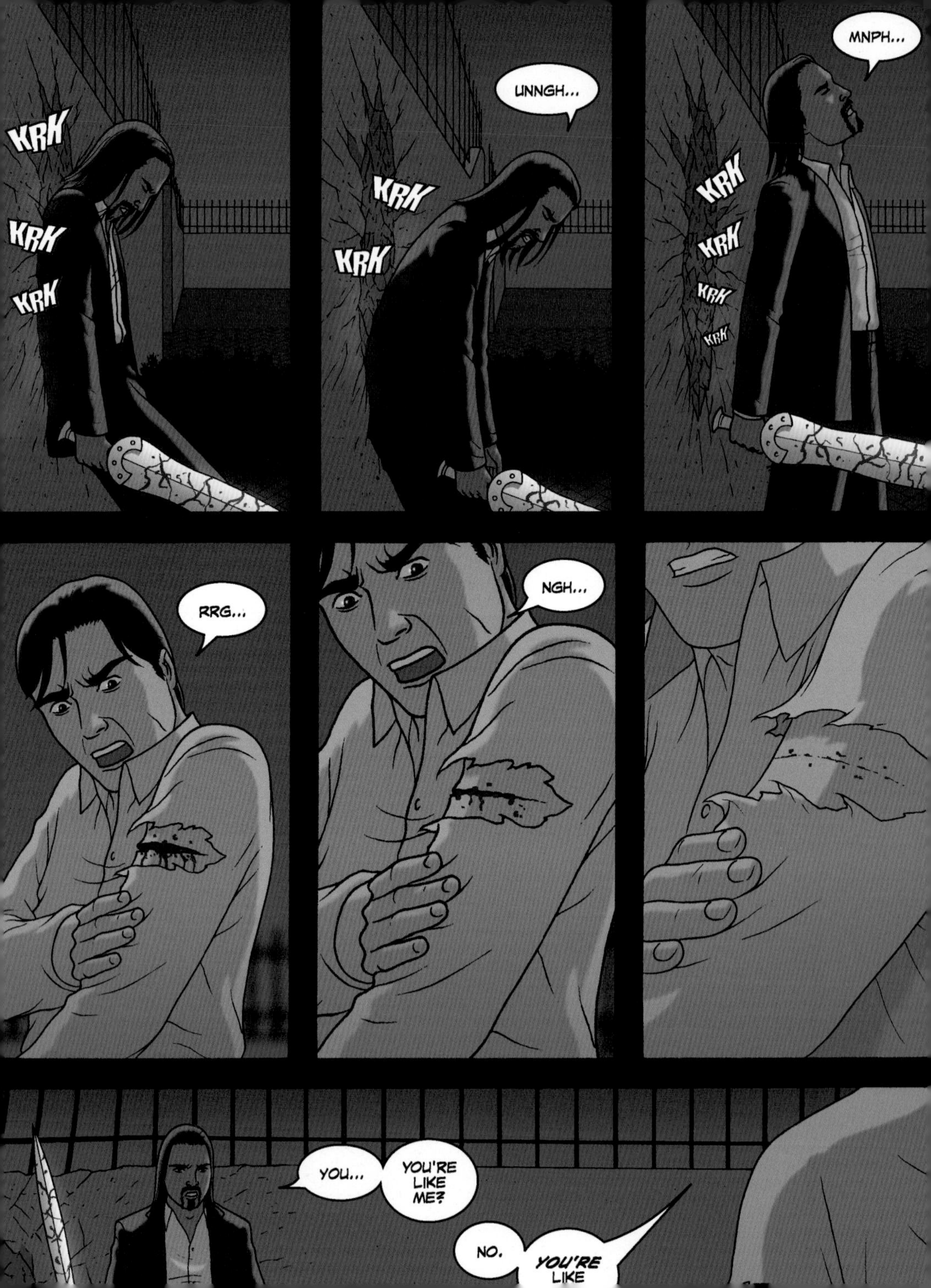
KRK
KRK
KRK
UNNGH...
KRK
KRK
MNPH...
KRK
KRK
KRK
KRK
RRG...
NGH...
YOU...
YOU'RE LIKE ME?
NO.
YOU'RE LIKE

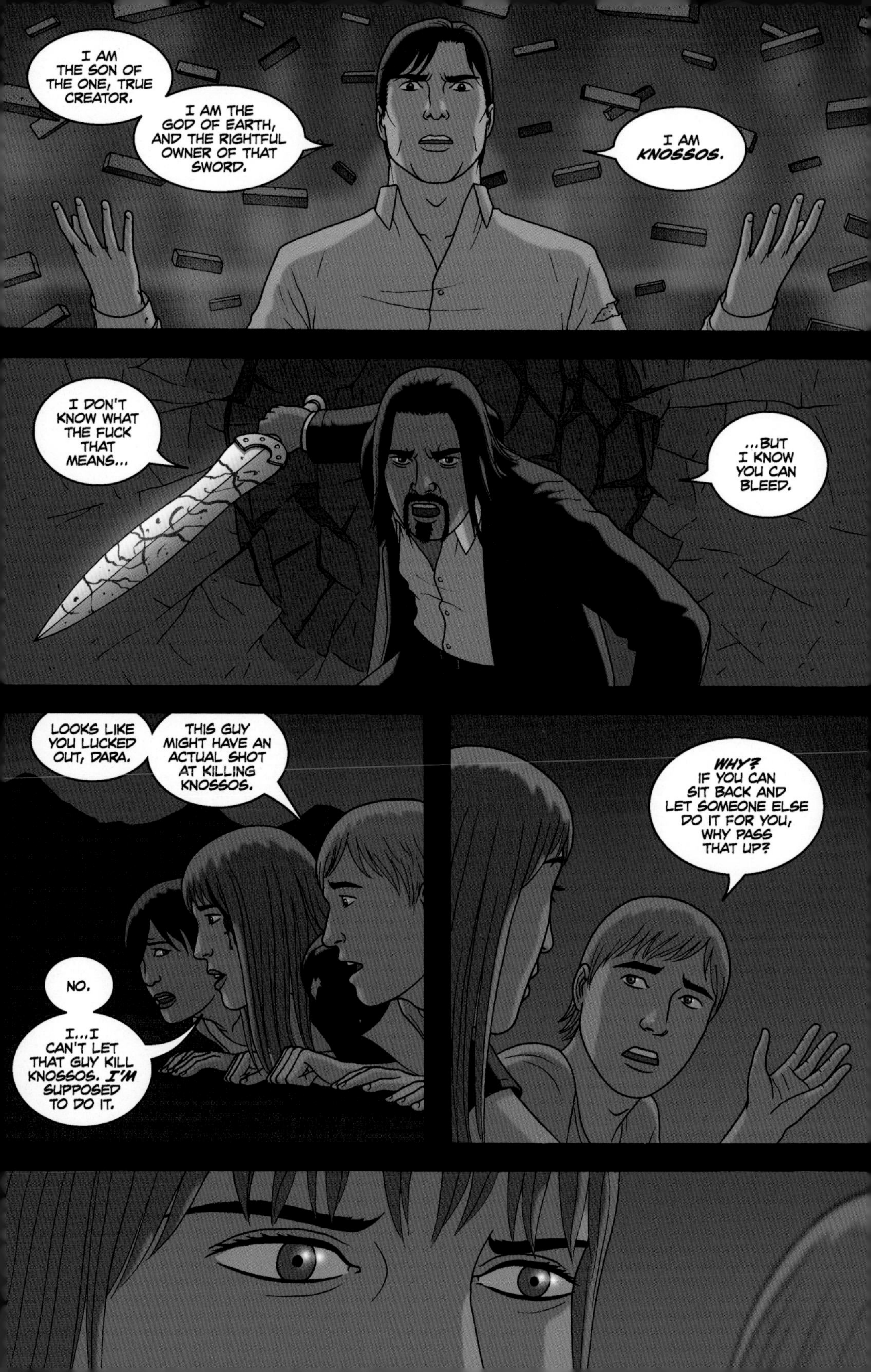

I AM THE SON OF THE ONE, TRUE CREATOR.
I AM THE GOD OF EARTH, AND THE RIGHTFUL OWNER OF THAT SWORD.
I AM *KNOSSOS.*
I DON'T KNOW WHAT THE FUCK THAT MEANS...
...BUT I KNOW YOU CAN BLEED.
LOOKS LIKE YOU LUCKED OUT, DARA.
THIS GUY MIGHT HAVE AN ACTUAL SHOT AT KILLING KNOSSOS.
NO.
I...I CAN'T LET THAT GUY KILL KNOSSOS. *I'M* SUPPOSED TO DO IT.
WHY? IF YOU CAN SIT BACK AND LET SOMEONE ELSE DO IT FOR YOU, WHY PASS THAT UP?

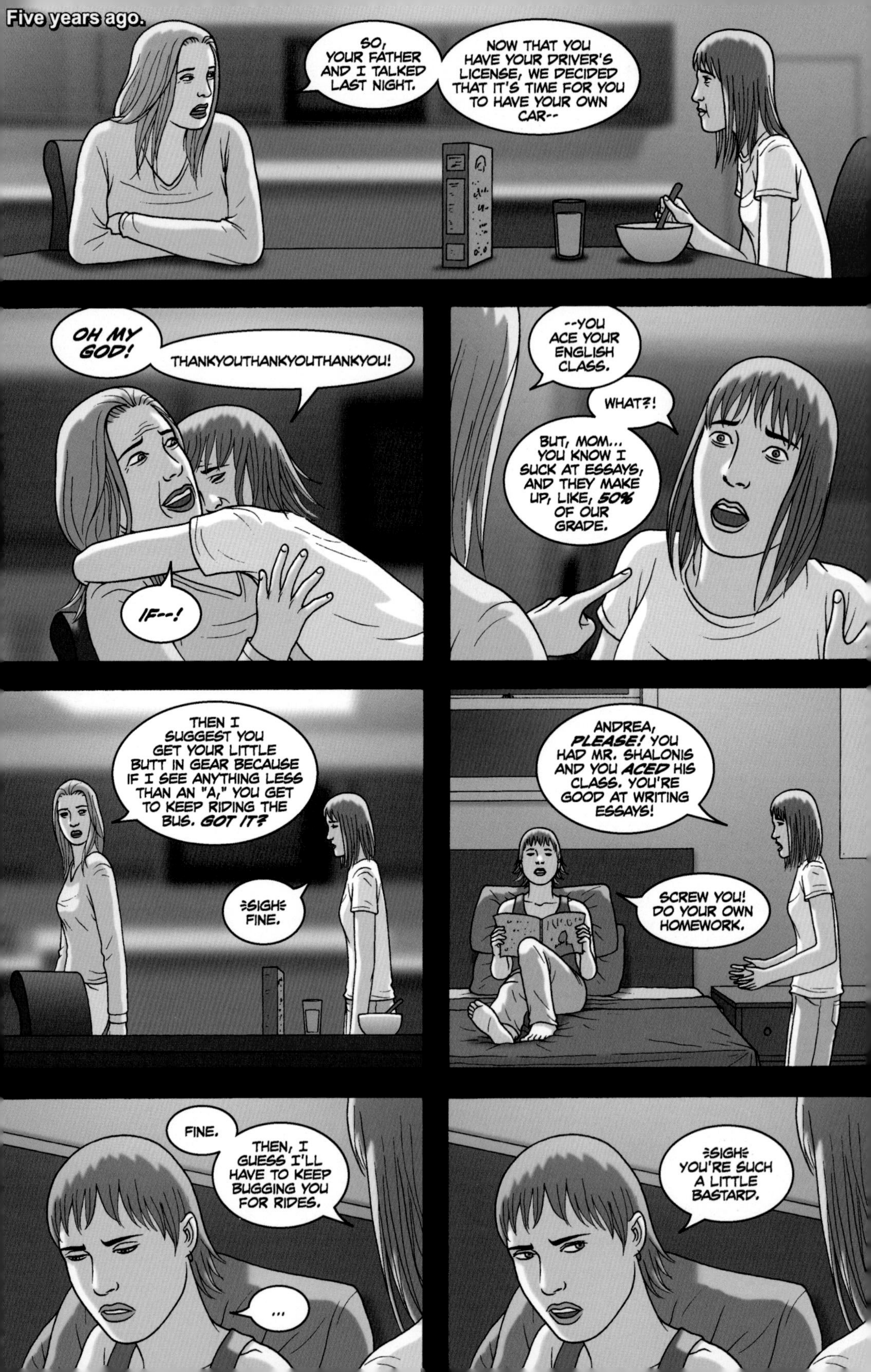
Five years ago.
SO, YOUR FATHER AND I TALKED LAST NIGHT.
NOW THAT YOU HAVE YOUR DRIVER'S LICENSE, WE DECIDED THAT IT'S TIME FOR YOU TO HAVE YOUR OWN CAR--
OH MY GOD!
THANKYOUTHANKYOUTHANKYOU!
IF--!
--YOU ACE YOUR ENGLISH CLASS.
WHAT?!
BUT, MOM... YOU KNOW I SUCK AT ESSAYS, AND THEY MAKE UP, LIKE, 50% OF OUR GRADE.
THEN I SUGGEST YOU GET YOUR LITTLE BUTT IN GEAR BECAUSE IF I SEE ANYTHING LESS THAN AN "A," YOU GET TO KEEP RIDING THE BUS. GOT IT?
SIGH FINE.
ANDREA, PLEASE! YOU HAD MR. SHALONIS AND YOU ACED HIS CLASS. YOU'RE GOOD AT WRITING ESSAYS!
SCREW YOU! DO YOUR OWN HOMEWORK.
FINE.
THEN, I GUESS I'LL HAVE TO KEEP BUGGING YOU FOR RIDES.
...
SIGH YOU'RE SUCH A LITTLE BASTARD.

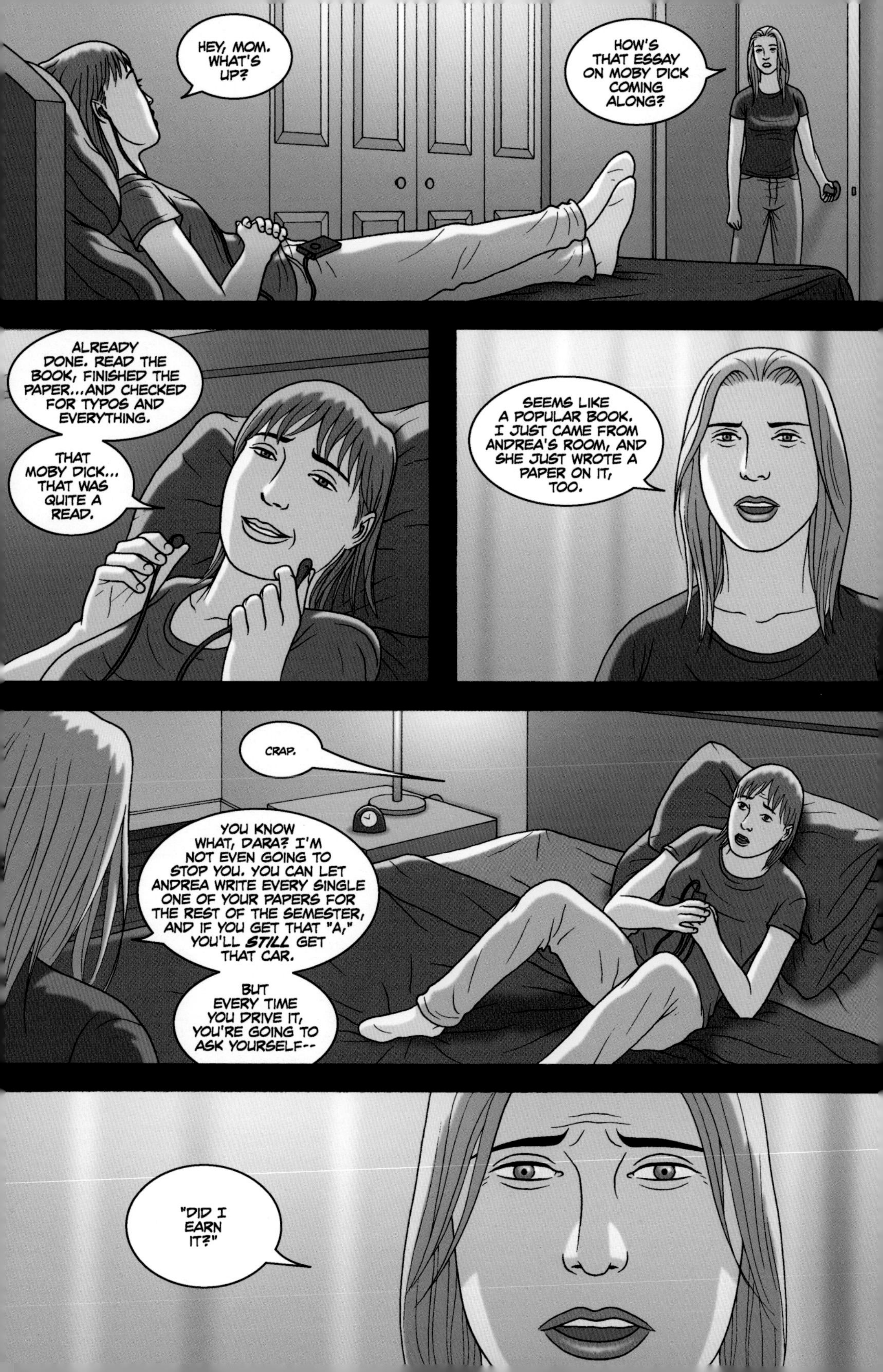
HEY, MOM. WHAT'S UP?
HOW'S THAT ESSAY ON MOBY DICK COMING ALONG?
ALREADY DONE. READ THE BOOK, FINISHED THE PAPER...AND CHECKED FOR TYPOS AND EVERYTHING.
THAT MOBY DICK... THAT WAS QUITE A READ.
SEEMS LIKE A POPULAR BOOK. I JUST CAME FROM ANDREA'S ROOM, AND SHE JUST WROTE A PAPER ON IT, TOO.
CRAP.
YOU KNOW WHAT, DARA? I'M NOT EVEN GOING TO STOP YOU. YOU CAN LET ANDREA WRITE EVERY SINGLE ONE OF YOUR PAPERS FOR THE REST OF THE SEMESTER, AND IF YOU GET THAT "A," YOU'LL *STILL* GET THAT CAR.
BUT EVERY TIME YOU DRIVE IT, YOU'RE GOING TO ASK YOURSELF--
"DID I EARN IT?"

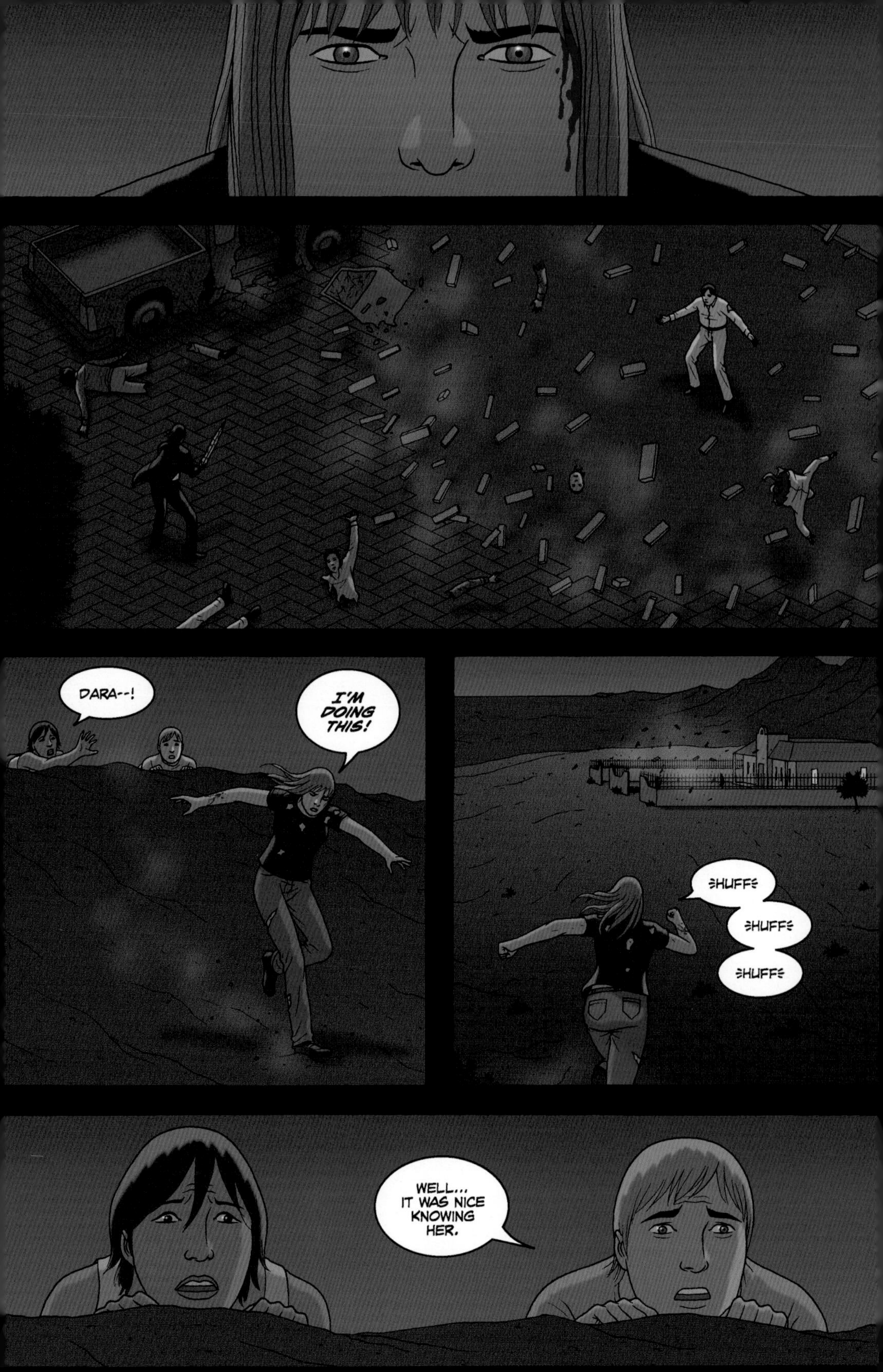
DARA--!
I'M DOING THIS!
HUFF
HUFF
HUFF
WELL... IT WAS NICE KNOWING HER.

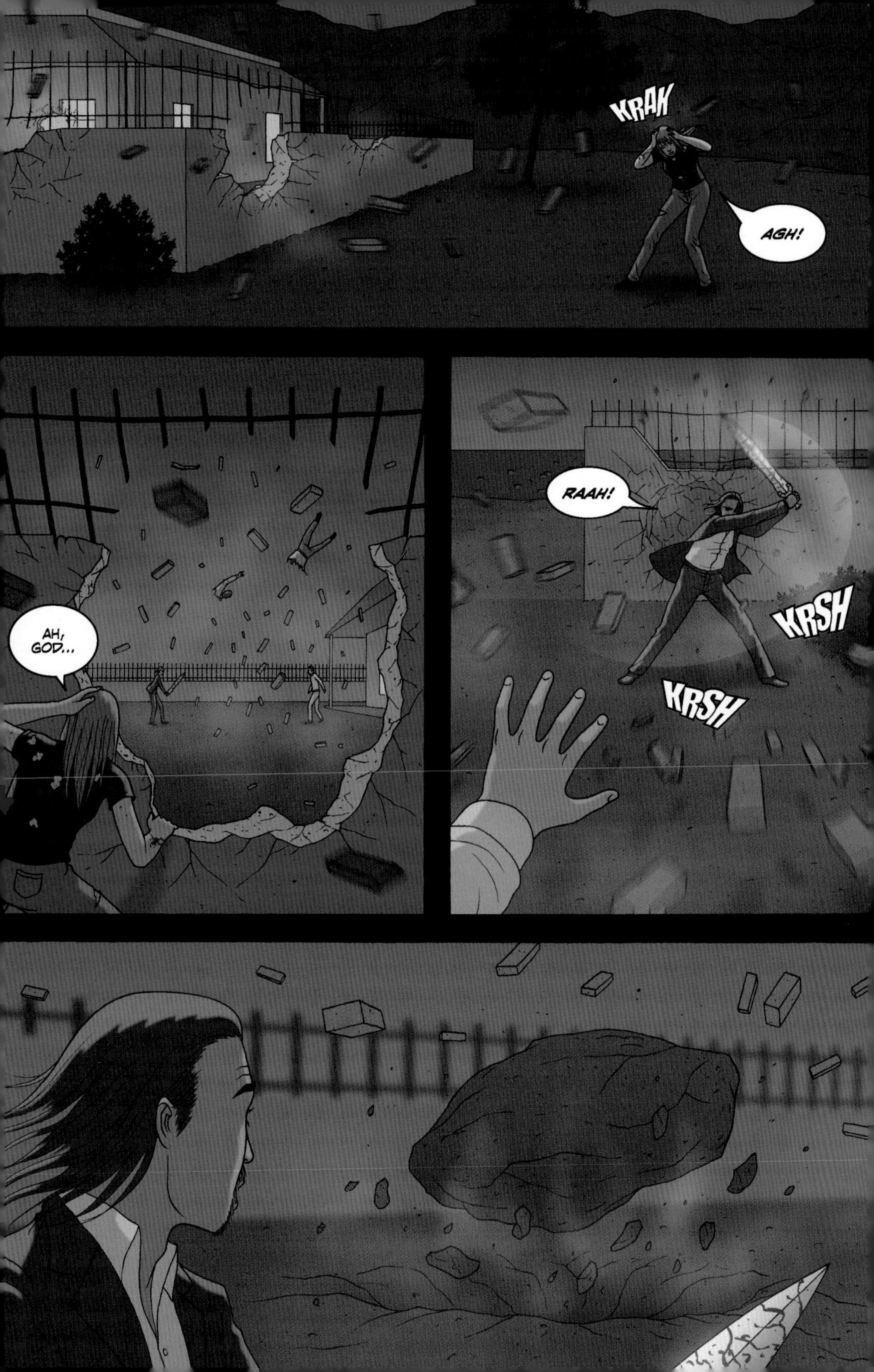
KRAK
AGH!
AH, GOD...
RAAH!
KRSH
KRSH

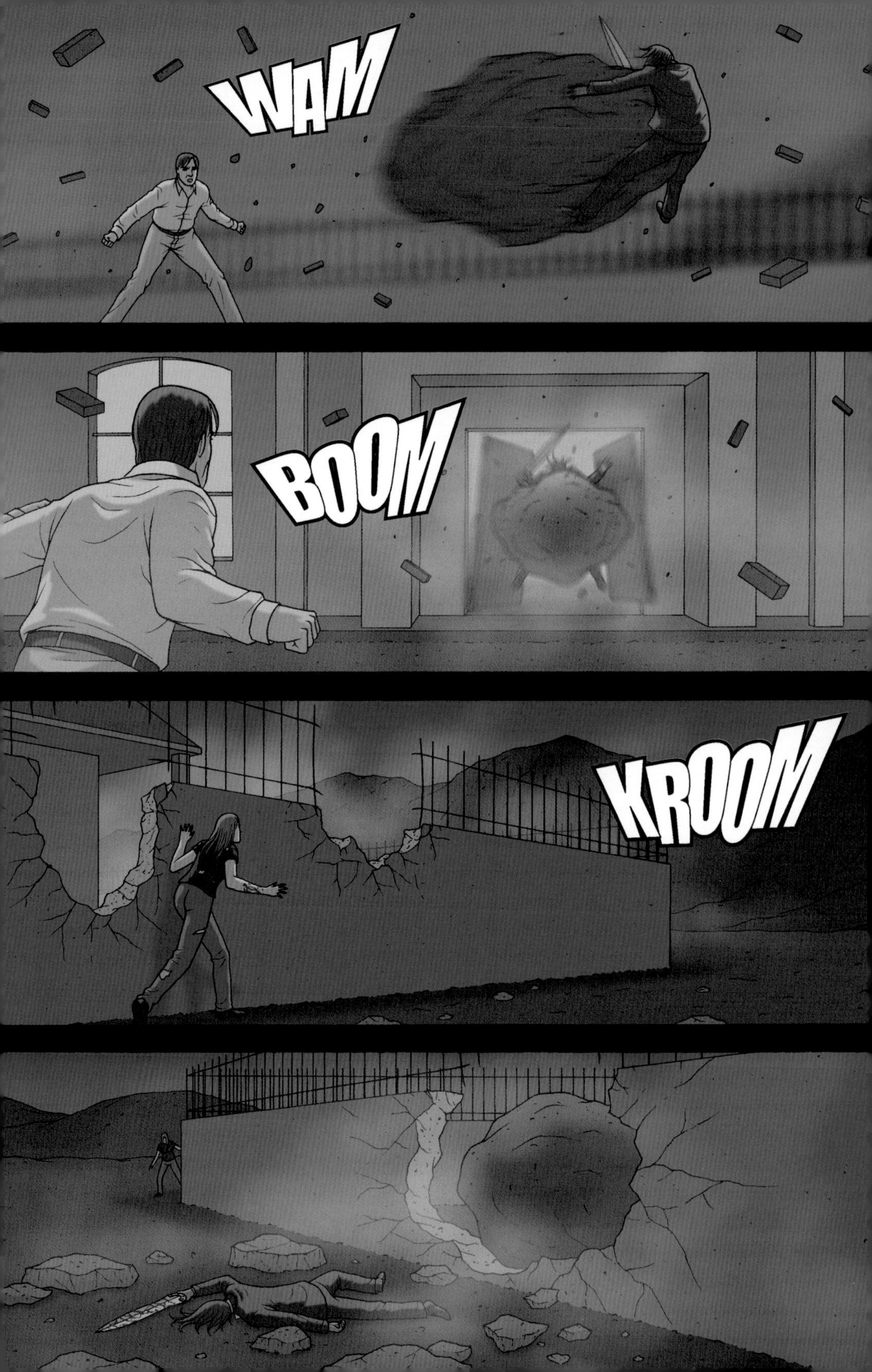
WAM
BOOM
KROOM

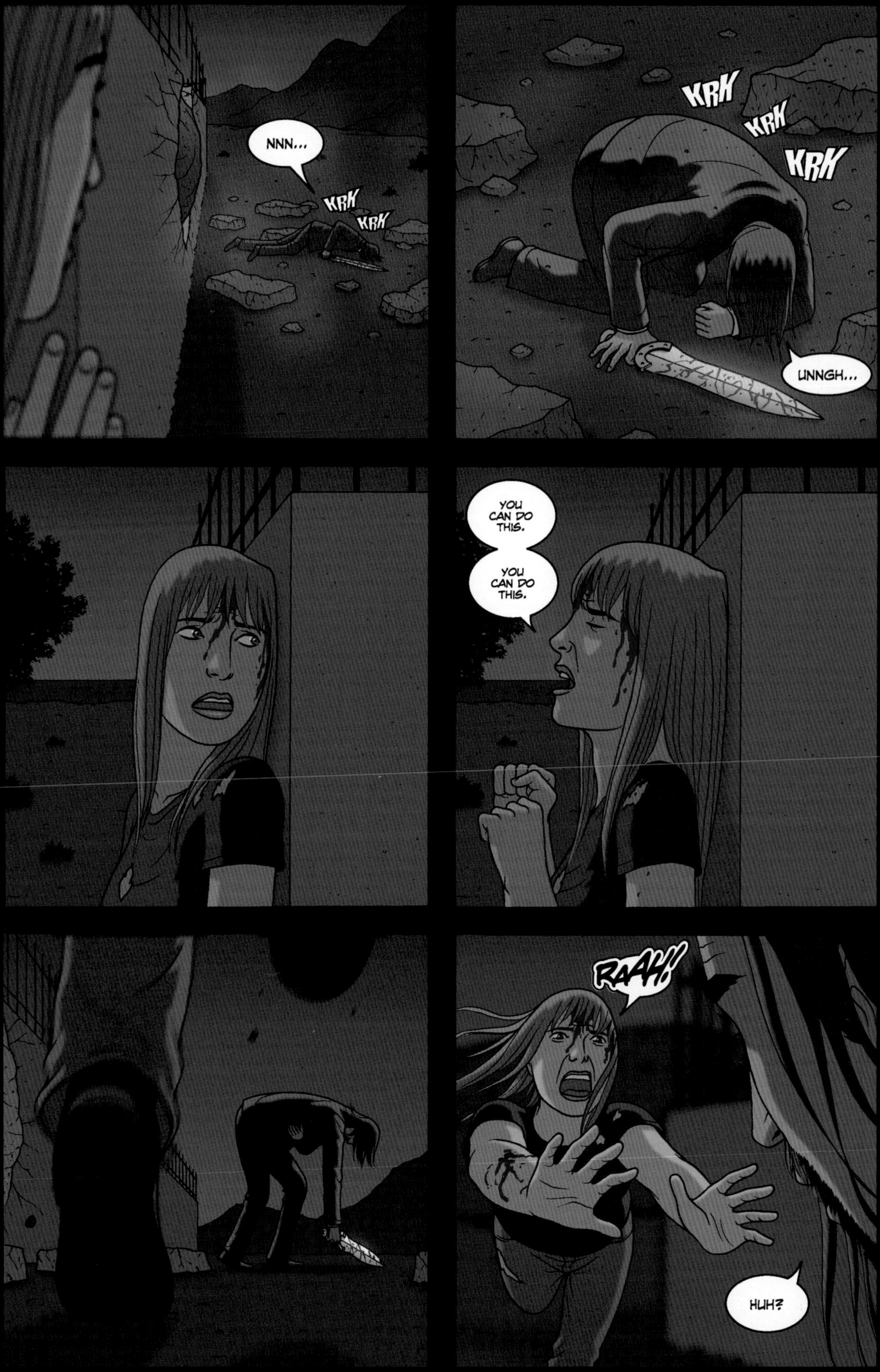
NNN...
KRK
KRK
KRK
KRK
KRK
UNNGH...
YOU CAN DO THIS.
YOU CAN DO THIS.
RAAH!
HUH?

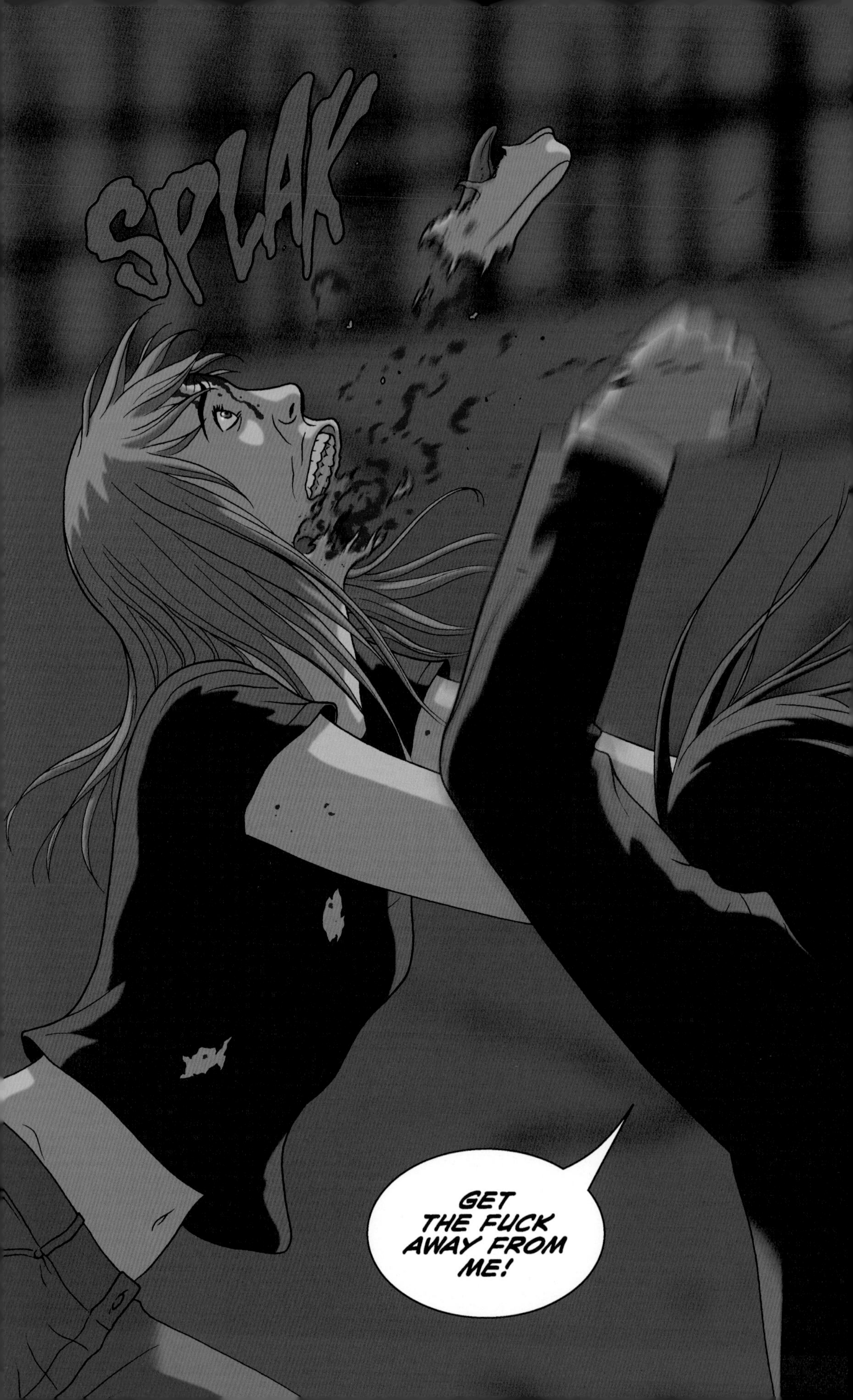
SPLAK
GET THE FUCK AWAY FROM ME!

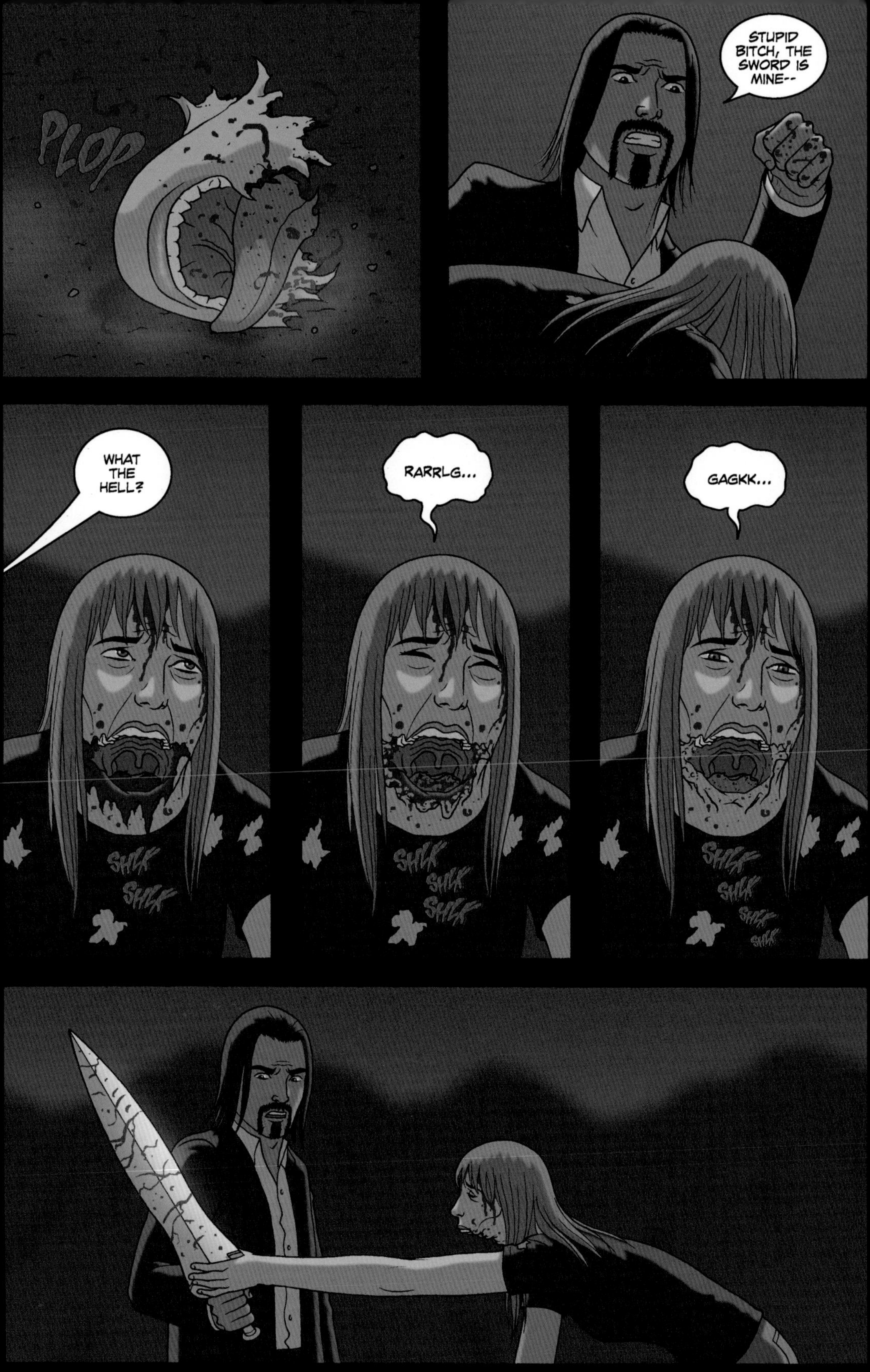
PLOP
STUPID BITCH, THE SWORD IS MINE--
WHAT THE HELL?
SHLK SHLK
RARRLG...
SHLK SHLK SHLK
GAGKK...
SHLK SHLK SHLK SHLK

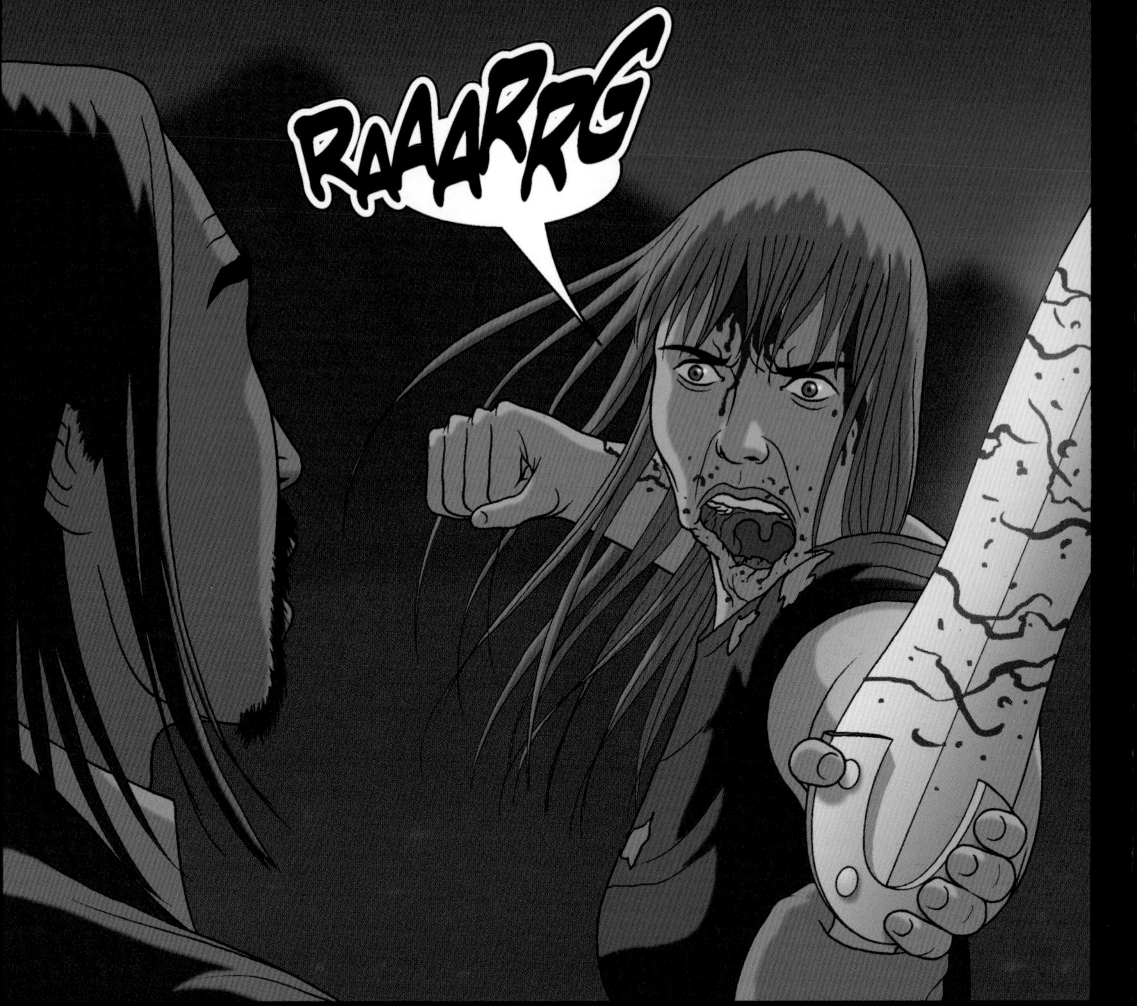
RAAARRG

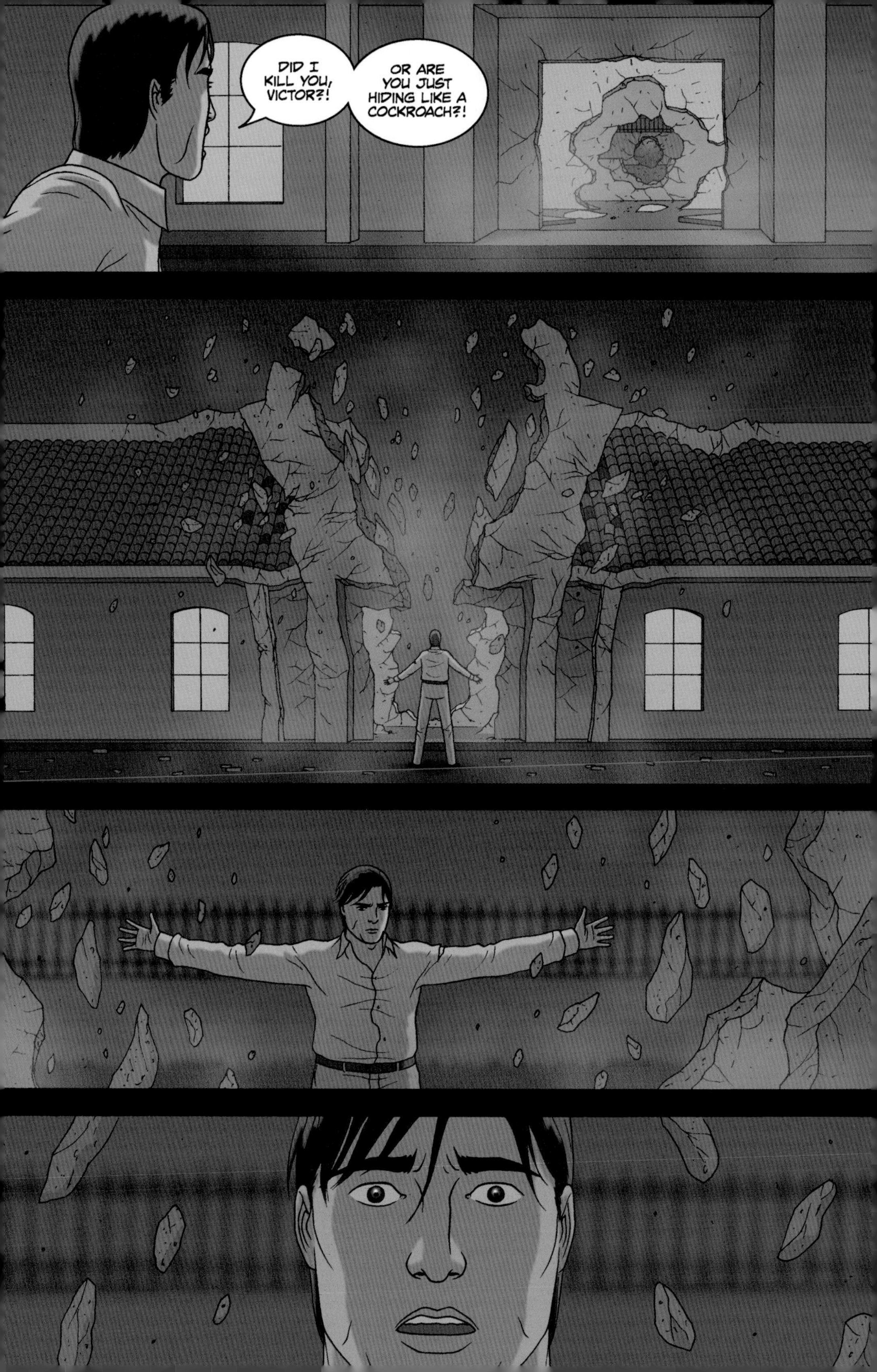
DID I KILL YOU, VICTOR?!
OR ARE YOU JUST HIDING LIKE A COCKROACH?!

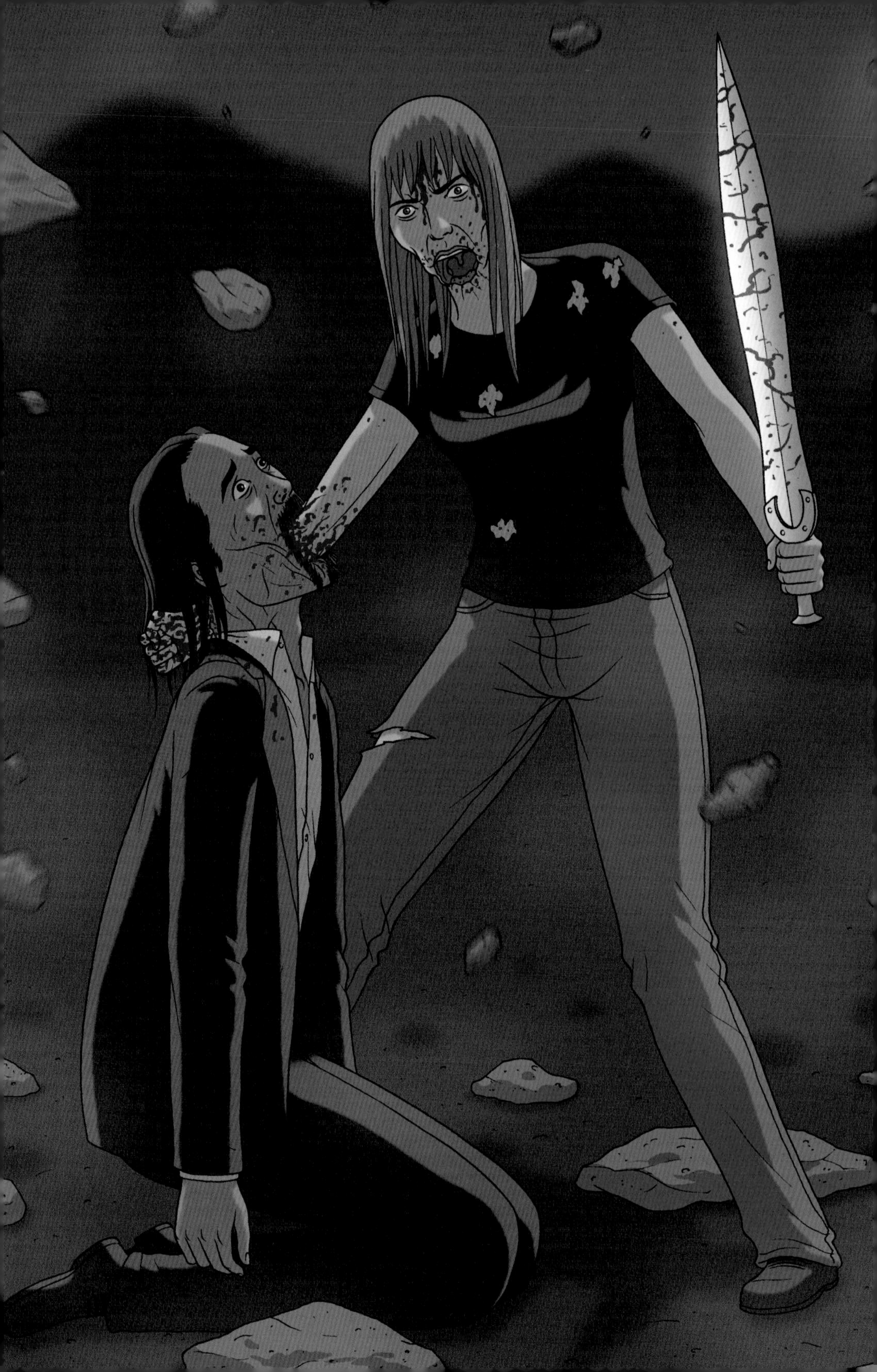

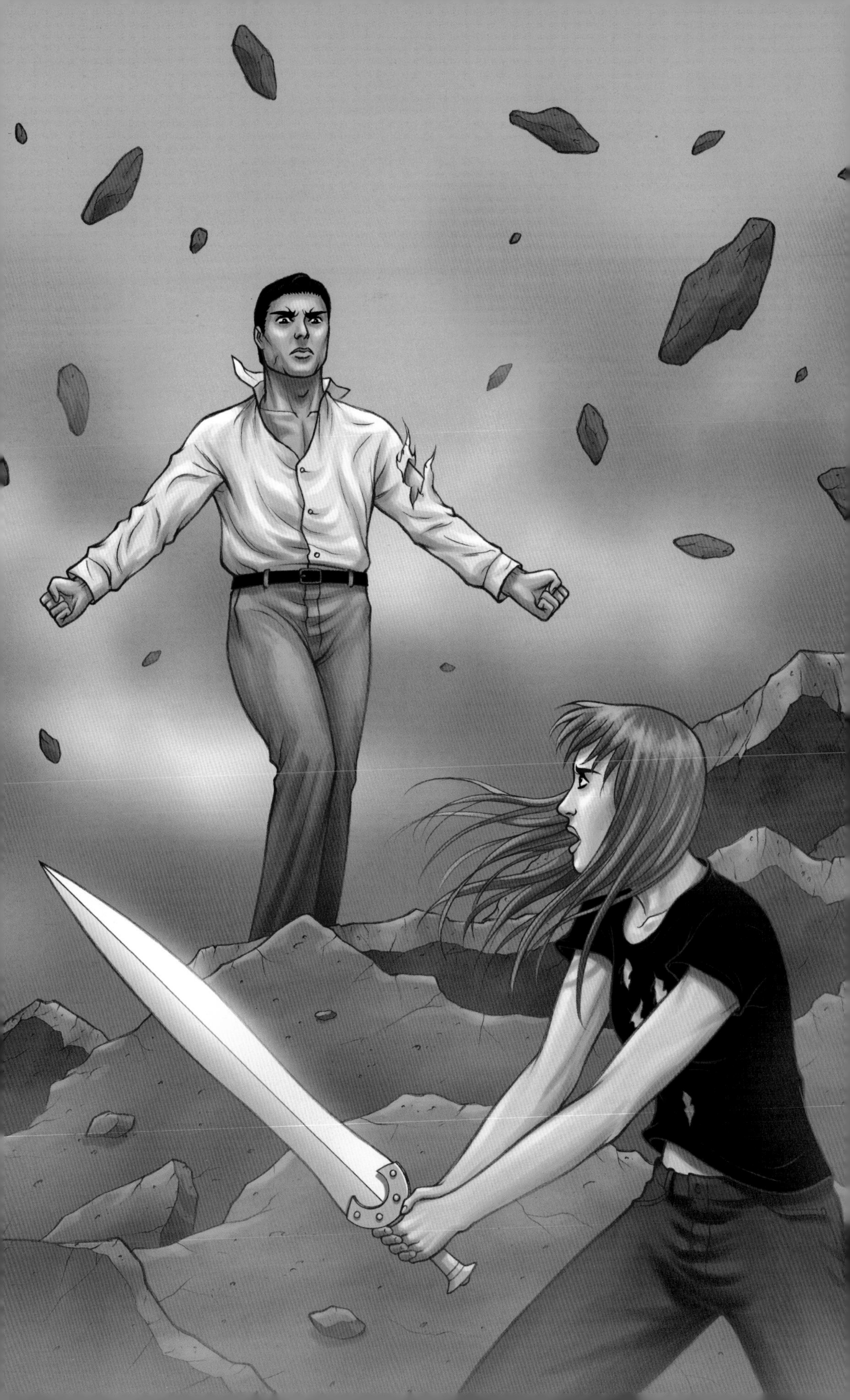

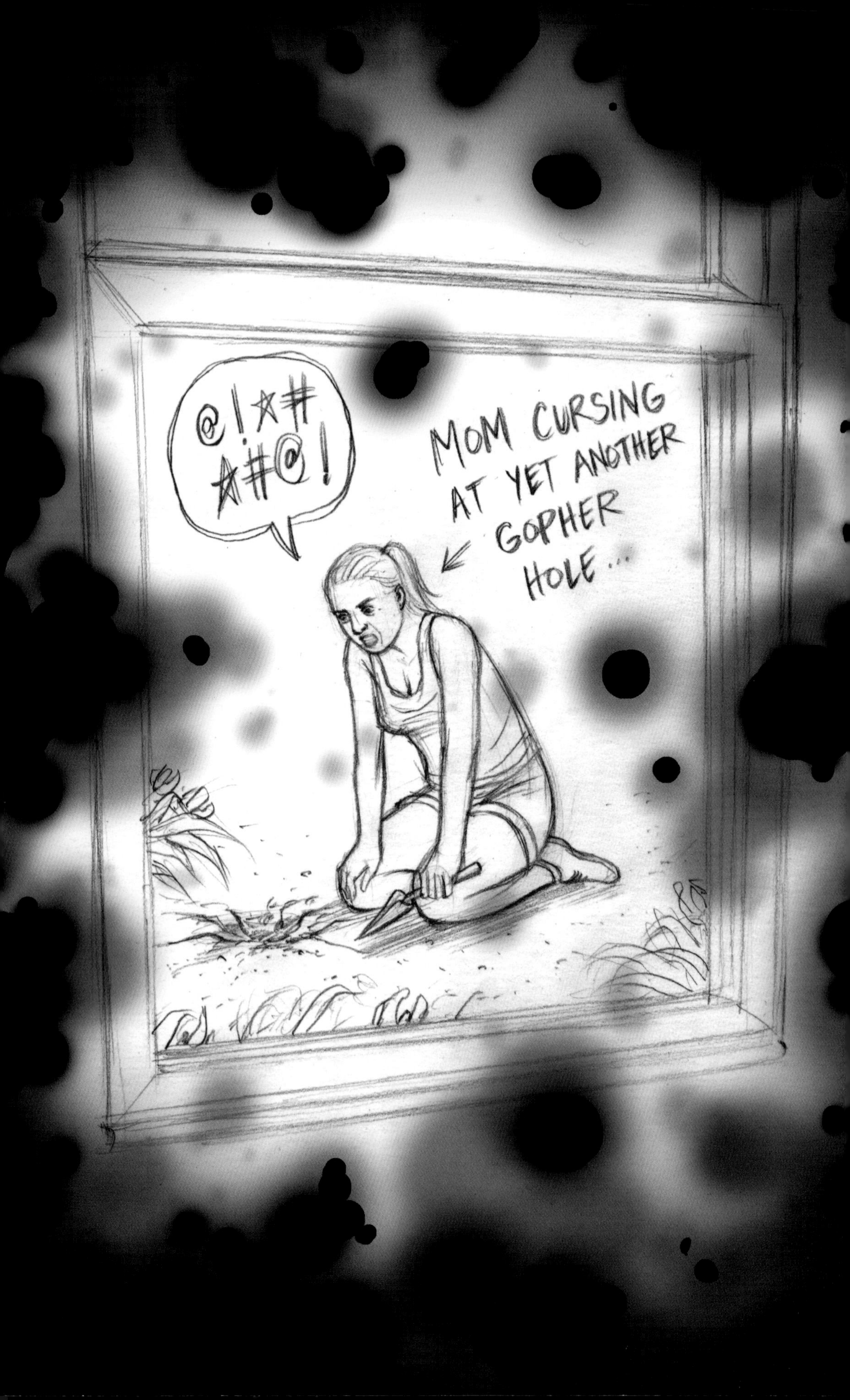
@!☆#
☆#@!
MOM CURSING AT YET ANOTHER GOPHER HOLE...

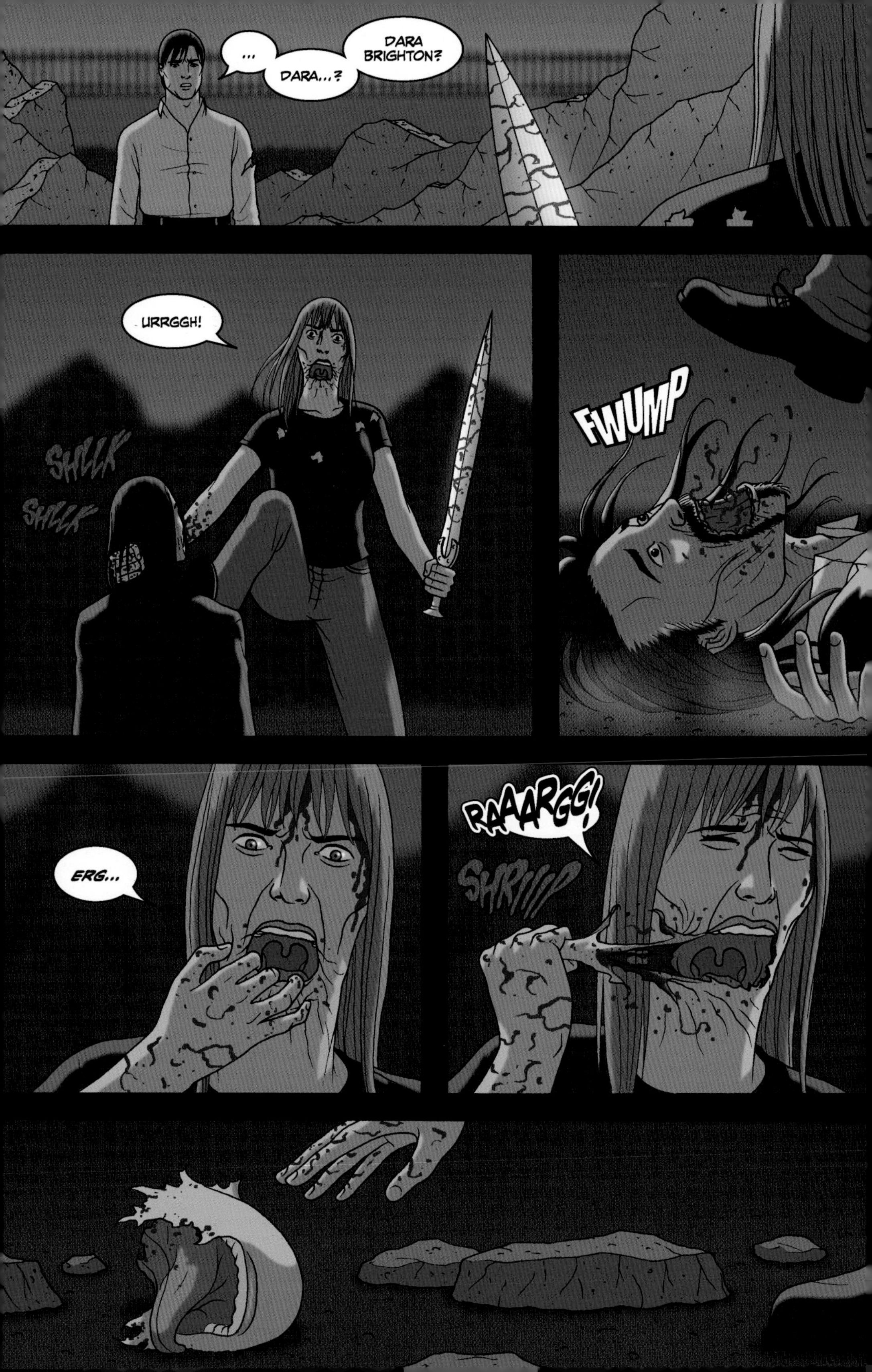
...
DARA...?
DARA BRIGHTON?
URRGGH!
SHLLK
SHLLK
FWUMP
ERG...
RAAARGG!
SHRIIIP

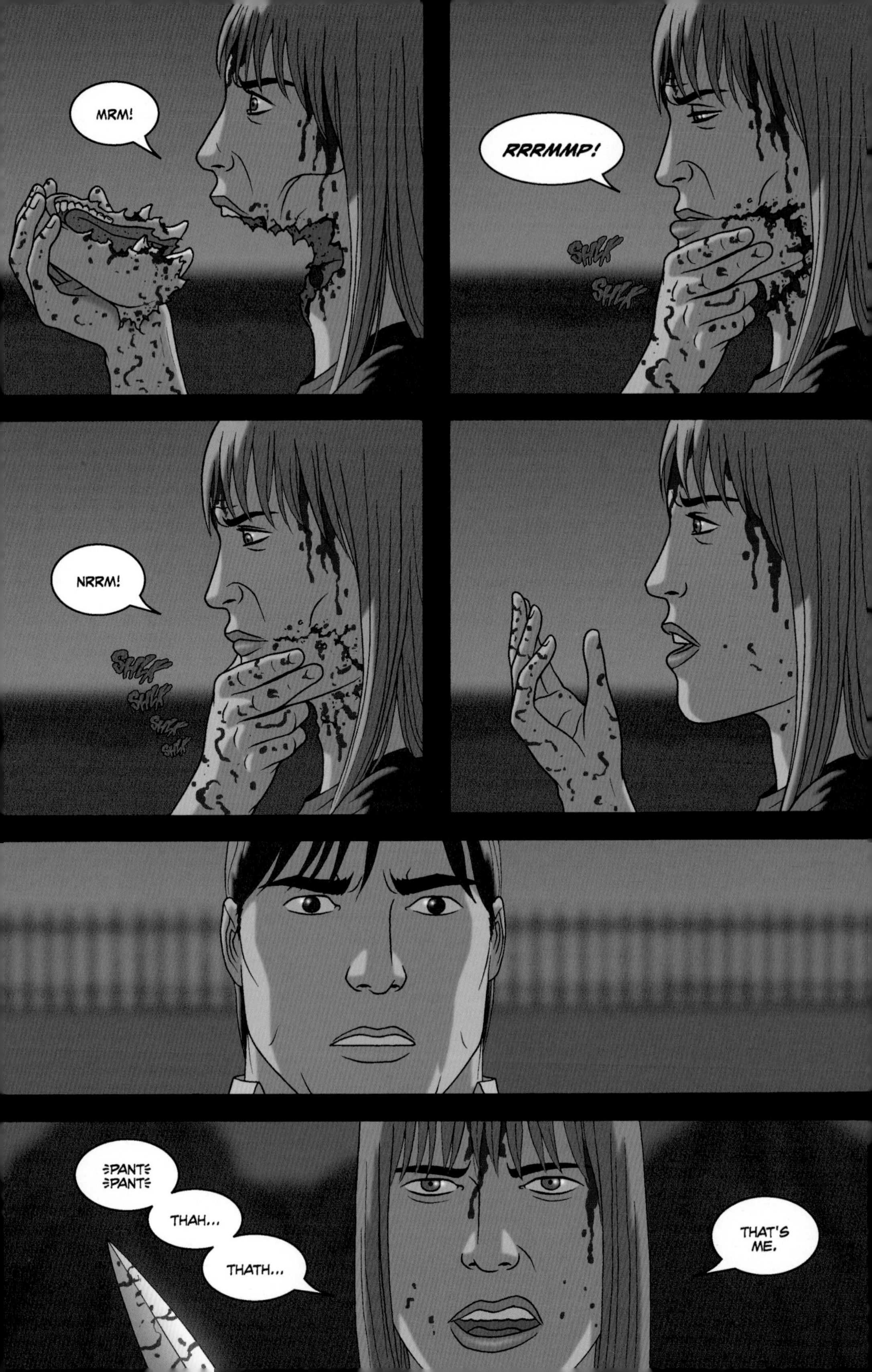
MRM!
RRRMMP!
SHLK
SHLK
NRRM!
SHLK
SHLK
SHLK
SHLK
PANT
PANT
THAH...
THATH...
THAT'S ME.

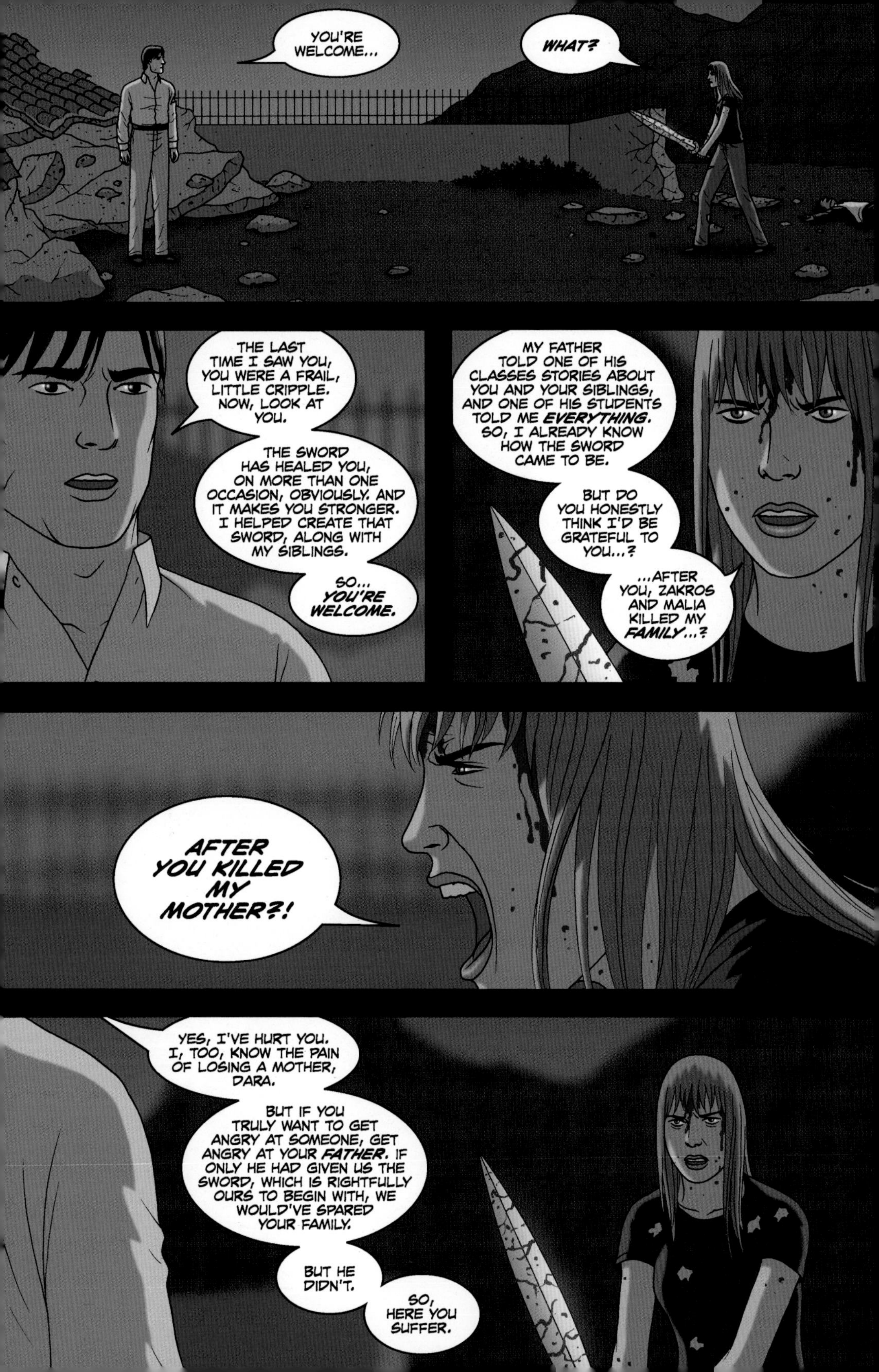
YOU'RE WELCOME...
WHAT?
THE LAST TIME I SAW YOU, YOU WERE A FRAIL, LITTLE CRIPPLE. NOW, LOOK AT YOU.
THE SWORD HAS HEALED YOU, ON MORE THAN ONE OCCASION, OBVIOUSLY. AND IT MAKES YOU STRONGER. I HELPED CREATE THAT SWORD, ALONG WITH MY SIBLINGS.
SO... YOU'RE WELCOME.
MY FATHER TOLD ONE OF HIS CLASSES STORIES ABOUT YOU AND YOUR SIBLINGS, AND ONE OF HIS STUDENTS TOLD ME EVERYTHING. SO, I ALREADY KNOW HOW THE SWORD CAME TO BE.
BUT DO YOU HONESTLY THINK I'D BE GRATEFUL TO YOU...?
...AFTER YOU, ZAKROS AND MALIA KILLED MY FAMILY...?
AFTER YOU KILLED MY MOTHER?!
YES, I'VE HURT YOU. I, TOO, KNOW THE PAIN OF LOSING A MOTHER, DARA.
BUT IF YOU TRULY WANT TO GET ANGRY AT SOMEONE, GET ANGRY AT YOUR FATHER. IF ONLY HE HAD GIVEN US THE SWORD, WHICH IS RIGHTFULLY OURS TO BEGIN WITH, WE WOULD'VE SPARED YOUR FAMILY.
BUT HE DIDN'T.
SO, HERE YOU SUFFER.

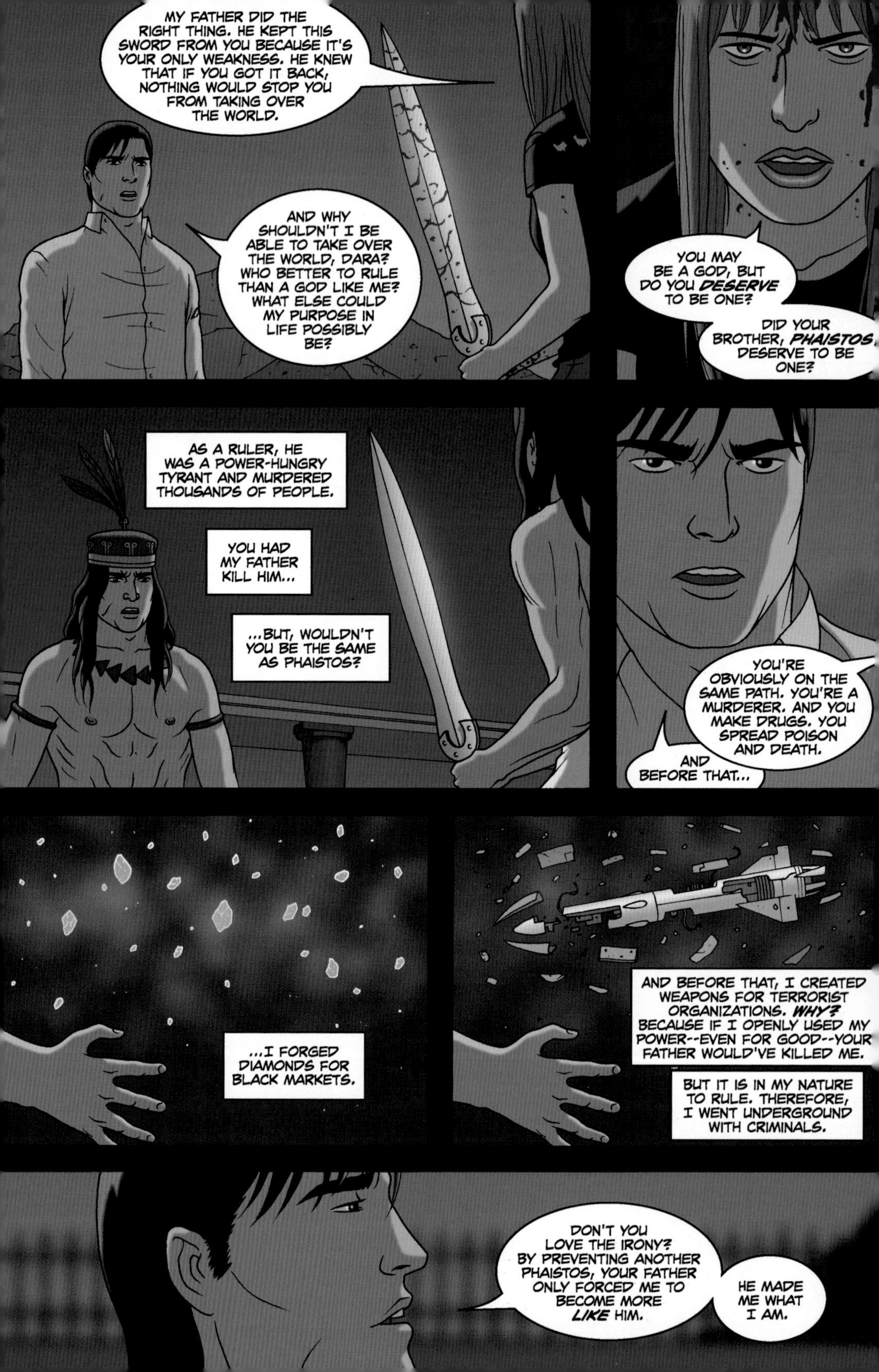
MY FATHER DID THE RIGHT THING. HE KEPT THIS SWORD FROM YOU BECAUSE IT'S YOUR ONLY WEAKNESS. HE KNEW THAT IF YOU GOT IT BACK, NOTHING WOULD STOP YOU FROM TAKING OVER THE WORLD.
AND WHY SHOULDN'T I BE ABLE TO TAKE OVER THE WORLD, DARA? WHO BETTER TO RULE THAN A GOD LIKE ME? WHAT ELSE COULD MY PURPOSE IN LIFE POSSIBLY BE?
YOU MAY BE A GOD, BUT DO YOU *DESERVE* TO BE ONE?
DID YOUR BROTHER, *PHAISTOS*, DESERVE TO BE ONE?
AS A RULER, HE WAS A POWER-HUNGRY TYRANT AND MURDERED THOUSANDS OF PEOPLE.
YOU HAD MY FATHER KILL HIM...
...BUT, WOULDN'T YOU BE THE SAME AS PHAISTOS?
YOU'RE OBVIOUSLY ON THE SAME PATH. YOU'RE A MURDERER. AND YOU MAKE DRUGS. YOU SPREAD POISON AND DEATH.
AND BEFORE THAT...
...I FORGED DIAMONDS FOR BLACK MARKETS.
AND BEFORE THAT, I CREATED WEAPONS FOR TERRORIST ORGANIZATIONS. *WHY?* BECAUSE IF I OPENLY USED MY POWER--EVEN FOR GOOD--YOUR FATHER WOULD'VE KILLED ME.
BUT IT IS IN MY NATURE TO RULE. THEREFORE, I WENT UNDERGROUND WITH CRIMINALS.
DON'T YOU LOVE THE IRONY? BY PREVENTING ANOTHER PHAISTOS, YOUR FATHER ONLY FORCED ME TO BECOME MORE *LIKE* HIM.
HE MADE ME WHAT I AM.

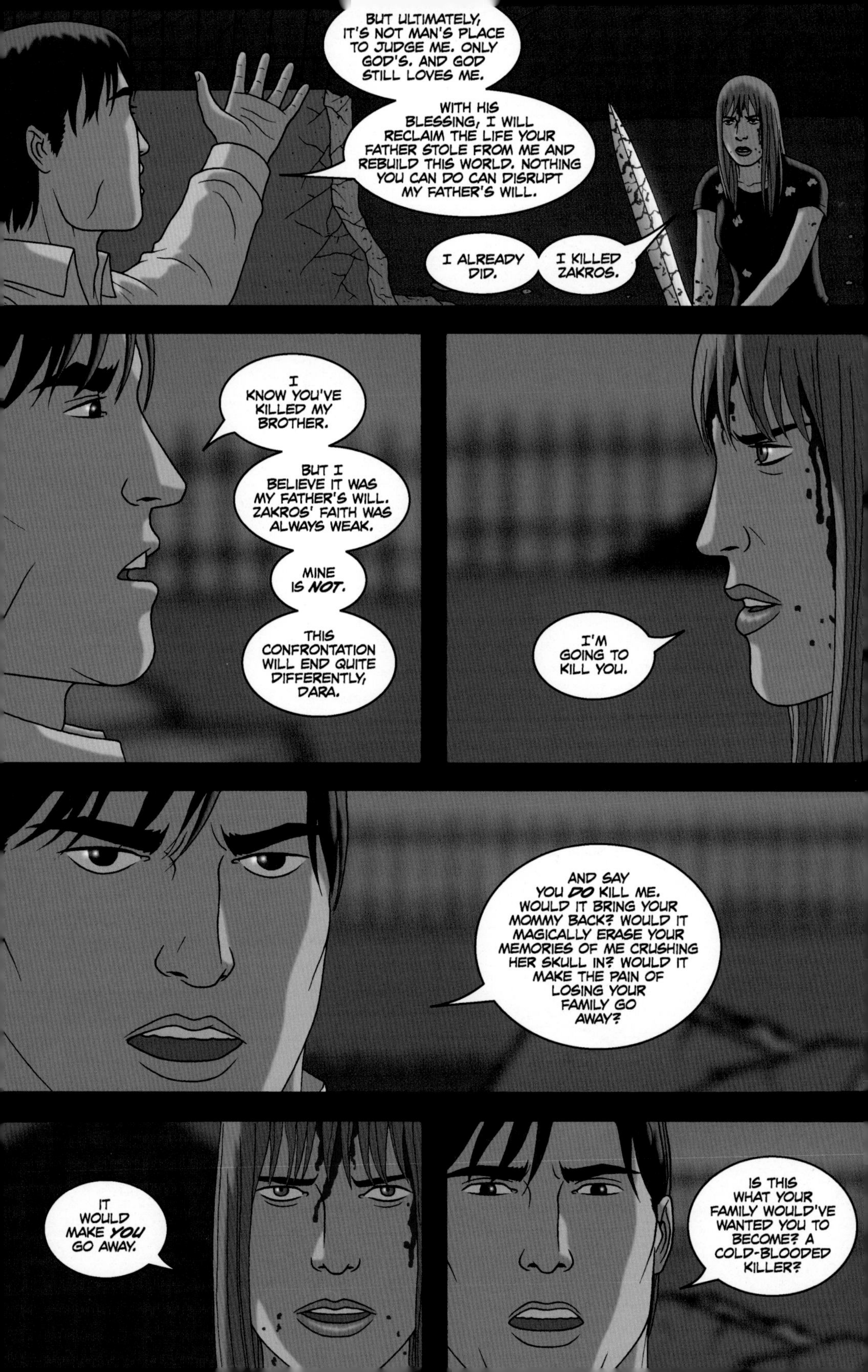
BUT ULTIMATELY, IT'S NOT MAN'S PLACE TO JUDGE ME. ONLY GOD'S. AND GOD STILL LOVES ME.
WITH HIS BLESSING, I WILL RECLAIM THE LIFE YOUR FATHER STOLE FROM ME AND REBUILD THIS WORLD. NOTHING YOU CAN DO CAN DISRUPT MY FATHER'S WILL.
I ALREADY DID.
I KILLED ZAKROS.
I KNOW YOU'VE KILLED MY BROTHER.
BUT I BELIEVE IT WAS MY FATHER'S WILL. ZAKROS' FAITH WAS ALWAYS WEAK.
MINE IS ***NOT***.
THIS CONFRONTATION WILL END QUITE DIFFERENTLY, DARA.
I'M GOING TO KILL YOU.
AND SAY YOU ***DO*** KILL ME. WOULD IT BRING YOUR MOMMY BACK? WOULD IT MAGICALLY ERASE YOUR MEMORIES OF ME CRUSHING HER SKULL IN? WOULD IT MAKE THE PAIN OF LOSING YOUR FAMILY GO AWAY?
IT WOULD MAKE ***YOU*** GO AWAY.
IS THIS WHAT YOUR FAMILY WOULD'VE WANTED YOU TO BECOME? A COLD-BLOODED KILLER?

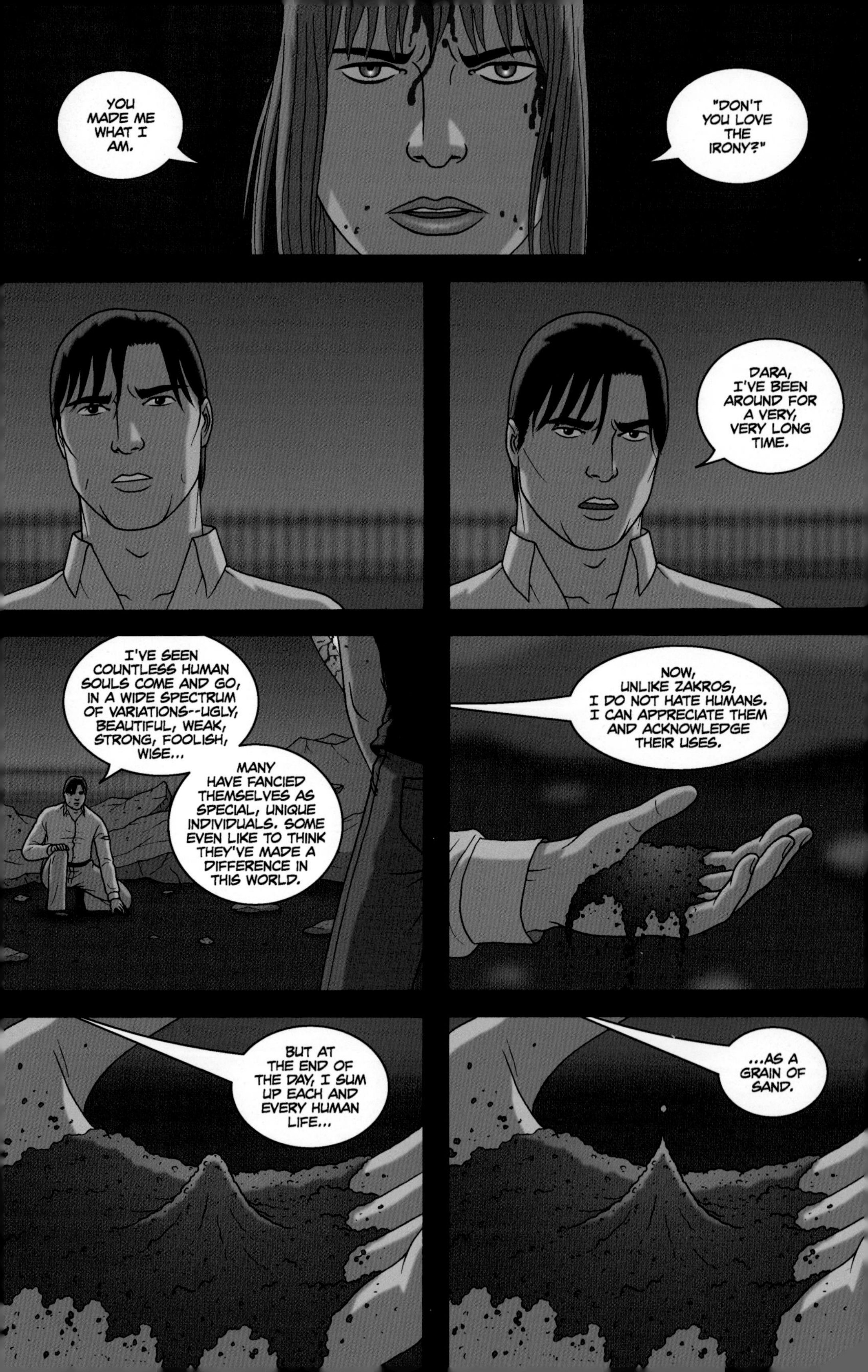
YOU MADE ME WHAT I AM.
"DON'T YOU LOVE THE IRONY?"
DARA, I'VE BEEN AROUND FOR A VERY, VERY LONG TIME.
I'VE SEEN COUNTLESS HUMAN SOULS COME AND GO, IN A WIDE SPECTRUM OF VARIATIONS--UGLY, BEAUTIFUL, WEAK, STRONG, FOOLISH, WISE...
MANY HAVE FANCIED THEMSELVES AS SPECIAL, UNIQUE INDIVIDUALS. SOME EVEN LIKE TO THINK THEY'VE MADE A DIFFERENCE IN THIS WORLD.
NOW, UNLIKE ZAKROS, I DO NOT HATE HUMANS. I CAN APPRECIATE THEM AND ACKNOWLEDGE THEIR USES.
BUT AT THE END OF THE DAY, I SUM UP EACH AND EVERY HUMAN LIFE...
...AS A GRAIN OF SAND.

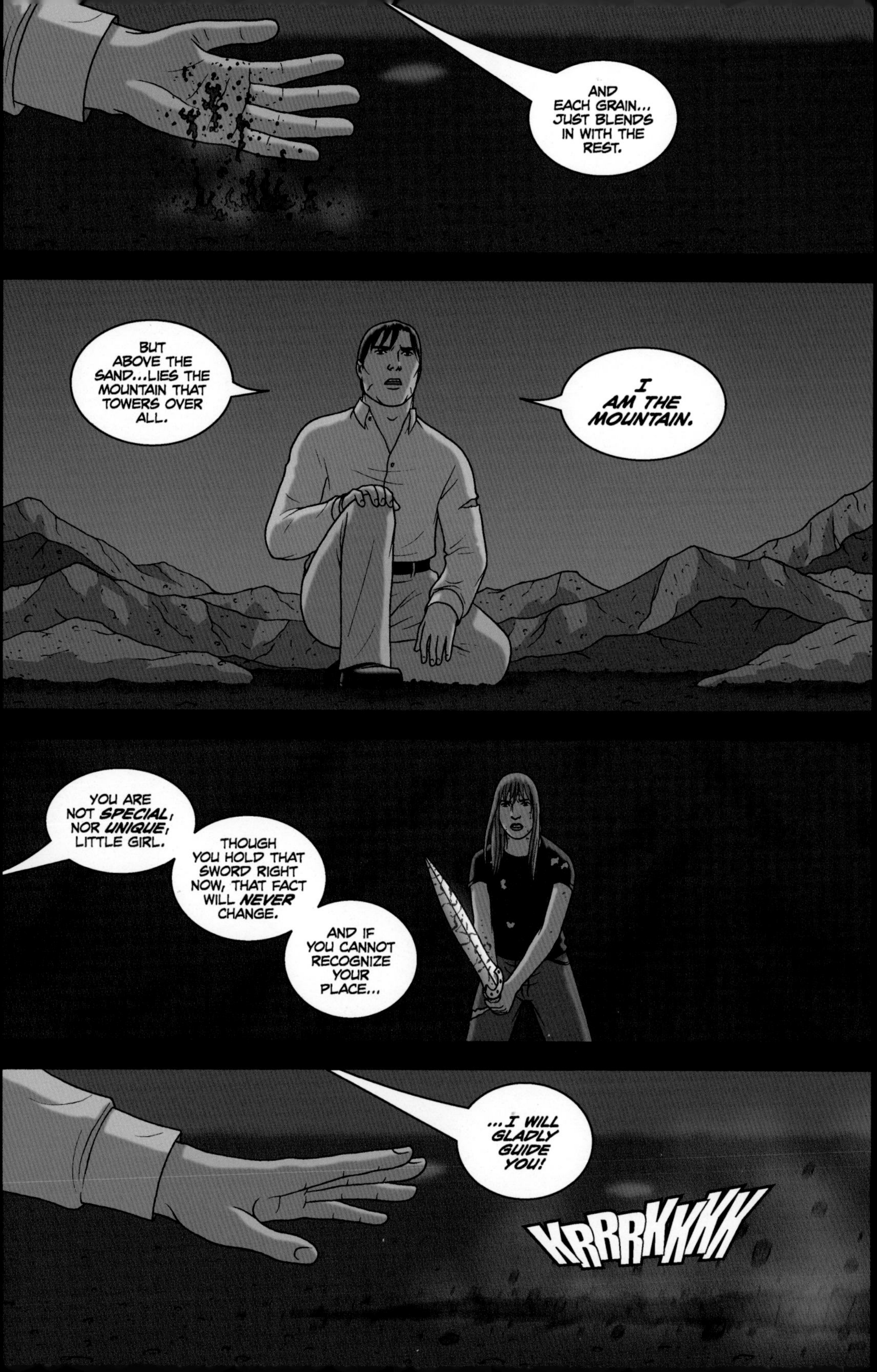
AND EACH GRAIN... JUST BLENDS IN WITH THE REST.
BUT ABOVE THE SAND...LIES THE MOUNTAIN THAT TOWERS OVER ALL.
I AM THE MOUNTAIN.
YOU ARE NOT SPECIAL, NOR UNIQUE, LITTLE GIRL.
THOUGH YOU HOLD THAT SWORD RIGHT NOW, THAT FACT WILL NEVER CHANGE.
AND IF YOU CANNOT RECOGNIZE YOUR PLACE...
...I WILL GLADLY GUIDE YOU!
KRRRKKKK

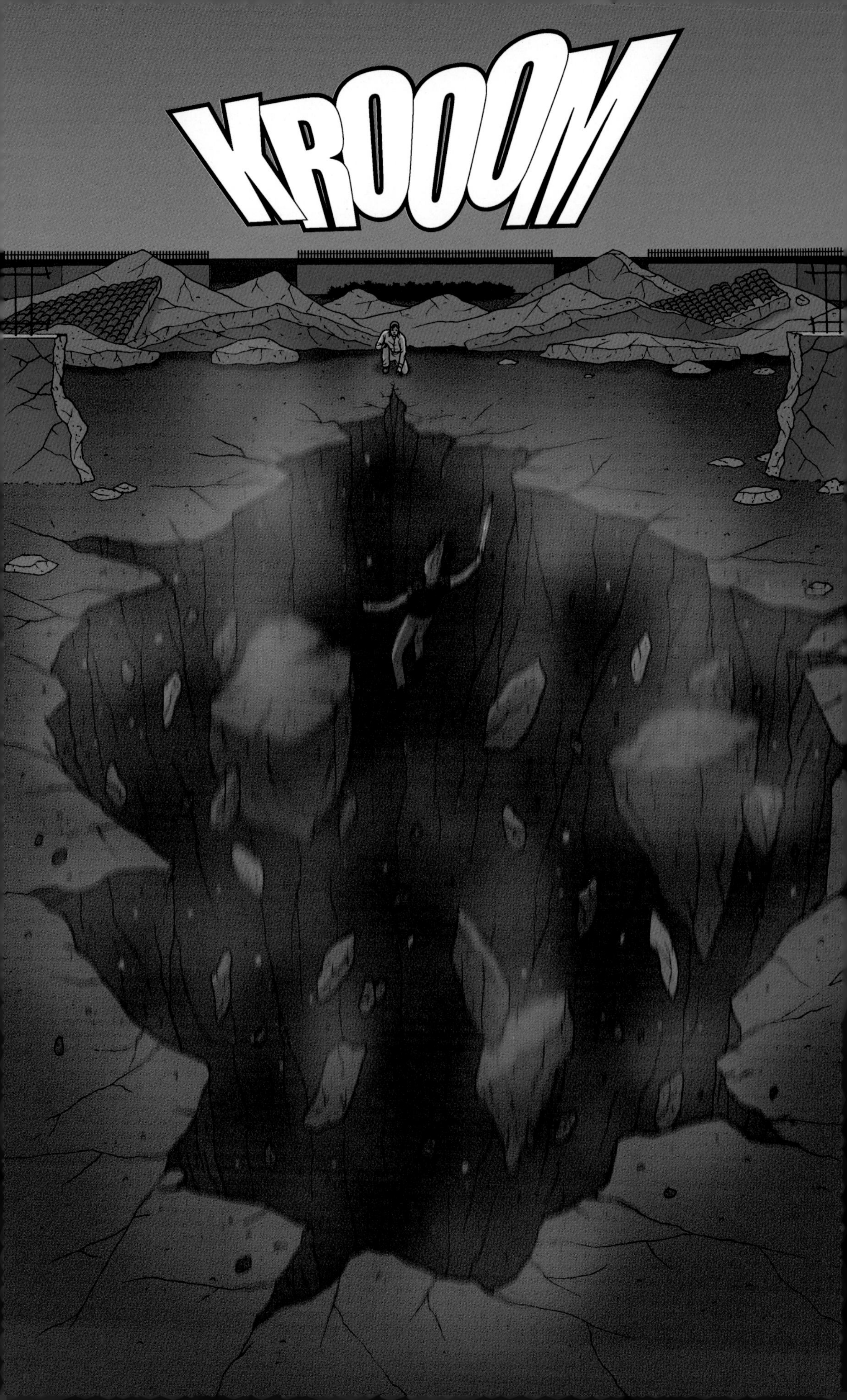
KROOOM

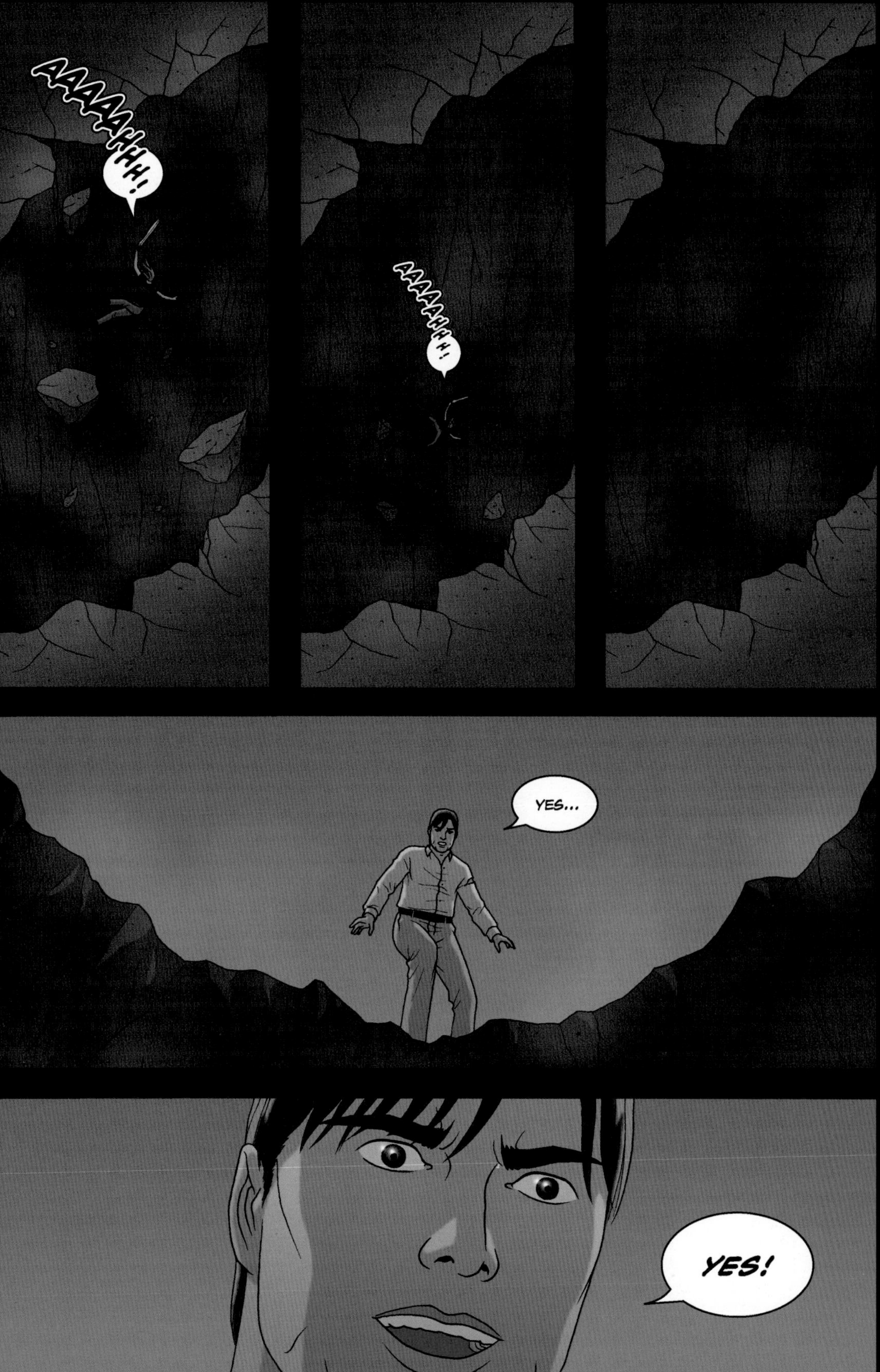
AAAAAHHH!
AAAAAHHH!
YES...
YES!

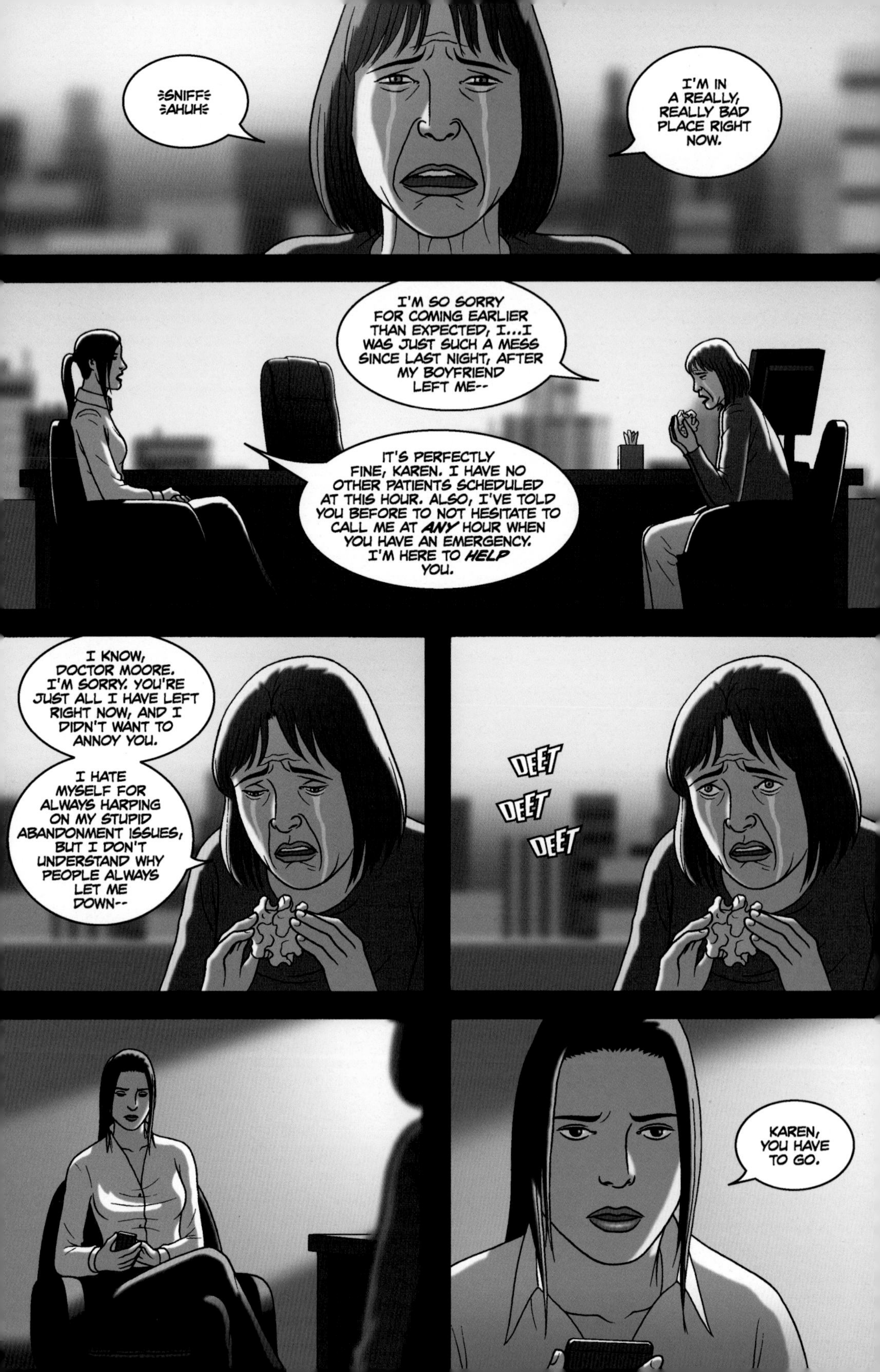

SNIFF AHUH
I'M IN A REALLY, REALLY BAD PLACE RIGHT NOW.
I'M SO SORRY FOR COMING EARLIER THAN EXPECTED, I...I WAS JUST SUCH A MESS SINCE LAST NIGHT, AFTER MY BOYFRIEND LEFT ME--
IT'S PERFECTLY FINE, KAREN. I HAVE NO OTHER PATIENTS SCHEDULED AT THIS HOUR. ALSO, I'VE TOLD YOU BEFORE TO NOT HESITATE TO CALL ME AT ANY HOUR WHEN YOU HAVE AN EMERGENCY. I'M HERE TO HELP YOU.
I KNOW, DOCTOR MOORE. I'M SORRY. YOU'RE JUST ALL I HAVE LEFT RIGHT NOW, AND I DIDN'T WANT TO ANNOY YOU.
I HATE MYSELF FOR ALWAYS HARPING ON MY STUPID ABANDONMENT ISSUES, BUT I DON'T UNDERSTAND WHY PEOPLE ALWAYS LET ME DOWN--
DEET
DEET
DEET
KAREN, YOU HAVE TO GO.

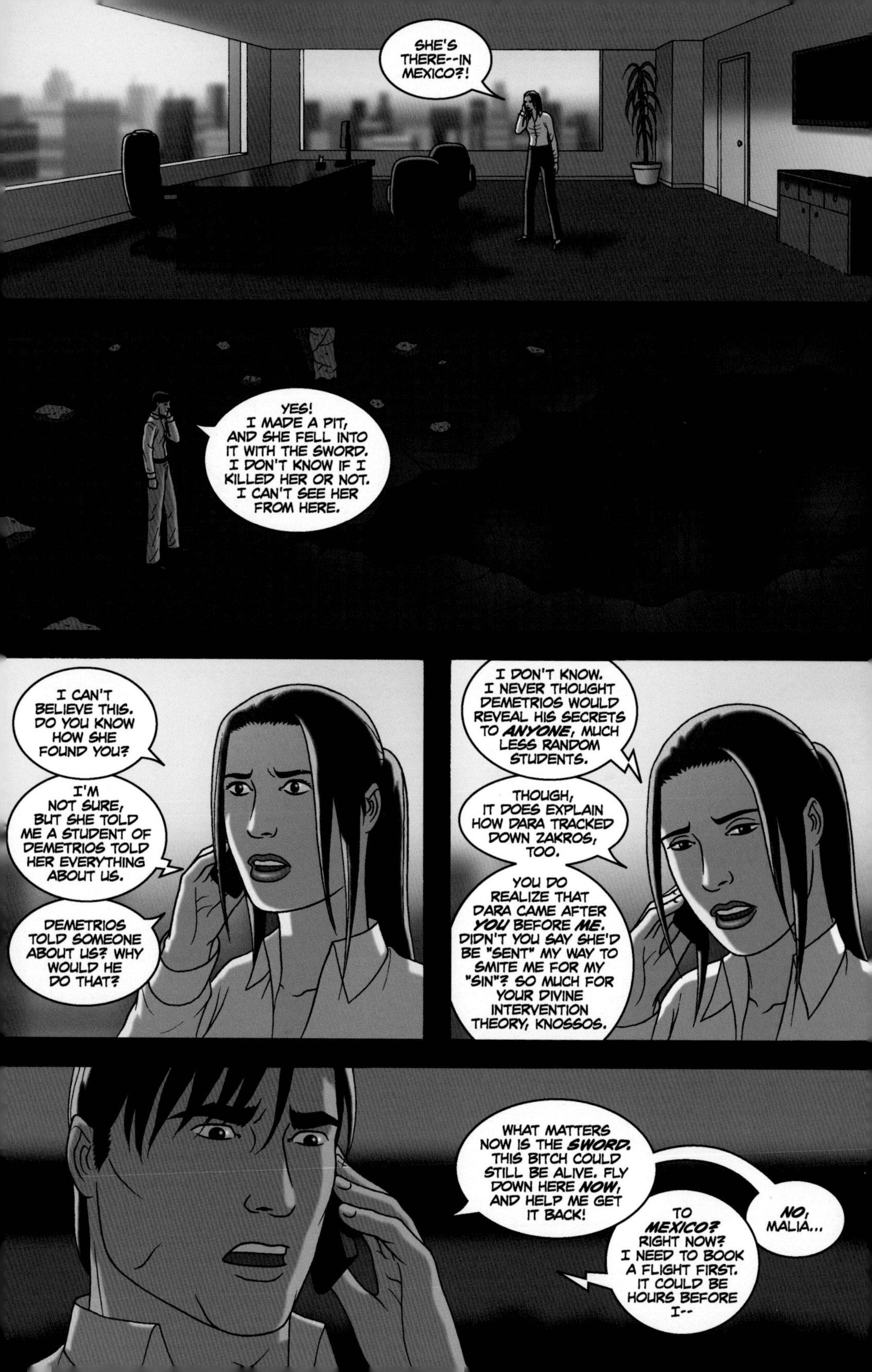
SHE'S THERE--IN MEXICO?!
YES! I MADE A PIT, AND SHE FELL INTO IT WITH THE SWORD. I DON'T KNOW IF I KILLED HER OR NOT. I CAN'T SEE HER FROM HERE.
I CAN'T BELIEVE THIS. DO YOU KNOW HOW SHE FOUND YOU?
I'M NOT SURE, BUT SHE TOLD ME A STUDENT OF DEMETRIOS TOLD HER EVERYTHING ABOUT US.
DEMETRIOS TOLD SOMEONE ABOUT US? WHY WOULD HE DO THAT?
I DON'T KNOW. I NEVER THOUGHT DEMETRIOS WOULD REVEAL HIS SECRETS TO ANYONE, MUCH LESS RANDOM STUDENTS.
THOUGH, IT DOES EXPLAIN HOW DARA TRACKED DOWN ZAKROS, TOO.
YOU DO REALIZE THAT DARA CAME AFTER YOU BEFORE ME. DIDN'T YOU SAY SHE'D BE "SENT" MY WAY TO SMITE ME FOR MY "SIN"? SO MUCH FOR YOUR DIVINE INTERVENTION THEORY, KNOSSOS.
WHAT MATTERS NOW IS THE SWORD. THIS BITCH COULD STILL BE ALIVE. FLY DOWN HERE NOW, AND HELP ME GET IT BACK!
TO MEXICO? RIGHT NOW? I NEED TO BOOK A FLIGHT FIRST. IT COULD BE HOURS BEFORE I--
NO, MALIA...

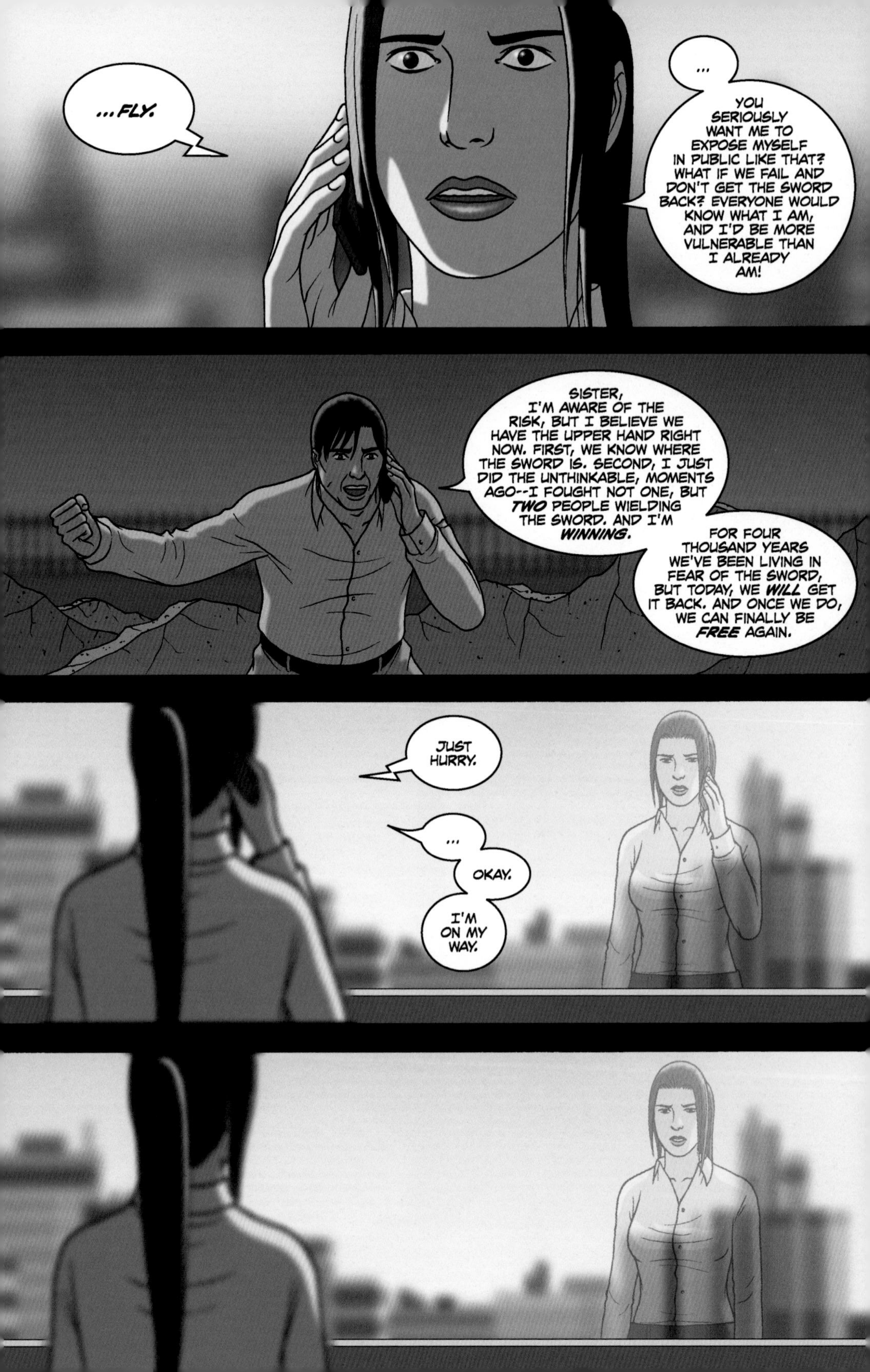
...FLY.
...
YOU SERIOUSLY WANT ME TO EXPOSE MYSELF IN PUBLIC LIKE THAT? WHAT IF WE FAIL AND DON'T GET THE SWORD BACK? EVERYONE WOULD KNOW WHAT I AM, AND I'D BE MORE VULNERABLE THAN I ALREADY AM!
SISTER, I'M AWARE OF THE RISK, BUT I BELIEVE WE HAVE THE UPPER HAND RIGHT NOW. FIRST, WE KNOW WHERE THE SWORD IS. SECOND, I JUST DID THE UNTHINKABLE, MOMENTS AGO--I FOUGHT NOT ONE, BUT *TWO* PEOPLE WIELDING THE SWORD. AND I'M *WINNING*.
FOR FOUR THOUSAND YEARS WE'VE BEEN LIVING IN FEAR OF THE SWORD, BUT TODAY, WE *WILL* GET IT BACK. AND ONCE WE DO, WE CAN FINALLY BE *FREE* AGAIN.
JUST HURRY.
...
OKAY.
I'M ON MY WAY.

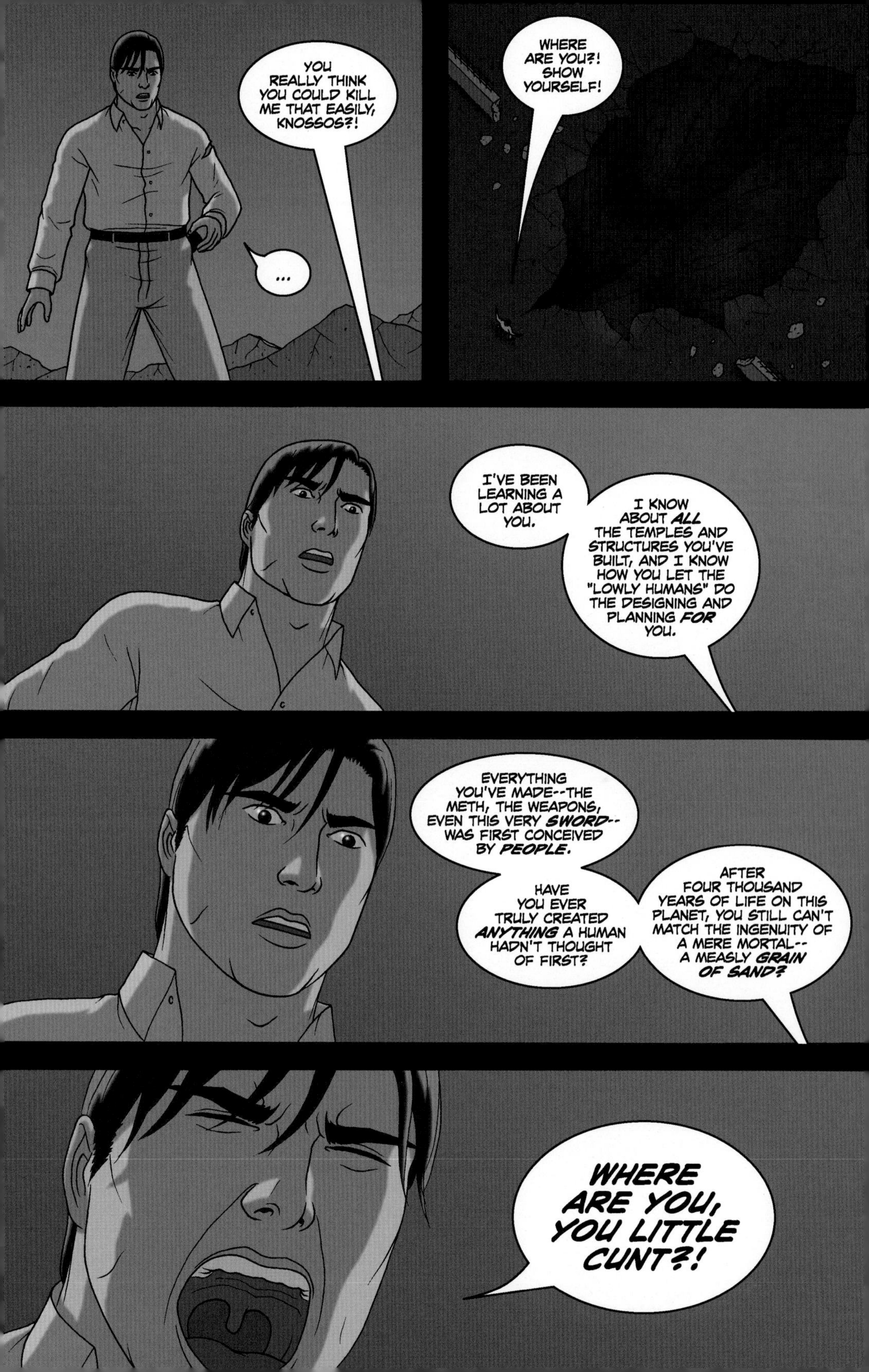
YOU REALLY THINK YOU COULD KILL ME THAT EASILY, KNOSSOS?!
...
WHERE ARE YOU?! SHOW YOURSELF!
I'VE BEEN LEARNING A LOT ABOUT YOU.
I KNOW ABOUT *ALL* THE TEMPLES AND STRUCTURES YOU'VE BUILT, AND I KNOW HOW YOU LET THE "LOWLY HUMANS" DO THE DESIGNING AND PLANNING *FOR* YOU.
EVERYTHING YOU'VE MADE--THE METH, THE WEAPONS, EVEN THIS VERY *SWORD*--WAS FIRST CONCEIVED BY *PEOPLE*.
HAVE YOU EVER TRULY CREATED *ANYTHING* A HUMAN HADN'T THOUGHT OF FIRST?
AFTER FOUR THOUSAND YEARS OF LIFE ON THIS PLANET, YOU STILL CAN'T MATCH THE INGENUITY OF A MERE MORTAL--A MEASLY *GRAIN OF SAND*?
WHERE ARE YOU, YOU LITTLE CUNT?!

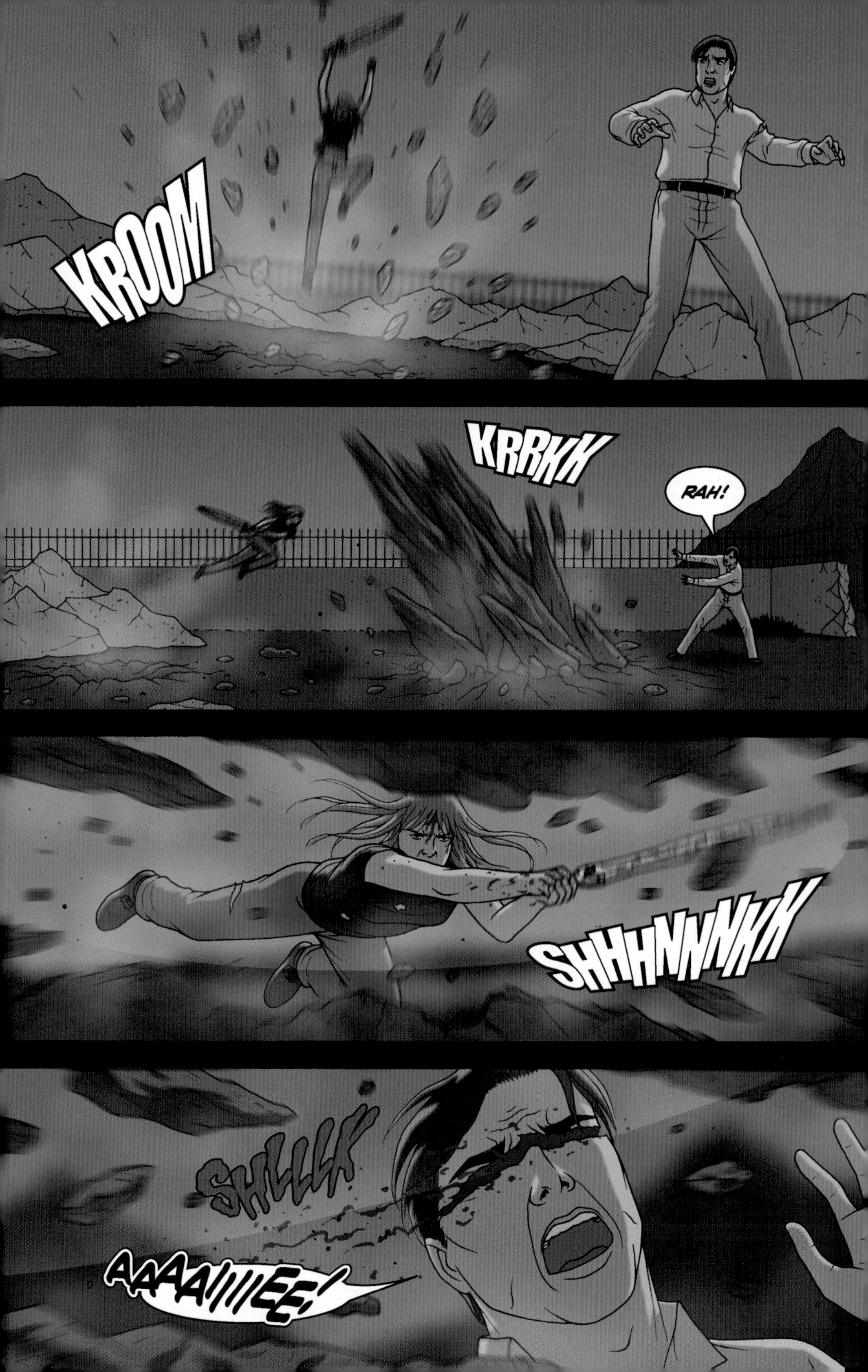
KROOM
KRRKK
RAH!
SHHHNNNKK
SHLLK
AAAAIIIIEE!

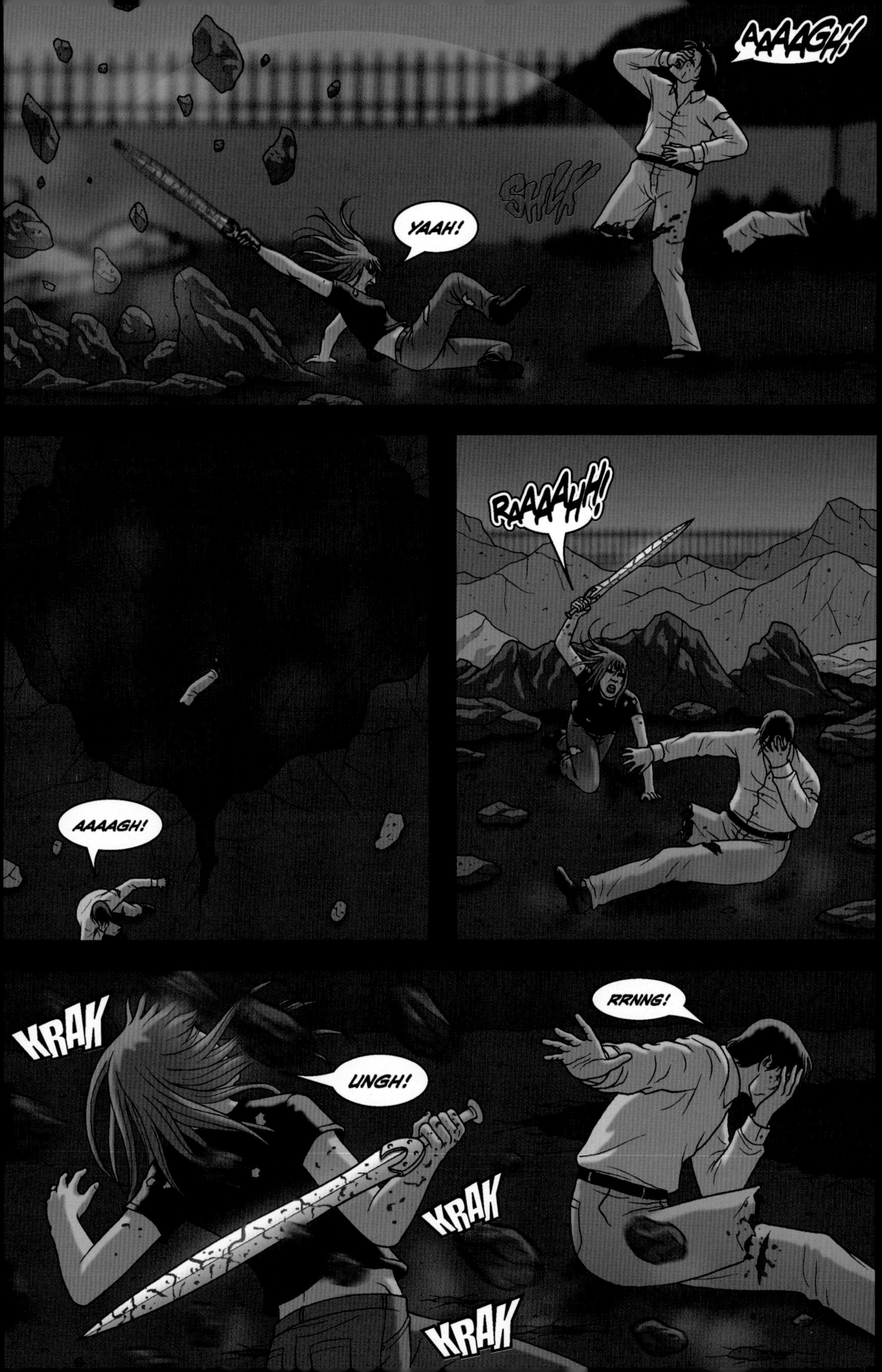
AAAAGH!
SHLK
YAAH!
AAAAGH!
RAAAAHH!
RRNNG!
KRAK
UNGH!
KRAK
KRAK

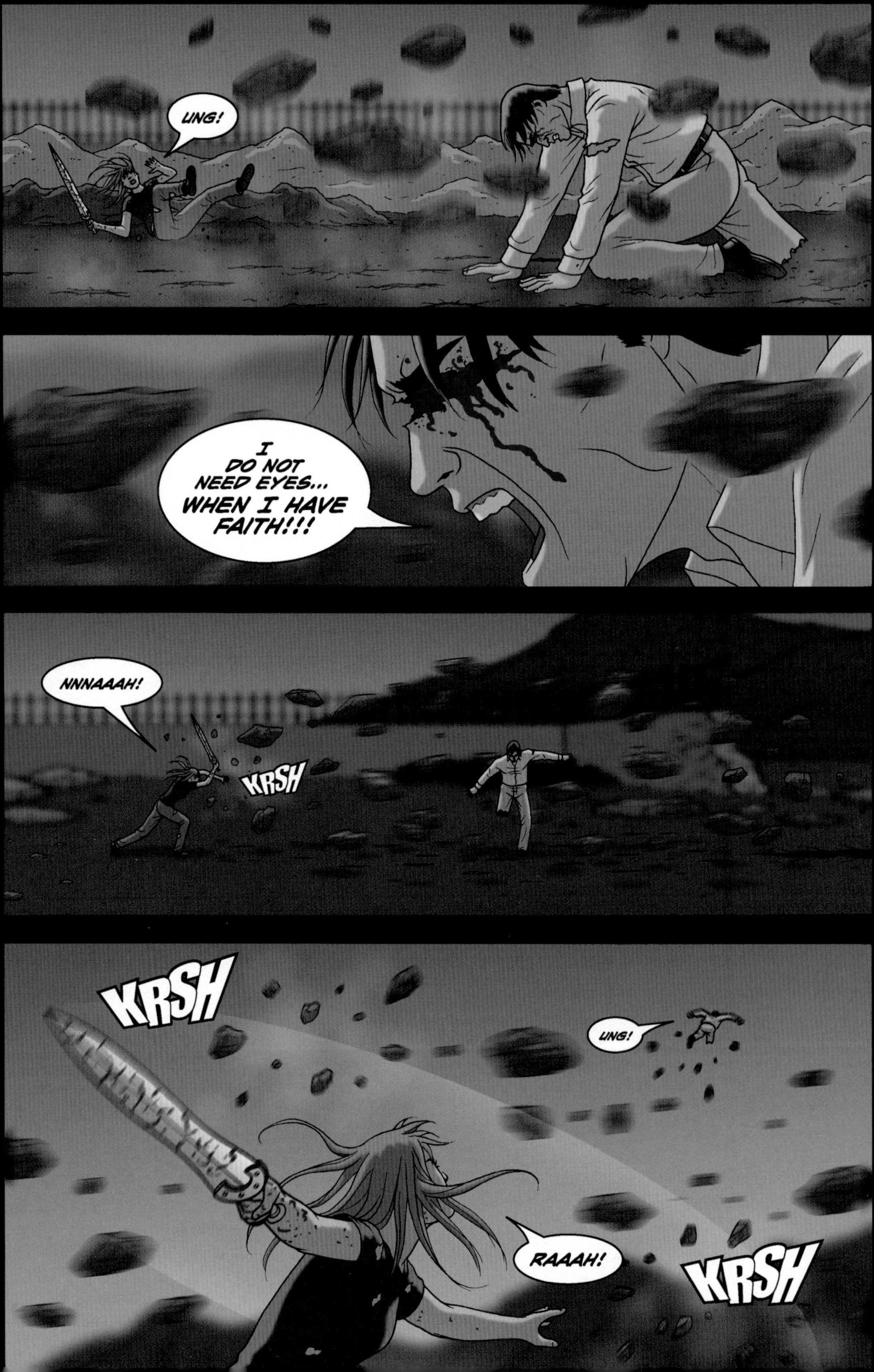
UNG!
I DO NOT NEED EYES... WHEN I HAVE FAITH!!!
NNNAAAH!
KRSH
KRSH
UNG!
RAAAH!
KRSH

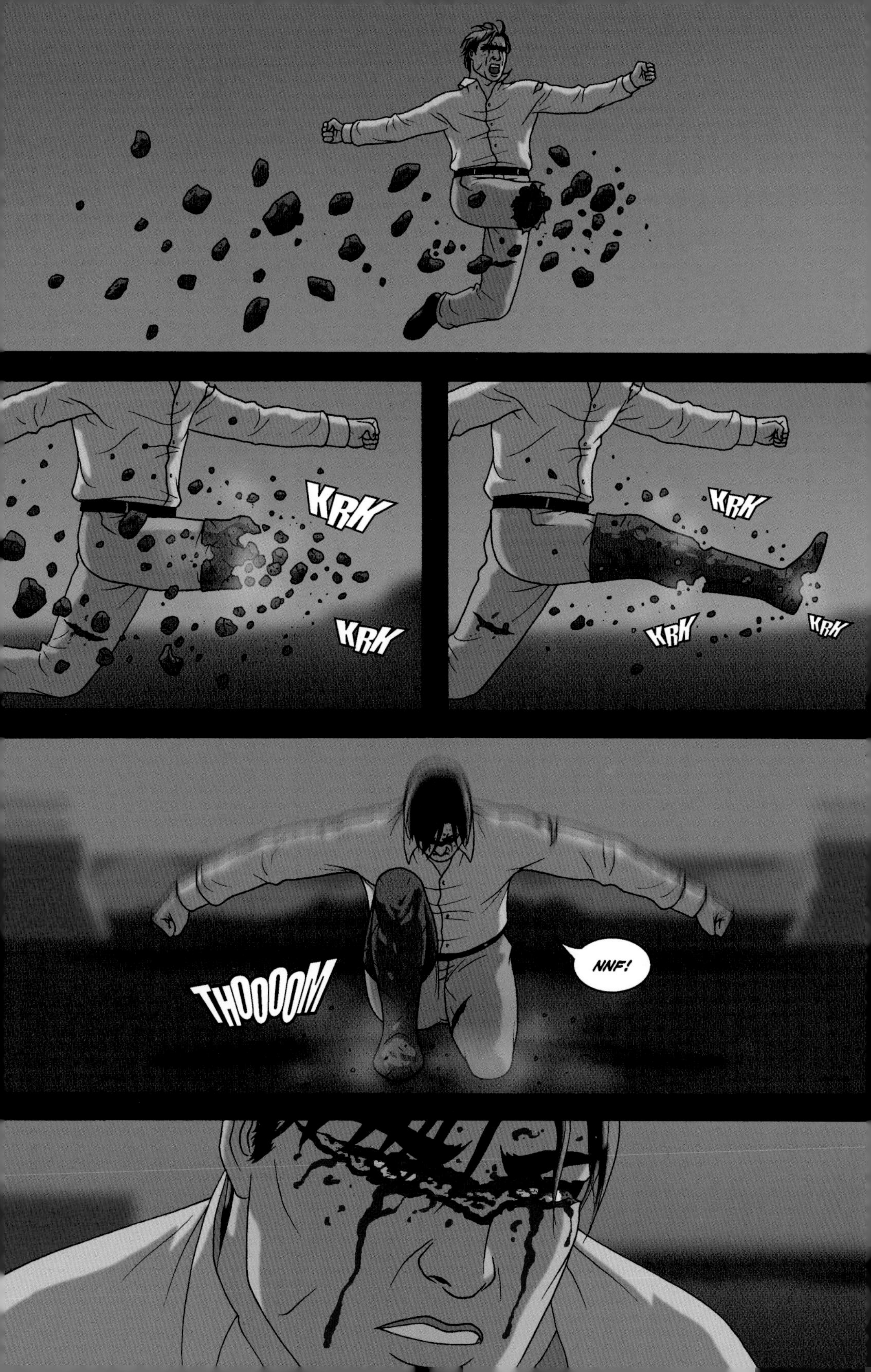
KRK
KRK
KRK
KRK
KRK
THOOOOM
NNF!

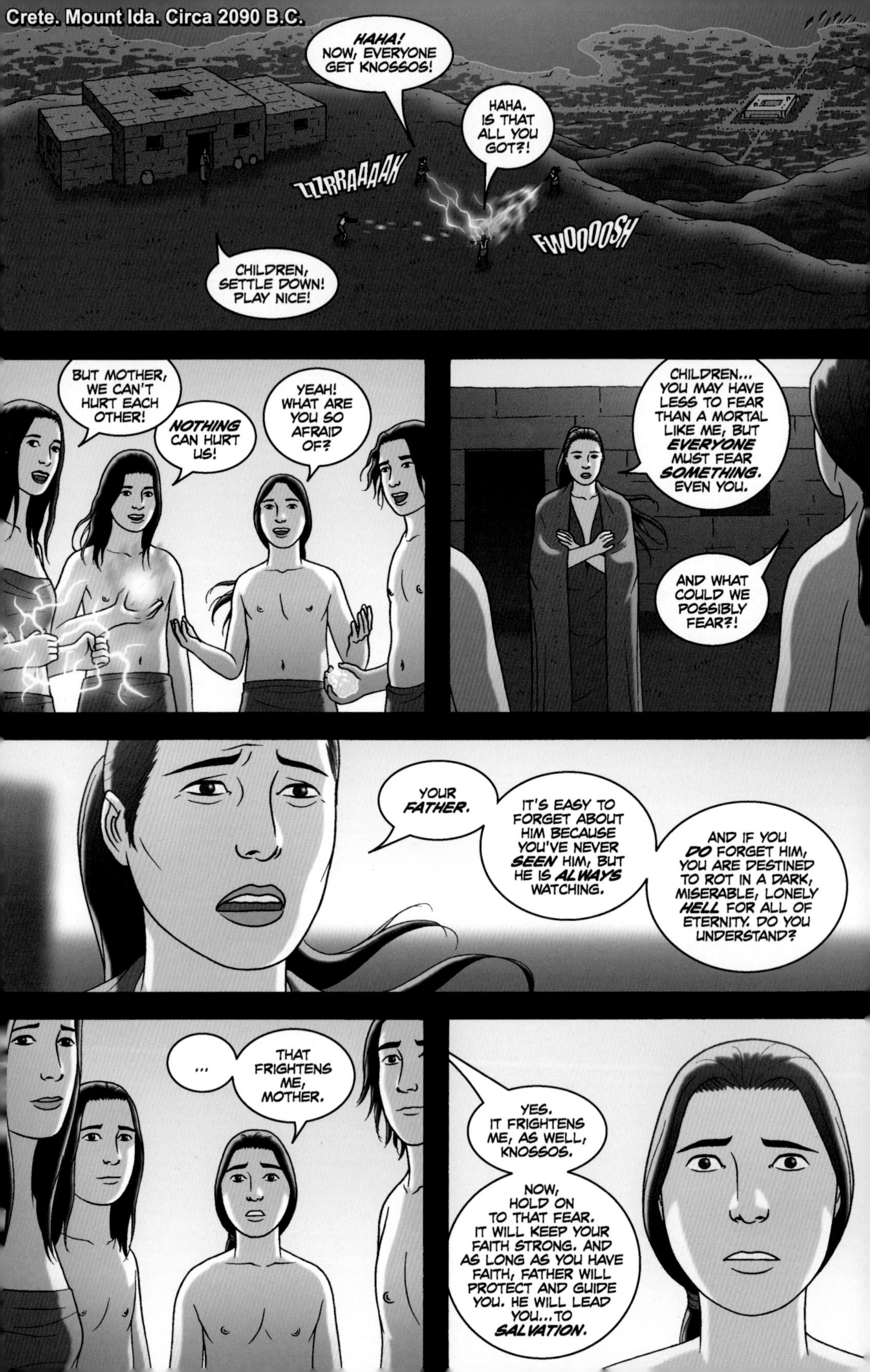
Crete. Mount Ida. Circa 2090 B.C.
HAHA! NOW, EVERYONE GET KNOSSOS!
HAHA. IS THAT ALL YOU GOT?!
ZZZRRAAAAK
FWOOOOSH
CHILDREN, SETTLE DOWN! PLAY NICE!
BUT MOTHER, WE CAN'T HURT EACH OTHER!
NOTHING CAN HURT US!
YEAH! WHAT ARE YOU SO AFRAID OF?
CHILDREN... YOU MAY HAVE LESS TO FEAR THAN A MORTAL LIKE ME, BUT EVERYONE MUST FEAR SOMETHING. EVEN YOU.
AND WHAT COULD WE POSSIBLY FEAR?!
YOUR FATHER.
IT'S EASY TO FORGET ABOUT HIM BECAUSE YOU'VE NEVER SEEN HIM, BUT HE IS ALWAYS WATCHING.
AND IF YOU DO FORGET HIM, YOU ARE DESTINED TO ROT IN A DARK, MISERABLE, LONELY HELL FOR ALL OF ETERNITY. DO YOU UNDERSTAND?
...
THAT FRIGHTENS ME, MOTHER.
YES. IT FRIGHTENS ME, AS WELL, KNOSSOS.
NOW, HOLD ON TO THAT FEAR. IT WILL KEEP YOUR FAITH STRONG. AND AS LONG AS YOU HAVE FAITH, FATHER WILL PROTECT AND GUIDE YOU. HE WILL LEAD YOU...TO SALVATION.

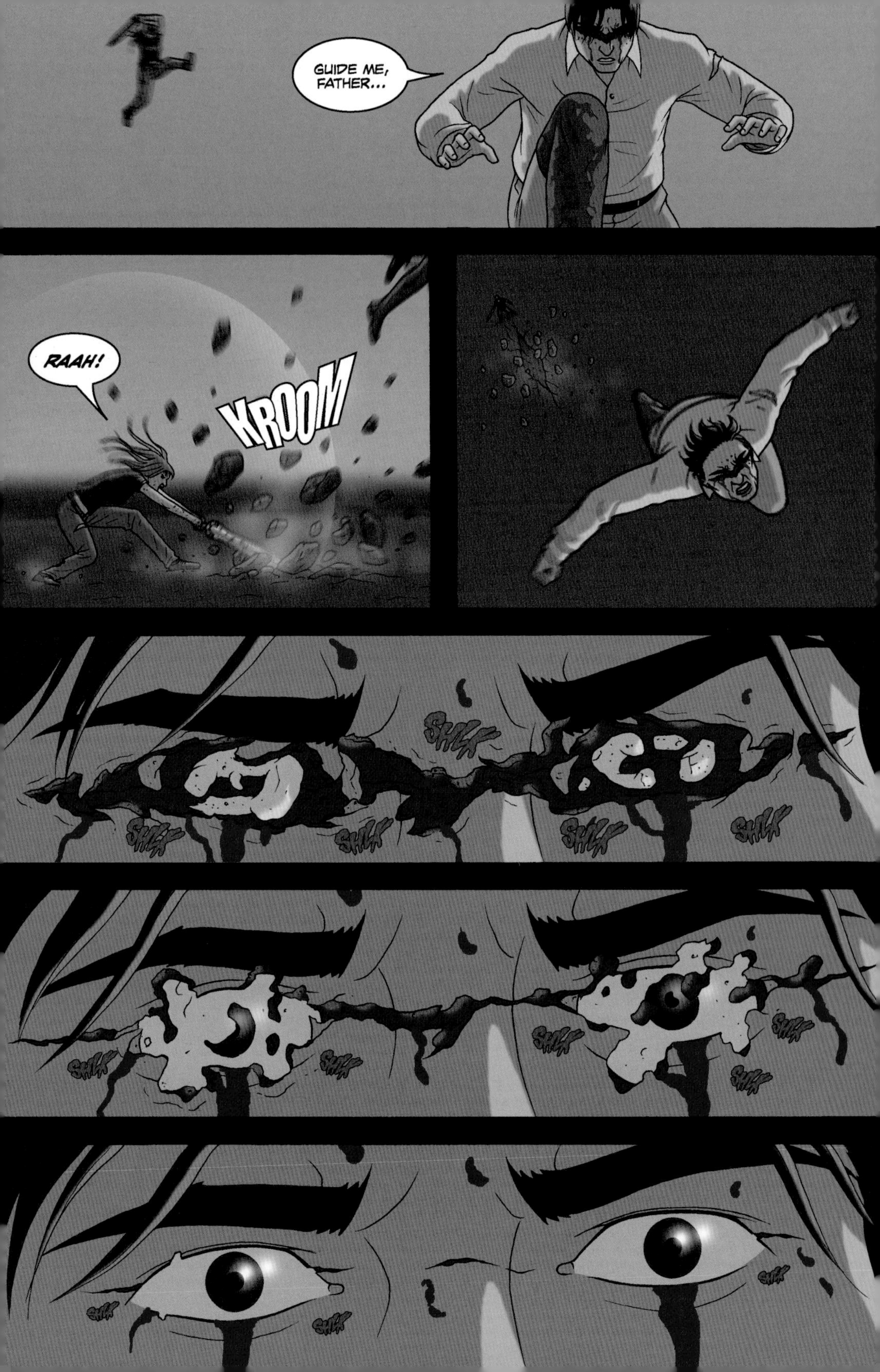
GUIDE ME, FATHER...
RAAH!
KROOM
SHLK
SHLK
SHLK
SHLK
SHLK
SHLK
SHLK
SHLK
SHLK
SHLK
SHLK
SHLK
SHLK
SHLK

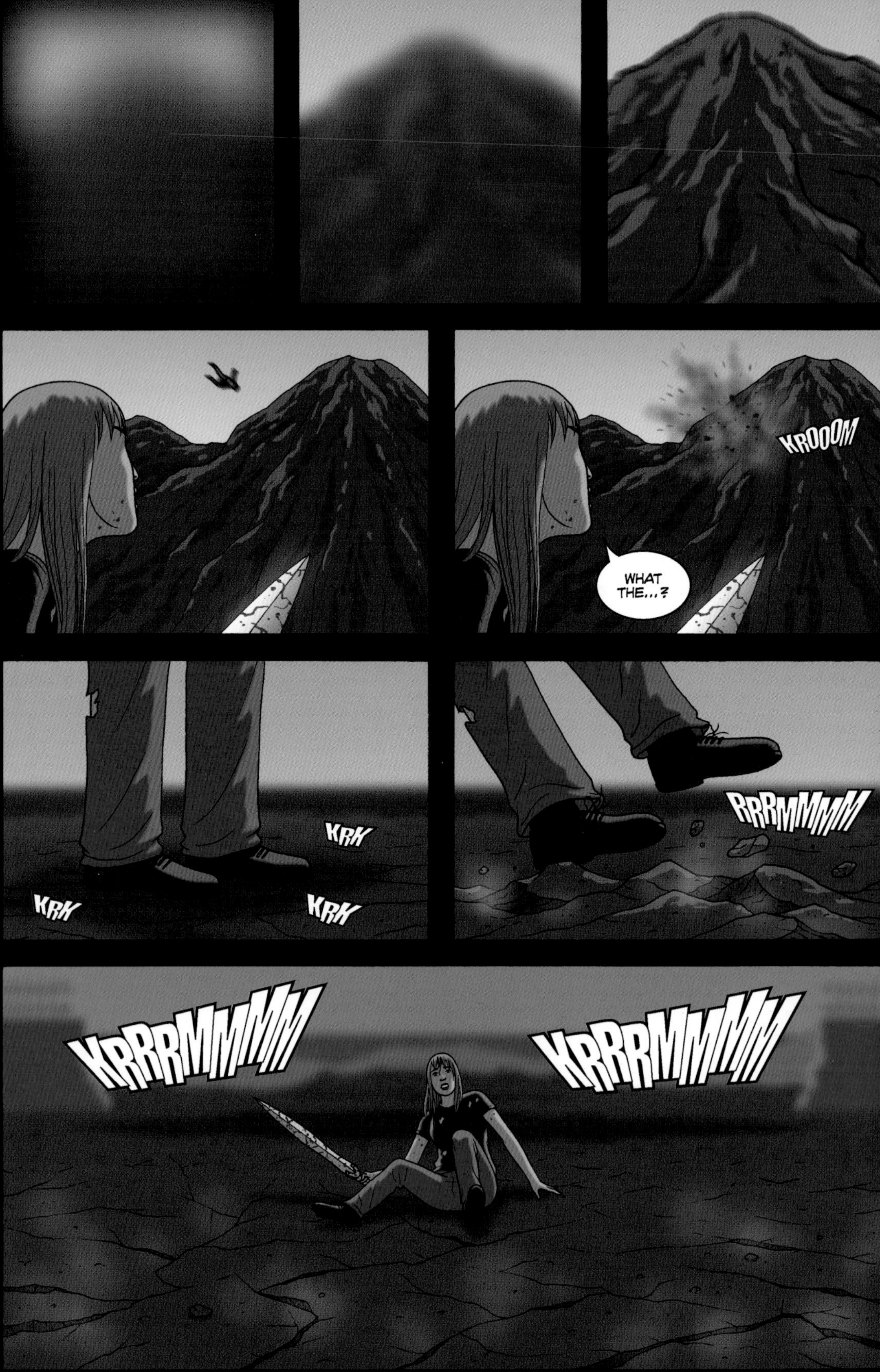
KROOOM
WHAT THE...?
KRK
KRK
KRK
RRRMMMM
KRRRMMMM
KRRRMMMM

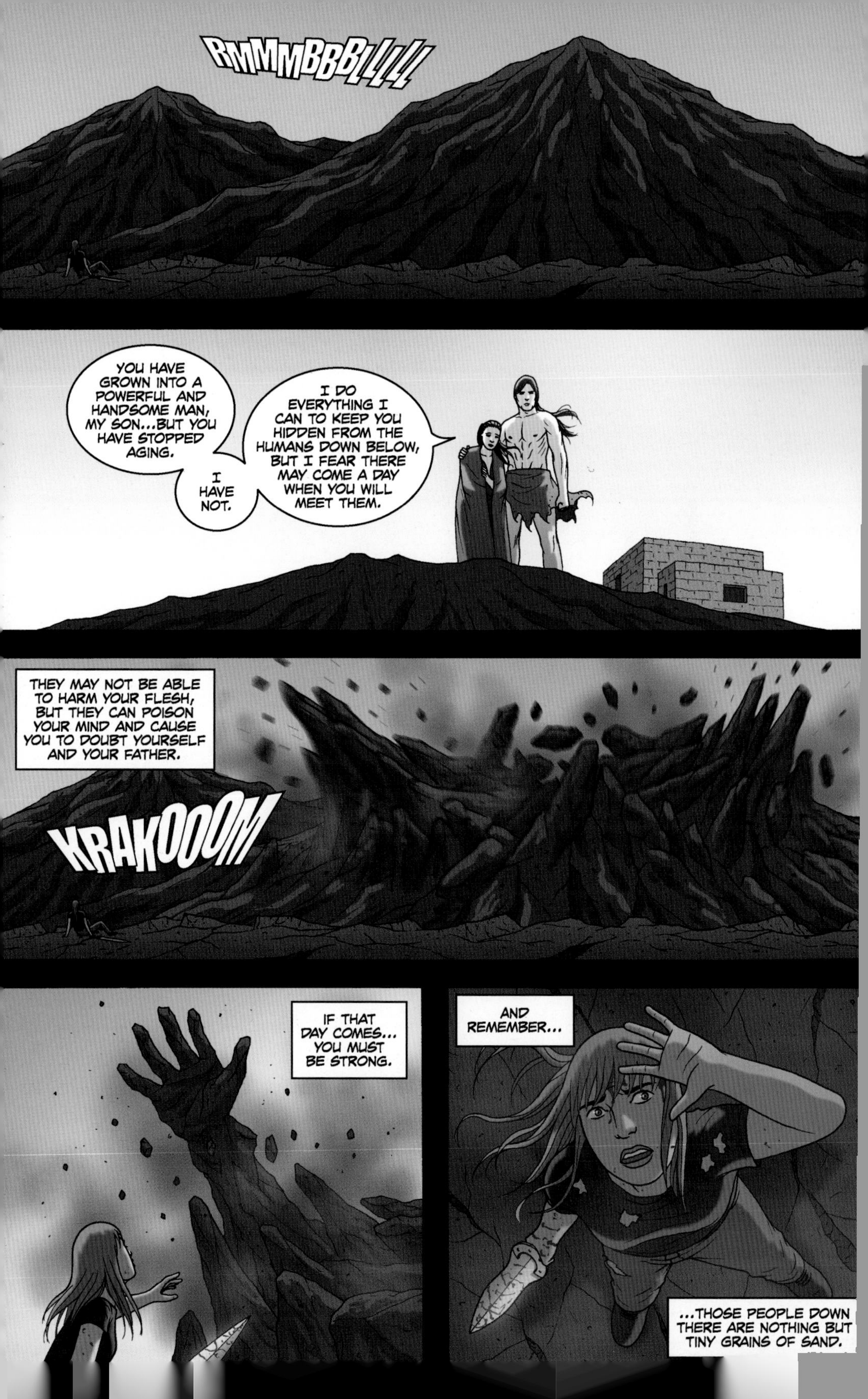
RMMMBBBLLLLL
YOU HAVE GROWN INTO A POWERFUL AND HANDSOME MAN, MY SON...BUT YOU HAVE STOPPED AGING.
I HAVE NOT.
I DO EVERYTHING I CAN TO KEEP YOU HIDDEN FROM THE HUMANS DOWN BELOW, BUT I FEAR THERE MAY COME A DAY WHEN YOU WILL MEET THEM.
THEY MAY NOT BE ABLE TO HARM YOUR FLESH, BUT THEY CAN POISON YOUR MIND AND CAUSE YOU TO DOUBT YOURSELF AND YOUR FATHER.
KRAKOOOM
IF THAT DAY COMES... YOU MUST BE STRONG.
AND REMEMBER...
...THOSE PEOPLE DOWN THERE ARE NOTHING BUT TINY GRAINS OF SAND.

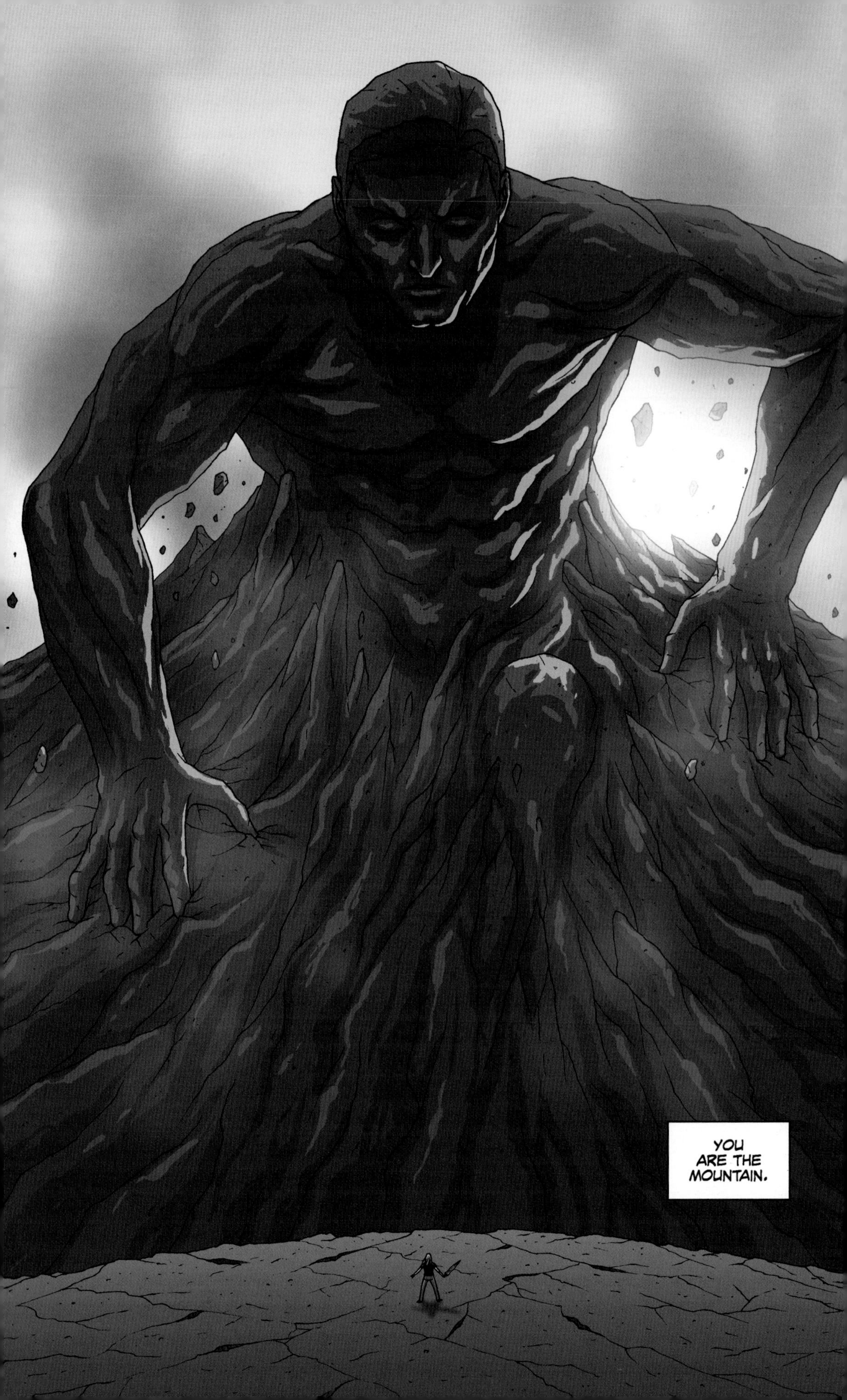
YOU ARE THE MOUNTAIN.

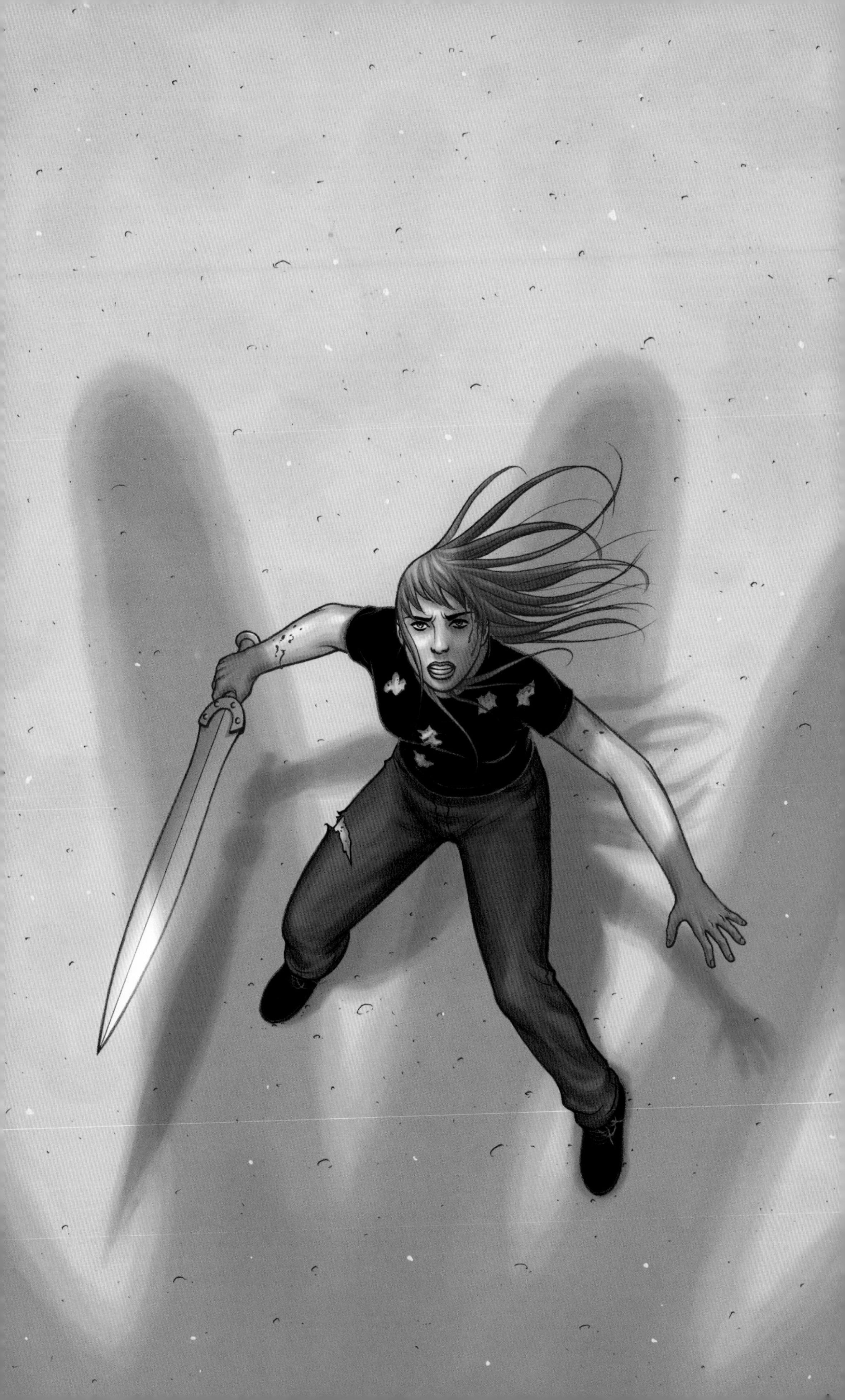

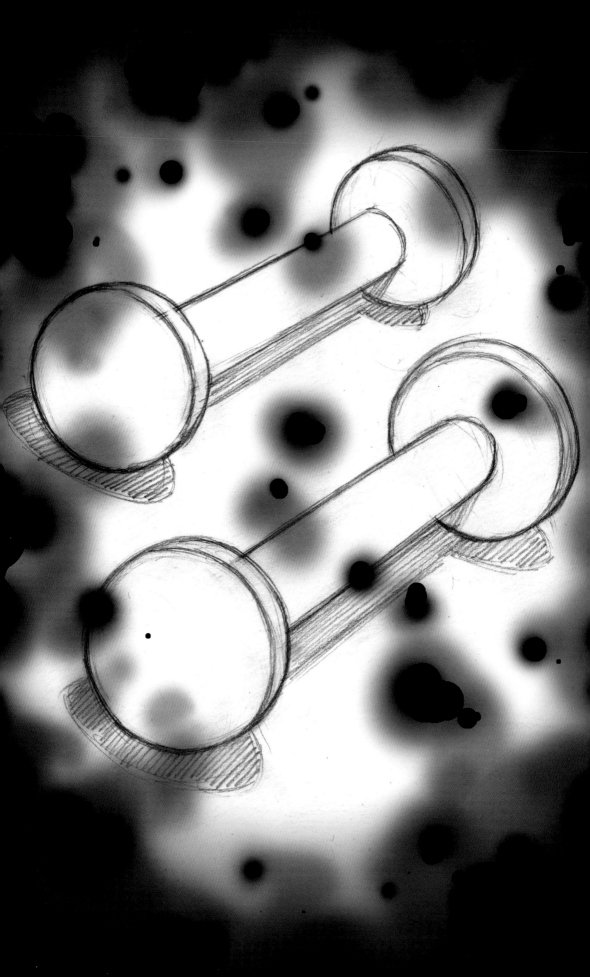

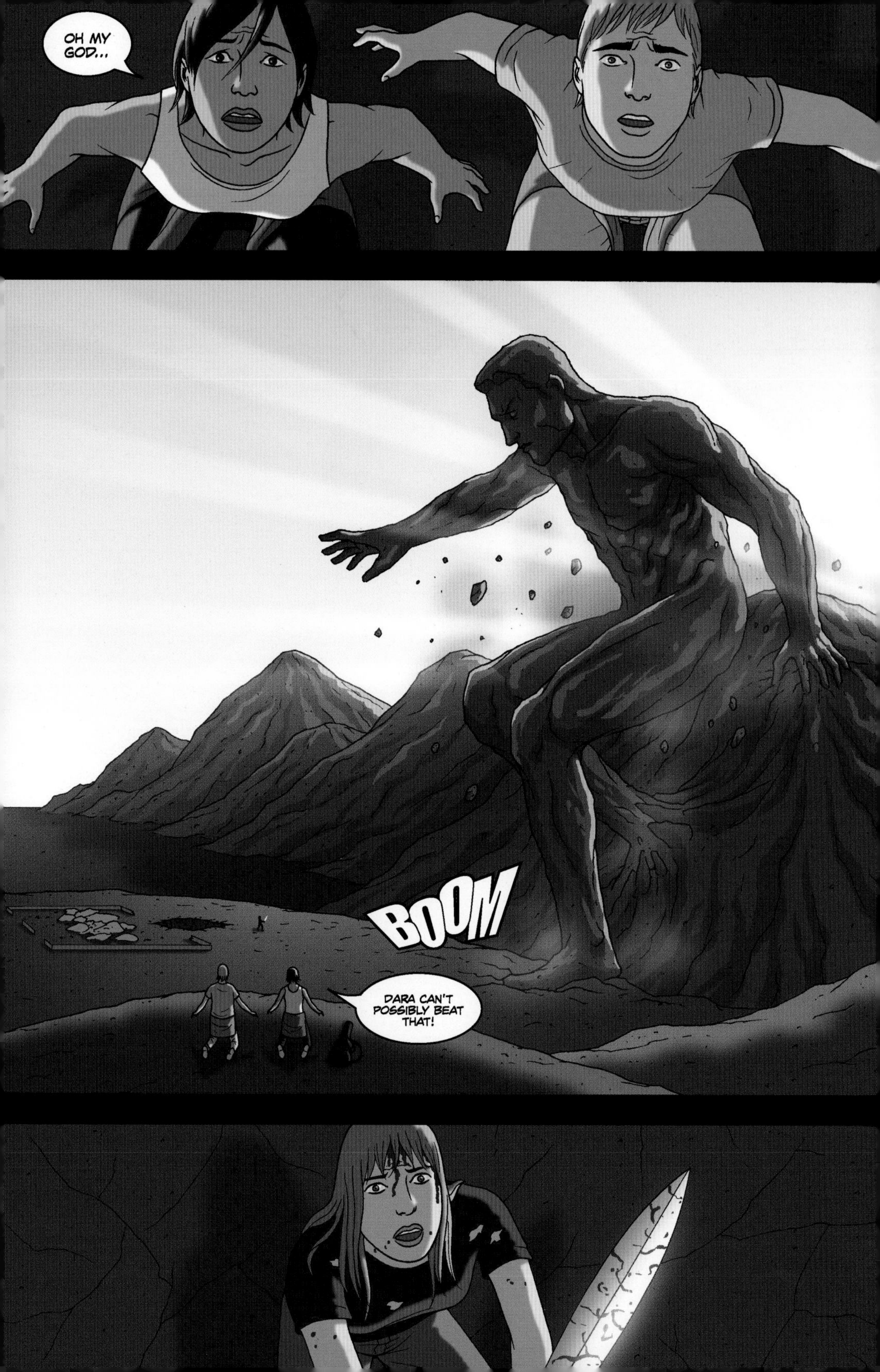
OH MY GOD...
BOOM
DARA CAN'T POSSIBLY BEAT THAT!

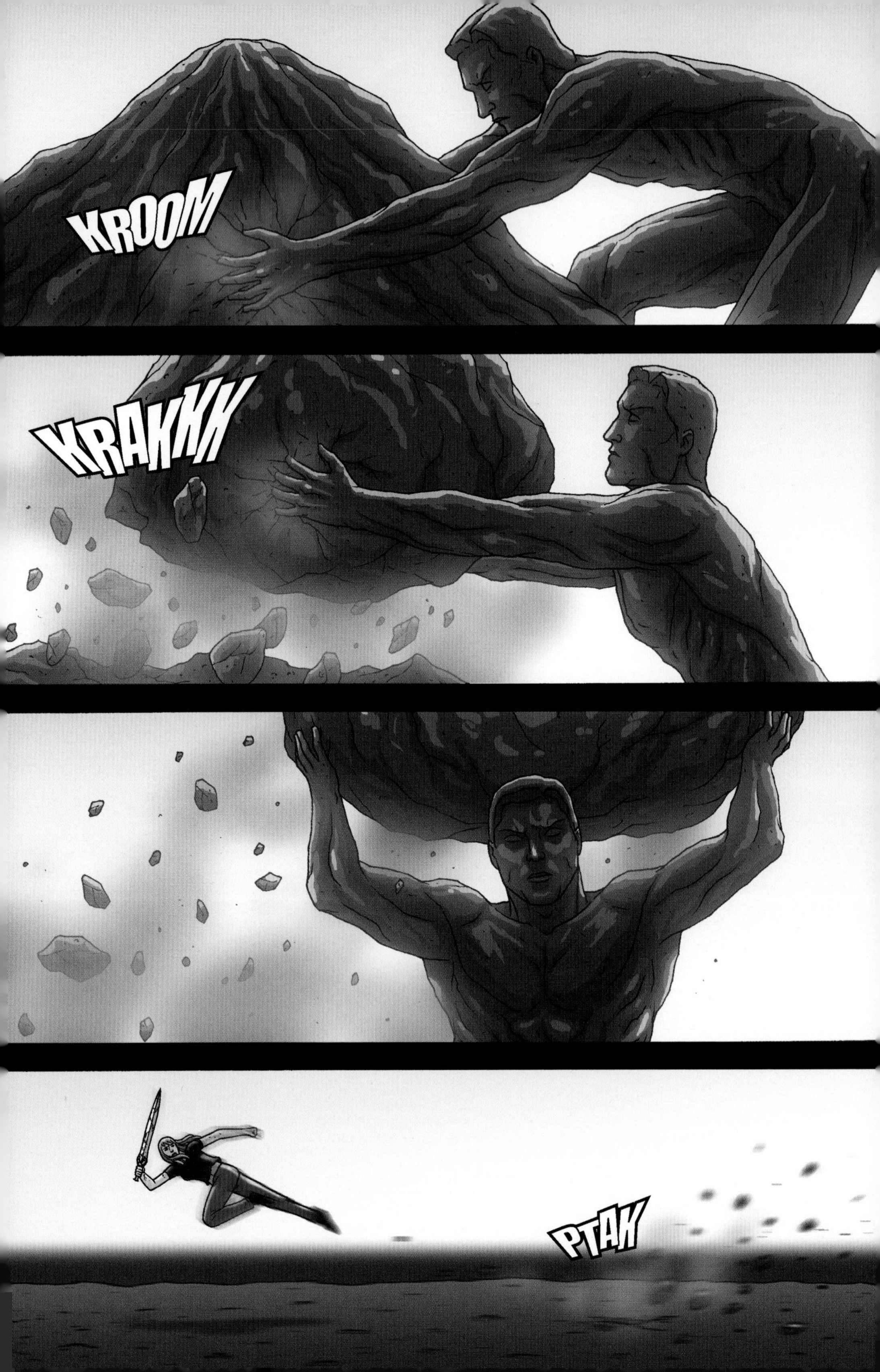
KROOM
KRAKKK
PTAK

PTAK

PTAK

PTAK

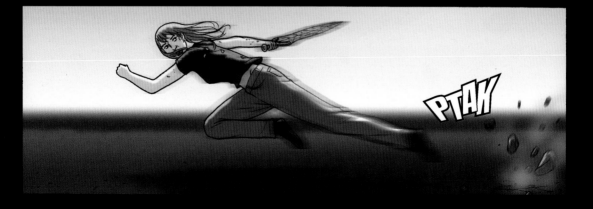

PTAK

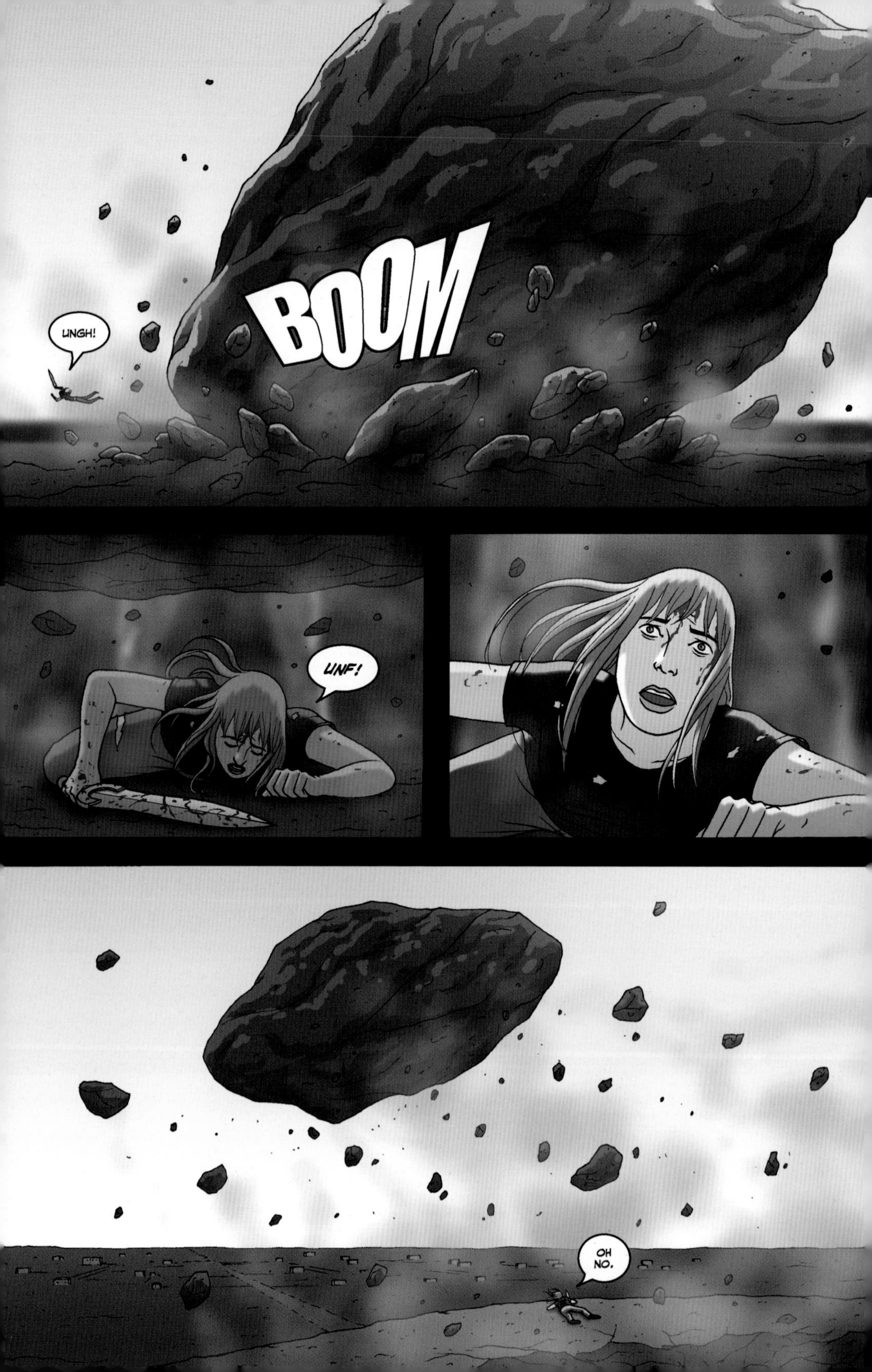
UNGH!
BOOM
UNF!
OH NO.

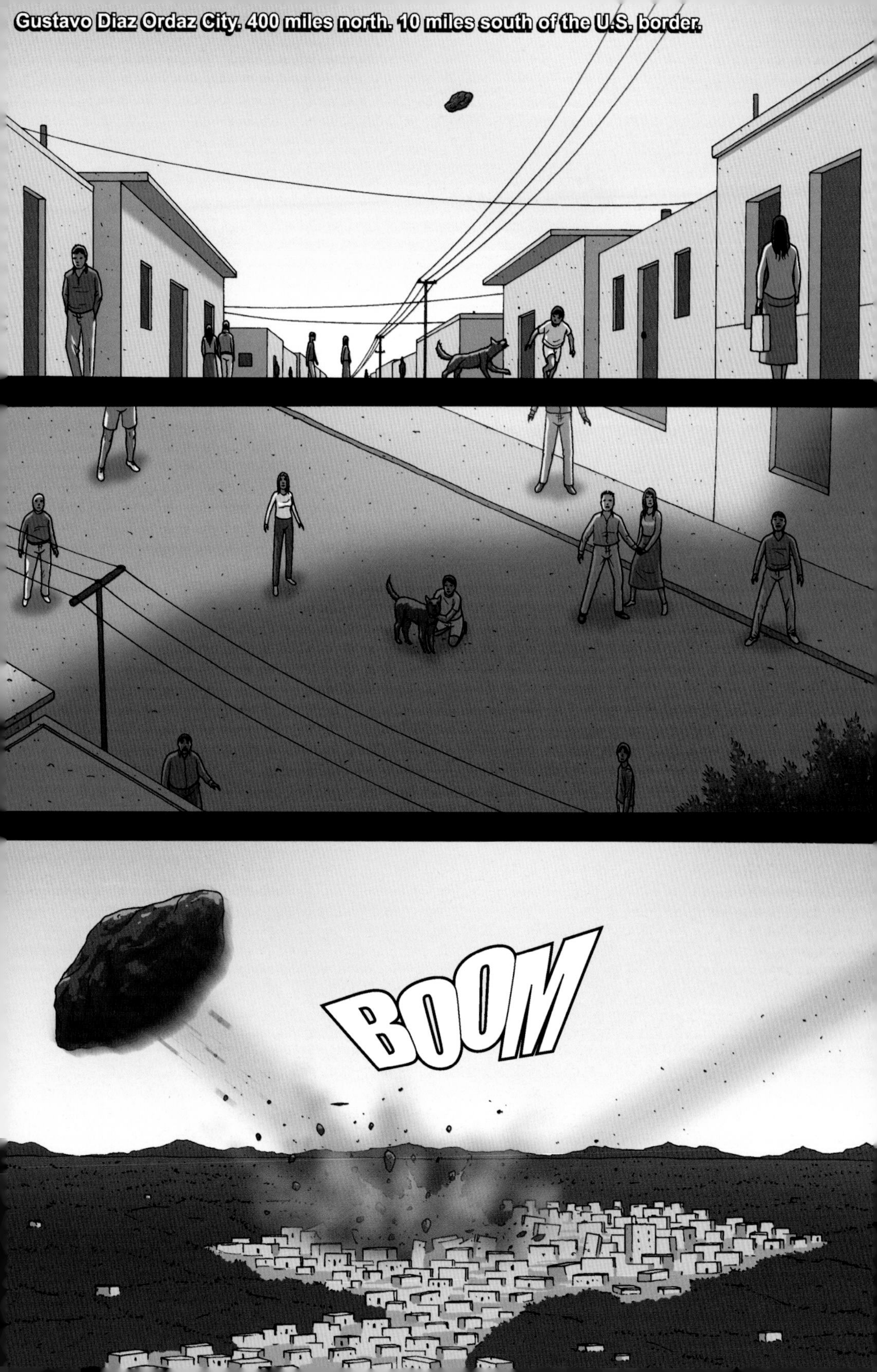
Gustavo Diaz Ordaz City. 400 miles north. 10 miles south of the U.S. border.
BOOM

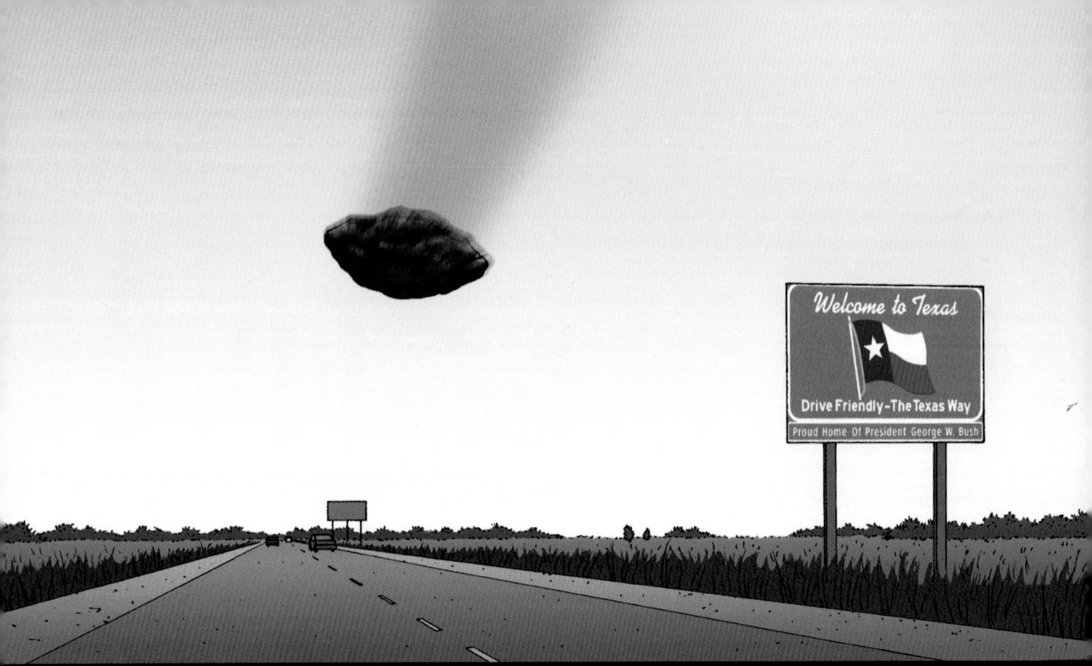
Welcome to Texas
Drive Friendly–The Texas Way
Proud Home Of President George W. Bush

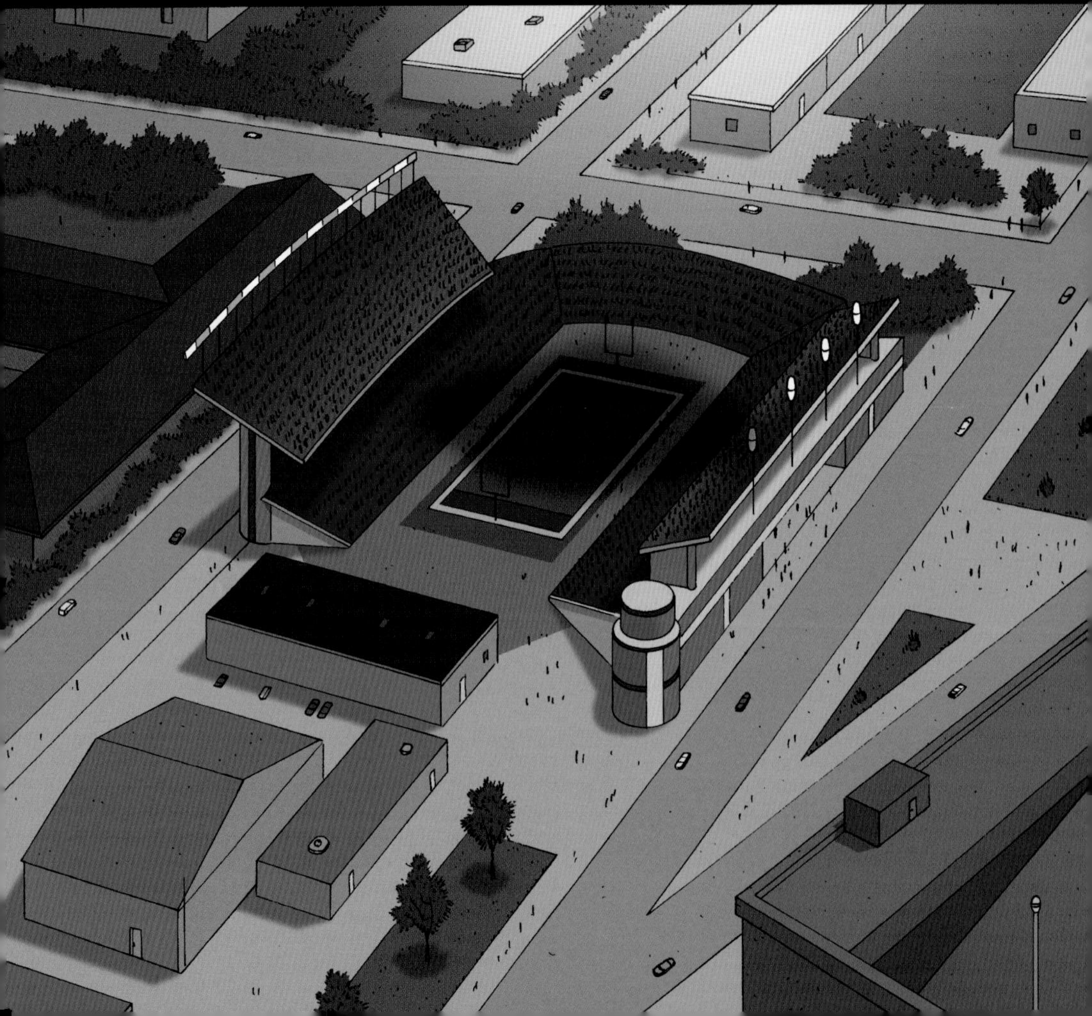

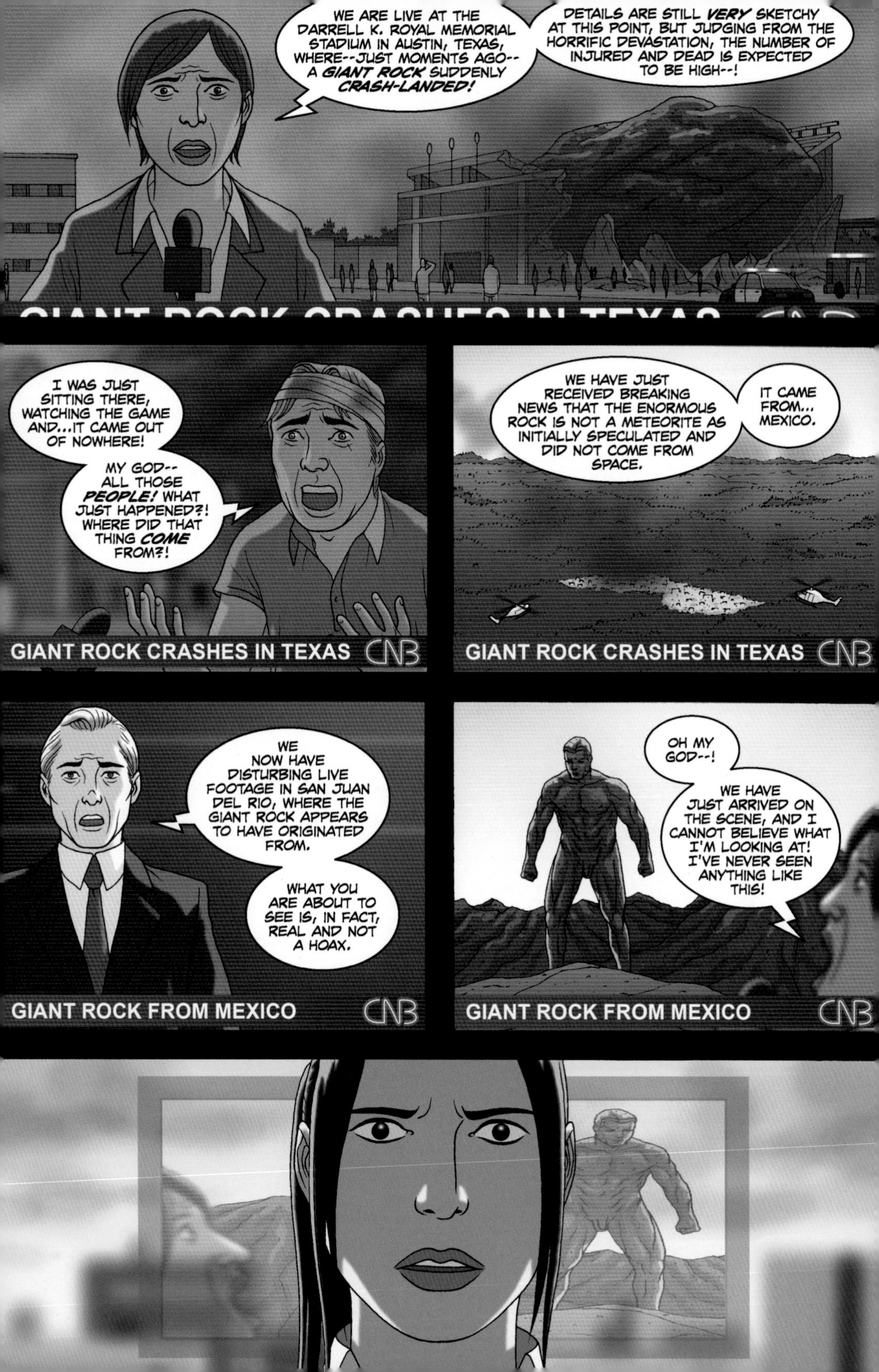
WE ARE LIVE AT THE DARRELL K. ROYAL MEMORIAL STADIUM IN AUSTIN, TEXAS, WHERE--JUST MOMENTS AGO--A GIANT ROCK SUDDENLY CRASH-LANDED!
DETAILS ARE STILL VERY SKETCHY AT THIS POINT, BUT JUDGING FROM THE HORRIFIC DEVASTATION, THE NUMBER OF INJURED AND DEAD IS EXPECTED TO BE HIGH--!
I WAS JUST SITTING THERE, WATCHING THE GAME AND...IT CAME OUT OF NOWHERE!
MY GOD--ALL THOSE PEOPLE! WHAT JUST HAPPENED?! WHERE DID THAT THING COME FROM?!
GIANT ROCK CRASHES IN TEXAS
WE HAVE JUST RECEIVED BREAKING NEWS THAT THE ENORMOUS ROCK IS NOT A METEORITE AS INITIALLY SPECULATED AND DID NOT COME FROM SPACE.
IT CAME FROM... MEXICO.
GIANT ROCK CRASHES IN TEXAS
WE NOW HAVE DISTURBING LIVE FOOTAGE IN SAN JUAN DEL RIO, WHERE THE GIANT ROCK APPEARS TO HAVE ORIGINATED FROM.
WHAT YOU ARE ABOUT TO SEE IS, IN FACT, REAL AND NOT A HOAX.
GIANT ROCK FROM MEXICO
OH MY GOD--!
WE HAVE JUST ARRIVED ON THE SCENE, AND I CANNOT BELIEVE WHAT I'M LOOKING AT! I'VE NEVER SEEN ANYTHING LIKE THIS!
GIANT ROCK FROM MEXICO

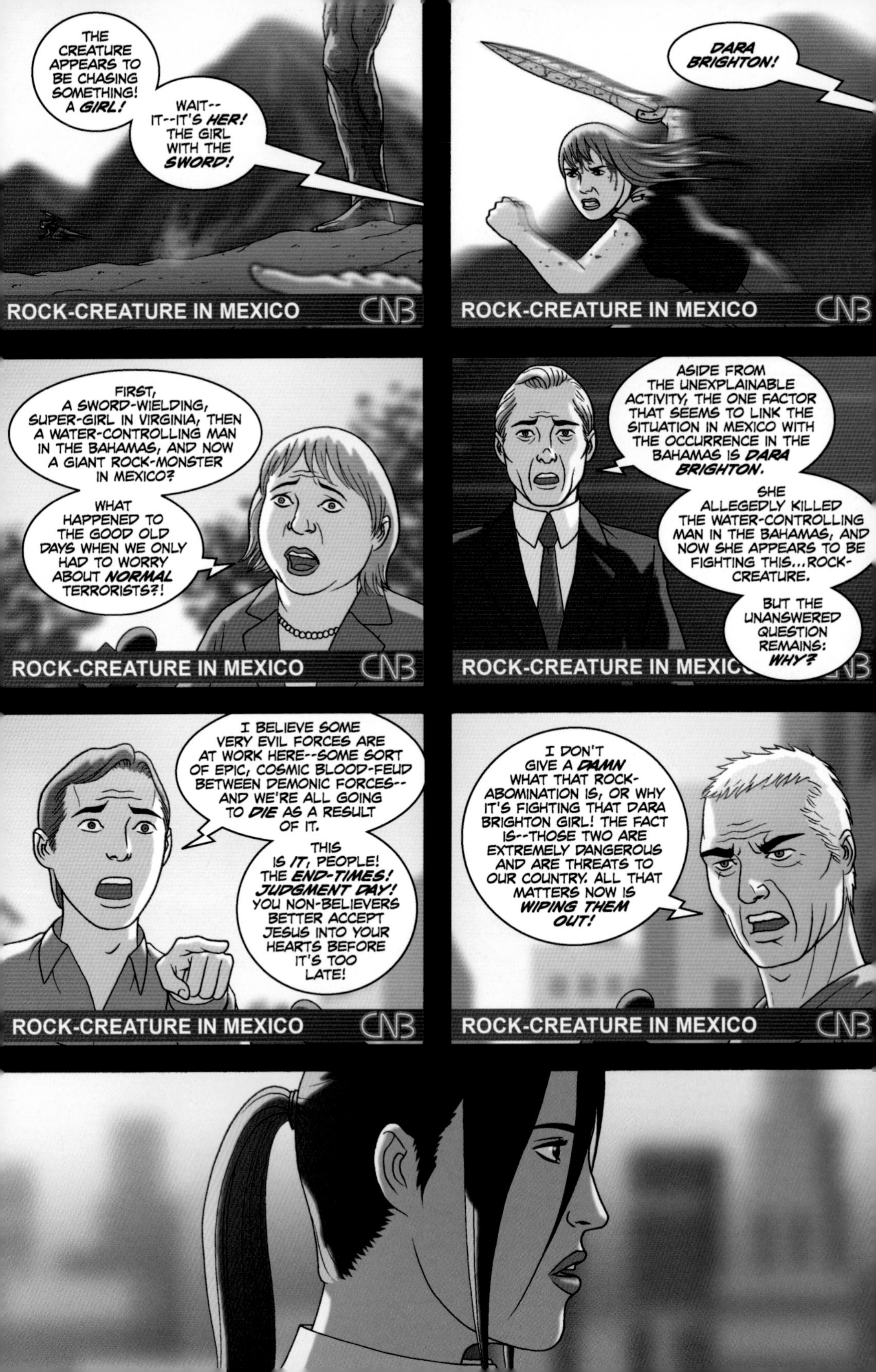
THE CREATURE APPEARS TO BE CHASING SOMETHING! A GIRL!
WAIT-- IT--IT'S HER! THE GIRL WITH THE SWORD!
ROCK-CREATURE IN MEXICO
CNB
DARA BRIGHTON!
ROCK-CREATURE IN MEXICO
CNB
FIRST, A SWORD-WIELDING, SUPER-GIRL IN VIRGINIA, THEN A WATER-CONTROLLING MAN IN THE BAHAMAS, AND NOW A GIANT ROCK-MONSTER IN MEXICO?
WHAT HAPPENED TO THE GOOD OLD DAYS WHEN WE ONLY HAD TO WORRY ABOUT NORMAL TERRORISTS?!
ROCK-CREATURE IN MEXICO
CNB
ASIDE FROM THE UNEXPLAINABLE ACTIVITY, THE ONE FACTOR THAT SEEMS TO LINK THE SITUATION IN MEXICO WITH THE OCCURRENCE IN THE BAHAMAS IS DARA BRIGHTON.
SHE ALLEGEDLY KILLED THE WATER-CONTROLLING MAN IN THE BAHAMAS, AND NOW SHE APPEARS TO BE FIGHTING THIS...ROCK-CREATURE.
BUT THE UNANSWERED QUESTION REMAINS: WHY?
ROCK-CREATURE IN MEXICO
I BELIEVE SOME VERY EVIL FORCES ARE AT WORK HERE--SOME SORT OF EPIC, COSMIC BLOOD-FEUD BETWEEN DEMONIC FORCES--AND WE'RE ALL GOING TO DIE AS A RESULT OF IT.
THIS IS IT, PEOPLE! THE END-TIMES! JUDGMENT DAY! YOU NON-BELIEVERS BETTER ACCEPT JESUS INTO YOUR HEARTS BEFORE IT'S TOO LATE!
ROCK-CREATURE IN MEXICO
CNB
I DON'T GIVE A DAMN WHAT THAT ROCK-ABOMINATION IS, OR WHY IT'S FIGHTING THAT DARA BRIGHTON GIRL! THE FACT IS--THOSE TWO ARE EXTREMELY DANGEROUS AND ARE THREATS TO OUR COUNTRY. ALL THAT MATTERS NOW IS WIPING THEM OUT!
ROCK-CREATURE IN MEXICO
CNB

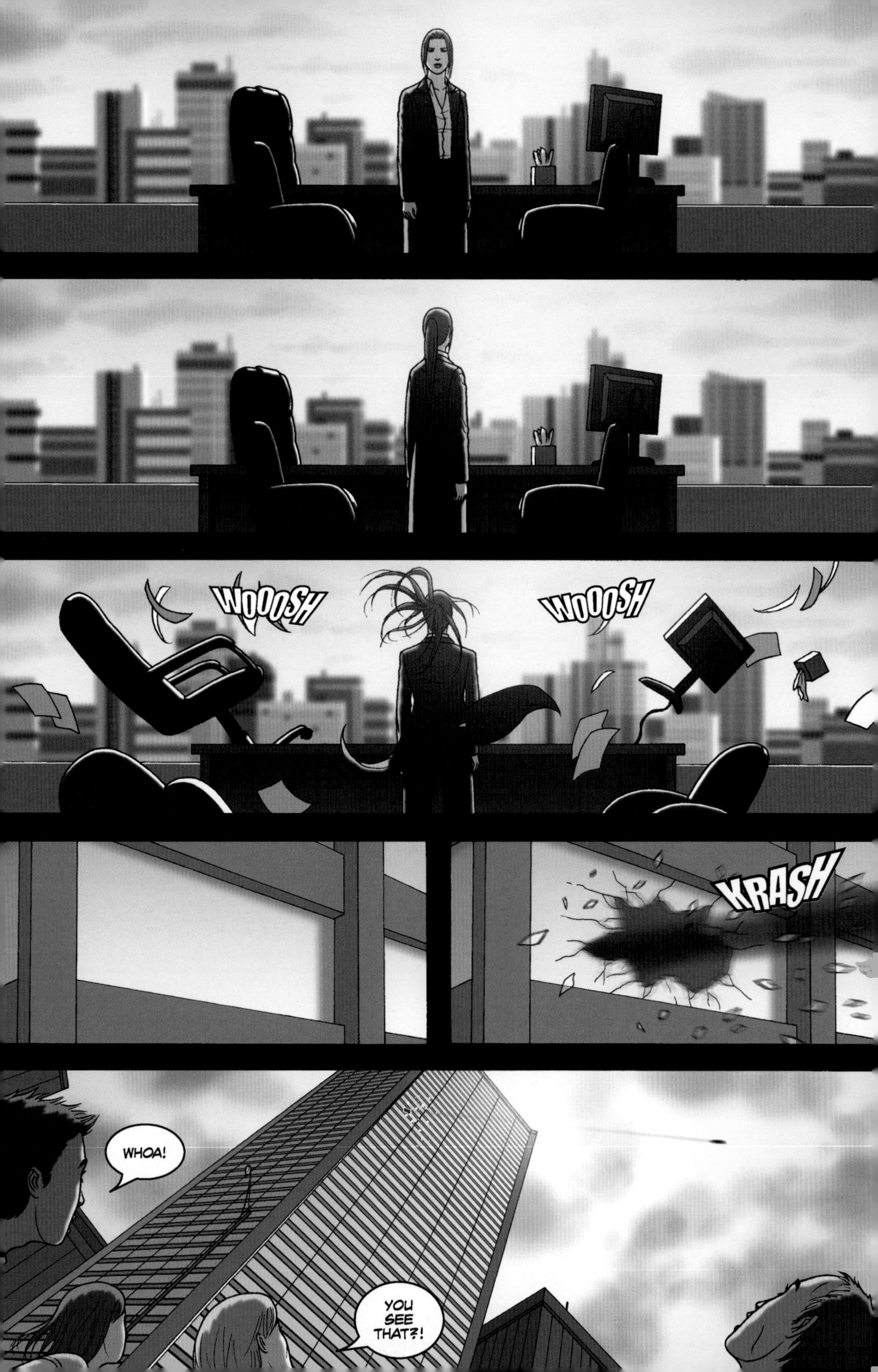
WOOOSH
WOOOSH
KRASH
WHOA!
YOU SEE THAT?!

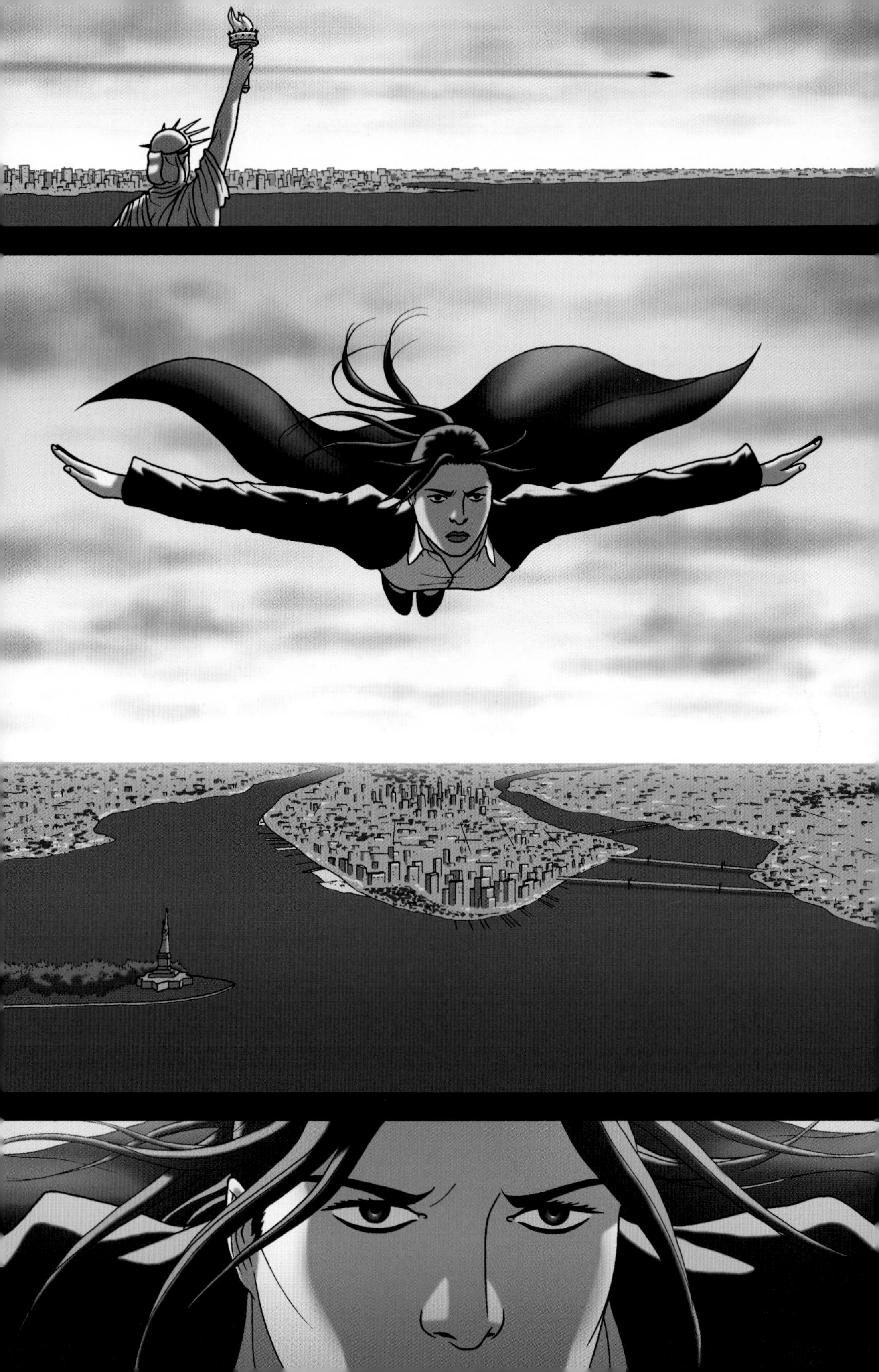

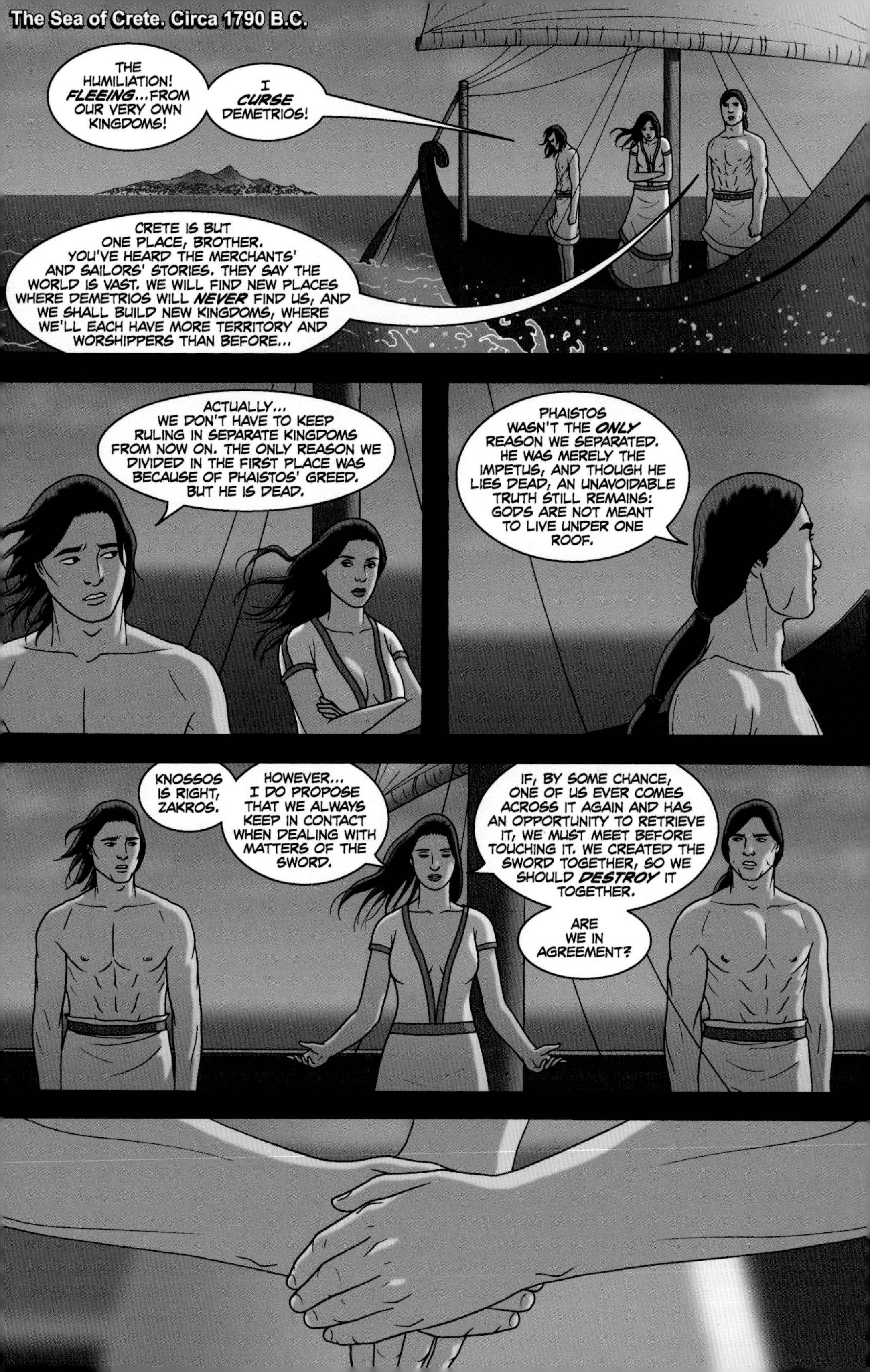
The Sea of Crete. Circa 1790 B.C.
THE HUMILIATION! FLEEING...FROM OUR VERY OWN KINGDOMS!
I CURSE DEMETRIOS!
CRETE IS BUT ONE PLACE, BROTHER. YOU'VE HEARD THE MERCHANTS' AND SAILORS' STORIES. THEY SAY THE WORLD IS VAST. WE WILL FIND NEW PLACES WHERE DEMETRIOS WILL NEVER FIND US, AND WE SHALL BUILD NEW KINGDOMS, WHERE WE'LL EACH HAVE MORE TERRITORY AND WORSHIPPERS THAN BEFORE...
ACTUALLY... WE DON'T HAVE TO KEEP RULING IN SEPARATE KINGDOMS FROM NOW ON. THE ONLY REASON WE DIVIDED IN THE FIRST PLACE WAS BECAUSE OF PHAISTOS' GREED. BUT HE IS DEAD.
PHAISTOS WASN'T THE ONLY REASON WE SEPARATED. HE WAS MERELY THE IMPETUS, AND THOUGH HE LIES DEAD, AN UNAVOIDABLE TRUTH STILL REMAINS: GODS ARE NOT MEANT TO LIVE UNDER ONE ROOF.
KNOSSOS IS RIGHT, ZAKROS.
HOWEVER... I DO PROPOSE THAT WE ALWAYS KEEP IN CONTACT WHEN DEALING WITH MATTERS OF THE SWORD.
IF, BY SOME CHANCE, ONE OF US EVER COMES ACROSS IT AGAIN AND HAS AN OPPORTUNITY TO RETRIEVE IT, WE MUST MEET BEFORE TOUCHING IT. WE CREATED THE SWORD TOGETHER, SO WE SHOULD DESTROY IT TOGETHER.
ARE WE IN AGREEMENT?

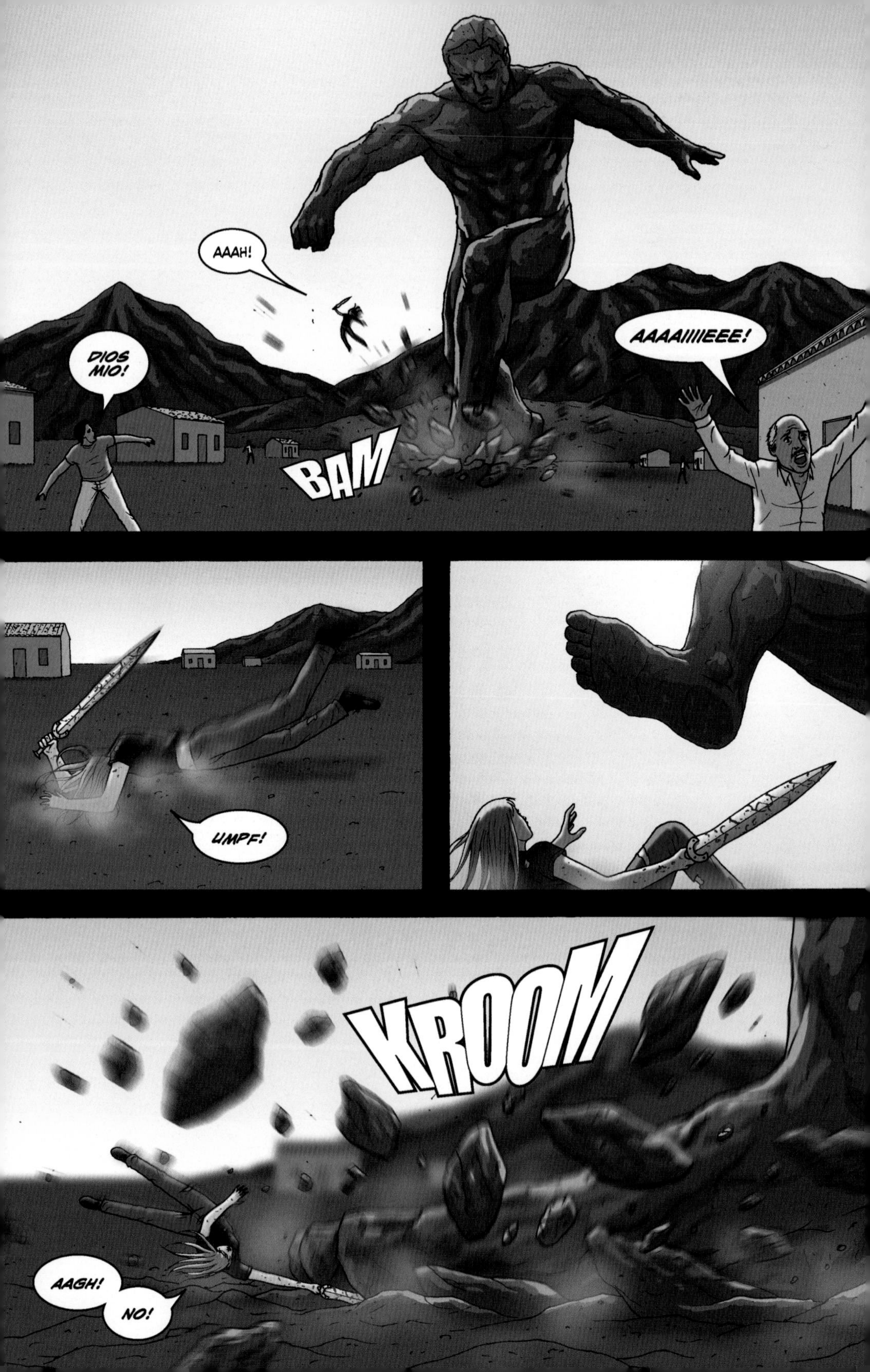
AAAH!
DIOS MIO!
AAAAIIIIIEEE!
BAM
UMPF!
KROOM
AAGH!
NO!

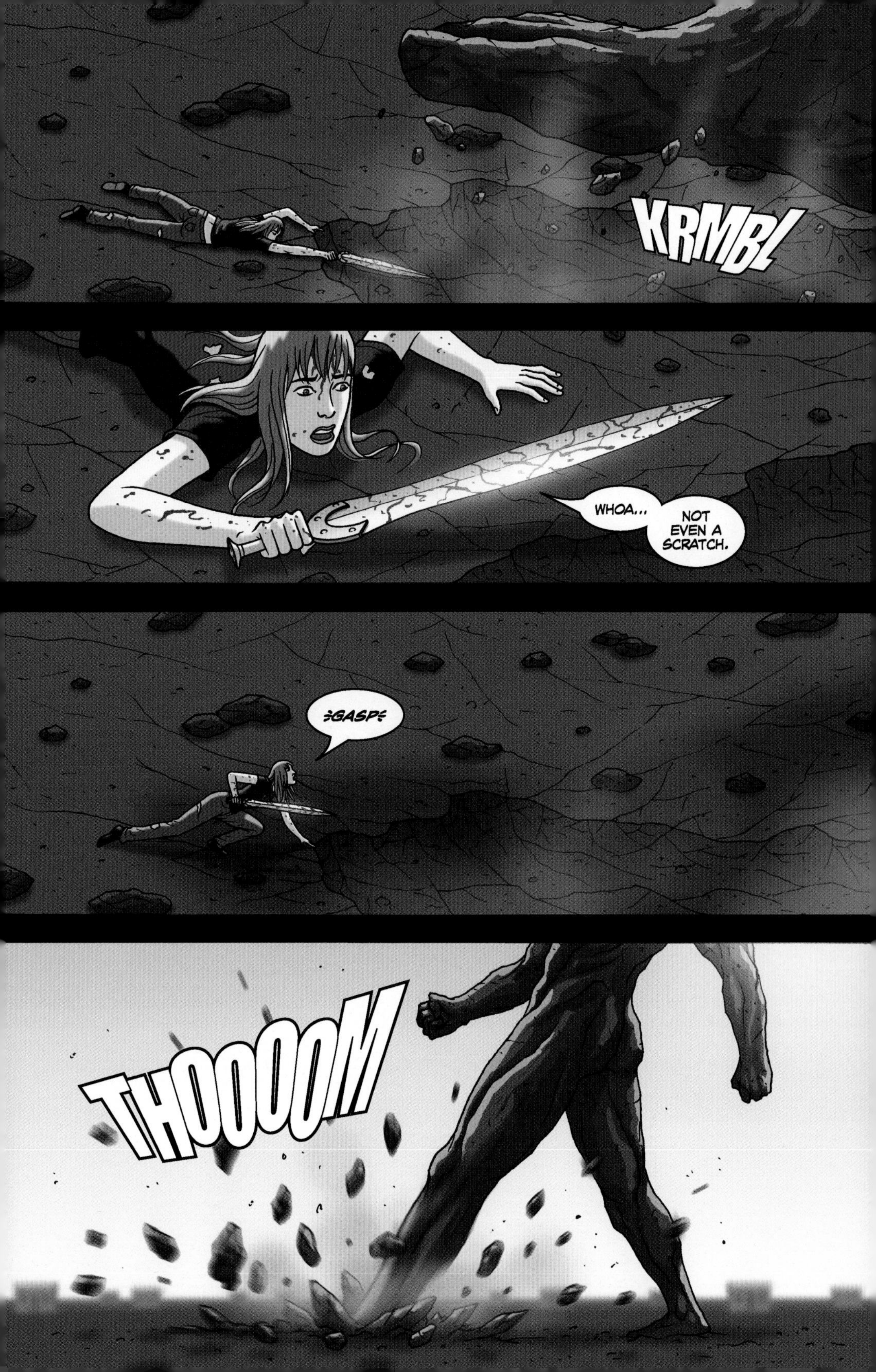
KRMBL
WHOA...
NOT EVEN A SCRATCH.
GASP
THOOOOM

KRRRKKK

AAAAGH!

KRRRKKK

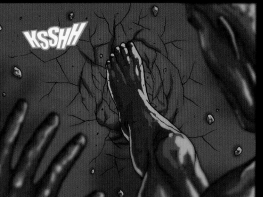

KSSHH

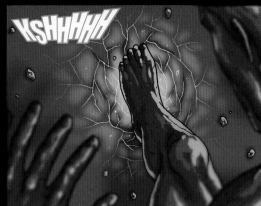

KSHHHHH

NO...!

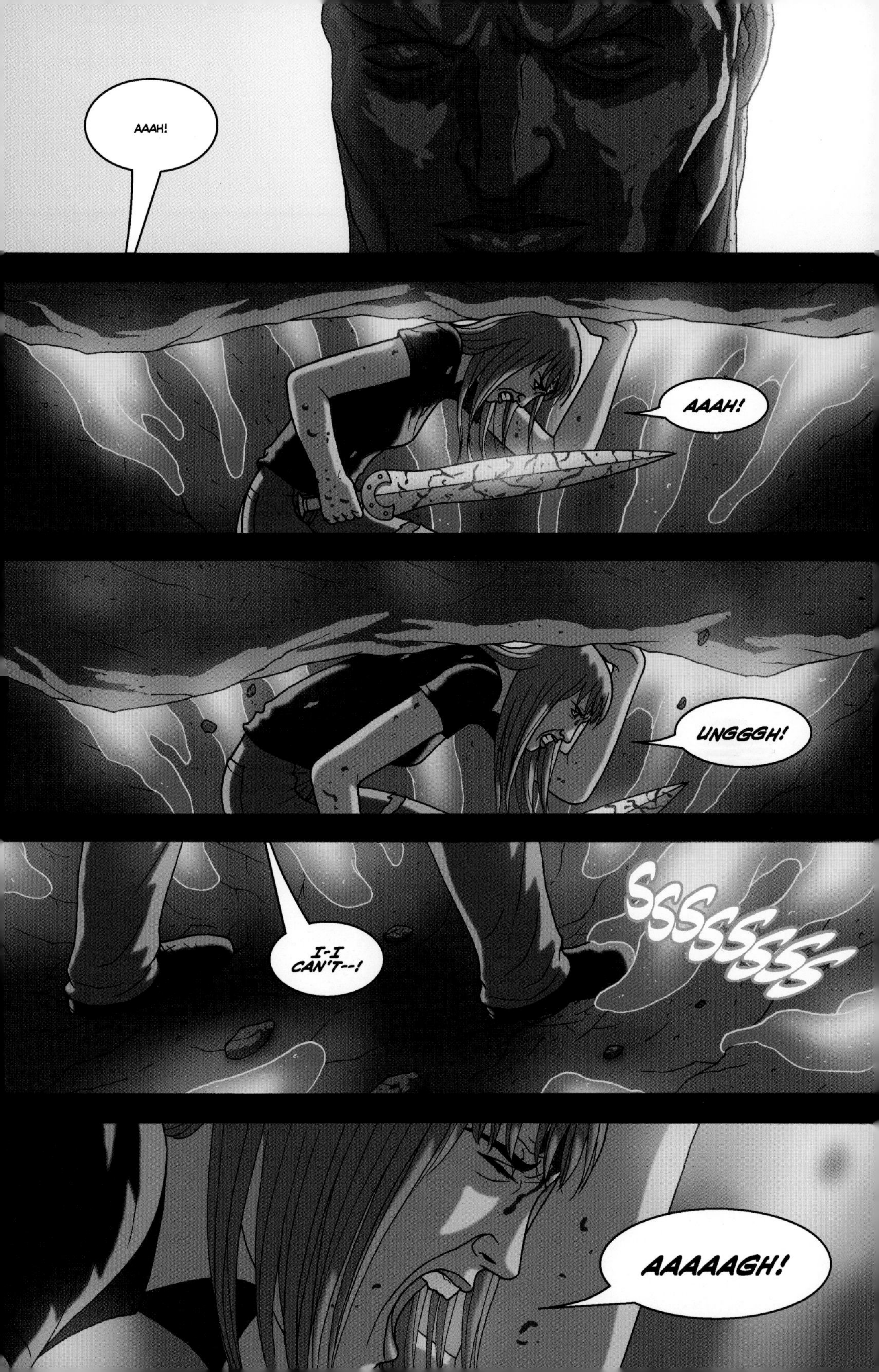
AAAH!
AAAH!
UNGGGH!
I-I CAN'T--!
SSSSSSSSS
AAAAAGH!

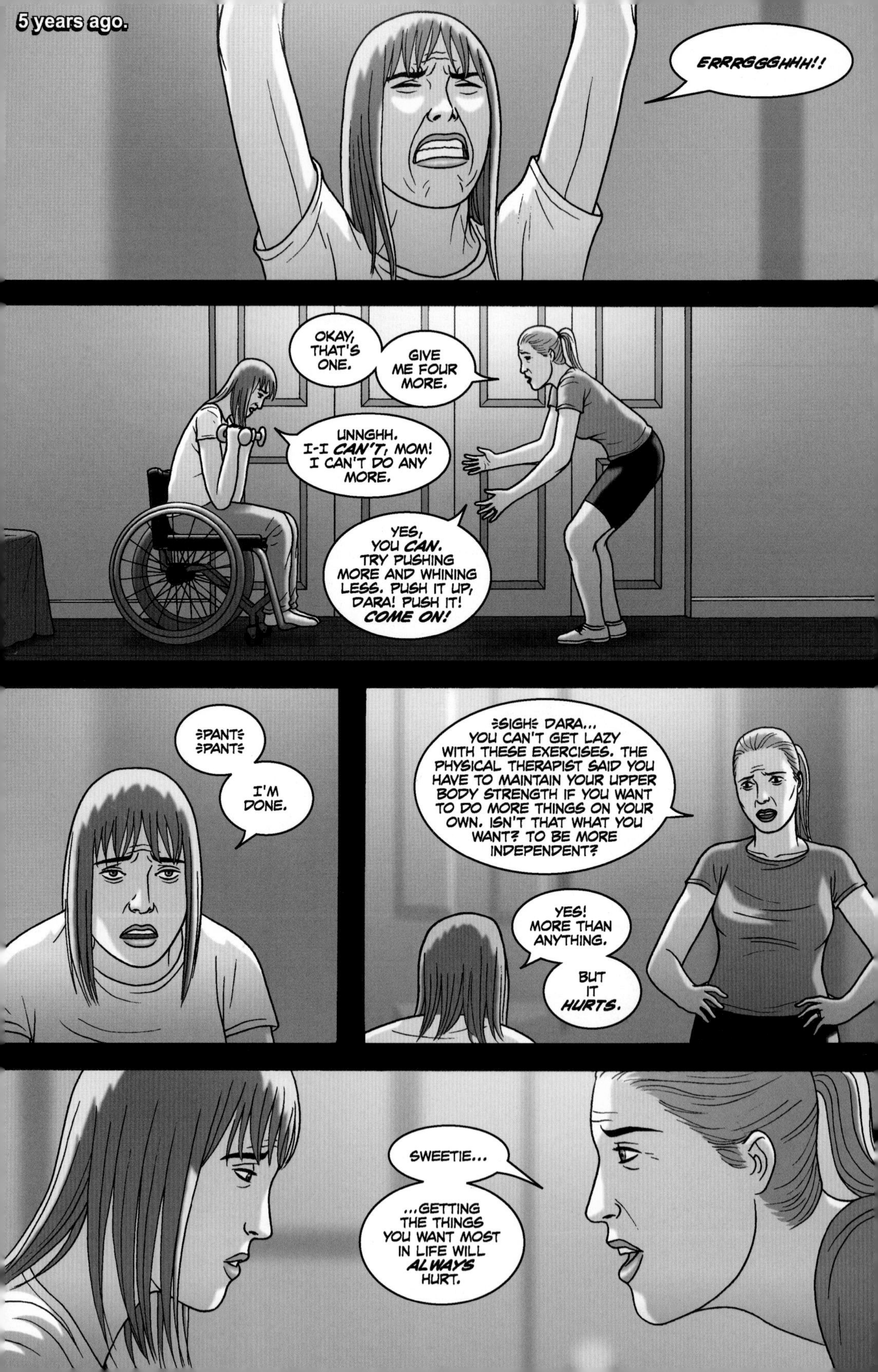
5 years ago.
ERRRGGGHHH!!
OKAY, THAT'S ONE.
GIVE ME FOUR MORE.
UNNGHH. I-I CAN'T, MOM! I CAN'T DO ANY MORE.
YES, YOU CAN. TRY PUSHING MORE AND WHINING LESS. PUSH IT UP, DARA! PUSH IT! COME ON!
=PANT= =PANT=
I'M DONE.
=SIGH= DARA... YOU CAN'T GET LAZY WITH THESE EXERCISES. THE PHYSICAL THERAPIST SAID YOU HAVE TO MAINTAIN YOUR UPPER BODY STRENGTH IF YOU WANT TO DO MORE THINGS ON YOUR OWN. ISN'T THAT WHAT YOU WANT? TO BE MORE INDEPENDENT?
YES! MORE THAN ANYTHING.
BUT IT HURTS.
SWEETIE...
...GETTING THE THINGS YOU WANT MOST IN LIFE WILL ALWAYS HURT.

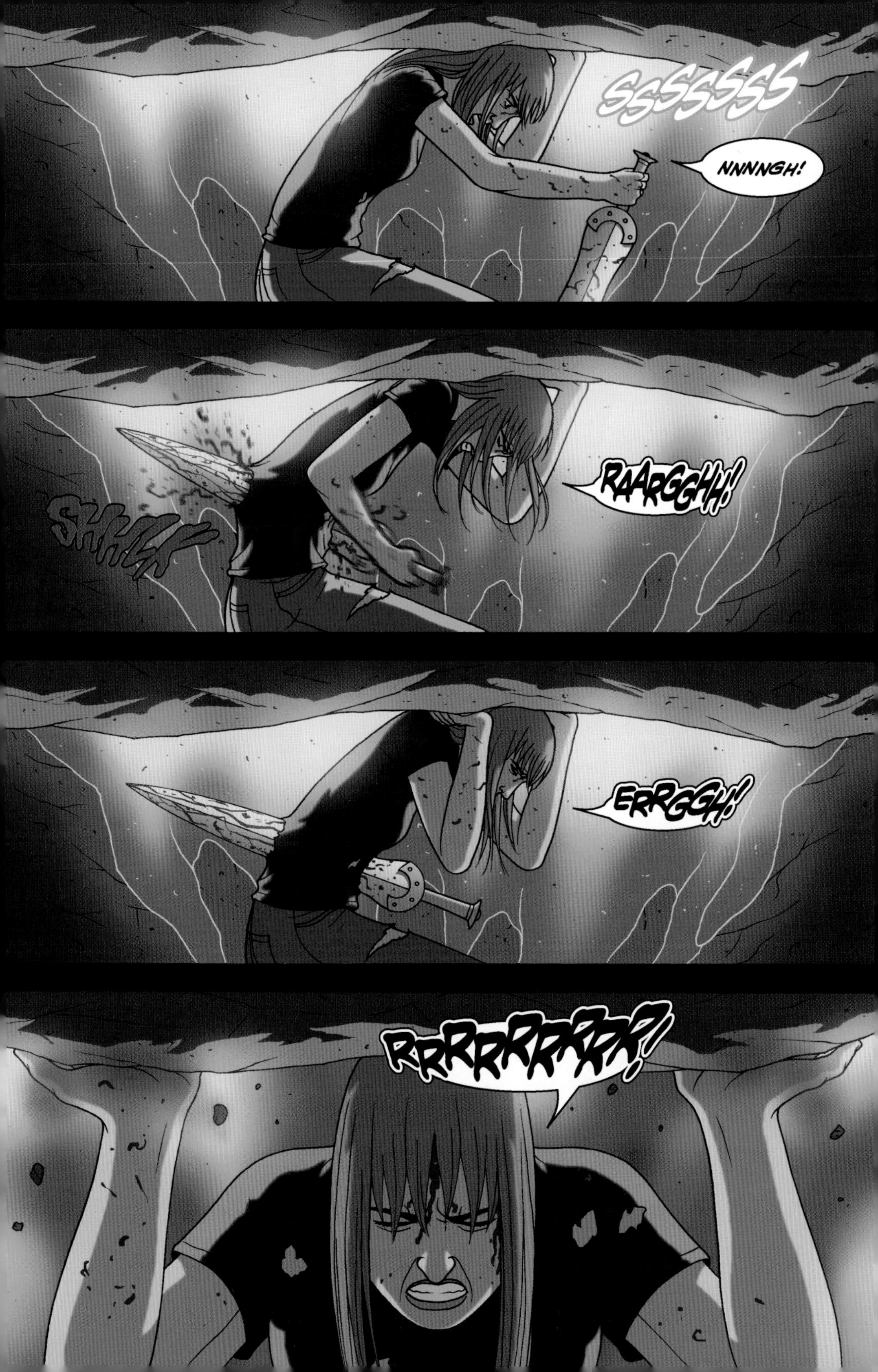
SSSSSSS
NNNNGH!
RAARGGHH!
SHHLK
ERRGGH!
RRRRRRRRR!

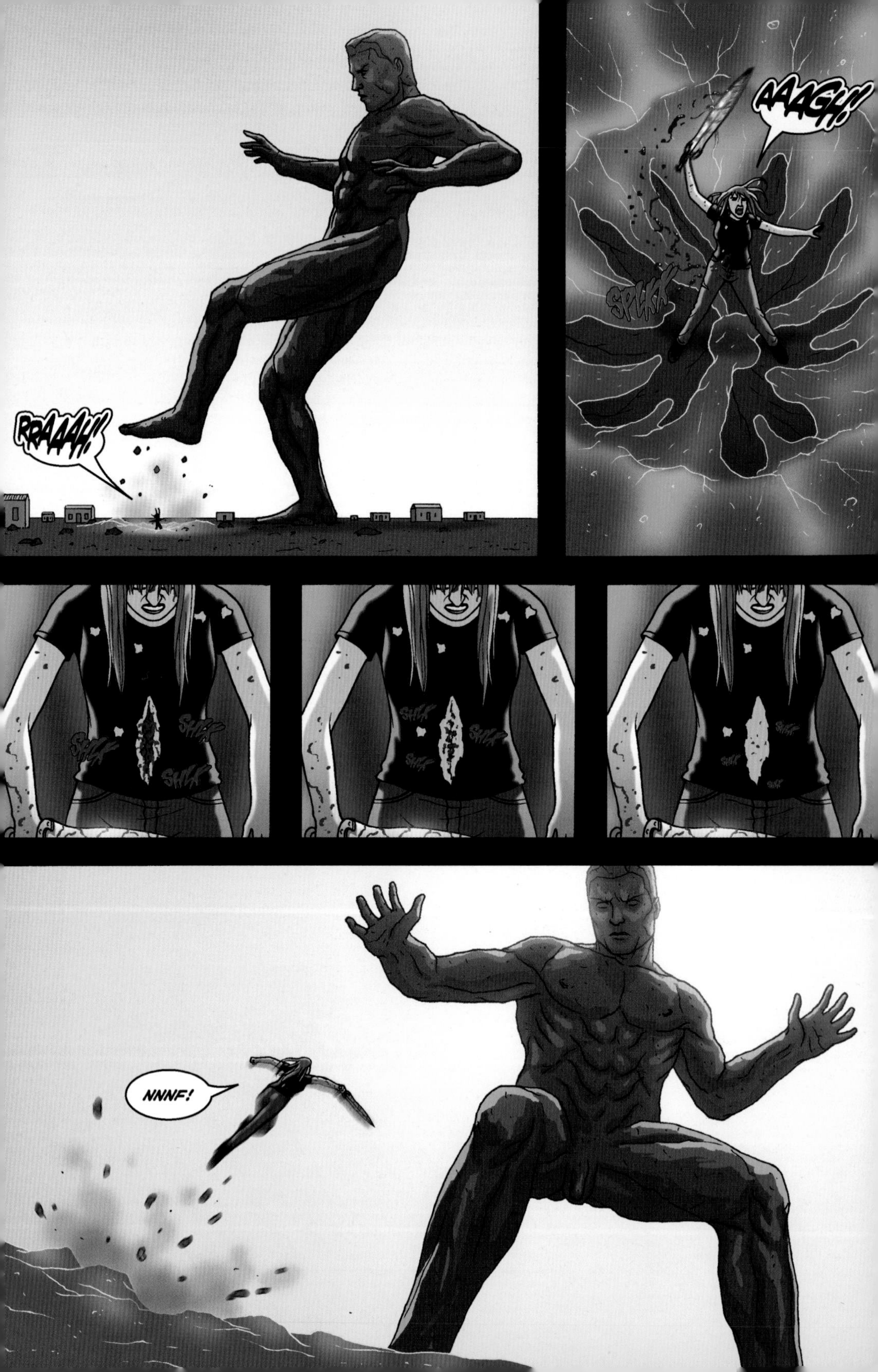
RRAAAH!!
AAAGH!!
SPLKT
SHLK
SHLK
SHLK
SHLK
SHLK
SHLK
SHLK
SHLK
SHLK
NNNF!

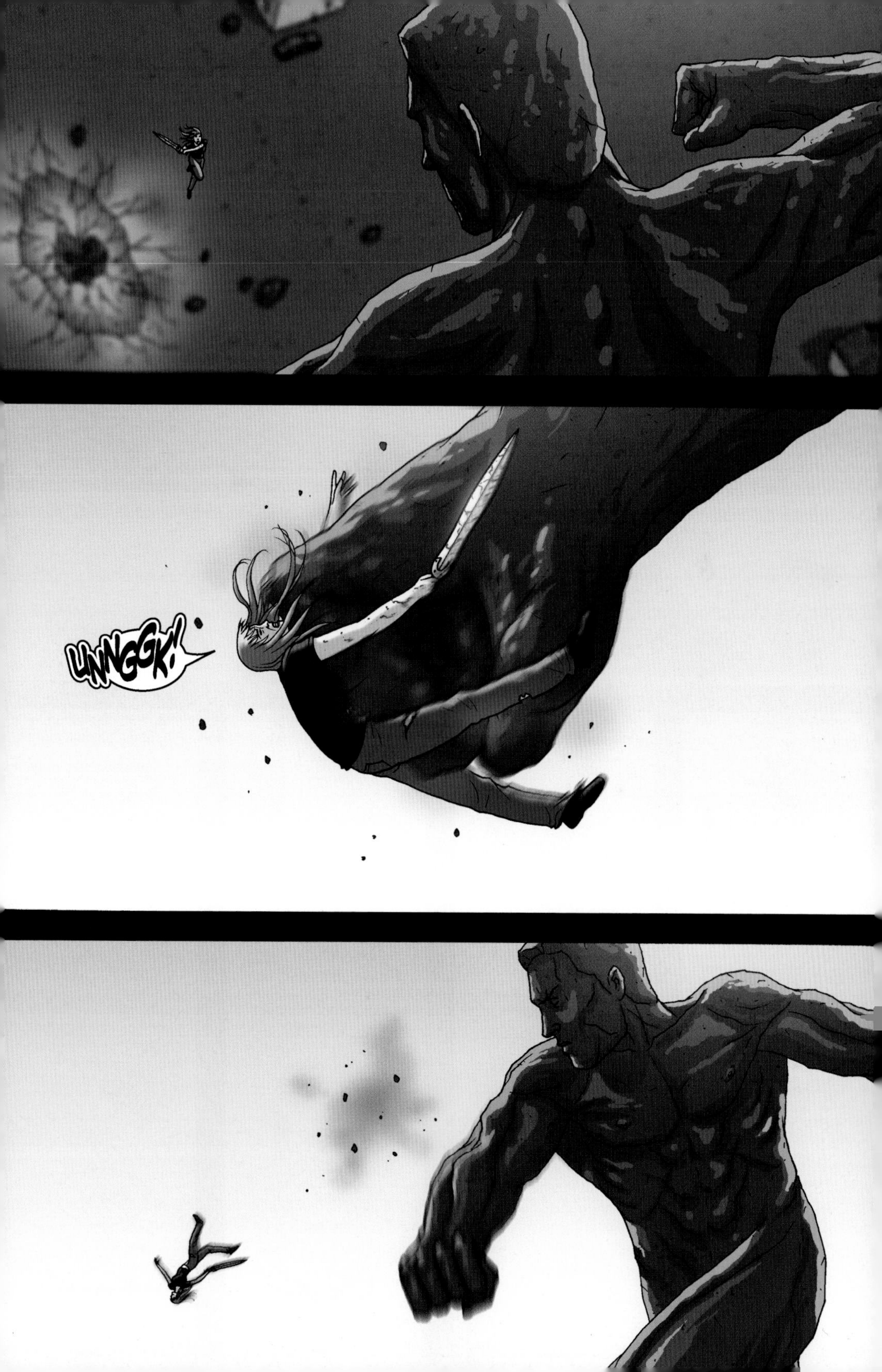
UNNGGK!

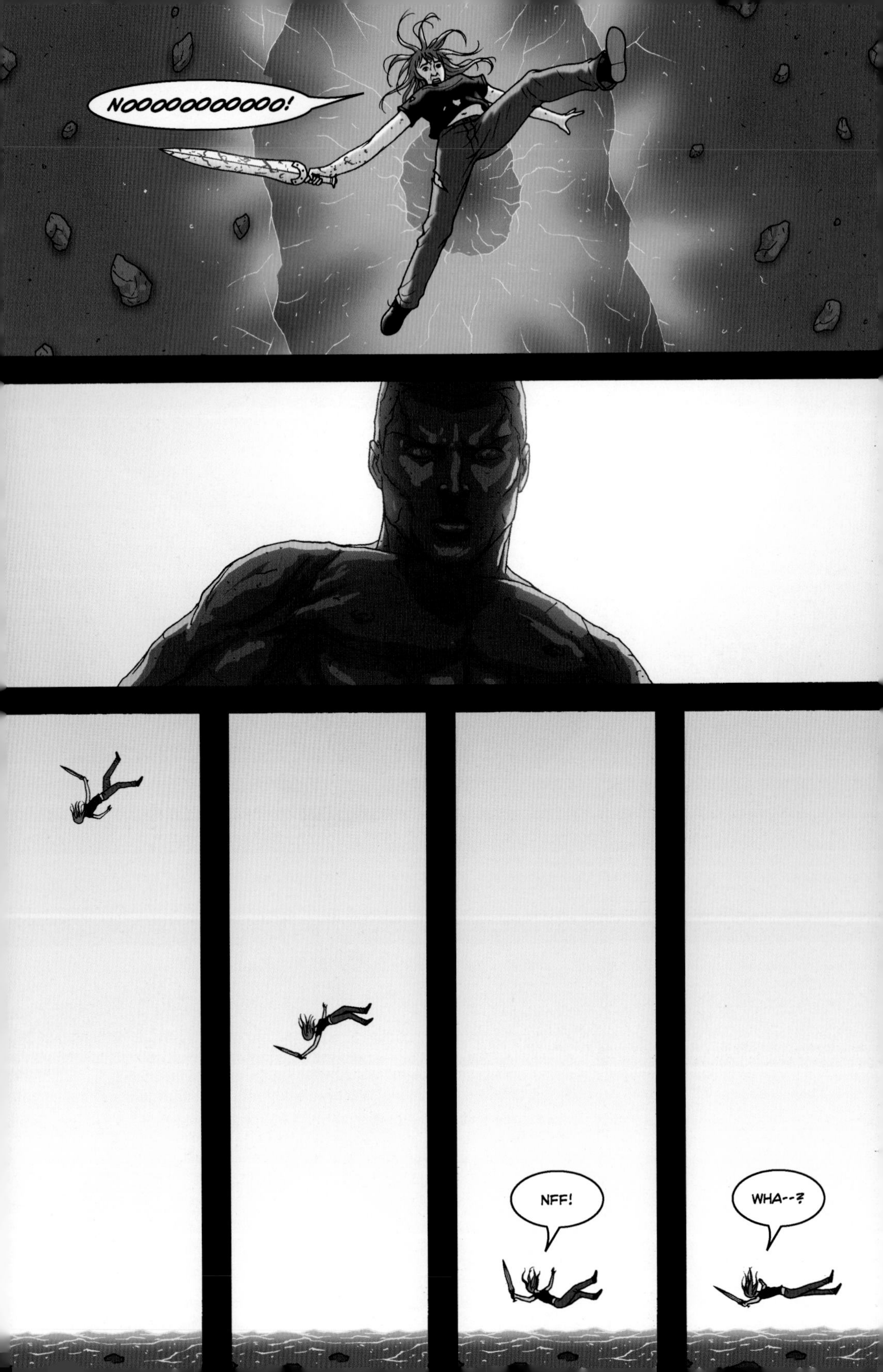
NOOOOOOOOOOO!
NFF!
WHA--?

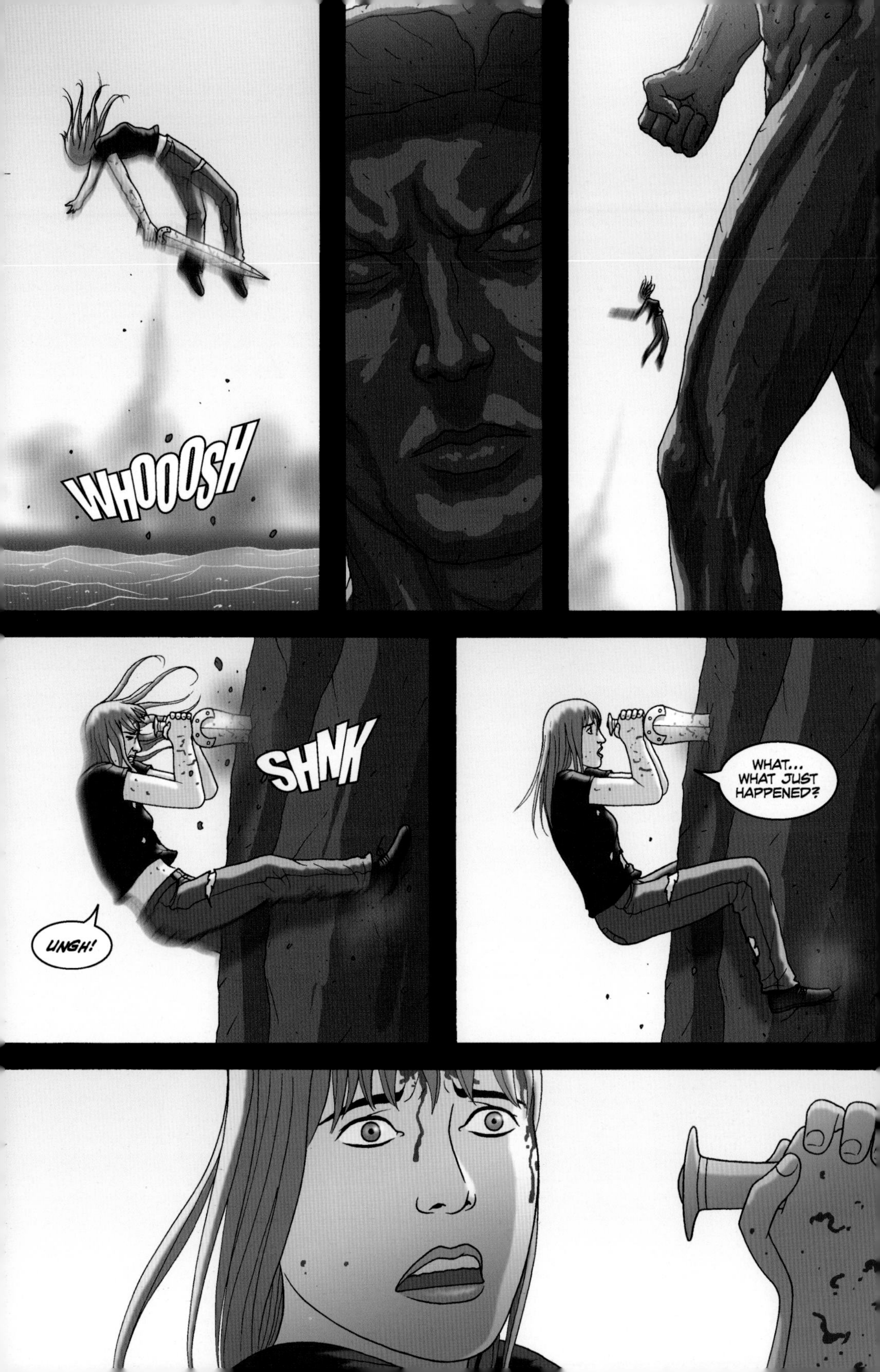
WHOOOSH
SHNK
UNGH!
WHAT... WHAT JUST HAPPENED?

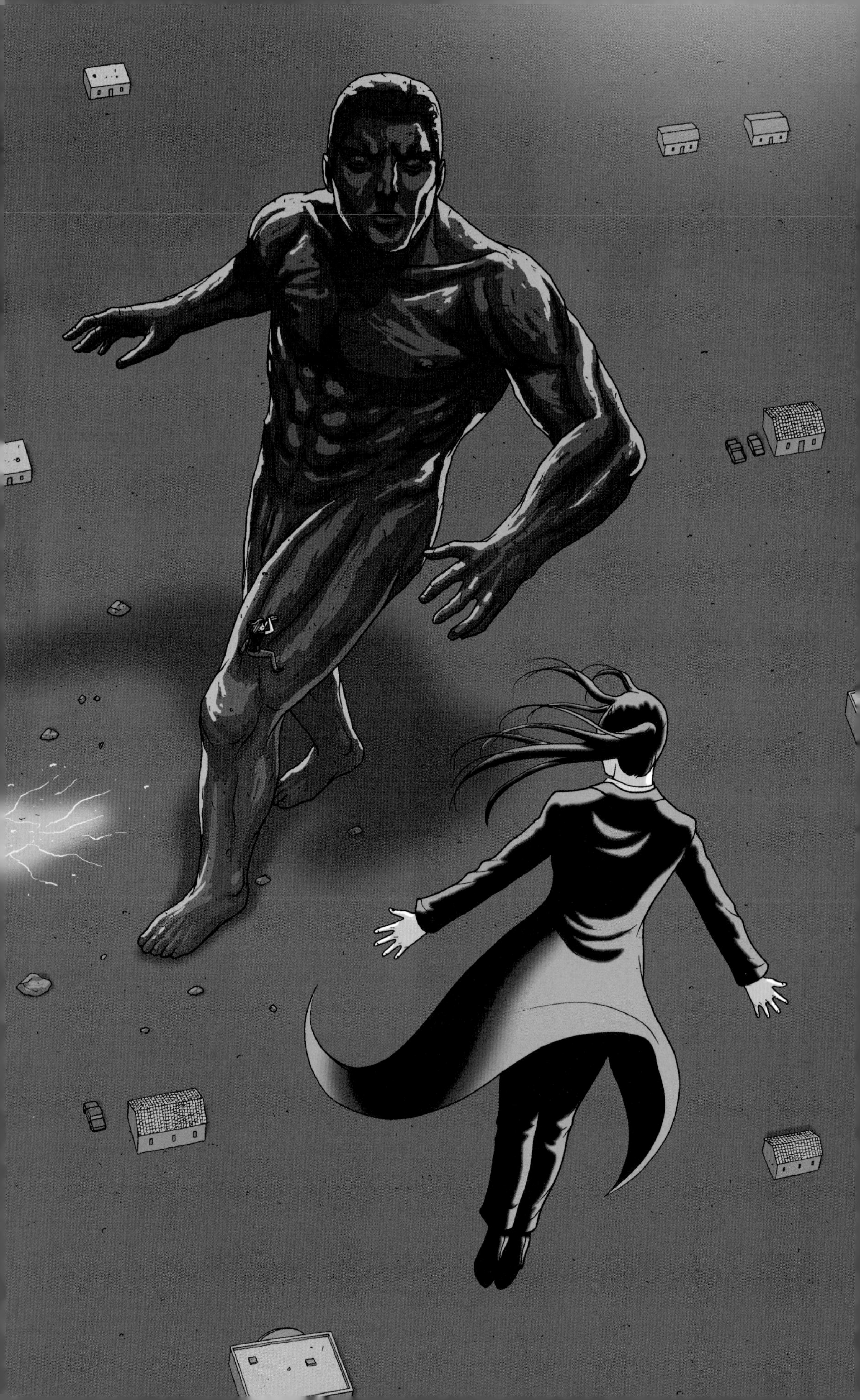

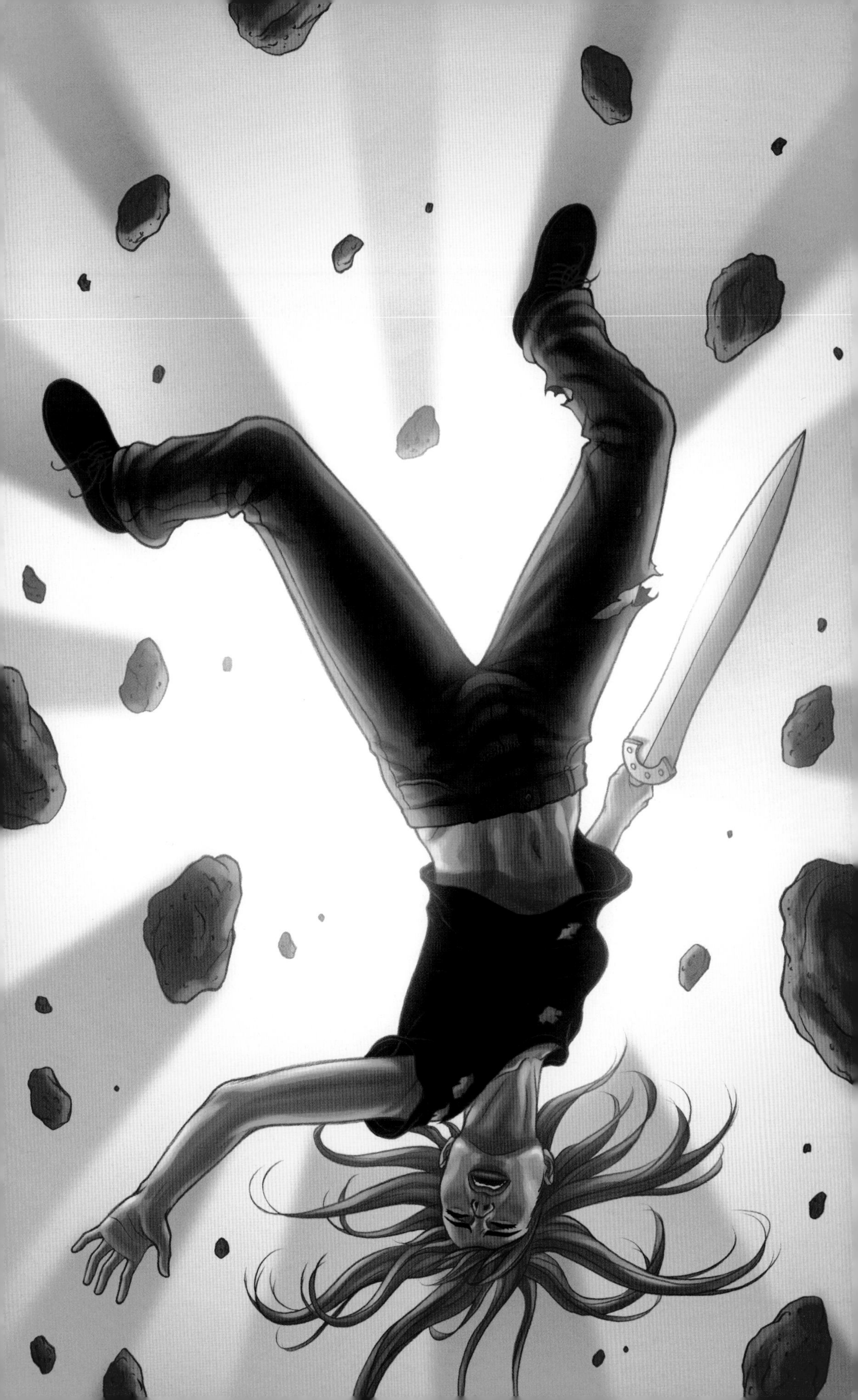

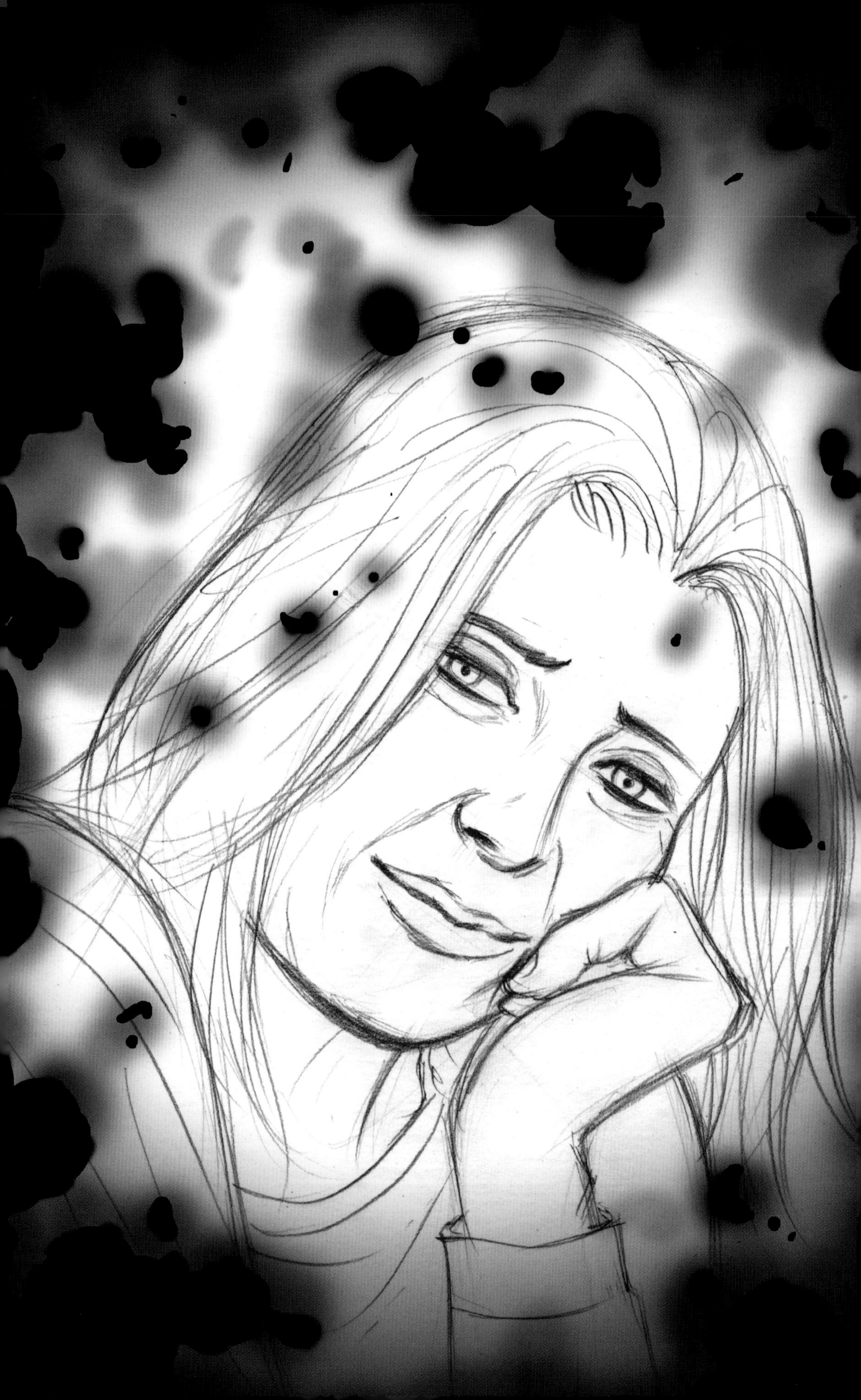

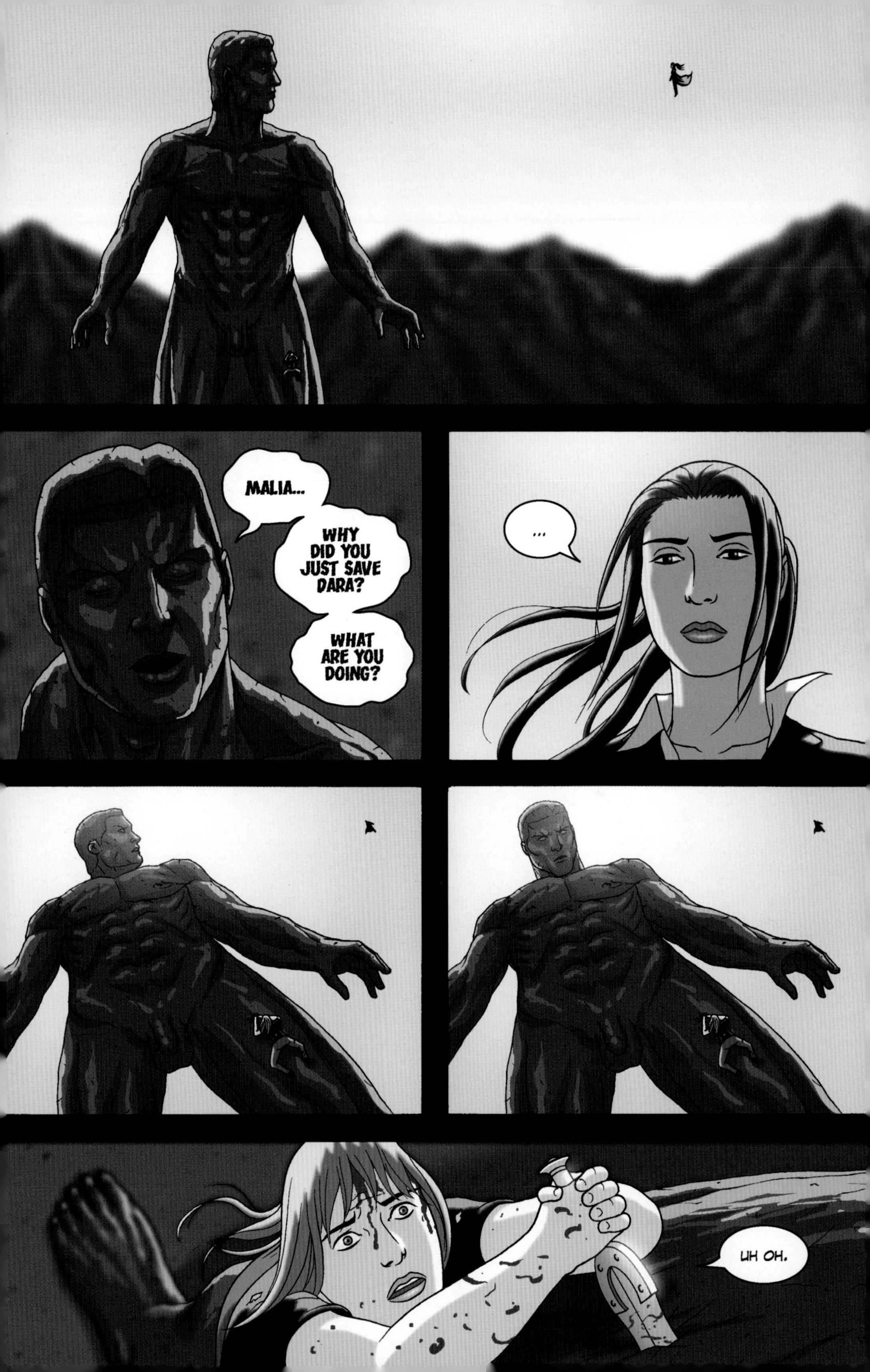

MALIA...
WHY DID YOU JUST SAVE DARA?
WHAT ARE YOU DOING?
...
UH OH.

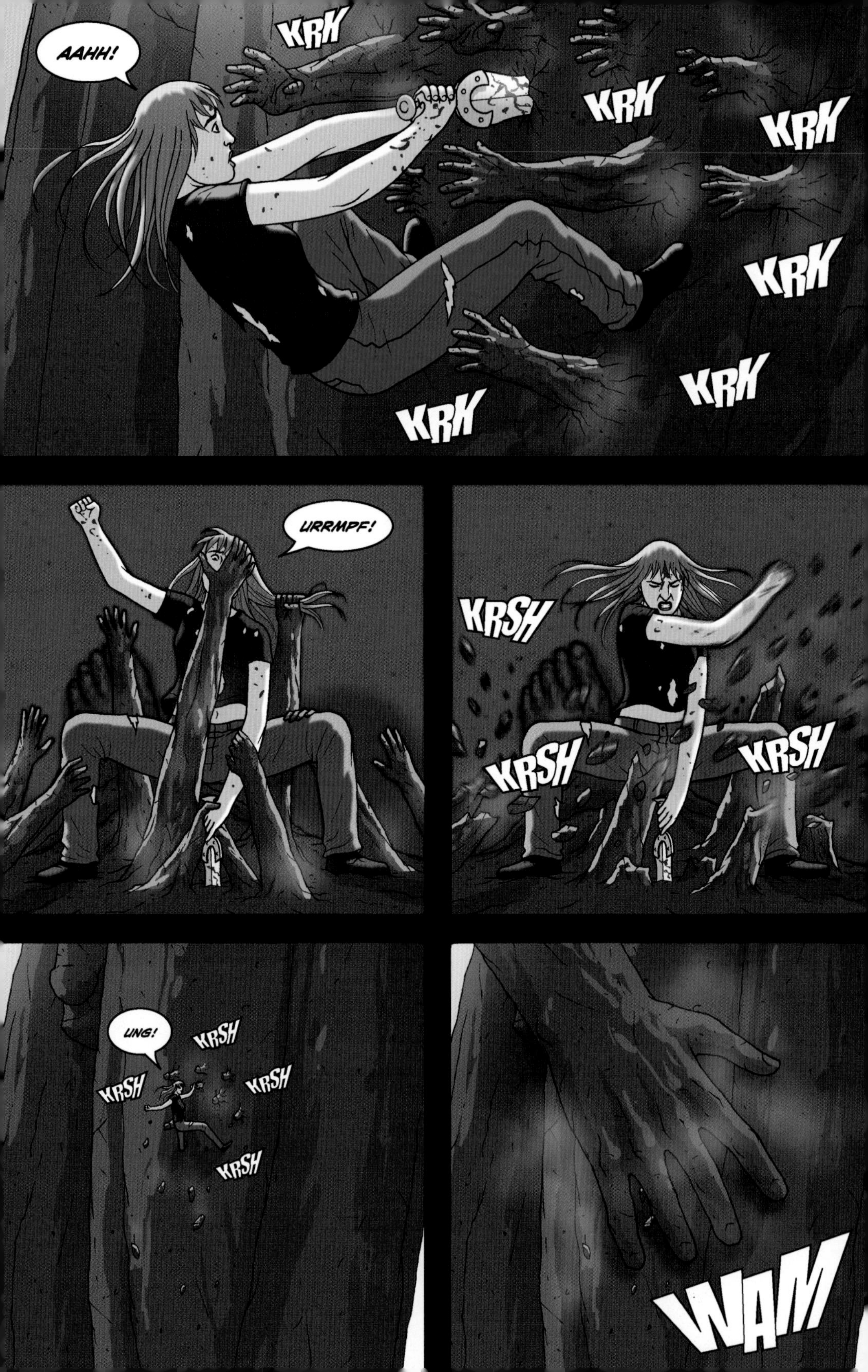
AAHH!
KRK
KRK
KRK
KRK
KRK
KRK
URRMPF!
KRSH
KRSH
KRSH
UNG!
KRSH
KRSH
KRSH
KRSH
WAM

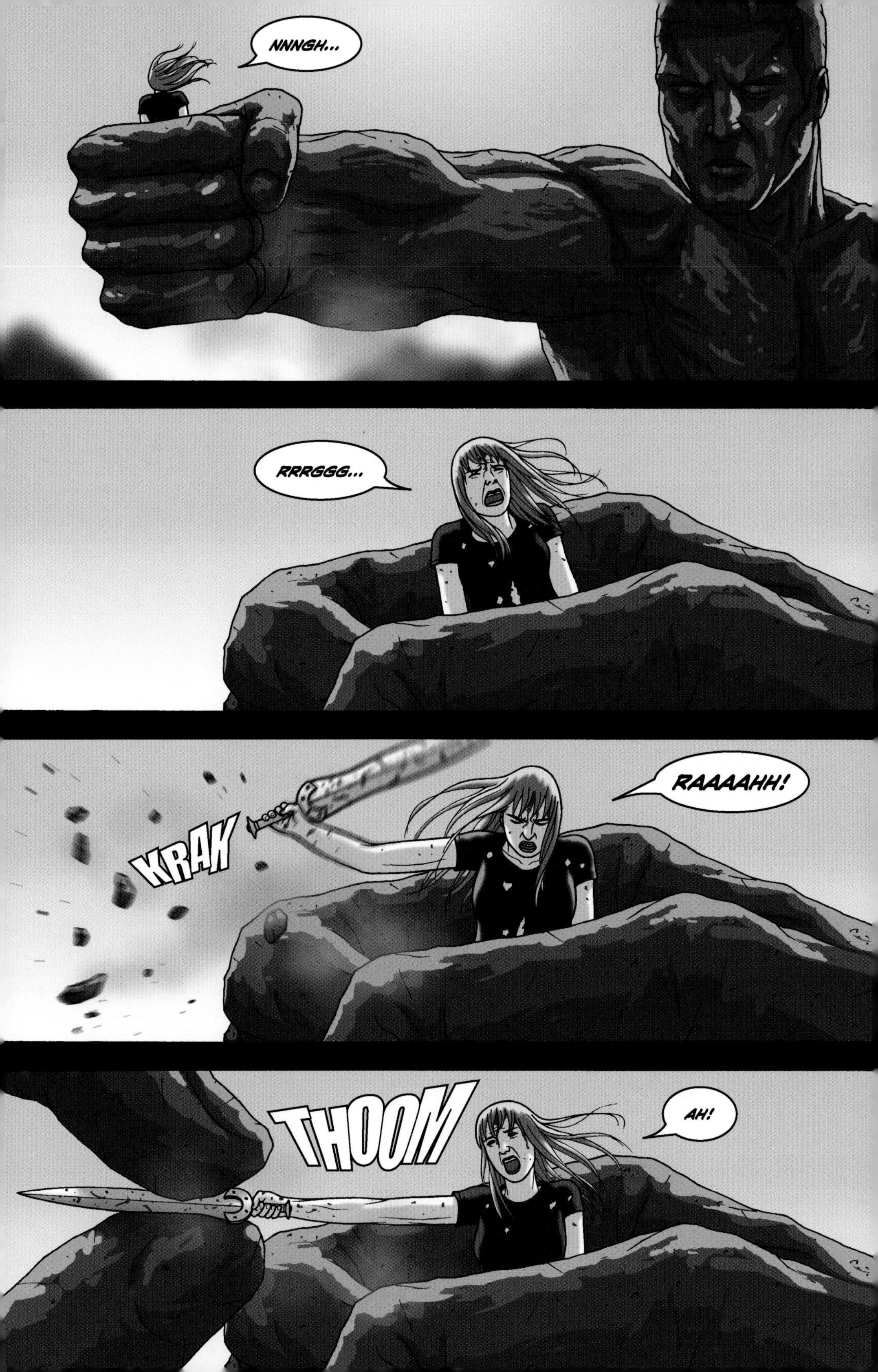
NNNGH...
RRRGGG...
KRAK
RAAAAHH!
THOOM
AH!

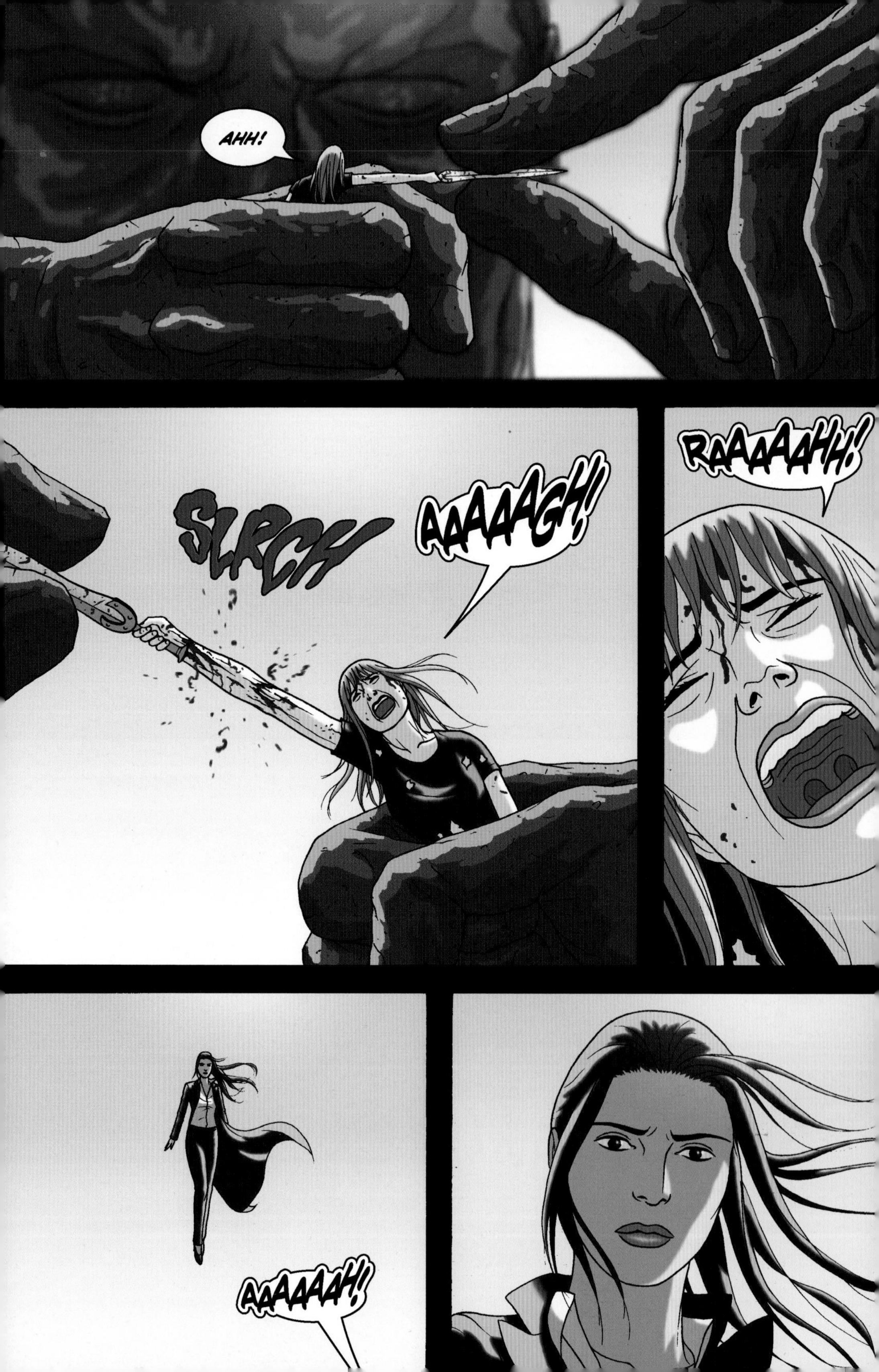
AHH!
SLRCH
AAAAAGH!
RAAAAAHH!
AAAAAAH!

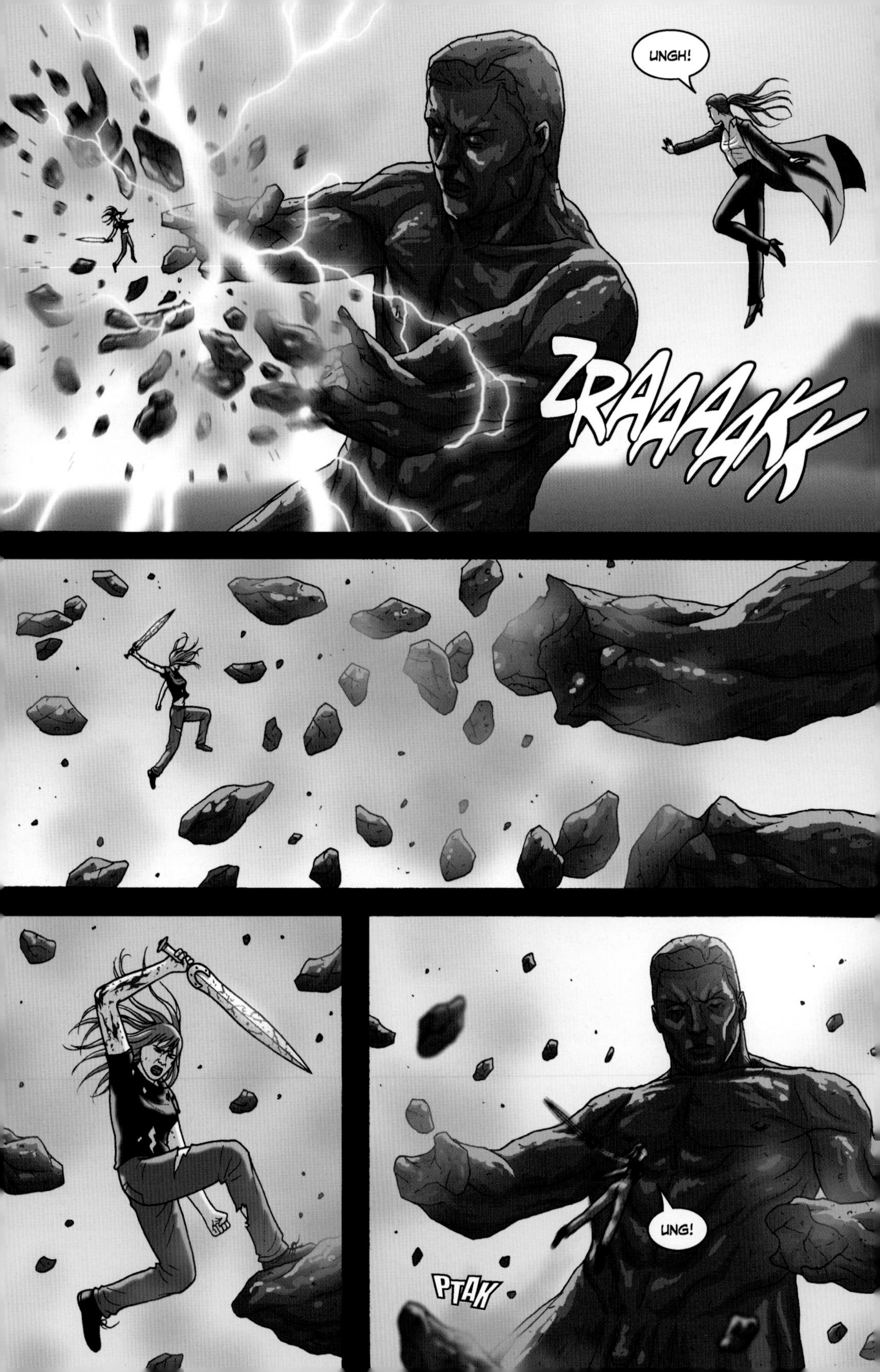
UNGH!
ZRAAAAK
UNG!
PTAK

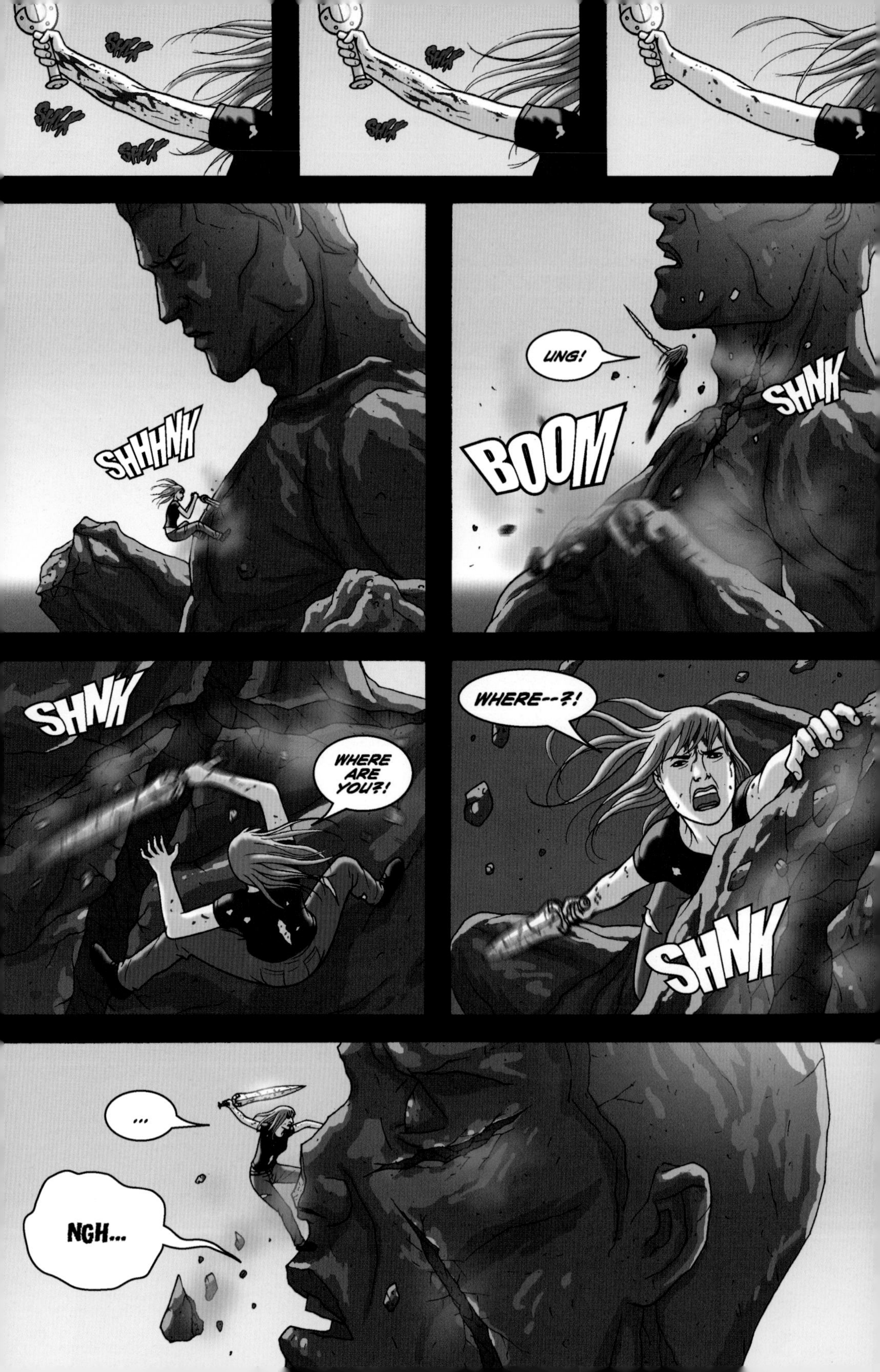
SHKK
SHKK
SHKK
SHKK
SHKK
SHHHNK
UNG!
BOOM
SHNK
SHNK
WHERE ARE YOU?!
WHERE--?!
SHNK
...
NGH...

...
KRK
KRK
KRK
KRK
KRK
KRK
KRK
KRK
KRK
KRK
KRK
KRK
KRK

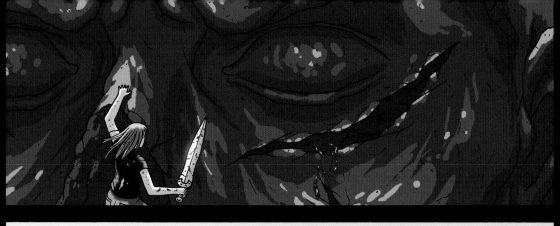

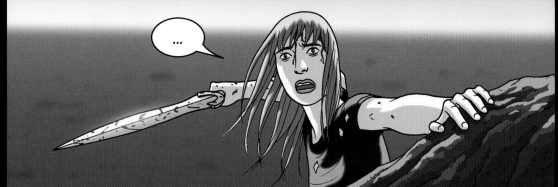

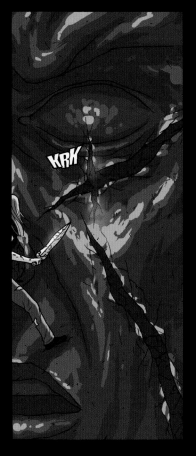

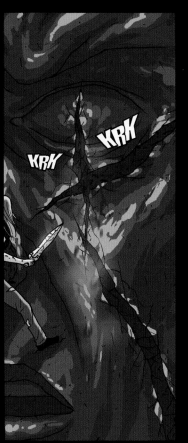

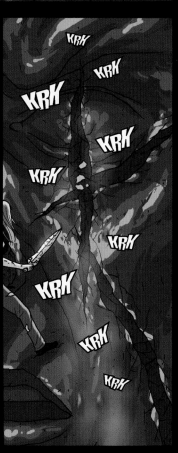

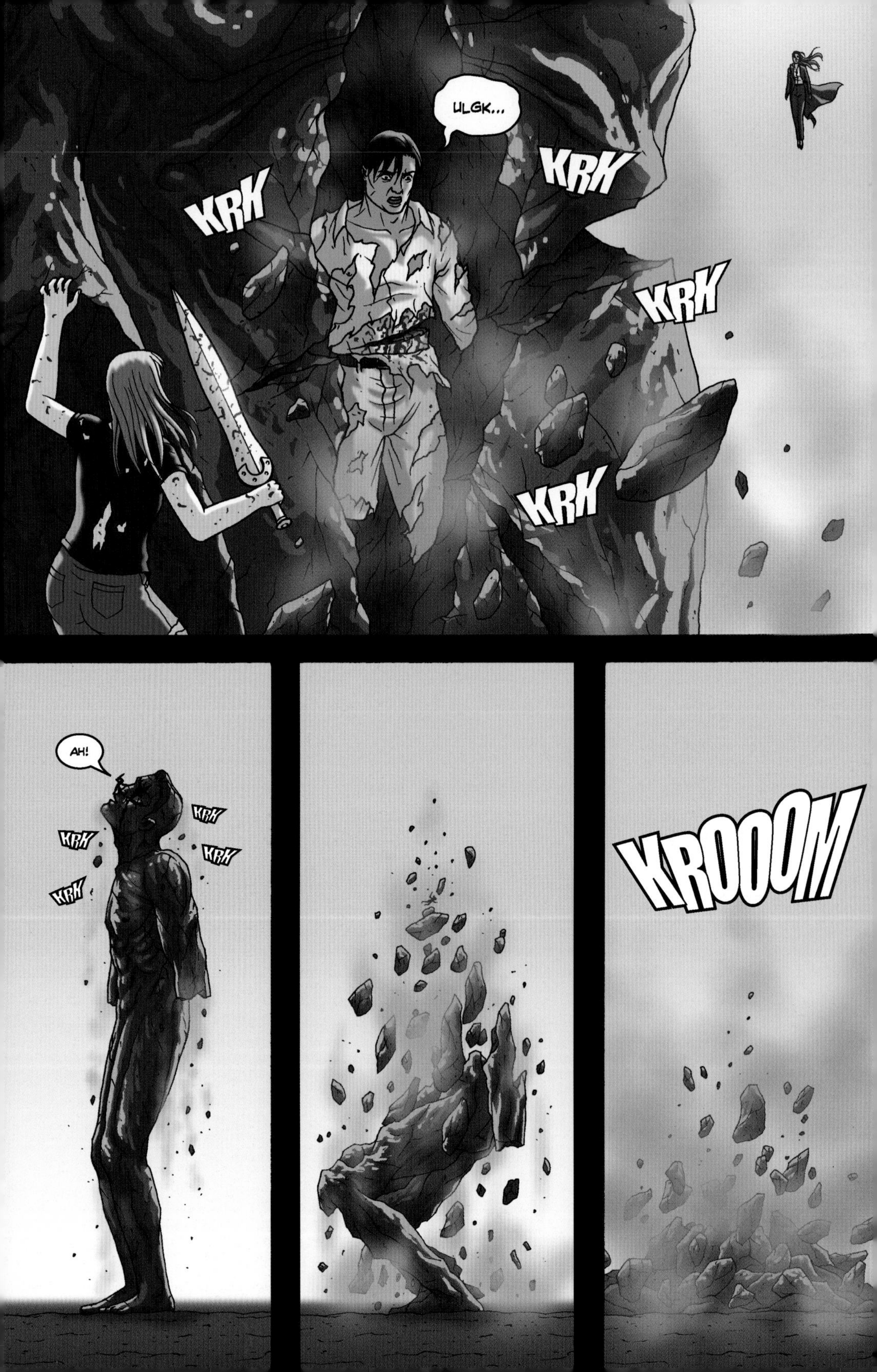
ULGK...
KRK
KRK
KRK
KRK
AH!
KRK
KRK
KRK
KRK
KROOOM

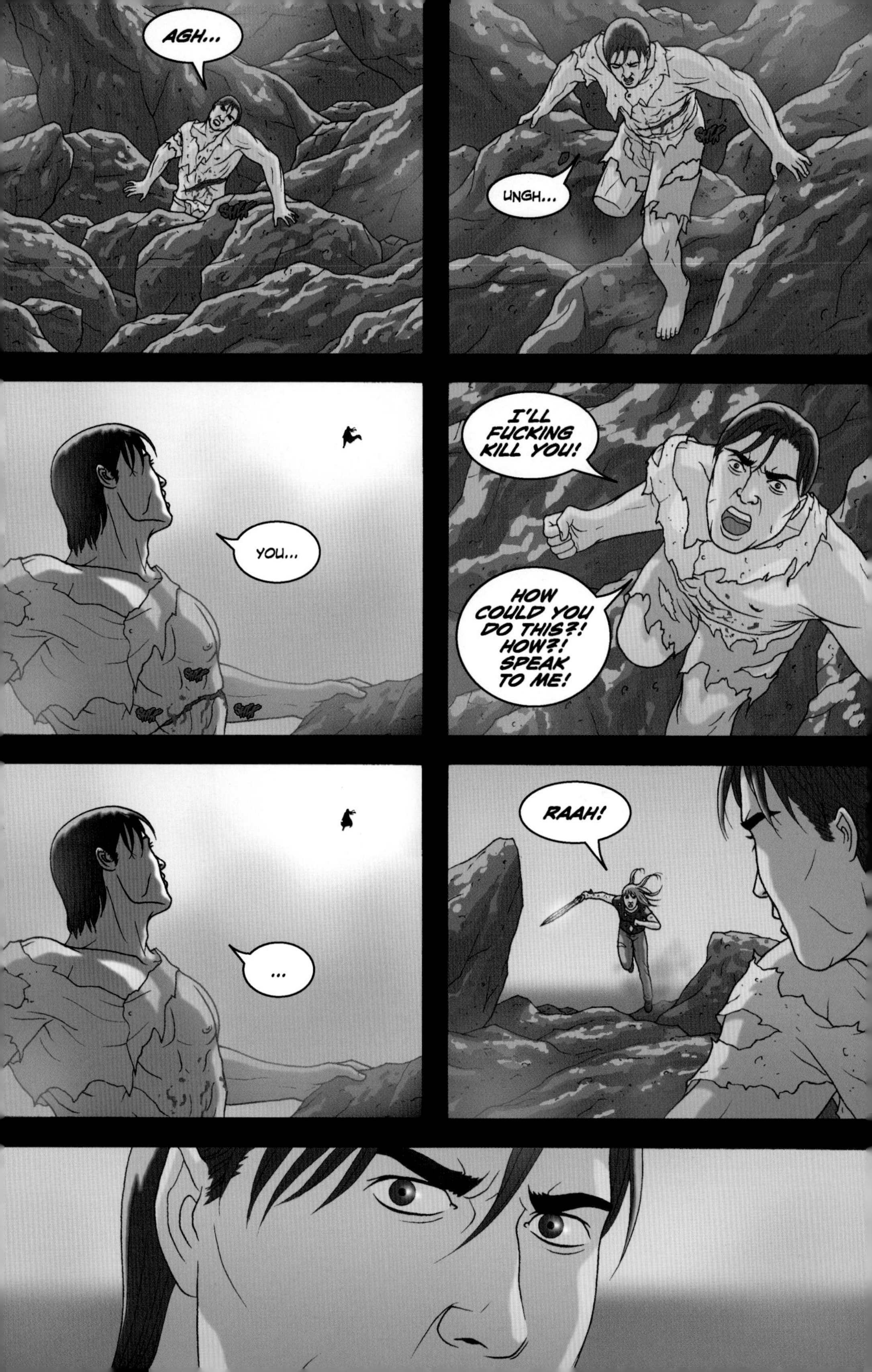
AGH...
UNGH...
YOU...
I'LL FUCKING KILL YOU!
HOW COULD YOU DO THIS?! HOW?! SPEAK TO ME!
...
RAAH!

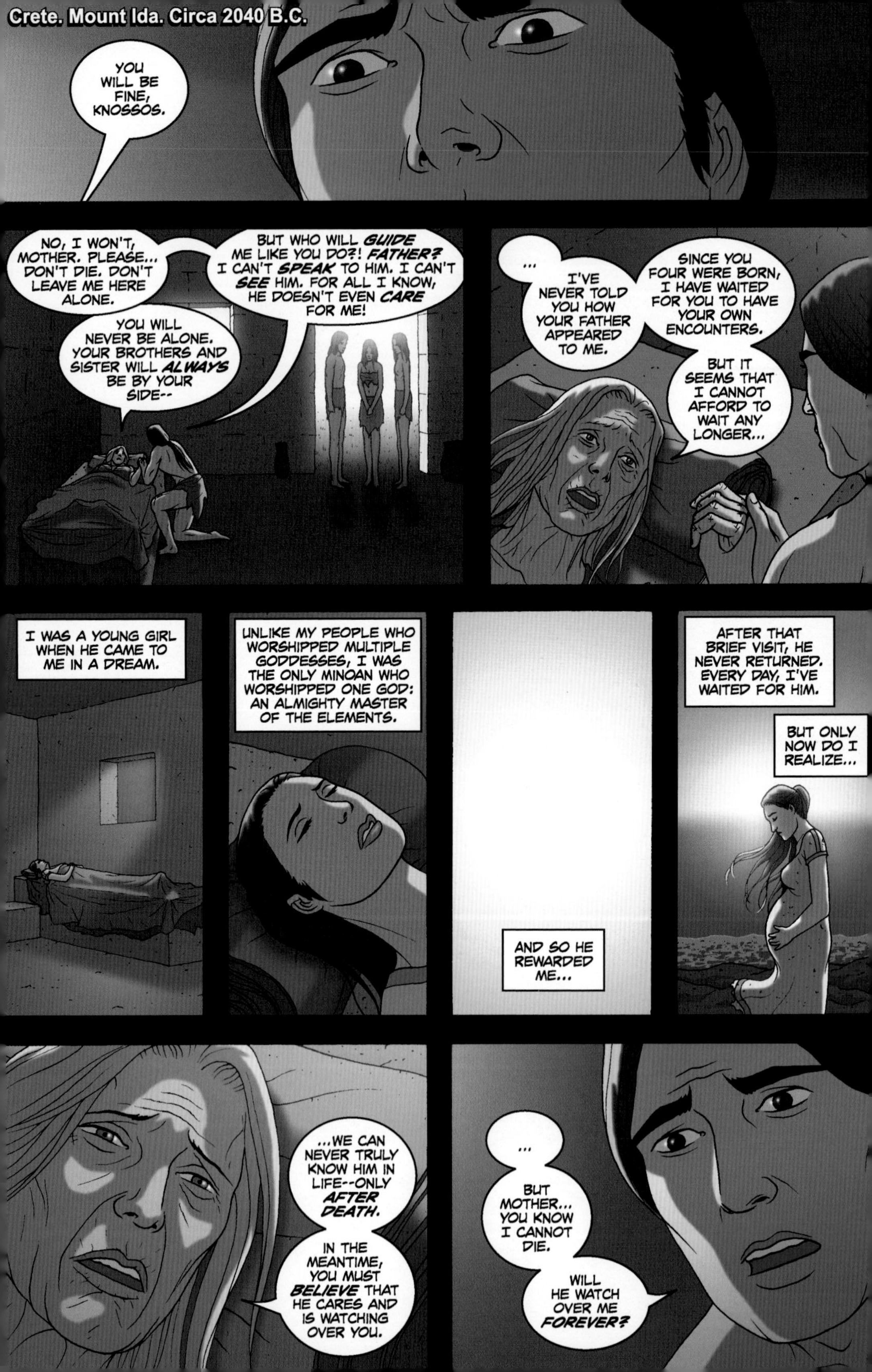

Crete. Mount Ida. Circa 2040 B.C.
YOU WILL BE FINE, KNOSSOS.
NO, I WON'T, MOTHER. PLEASE... DON'T DIE. DON'T LEAVE ME HERE ALONE.
BUT WHO WILL GUIDE ME LIKE YOU DO?! FATHER? I CAN'T SPEAK TO HIM. I CAN'T SEE HIM. FOR ALL I KNOW, HE DOESN'T EVEN CARE FOR ME!
YOU WILL NEVER BE ALONE. YOUR BROTHERS AND SISTER WILL ALWAYS BE BY YOUR SIDE--
...
I'VE NEVER TOLD YOU HOW YOUR FATHER APPEARED TO ME.
SINCE YOU FOUR WERE BORN, I HAVE WAITED FOR YOU TO HAVE YOUR OWN ENCOUNTERS.
BUT IT SEEMS THAT I CANNOT AFFORD TO WAIT ANY LONGER...
I WAS A YOUNG GIRL WHEN HE CAME TO ME IN A DREAM.
UNLIKE MY PEOPLE WHO WORSHIPPED MULTIPLE GODDESSES, I WAS THE ONLY MINOAN WHO WORSHIPPED ONE GOD: AN ALMIGHTY MASTER OF THE ELEMENTS.
AND SO HE REWARDED ME...
AFTER THAT BRIEF VISIT, HE NEVER RETURNED. EVERY DAY, I'VE WAITED FOR HIM.
BUT ONLY NOW DO I REALIZE...
...WE CAN NEVER TRULY KNOW HIM IN LIFE--ONLY AFTER DEATH.
IN THE MEANTIME, YOU MUST BELIEVE THAT HE CARES AND IS WATCHING OVER YOU.
...
BUT MOTHER... YOU KNOW I CANNOT DIE.
WILL HE WATCH OVER ME FOREVER?

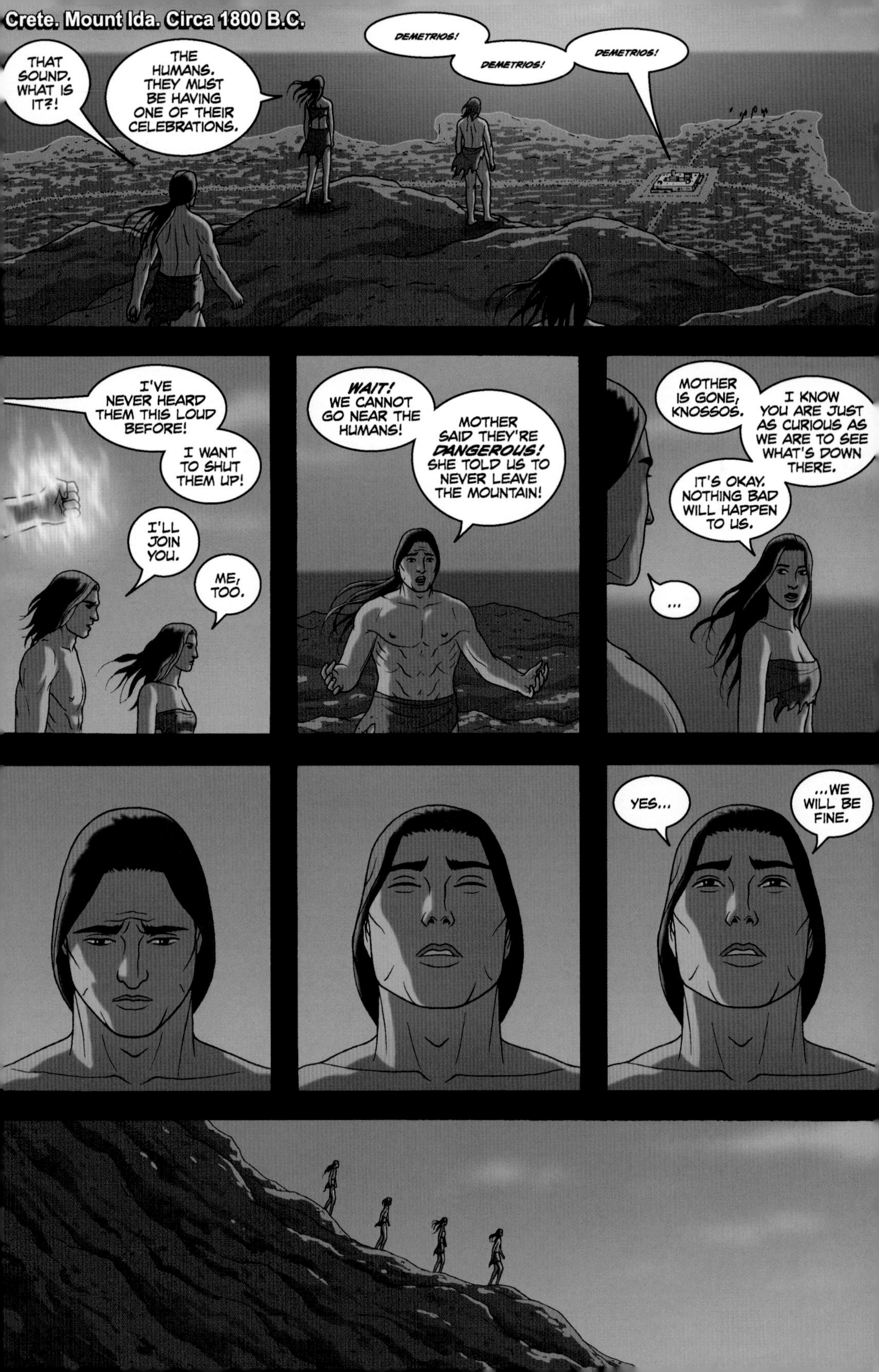

Crete. Mount Ida. Circa 1800 B.C.
THAT SOUND. WHAT IS IT?!
THE HUMANS. THEY MUST BE HAVING ONE OF THEIR CELEBRATIONS.
DEMETRIOS!
DEMETRIOS!
DEMETRIOS!
I'VE NEVER HEARD THEM THIS LOUD BEFORE!
I WANT TO SHUT THEM UP!
I'LL JOIN YOU.
ME, TOO.
WAIT! WE CANNOT GO NEAR THE HUMANS!
MOTHER SAID THEY'RE DANGEROUS! SHE TOLD US TO NEVER LEAVE THE MOUNTAIN!
MOTHER IS GONE, KNOSSOS.
I KNOW YOU ARE JUST AS CURIOUS AS WE ARE TO SEE WHAT'S DOWN THERE.
IT'S OKAY. NOTHING BAD WILL HAPPEN TO US.
...
YES...
...WE WILL BE FINE.

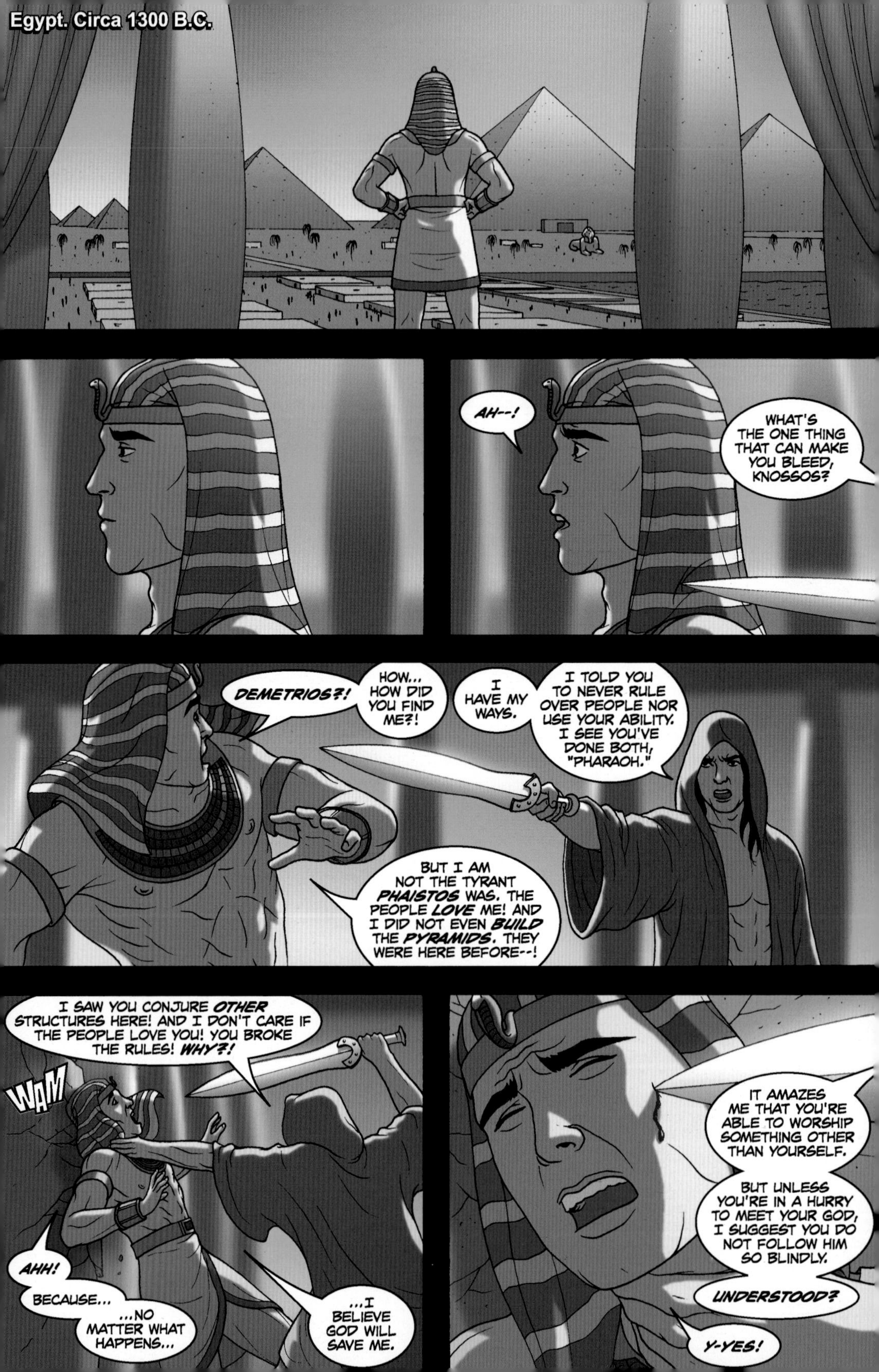

Egypt. Circa 1300 B.C.
AH--!
WHAT'S THE ONE THING THAT CAN MAKE YOU BLEED, KNOSSOS?
DEMETRIOS?!
HOW... HOW DID YOU FIND ME?!
I HAVE MY WAYS.
I TOLD YOU TO NEVER RULE OVER PEOPLE NOR USE YOUR ABILITY. I SEE YOU'VE DONE BOTH, "PHARAOH."
BUT I AM NOT THE TYRANT PHAISTOS WAS. THE PEOPLE LOVE ME! AND I DID NOT EVEN BUILD THE PYRAMIDS. THEY WERE HERE BEFORE--!
I SAW YOU CONJURE OTHER STRUCTURES HERE! AND I DON'T CARE IF THE PEOPLE LOVE YOU! YOU BROKE THE RULES! WHY?!
WAM
AHH!
BECAUSE...
...NO MATTER WHAT HAPPENS...
...I BELIEVE GOD WILL SAVE ME.
IT AMAZES ME THAT YOU'RE ABLE TO WORSHIP SOMETHING OTHER THAN YOURSELF.
BUT UNLESS YOU'RE IN A HURRY TO MEET YOUR GOD, I SUGGEST YOU DO NOT FOLLOW HIM SO BLINDLY.
UNDERSTOOD?
Y-YES!

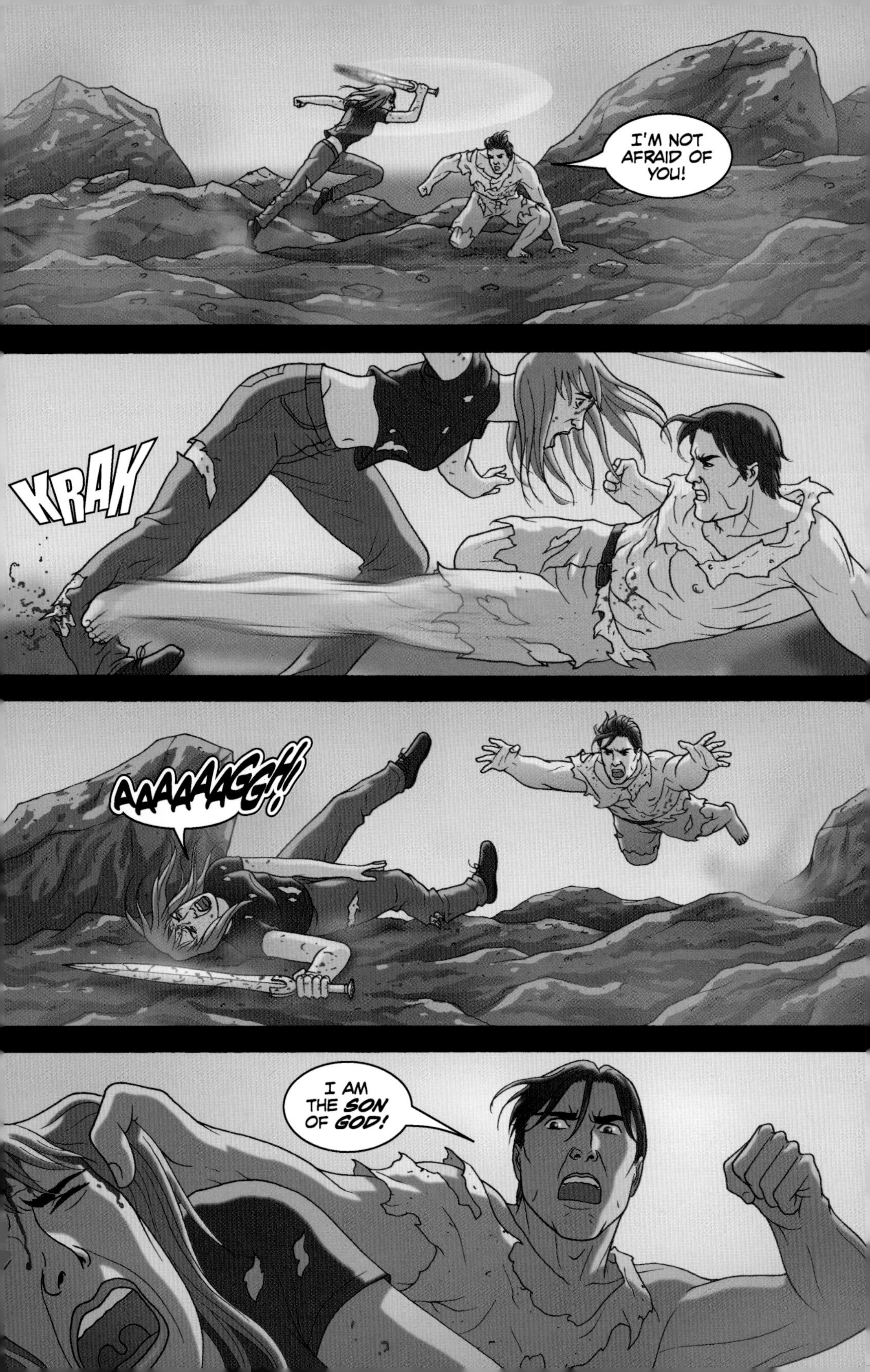
I'M NOT AFRAID OF YOU!
KRAK
AAAAAAGGH!
I AM THE SON OF GOD!

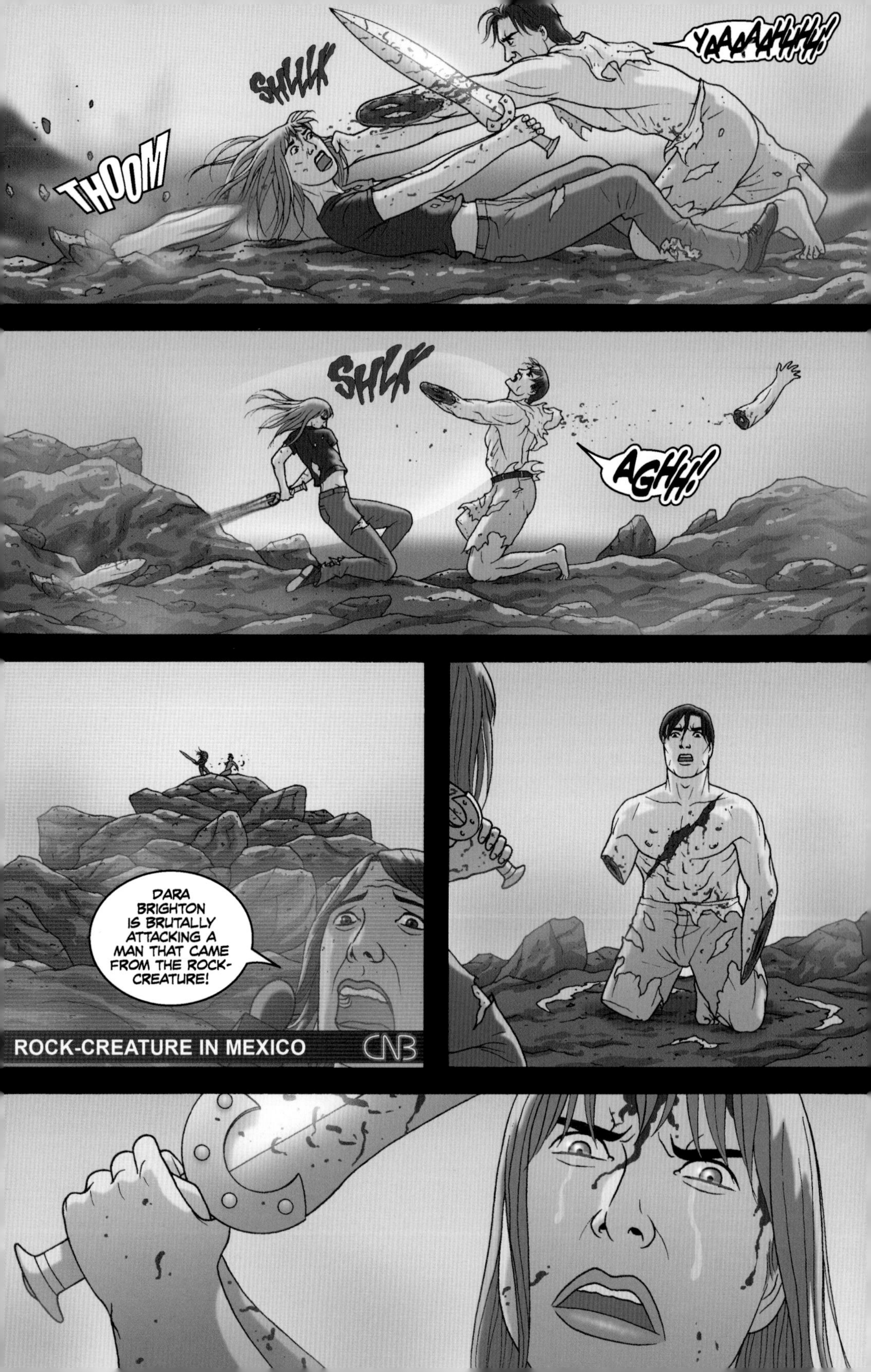
YAAAAAHHHH!
SHLLK
THOOM
SHLK
AGHH!
DARA BRIGHTON IS BRUTALLY ATTACKING A MAN THAT CAME FROM THE ROCK-CREATURE!
ROCK-CREATURE IN MEXICO
CNB

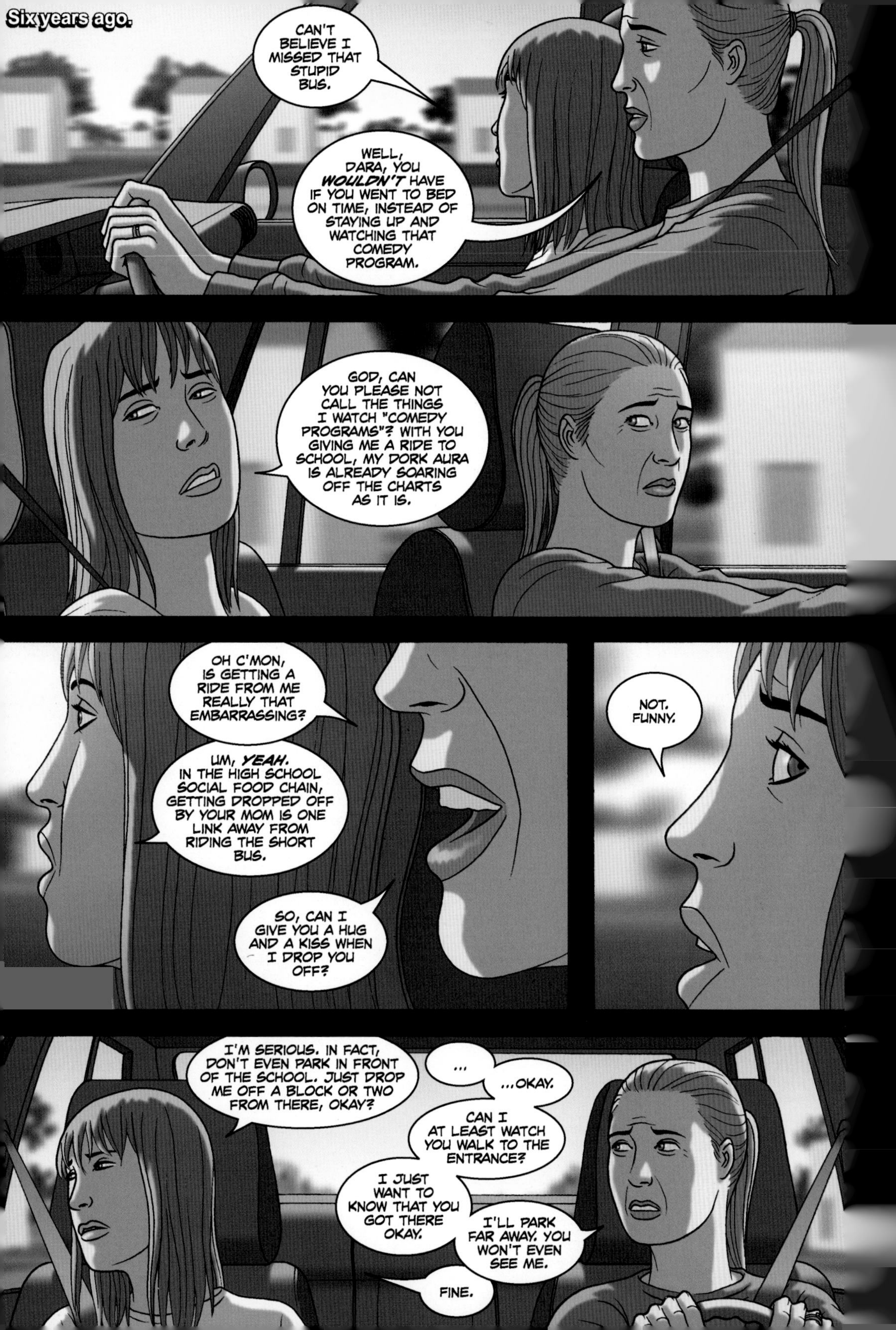
Six years ago.
CAN'T BELIEVE I MISSED THAT STUPID BUS.
WELL, DARA, YOU *WOULDN'T* HAVE IF YOU WENT TO BED ON TIME, INSTEAD OF STAYING UP AND WATCHING THAT COMEDY PROGRAM.
GOD, CAN YOU PLEASE NOT CALL THE THINGS I WATCH "COMEDY PROGRAMS"? WITH YOU GIVING ME A RIDE TO SCHOOL, MY DORK AURA IS ALREADY SOARING OFF THE CHARTS AS IT IS.
OH C'MON, IS GETTING A RIDE FROM ME REALLY THAT EMBARRASSING?
UM, *YEAH.* IN THE HIGH SCHOOL SOCIAL FOOD CHAIN, GETTING DROPPED OFF BY YOUR MOM IS ONE LINK AWAY FROM RIDING THE SHORT BUS.
SO, CAN I GIVE YOU A HUG AND A KISS WHEN I DROP YOU OFF?
NOT. FUNNY.
I'M SERIOUS. IN FACT, DON'T EVEN PARK IN FRONT OF THE SCHOOL. JUST DROP ME OFF A BLOCK OR TWO FROM THERE, OKAY?
...
...OKAY.
CAN I AT LEAST WATCH YOU WALK TO THE ENTRANCE?
I JUST WANT TO KNOW THAT YOU GOT THERE OKAY.
I'LL PARK FAR AWAY. YOU WON'T EVEN SEE ME.
FINE.

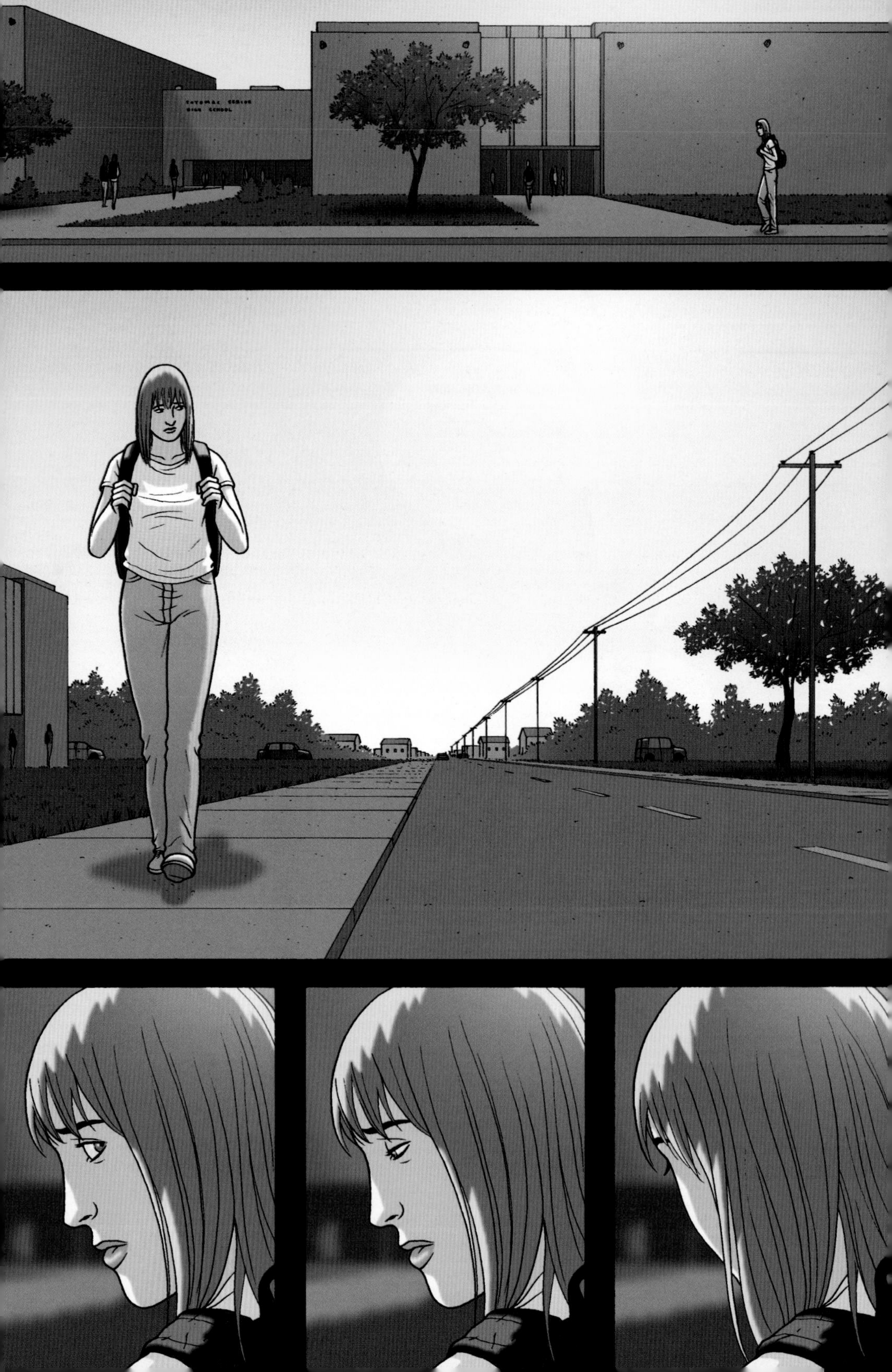

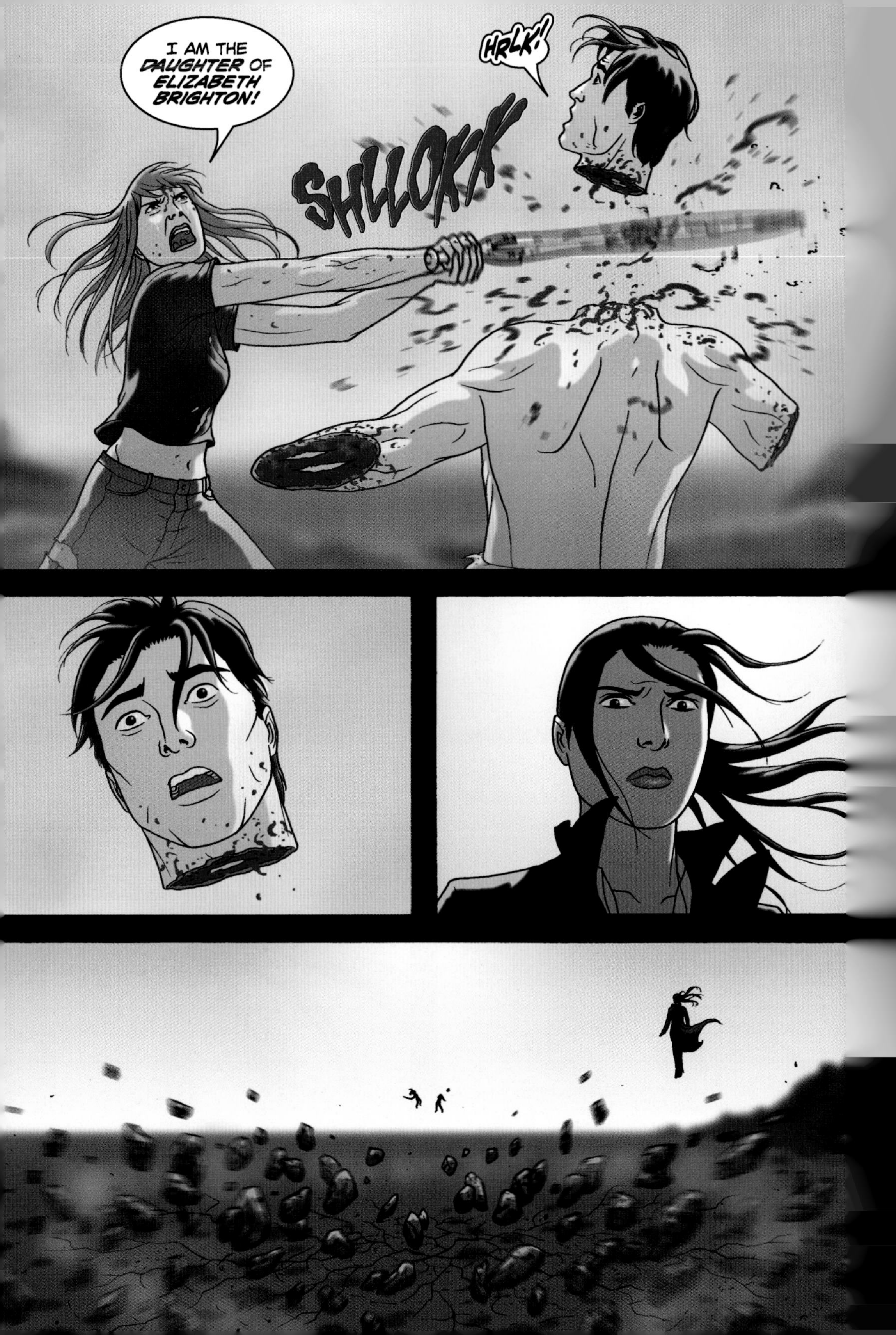
I AM THE DAUGHTER OF ELIZABETH BRIGHTON!
HRLK!
SHLLOKK

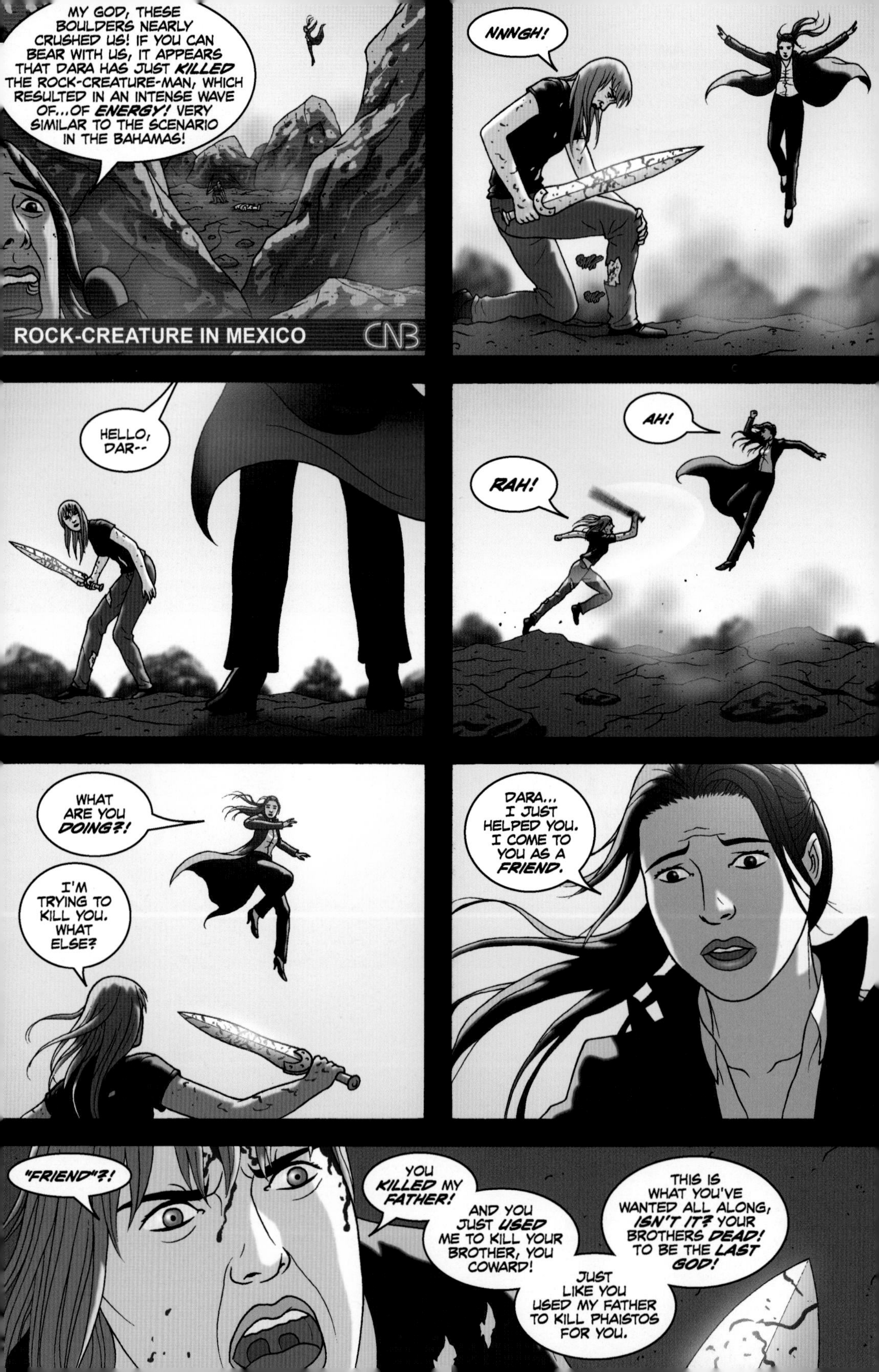
MY GOD, THESE BOULDERS NEARLY CRUSHED US! IF YOU CAN BEAR WITH US, IT APPEARS THAT DARA HAS JUST KILLED THE ROCK-CREATURE-MAN, WHICH RESULTED IN AN INTENSE WAVE OF...OF ENERGY! VERY SIMILAR TO THE SCENARIO IN THE BAHAMAS!
ROCK-CREATURE IN MEXICO
CNB
NNNGH!
HELLO, DAR--
AH!
RAH!
WHAT ARE YOU DOING?!
I'M TRYING TO KILL YOU. WHAT ELSE?
DARA... I JUST HELPED YOU. I COME TO YOU AS A FRIEND.
"FRIEND"?!
YOU KILLED MY FATHER!
AND YOU JUST USED ME TO KILL YOUR BROTHER, YOU COWARD!
JUST LIKE YOU USED MY FATHER TO KILL PHAISTOS FOR YOU.
THIS IS WHAT YOU'VE WANTED ALL ALONG, ISN'T IT? YOUR BROTHERS DEAD! TO BE THE LAST GOD!

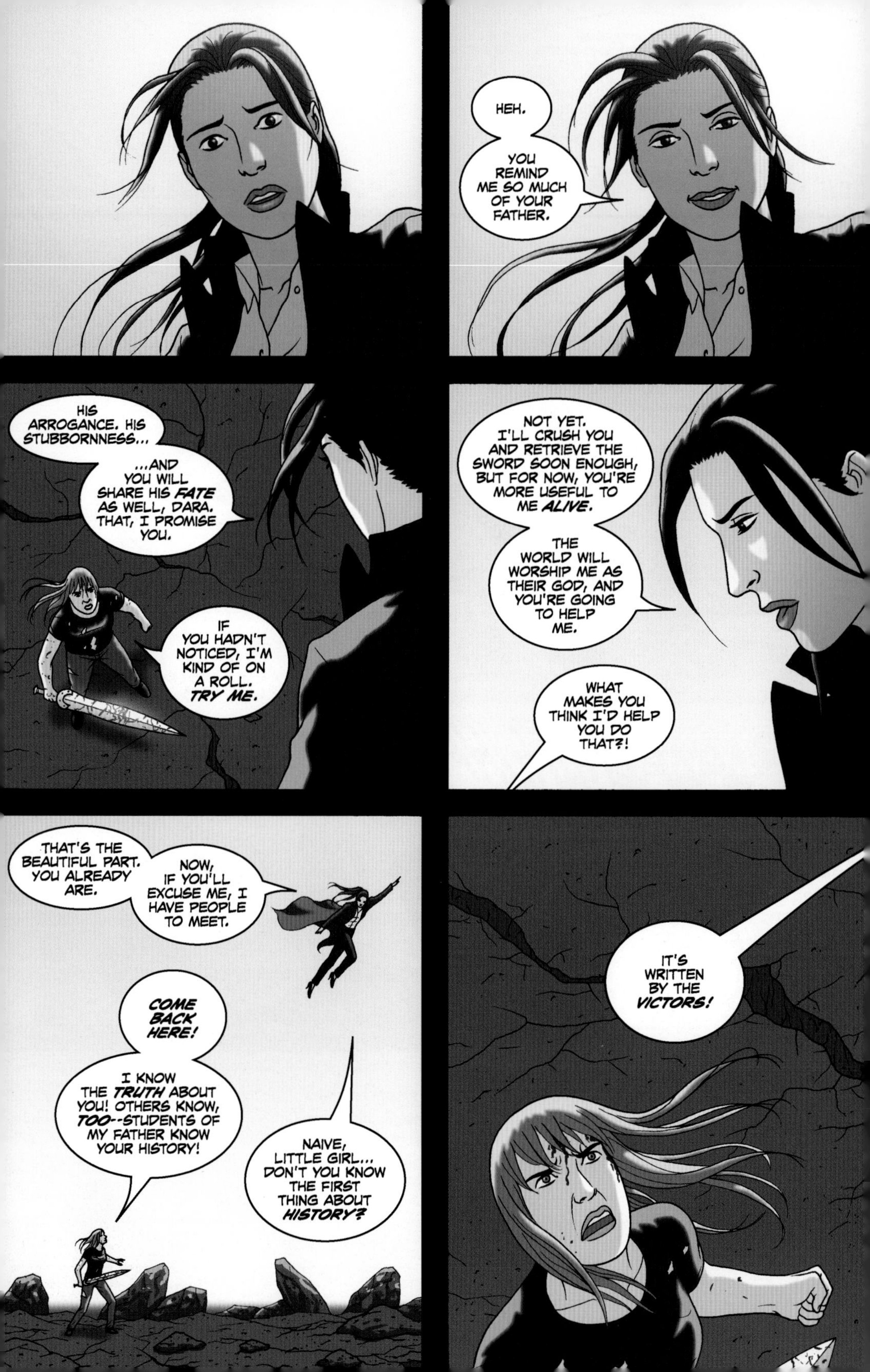

HEH.
YOU REMIND ME SO MUCH OF YOUR FATHER.
HIS ARROGANCE. HIS STUBBORNNESS...
...AND YOU WILL SHARE HIS FATE AS WELL, DARA. THAT, I PROMISE YOU.
IF YOU HADN'T NOTICED, I'M KIND OF ON A ROLL. TRY ME.
NOT YET. I'LL CRUSH YOU AND RETRIEVE THE SWORD SOON ENOUGH, BUT FOR NOW, YOU'RE MORE USEFUL TO ME ALIVE.
THE WORLD WILL WORSHIP ME AS THEIR GOD, AND YOU'RE GOING TO HELP ME.
WHAT MAKES YOU THINK I'D HELP YOU DO THAT?!
THAT'S THE BEAUTIFUL PART. YOU ALREADY ARE.
NOW, IF YOU'LL EXCUSE ME, I HAVE PEOPLE TO MEET.
COME BACK HERE!
I KNOW THE TRUTH ABOUT YOU! OTHERS KNOW, TOO--STUDENTS OF MY FATHER KNOW YOUR HISTORY!
NAIVE, LITTLE GIRL... DON'T YOU KNOW THE FIRST THING ABOUT HISTORY?
IT'S WRITTEN BY THE VICTORS!

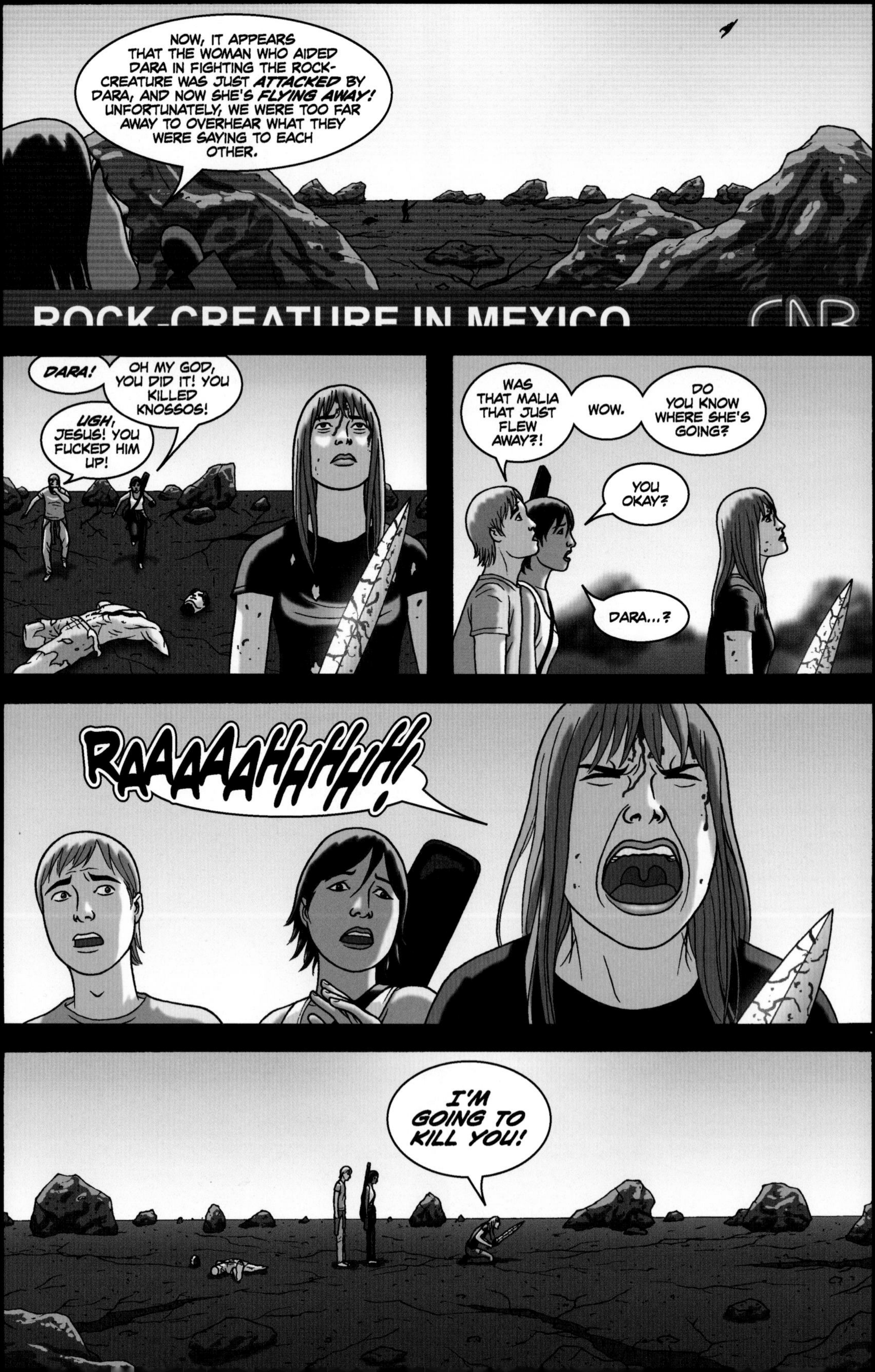
NOW, IT APPEARS THAT THE WOMAN WHO AIDED DARA IN FIGHTING THE ROCK-CREATURE WAS JUST ATTACKED BY DARA, AND NOW SHE'S FLYING AWAY! UNFORTUNATELY, WE WERE TOO FAR AWAY TO OVERHEAR WHAT THEY WERE SAYING TO EACH OTHER.
ROCK-CREATURE IN MEXICO
DARA!
OH MY GOD, YOU DID IT! YOU KILLED KNOSSOS!
UGH, JESUS! YOU FUCKED HIM UP!
WAS THAT MALIA THAT JUST FLEW AWAY?!
WOW.
DO YOU KNOW WHERE SHE'S GOING?
YOU OKAY?
DARA...?
RAAAAAHHHHH!
I'M GOING TO KILL YOU!

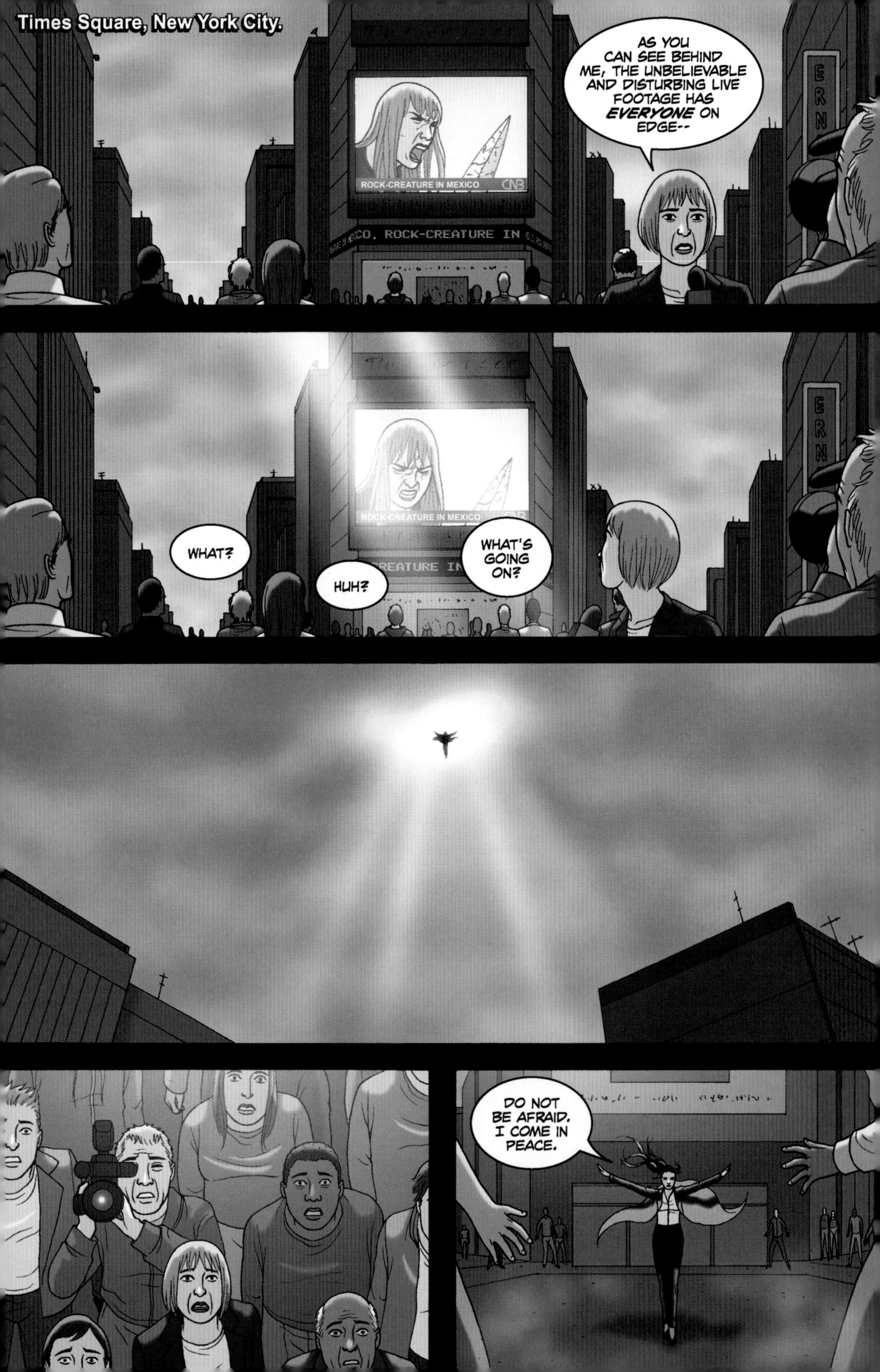

Times Square, New York City.
ROCK-CREATURE IN MEXICO
CO. ROCK-CREATURE IN
AS YOU CAN SEE BEHIND ME, THE UNBELIEVABLE AND DISTURBING LIVE FOOTAGE HAS EVERYONE ON EDGE--
ROCK-CREATURE IN MEXICO
WHAT?
HUH?
WHAT'S GOING ON?
DO NOT BE AFRAID. I COME IN PEACE.

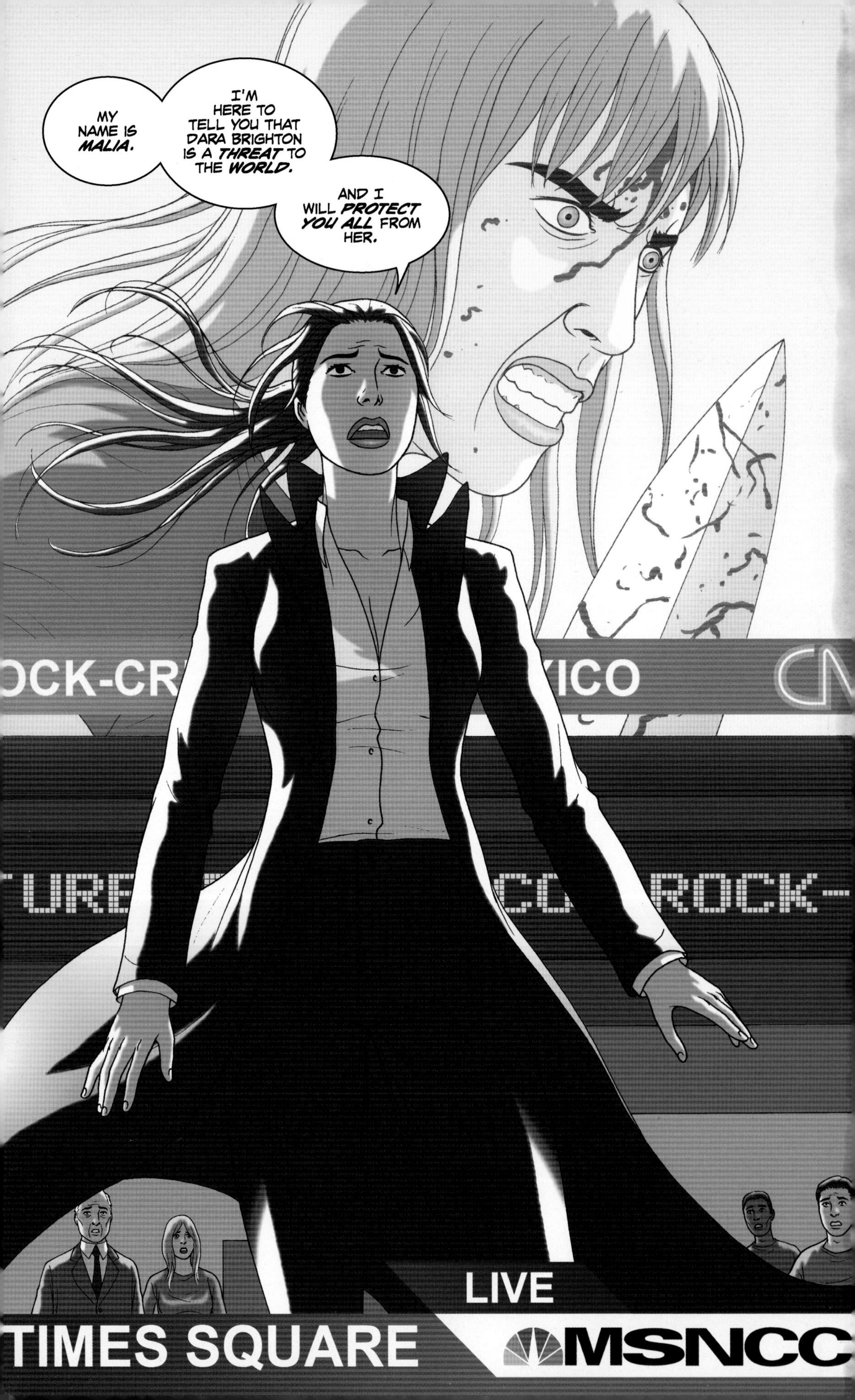
MY NAME IS *MALIA*.
I'M HERE TO TELL YOU THAT DARA BRIGHTON IS A *THREAT* TO THE *WORLD*.
AND I WILL *PROTECT YOU ALL* FROM HER.
LIVE
TIMES SQUARE
MSNCC

TO BE CONTINUED...

MORE GREAT IMAGE BOOKS FROM
THE LUNA BROTHERS

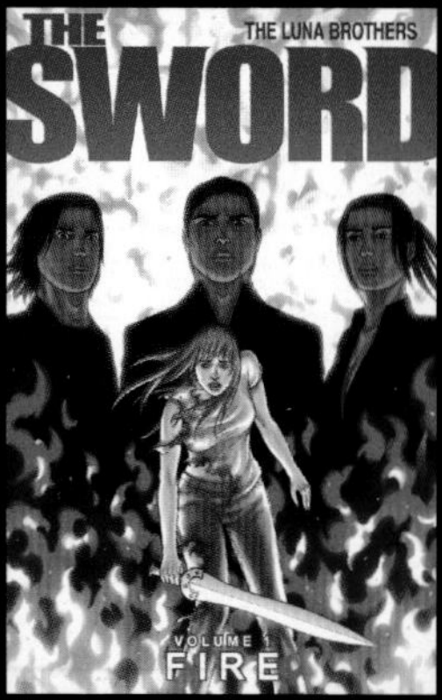
THE SWORD
THE LUNA BROTHERS
VOLUME 1
FIRE

THE SWORD
Vol. 1: FIRE
Trade Paperback
$14.99
ISBN: 978-1-58240-879-8
Collects THE SWORD #1-6
152 Pages

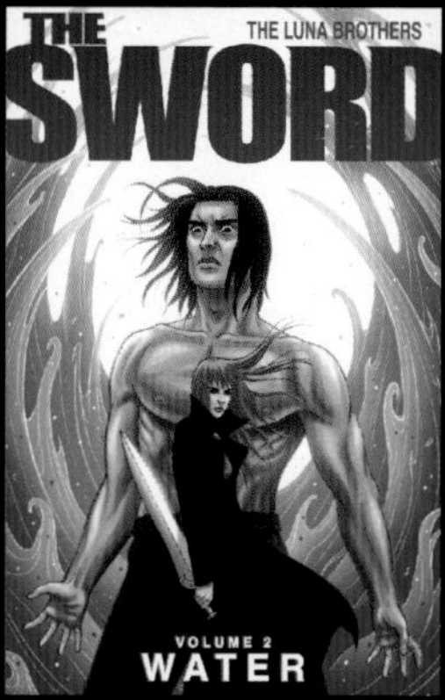
THE SWORD
THE LUNA BROTHERS
VOLUME 2
WATER

THE SWORD
Vol. 2: WATER
Trade Paperback
$14.99
ISBN: 978-1-58240-976-4
Collects THE SWORD #7-12
152 Pages

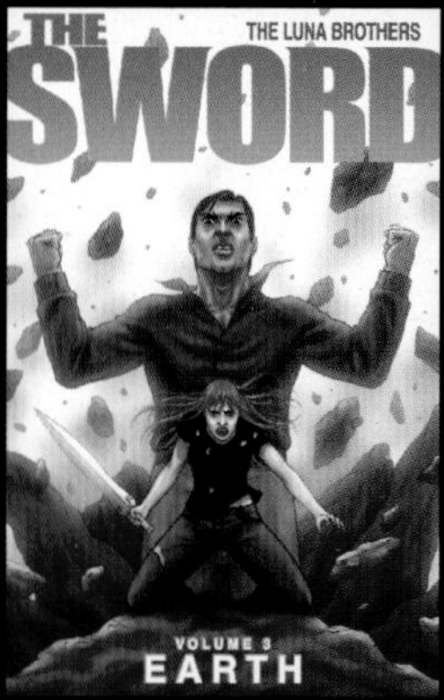
THE SWORD
THE LUNA BROTHERS
VOLUME 3
EARTH

THE SWORD
Vol. 3: EARTH
Trade Paperback
$14.99
ISBN: 978-1-60706-073-4
Collects THE SWORD #13-18
152 Pages

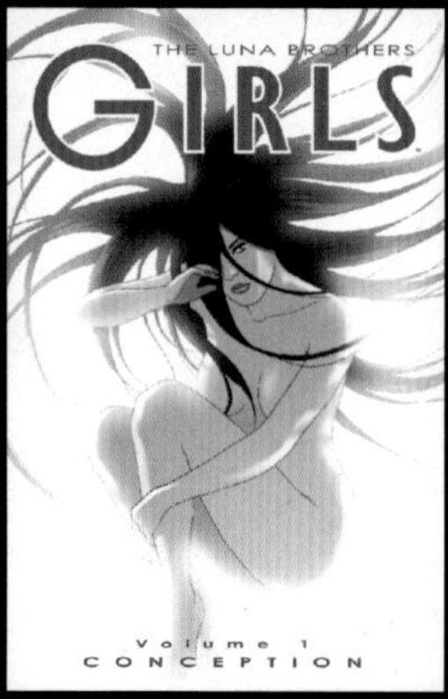
THE LUNA BROTHERS
GIRLS
Volume 1
CONCEPTION

GIRLS
Vol. 1: CONCEPTION
Trade Paperback
$14.99
ISBN: 978-1-58240-529-2
Collects GIRLS #1-6
152 Pages

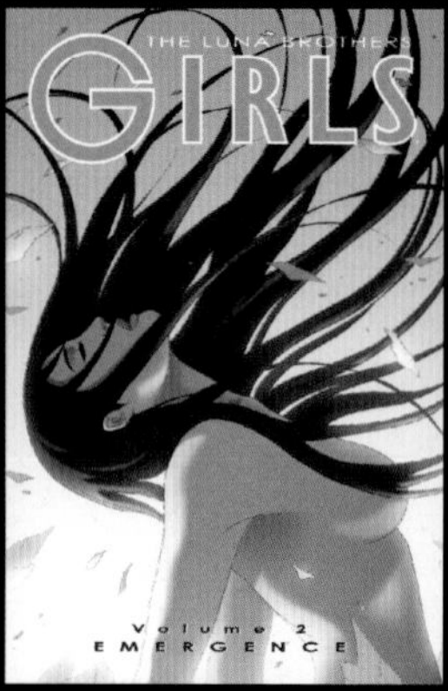
THE LUNA BROTHERS
GIRLS
Volume 2
EMERGENCE

GIRLS
Vol. 2: EMERGENCE
Trade Paperback
$14.99
ISBN: 978-1-58240-608-4
Collects GIRLS #7-12
152 Pages

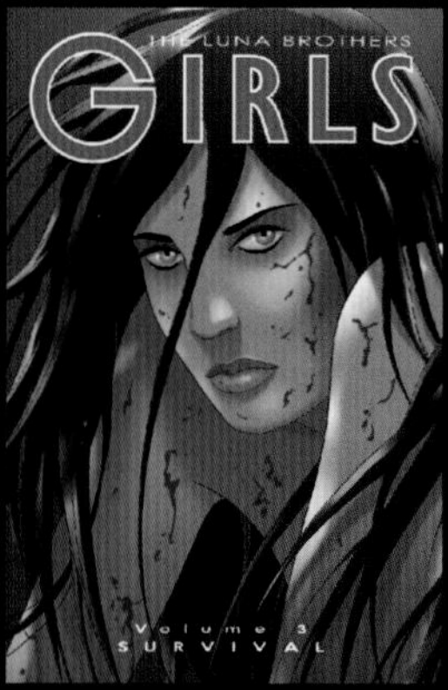
THE LUNA BROTHERS
GIRLS
Volume 3
SURVIVAL

GIRLS
Vol. 3: SURVIVAL
Trade Paperback
$14.99
ISBN: 978-1-58240-703-6
Collects GIRLS #13-18
152 Pages

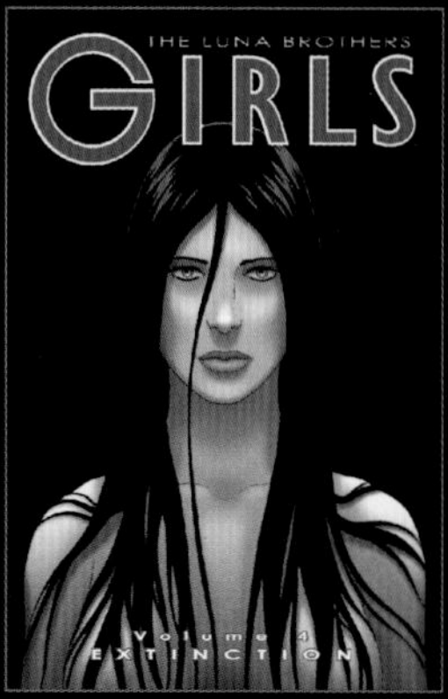
THE LUNA BROTHERS
GIRLS
Volume 4
EXTINCTION

GIRLS
Vol. 4: EXTINCTION
Trade Paperback
$14.99
ISBN: 978-1-58240-790-6
Collects GIRLS #19-24
168 Pages

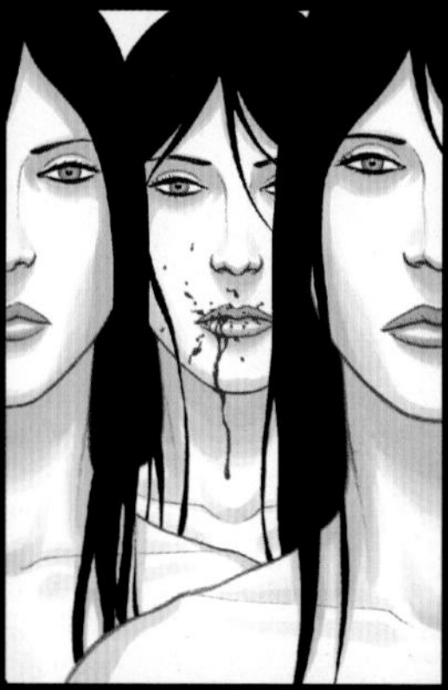

GIRLS
THE COMPLETE
COLLECTION DELUXE HC
$99.99
ISBN: 978-1-58240-826-2
Collects GIRLS #1-24
624 Pages

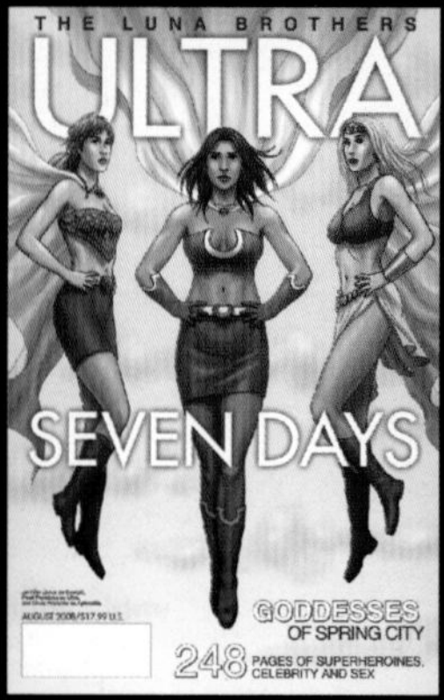
THE LUNA BROTHERS
ULTRA
SEVEN DAYS
GODDESSES OF SPRING CITY
248 PAGES OF SUPERHEROINES, CELEBRITY AND SEX

ULTRA
SEVEN DAYS
Trade Paperback
$17.99
ISBN: 978-1-58240-483-7
Collects ULTRA #1-8
248 Pages

For a comic shop near you carrying graphic novels from Image Comics, please call toll free: 1-888-COMIC-BOOK